WOLF
TRAP

"What gives this thrill-a-minute World War II story its special resonance is the genuine research that infuses its every twist and turn . . . There's an appealing love story woven into the web of terror and suspense. Nolan wrote THE ALGONQUIN PROJECT, A PROMISE OF GLORY and other highly acclaimed thrillers."
—*Publishers Weekly*

"Tense, behind-the-scenes war thriller . . . A story of the furious rivalries within the complex Nazi intelligence system . . . Nolan paints a detailed portrait of the Nazi system, featuring the top figures of the SS, the Gestapo, Abwehr and the Criminal Police. Nolan's plotting is filled with surprises, but what takes WOLF TRAP beyond the average thriller is how the author used honest research and restrained imagination to create a plausible picture of the Nazi machine more detailed than the facts will ever be able to supply."
—*Richmond Times-Dispatch*

WOLF TRAP

FREDERICK NOLAN

St. Martin's Press · New York

ISBN: 0-312-90393-6

Mass Market edition/April 1986

For Nick Austin
Supporter · Encourager · Contributor

WOLF TRAP

Munich, June 30, 1934

The old man was playing the cello when the SS squad kicked down the door and burst into the room like an explosion. He stared at them uncomprehendingly for a moment as they fanned out around him, their faces set in an anger whose cause he did not know. Two of them grabbed him and jerked him roughly to his feet, pulling him across the room to stand in front of a burly, thick-necked Major whose uniform bore the black sleeve-diamond of the Sicherheitsdienst. *The old man winced as the beautifully kept cello clattered to the polished wood-block floor. He bent down to pick it up, the bow still in his hand.*

"Leave it!" the SS Major snapped.

He was a big man, his face shiny with the sweat of exertion. He had the thick, heavy hands of a manual worker. Thugs, the old man thought, drawing himself up to his full height. Nazi thugs.

"What is the meaning of this?" he said, wrestling angrily free of the grip of the two SS troopers who had been holding him. "Do you know who I am?"

"I know who you are, Scheisse!" the SS Major shouted. Without any warning he hit the old man in the face with his fist. The old man reeled back, colliding with the two troopers who had been holding him. He fell to the floor, his eyes filmed by shock. He touched his smashed mouth with a trembling hand.

"What have I done?" he said. There were tears in his eyes. All the anger was gone from his voice. Nothing was left but fear.

"Pick him up and get him out of here!" the SS Major snapped, his eyes cold with hatred. The guards jerked the old man to his feet and bundled him towards the door. Just as they reached the doorway, the double doors burst open and a young man with blond hair hurled himself at them. His right fist hit

1

one of the troopers a looping, glancing blow on the hinge of the jaw. The man went down in a sprawling heap, his steel helmet banging metallically on the floor.

"Grab him!" the SS Major shouted to the other four troopers. They swarmed all over the young man, pinioning his arms and bearing him, kicking and fighting, to the floor by sheer weight of numbers. The old man watched all this as though it were happening in a film that did not interest him. The young man lay on the floor, spreadeagled by the panting soldiers. His eyes were full of angry loathing.

The SS major stood with his hands on his hips and frowned down at the prostrate prisoner. Twenty-four, twenty-five, maybe. Must be the old man's son.

"Where are you taking my father?" the young man shouted, writhing against the restraining hands of the troopers. "What are you doing here? Let me stand up, damn you!"

The Major nodded, and the soldiers allowed the young man to get to his feet. He stood glaring at the soldiers, the Major.

"Your father is under arrest," the SS Major said. "For high treason."

"What?" the young man shouted. "Treason? Do you know who this is, for God's sake?"

"I know, all right," the Major said. "And my orders are to take him to Stadelheim prison."

"Major, there must be some mistake!" the young man said. "If you can just wait while I make a telephone call—"

"I don't wait for you nor nobody else!" the SS Major snapped, surlily. "And if you hold me up any longer, I'll be damned if I don't arrest you and take you along as well!"

"Who is your superior?" the young man snapped. He had a very military way with him, the Major thought. Junkerschule, probably. A lot of nobs sent their sons there.

"I insist on speaking to your superior!" the young man said. The SS Major's patience was thin at best; now it snapped.

"Enough of this shit!" he growled. "Beck! Gross! Take the old man!" The two soldiers who had lifted the old man to his feet earlier grabbed him again. He looked from one to the other, as though still uncomprehending.

"No, damn you!" the young man shouted. He threw himself at the nearer of the two soldiers, trying to wrest the old man free from his grasp. The SS Major gave an impatient shrug. He took the Luger from his holster and hit the young man with the barrel. The young man fell to his knees, head lolling. He turned, blindly, hands groping for the Major's boots.

"Ach!" the Major said, angrily. He hit the kneeling man again. The man fell unconscious to the polished wood floor, blood trickling from his mouth, as the SS troopers ran the old man out of the room and down the stairs, banging him against the walls and banisters, and against the doors as they went out into the street, a black-clad phalanx of grim-faced men from whose path pedestrians scattered like leaves before a November gale. A moment later their truck roared off up the Schulstrasse.

Two days later, a sealed coffin was delivered to the house by a narrow-faced doctor from Dachau concentration camp. He told them that since it contained the body of a man executed for treason, it could under no circumstances be opened. He said that arrangements had already been made for it to be cremated. No marker or gravestone would be permitted. They did not need to be told he was Gestapo; you could smell it on him. He left them alone at no time. They said their goodbyes to the old man with dry eyes. The coffin was taken away on a van.

A week passed, then a visitor arrived at the house. He wore the black uniform of an SS-Oberführer, a tall, blond man with the eyes of a lynx. He came to them, he said, at the express request of the Führer himself. There had been a dreadful mistake. The SS squad had been one of a great many sent out to arrest the conspirators in a plot to overthrow the Führer. The plot had been led by the degenerate criminal Ernst Röhm, leader of the SA. A dreadful mistake, he kept saying. No one's fault. Merely a confusion over the names, understandable in the circumstances. They had arrested the wrong man. The Führer was quite overcome with distress, and had withdrawn in solitude to a villa on the Tegernsee.

"I am here on his personal orders," the Oberführer told them. "To assure you that arrangements will be made for the family to receive financial assistance, and for you, gnädige Frau, to receive the pension due the wife of a German patriot."

"Filth!" the old woman said. "Get out of my house!"

Much later, they pieced together what had happened. Hitler learned that Ernst Röhm, one of his earliest adherents, and leader of the bully-boy Sturmabteilung, was plotting against

3

him. He acted without mercy. The Nazi newspaper coined a nice phrase to cover it: "The Führer has cleansed with fire and sword." Operation Hummingbird, they called it. They settled scores all over Germany: in Silesia, in Prussia, in Berlin, and here in Munich. Röhm and all the SA leaders had been executed at Stadelheim. Eighty-three men were dead, executed without even the vestiges of a trial, in the Night of the Long Knives. It was unfortunate, they said, that in such affairs innocent people sometimes got killed; a woman pushing a pram, an old man playing the cello. It was unfortunate, but it was necessary. There was no cause for further alarm: Germany was safe in the hands of the SS.

"Then God help us all!" the old man's son said.

Morgenrot, Morgenrot,
Leuchtest uns zu frühen Tod.
Gestern noch auf stolzem Rossen
Heute durch die Brust geschossen.

Berlin, December 20, 1940

"Well, Kramer, what do you think?"

Paul Kramer turned to see Kurt Bergmann standing next to him. Kurt was in full uniform, the all-black dress of an *SS-Sturmbannführer*. He was nearly forty now, seven years older than Paul. His face wore the unsmiling expression that had been habitual for as long as Paul could remember, his eyes the same distant coldness.

"It's a big decision," he replied. "To go to war with Russia. I always thought the Führer was against a two-front war."

"Ach, man, the Soviet Army is a joke!" Bergmann scoffed. "The Führer says we'll be in Leningrad in three weeks."

"I'm sure I remember him making a speech about never repeating Napoleon's Russian experience," Paul argued, deliberately provoking Bergmann.

"Yes, yes," Bergmann said. "But that was before it became clear that it would be inopportune to invade Britain this year."

Inopportune, Paul thought, was that the word they were using for it? They always dressed up failure to look like decision. The Army had been ready for the invasion, but Göring's Luftwaffe had failed to gain control of the skies over England. That was why Operation Sealion, the invasion of Britain, had been called off. Did Bergmann's Security Service masters think Military Intelligence knew nothing?

"The British will wait, hoping for help from America," Bergmann went on, speaking as if he had learned the words by rote. "Meanwhile, the Führer has decided to act."

"He's certainly got everyone in the Bendlerstrasse working overtime," Paul said. The High Command of the

Wehrmacht had its headquarters in a vast monolith of anonymous grey granite stretching from the Tirpitz Quay to the Tiergartenstrasse. Everyone in Berlin referred to it by the name of the street on which its main entrance stood.

"He's incredible!" Bergmann enthused. "You should see him at work, Kramer! The energy the man has! My God, he can out-think and out-general most of the High Command, and still find time for plans to redesign Berlin, Linz, Nürnberg! Look at this place: Speer built it, of course. But it was the Führer's conception!" He waved a proprietorial hand at the Long Hall of the Reichs Chancellery in which they were standing. The sound of his voice echoed from the high ceiling.

"It's the first time I've been in here," Paul said, glancing around. Hitler had ordered the building of the place at the beginning of 1938. There was only one condition: it had to be ready by the following January. It was given the highest priority. Nothing was allowed to interfere with its construction, not cost, not weather, not the lives of the slave labourers shipped into Berlin by the SS to work on it. Four and a half thousand men worked around the clock in two shifts. Speer finished it on time, a vast, featureless, three-storey block with a frontage of more than three hundred and fifty metres on Voss-strasse. Marble stucco walls, bronze sconces, twenty-foot high windows, mahogany doors, Gobelin tapestries. Cosy, Paul thought. And completely in keeping with Hitler's megalomania. Was the whole place built on such a vast scale to make everyone who entered it feel insignificant?

"Never been in the *Reichskanzlei*?" Bergmann said. "Of course, you *Abwehr* people prefer that damned rabbit warren of yours on the Tirpitzufer, don't you?"

"We aren't given the Führer's appropriations," Paul said, watching his mild sarcasm bounce off Bergmann, as he had known it would. Bergmann knew the vast Chancellery inside out, just as he knew all the Reich's corridors of power. He was firmly attached to the coattails of the glamour boy of the SS, Reinhard Heydrich, and so could hardly help but succeed. If you called that success.

"Would you care to have a look around?" Bergmann

said, with conscious magnanimity. "I'm sure it could be arranged." Even if it could, Paul thought, it's the last place I'd want to see. Let the SS have it, and welcome.

"I thought security would be stringent," he said.

"It is for most people," Bergmann said. "But there are those of us who can go anywhere." He opened the breast pocket of his uniform and produced a grey linen card which bore his photograph. On the outside it was decorated with a golden seal and a yellow diagonal bar. It was signed by Hitler's personal adjutant, General Brückner. "These are issued only by the Security Service."

"*L'état, c'est moi?*" Paul murmured.

"Not quite," Bergmann said, missing the irony, as he always did. Paul wondered whether there was any way of getting under the man's skin, or whether Bergmann had by now so conditioned his reflexes that personal insults meant nothing. Paul knew there were plenty like that in the SS. You could call them the filthiest name you could think of, and they would laugh. Make a mild joke about Hitler, and they would have you killed.

"I'll take up your offer another time, if I may," he said. "I really must get back to the office."

"Any time, my dear Kramer," Bergmann said, loftily. To tell the truth, he felt a little sorry for Paul. When they were kids, he had envied him. Paul had it all: wealthy parents, the right sort of schools, university, the officer corps. But what had it got him? Military intelligence, and an unsung corner of it, at that. Tracking down Communist radio operators, going to Embassy cocktail parties: where was the excitement in that? The Military Intelligence people were a dull crowd altogether, Bergmann had long since decided. Look at the *Abwehr* chief, Canaris! *Alt Weisskopf,* they called him, the name a play on words: old whitehead, but also old wisehead. A little fellow, not much over five feet tall, who preferred civilian clothes to uniform, and who always had a couple of smelly little dachshunds trailing along after him. Bergmann smiled to himself: imagine anyone daring to give Heydrich a nickname!

"Well," he said.

"Yes, I must be off," Paul said. "What time is it?"

"Seven-twenty."

"I'd better get back. This Russian offensive has us all on the hop."

"I know," Bergmann said. "I'm just going to a meeting with the *Reichsführer-SS.*"

"Himmler? You move in exalted circles these days."

"It's all part of the job," Bergmann said, deprecatingly. Paul knew Bergmann was secretly pleased by the pretended flattery. Poor Kurt, he thought, always impressed by the man above him, and always contemptuous of the one beneath. Even in the old days in Königsbrunn when, as young men, they had both joined the Party, afire to build a new Germany. Paul remembered that Himmler had visited the town, made a speech. He had dined at the Bergmann house afterwards. It was a very great honour, Kurt told Paul's father. Would Dr Kramer care to have *Reichsführer* Himmler call during his visit? Kurt was sure he could arrange it.

"Thank you, Kurt," Walter Kramer had said. "I am not an admirer of these people. I leave politics to others." He was from an earlier, more courtly world, the world of the Emperor Franz Josef, the world of Johann Strauss. He did not begin to understand the New Order. He did not want to. He wanted only to be left alone with his beloved music.

"One day, anyone who has shaken the *Reichsführer's* hand will be a famous man in Germany," Kurt said. "A pity you feel as you do, Herr Doctor." He had always been awed by Paul's father, by the famous people who came to the Kramer house: musicians, opera singers, film producers. But in that one refusal, his respect turned to contempt. He knew Himmler, Dr Kramer did not. He would be an important member of the *Reichsführer's* staff when Walter Kramer was just a name in a reference book. The future belonged to men who knew how things were going to be in Germany. Little fish grew into big fish.

Well, Bergmann was a big fish now, Paul thought. After the Himmler visit, Königsbrunn had become much too small a theatre for his ambitions. He moved to Berlin, joined the infant "Security Service" and the SS—he held one of the coveted five-figure numbers—and rose steadily through the SS hierarchy. He was Heydrich's trusted henchman, and Heydrich was head of the *Reichs-*

sicherheitshauptamt, the Main Security Office which controlled all police functions, as well as the Gestapo. Heydrich was, in turn, second-in-command to Himmler, the head of the SS. They said that the Führer saw Heydrich as his most likely successor. That was a thought to make the blood run cold, Paul thought.

"It was good to see you, Kramer," Bergmann said. "We must lunch at Horcher's. Soon. I'll give you a call."

The hell you will, Paul thought sourly. Kurt Bergmann was renowned for a lot of reasons around the Wilhelmstrasse, but generosity was not among them. As Hans Oster had remarked one day after Bergmann called in at the Tirpitzufer, if Bergmann ever found a generous bone in his body he would have it removed, and then make it pay an exit tax.

They shook hands without warmth and Paul went out of the west portal of the Chancellery into the Voss-strasse. Two immobile *Leibstandarte* sentries, wearing black uniforms with white belts and gloves, stared rigidly ahead, their backs to the massive columns flanking the thirteen steps. Thirty-five feet above their heads, the great eagle of the Third Reich glared balefully to its left. Paul grimaced: he was not an admirer of Speer's Fall-of-the-Roman-Empire style of architecture. It sometimes seemed as if not a week could pass without some architectural "improvement" being made to the old city. They ranged from the merely irritating, like the removal of the *Siegessäule* from in front of the Reichstag to the centre of the newly-widened Charlottenburger Chaussée, to the obscene, as when they had felled all the lime trees in the Unter den Linden to erect marble pilasters crowned with martial eagles to honour Hitler's fiftieth birthday.

Paul picked up a taxi in the Potsdamerplatz, and told the driver to take him to the Lehninerplatz on the Kurfurstendamm. As they sped through the darkening streets, his thoughts were on Hitler's decision to invade Russia. He had been present when General Halder told Admiral Canaris about it, immediately after the meeting of the chiefs of staff concluded on December 5.

It was no surprise; Foreign Armies East had been bombarding the *Abwehr* with requests for information on Soviet units in Eastern Europe since early September. Such requests could only mean one thing: war with Russia. Canaris was appalled by the decision, and was sure that disaster would result.

"Our armies will bleed to death on the icy plains of Russia," Canaris said, in that quiet, lisping voice of his, during one of the very first "Barbarossa" conferences. "Two years, and there won't be anything left of them."

"Nevertheless, Canaris," General Halder said. "It's Russia, Russia, nothing but Russia!" Short, crew-cut, pince-nézed, Halder was one of the old brigade. He hated the Nazis and detested Hitler, yet still served as the Führer's chief of staff. A reflective man, laconic, quietly-spoken, he was a good planner, a sound technician. He simply couldn't 'shake it out of his sleeve' the way some of his fellow generals could. No charisma, Paul thought. Charisma was very important at the *Reichskanzlei*.

Canaris had never admitted to the chiefs of staff that the *Abwehr* knew next to nothing about Russia. Hitler had decreed following the signing of the German-Soviet non-aggression pact in August '39 that nothing must be done to offend the Russians. Canaris had obeyed that directive to the letter; from that date, German Military Intelligence had ceased to operate inside Russia. The consequence of which was that all hell had broken loose on the Tirpitzufer subsequent to the Führer's decision to attack.

"He announced his decision on December 5," Halder said, in that leaf-dry, disdainful way he had. "And demanded we deliver the revised plan for the attack by December 17. Ten days! Ten days to prepare for the conquest of Asia!"

It was done, of course. Anything else would have been unthinkable. From the masses of intelligence reports, Polish analyses, radio transmissions, Army reconnaissances, agents' appraisals, a preliminary assessment had been made. It would, of course, be regularly updated and an abstract, prepared on the special large-face typewriter used for all documents presented to the Führer—who did not like to wear or be seen wearing glasses—would be delivered to the *Reichskanzlei* in a GKS folder identical to the one Paul had just delivered there.

12

The taxi stopped, brakes squealing slightly. A thin drizzle had begun to fall. Paul turned up the collar of his greatcoat and paid the driver. He walked up the Wilmersdorferstrasse, putting Russia out of his thoughts and turning his mind to Kurt Bergmann.

Bergmann had taken over the apartment of a Jewish lecturer at Berlin University, "inheriting" the old man's fine collection of classical literature. It was not that Bergmann was interested in classical literature; he was interested in possessions. Many of the books were first editions, in fine leather bindings: the kind of books a pseudo-intellectual like Kurt would want to own because they would infer an erudition which he did not in fact possess. As for the old Jew, he had paid his *Reichsfluchtsteuer,* the tax paid by Jews who wished to leave the country, and fled to join his son in America. Germany was no place for a Jew any more.

Housing was in short supply in Berlin, although people of Bergmann's rank rarely experienced any problem. The favoured suburbs were Grünewald and Schlachtensee. Charlottenburg, especially somewhere near the palace, was the sought-after district in town. Bergmann's apartment was on the Friedrich Karlplatz, directly opposite the Schlossgarten. Paul wondered whether Erika would be there. She went out a lot: no point staying in, she always said. Kurt was forever working late, and there were always parties and dinner engagements.

He cut through a little park, stopping to light a cigarette. He stopped again by the school on the corner of the Scharrenstrasse. Old habits die hard, he thought, with a grin. It did not seem likely that anyone would be following him. He took the precaution of checking anyway. It did absolutely no harm if you were wrong. If you were right, it could save your neck. He came to the building and rang the bell. The buzzer released the door and he went up the stairs two at a time. She was waiting at the top, golden-blonde, lovely, wearing a silk dress the colour of fresh cream.

"Darling!" she said.

Berlin, January 12, 1941

The cinema ticket came in the morning post. There was no message with it, nothing. Sam Gray looked at it for a long time, his lower lip stuck pensively forward. Then he shrugged and put it into his wallet. It was for the evening performance of *Ohm Kruger,* a film about the Boer War which was playing at the Ufapalast.

"Eight-thirty," he muttered to himself, and shrugged again. He would have denied that it was a habit, yet he shrugged often, as though to say, *who knows?* He had not ordered any cinema ticket, nor was it likely that he would have been sent a complimentary one without some sort of covering note. Anyway, it wasn't a preview: the film had been playing more than a week. So?

"Only one way to find out," he told himself. He got to his feet, a big, wide-shouldered, sandy-haired man with large hands and feet. He was forty-four years of age, but he still had the guileless face of an American college boy: you almost expected freckles. It was a useful face, Sam always thought. Like his name. It was ordinary, and reliable, and unremarkable. It made people think he was just another naïve American, full of received opinions, and that was exactly how he wanted it. People talked much more freely if they didn't think you were very bright. Especially the Nazis, whose contempt increased in direct proportion to your inability to understand the German language. That was okay, too. Sam spoke perfect German, as well as Czech and French and Italian. He was perfectly happy to have people think he did not. They guarded their tongues less carefully, concealed their opinions less successfully, and that made his job much easier. If they wanted to dismiss him as 'that friendly commercial attaché from the American Embassy', that was all right, too. It wasn't much of a technique, but it was the best one he had.

He was in the cinema seat at the Ufapalast at exactly eight-twenty-five. The seats on both sides of him were empty, and remained so for almost an hour, during which Sam watched the Emil Jannings film with only minimal interest. Dr Goebbels was wasting no time attributing the invention of concentration camps to the British, he thought. Nazi propaganda was a long way short of subtle, but it seemed to do the trick on the Germans.

A man came down the steps and sat in the seat next to Sam. Sam did not look at him directly, and yet, had he been required to provide a police description, he would have been able to say that the man was about six feet tall, strongly-built, well dressed, clean-shaven, and in his mid-thirties. He wore a dark overcoat and the inevitable slouch felt hat with the brim turned down all the way around, the way everyone affected these days. Hair? Blond. Eyes? Hard to tell. Blue, maybe. Not a working man, Sam would have added.

The film drew towards its close. The man sitting next to him got up and as he did, dropped his gloves. He bent down to pick them up, and Sam heard him say "Look under the seat after I leave." Then he was gone. Sam waited until the film ended and left the cinema with the rest of the audience. He heard a woman saying it was disgraceful the way the British had treated the Boers. He wondered what she would say if he asked her how she felt about the way the Nazis were treating the Jews. He walked along the Kurfurstendamm, feeling the crackle of the envelope he had found beneath the cinema seat and slid into his pocket. He turned left into the Fasanenstrasse and then right, and right again. He stopped on the corner, watching the people who had been behind him pass by. They hurried along, breath ballooning in the frosty air, the freezing slush crunching beneath their winter boots. They all looked quite ordinary.

Sam walked back to the Kurfurstendamm and headed for the taxi rank in the Joachimplatz. He made no attempt to take the envelope out of his pocket. There was a saying in Berlin: half the taxi drivers work for the Gestapo, and not even the Gestapo knows which half. Thirty minutes later, he was in his apartment in Dahlem with the door locked, and a large Glenlivet poured into one of his heavy Waterford crystal glasses. He opened the brown manilla envelope. It contained an official-looking document in German, to which was paperclipped a typewritten note. *You are requested to ensure that the enclosed reaches British Intelligence in London by the fastest possible means,* it said. There was no name, nothing else. Sam opened the official document and laid it out flat on his desk. His hands shook slightly when he saw the heading.

FÜHRER AND SUPREME COMMANDER OF
THE ARMED FORCES
    FÜHRERHEADQUARTERS,
     10 December 1940
     9 copies.
DIRECTIVE No. 21: CASE "BARBAROSSA"

Sam read through the seven-page document with mounting astonishment. This was not some minor government document leaked by a disaffected civil servant. It was intelligence material of the highest order, a personal instruction issued by Hitler to the German High Command, ordering it to prepare for war against Russia.

Sam laid the documents down, frowning. Who was the man who had passed them to him? And how had he managed to get a copy of them? According to the heading, only nine had been prepared, which meant that the informant had access to the highest echelons of the German Army. And who knows enough about me to know I'd be the right person to pass something like this to? Sam wondered. He picked up the telephone and dialled a number.

"I need to see you," he said to the man who answered. "Right away."

"All right," the man said. "Why don't you come over?"

"No," Sam said. "At the office."

"I see." There was a pause. "It's that important?"

"Unquestionably."

"Half an hour, then." There was a click, followed by the dialling tone. Landis wasn't one to waste words. Sam Gray put the documents back into the envelope, and put on his jacket and topcoat. It was damned cold outside, and there were no taxis about. He hurried across to the U-Bahn, feeling strangely vulnerable. Twenty minutes later, the security guards let him into the Embassy, and he hurried to Landis's office. Landis was already behind his desk, hands folded neatly, eyes bright with interest. Nominally, Landis worked for the State Department. In fact, Sam knew, he was responsible to the Joint Intelligence Committee in Washington. The JIC reported directly to President Roosevelt. There had been some talk about setting up a separate, full-time intelligence agency but so far that was all it was, talk.

"All right," Landis said. He was a stocky man, with greying hair cut in that short, Cary Grant style. "What have we got?"

Sam handed the envelope across the desk. Landis slid the papers out and pulled his desk lamp across to see them better. He was silent as he read. Then he looked up.

"Jesus Christ, Sam!" he said.

Berlin, January 12, 1941

Five minutes after he left the cinema, Paul realised that he was being followed. He thought rapidly. Surveillance in itself meant little; it was almost a way of life in his business. The system worked like that. There were seven security agencies in the Reich: police, criminal police, security police, military intelligence, counter-espionage—the list went on and on, a web of *referaten* and sub-desks. The most pernicious, the most pervasive, and in his case, the most likely source of surveillance, Paul thought, was the secret State police, the Gestapo.

"God damn and blast it!" he muttered as he hurried along, head down, shoulders hunched against the biting wind. He might be under surveillance for any one of a dozen reasons, real or imagined, none of them remotely connected with the fact that he had visited the Ufapalast tonight. This might be the first time he had been followed, or the fiftieth. It made no difference. The agent, or agents, shadowing him would report his movements. He did not know whether they had seen him move to sit next to the big American, but he had to assume that they had. He did not want that fact, or his name, on any report going to 'Gestapo' Muller or his boss, Heydrich.

The first priority was to find out how many of them

there were. Usually, there was only one. He risked a glance over his shoulder. Too many people to be sure. Well, then. He went into a *tanzbar,* pushing through the heavy curtains into the smoke-fogged interior. There was a bar on the right. He went to it and ordered a beer he did not want. A girl came across, sat on the stool next to him.

"Hello," she said. "Buy me a drink."

Paul nodded to the barman."Champagne," the girl said. The barman poured her the wine. Cheap *sekt,* Paul thought, or even *spumante.* It was still worth it. He watched the curtained doorway.

"Why don't we go and sit somewhere more comfortable?" the girl said.

"In a minute," Paul told her. A man came in, eyes quickly scanning the room. He was about forty, thickset and dark-haired. He wore a long leather overcoat. *Gestapo,* Paul thought. The *spieler* at the door knew it, too. He was almost bent double in his desire to please. Gestapo waved him aside, went to a table, sat down. He did not look at Paul once. Yet Paul could not move without his seeing him do so. Paul smiled. They were a poisonous crowd, but they were predictable.

He got up and put on his coat.

"Hey," the girl said. "Hey!"

"Sorry, *Schatz,"* Paul said. "In a hurry."

He went out of the bar quickly, knowing Gestapo would follow. the question was, was there another of them outside? He crossed the street and stood looking in a darkened shop window. Nobody on the other side at all. Nobody watching, nobody crossing. Then Gestapo came out of the bar, looked up and down the street. He saw Paul on the opposite side, and took a pack of cigarettes from his pocket, lighting one. He would wait till Paul moved. Paul nodded. Only one, he thought.

He hurried up the Meinekenstrasse and turned right towards the Kaiser Wilhelm church. His mind was moving quickly. He had to ditch Gestapo somehow. It wasn't going to be easy, especially at this time of night. The best place would be the Ku-damm. There would be cafés open there. He smiled grimly again and headed west.

The first place he came to was packed with night birds, a

lot of them military. Here and there among the crowd he could see the black uniforms of SS officers. Nobody he knew, thank God. He looked around and saw a sulky-looking tart sitting alone at a table off to one side. He went across to her.

"Good evening," he said. "May I join you?"

"*Sitz' 'mal, Liebchen,*" the woman said, brightening up. "On the town, are you?" She spoke German with a French accent.

"I'm from Hamburg," Paul said. "Here on business."

"Looking for some fun, then?" she said, one eyebrow raised.

"What do you think?" Paul said, sitting down. "What's your name?"

"Marianna," she said. She was dark-haired and quite pretty. About twenty-five, he thought. Probably from Alsace: a lot of them were. He signalled a waiter and ordered wine. It would probably cost a leg and an arm; the waiters took ten per cent of the drinks the girls persuaded their 'Fritzes' to buy.

"I've got a place near here," she said, putting her hand on his thigh under the table. "Five minutes in a taxi."

"Sounds marvellous," he said. "We'll have a party."

"Mmmm," she said, with simulated yearning.

"Listen," he said. "I have to go outside. You know." She made a face. "Look, you pay for the wine. Then we'll be ready to leave." He slid a fifty Reichsmark note across the table, and her eyebrows rose.

"Don't be long," she said, grabbing the money.

He went through to the rear of the restaurant. Gestapo would be on the street, watching the front of the place. Paul went into the back yard of the café. It was littered with wooden crates. A pile of beer kegs stood against the wall. He wondered whether Gestapo had watched him through the window. He would assume Paul was in the toilet. A man didn't buy a twenty-Mark bottle of wine for a tart and then walk away.

Paul hurried along the alley to the street, conscious of the passing of seconds. There was a taxi at the rank on the corner of the Augsburgstrasse. He went around to the driver's side and knocked on the window.

19

"*Ja?*"

"I want to go to Gatow," Paul said.

"Get in, then," the driver said, boredom changing to cupidity. It was a good run out to Gatow.

"Could you help me with my trunk?" Paul gestured vaguely across the street, and heard the driver mutter a curse. He got out of the cab, hunching his shoulders against the wind, a short man, overweight, wearing a leather jacket.

"Where is it, then?" he grumbled.

They crossed the street. Paul waved towards a dark doorway and said "Here." The taxi driver stopped, frowning. As he peered into the doorway, Paul hit him mercilessly with the edge of his hand, the way he had been taught. The man grunted and dropped to his knees. Paul laid his fingers on the man's neck, pressed. The man sighed and stretched out. Paul dragged his body into the shadows. It took only a few minutes more to bind the man's hands and feet with his tie and belt, and to gag him with a handkerchief. Paul took the greasy-feeling leather wallet-purse from the man's pocket and put it in his own. Then he ran back across the street and got into the taxi. The keys were still in the ignition. He drove the car around the corner and parked it not far from the café. He locked it and left it there, walked briskly around the block, and was back in the café inside ten minutes. Marianna looked up, her face twisted with impatience.

"Thought you'd fallen in, darling," she said, peevishly. "I've finish' th' wine."

"There's a place round the corner," Paul said. "We can get a bottle of champagne and take it back to your place."

"Well," she said, mollified. "Thass what I like, man who doesn' mind spennnin' a few Marks." She was a little drunk, which was perfect for what Paul had in mind. He felt a twinge of pity. It wasn't her fault that she had got into this. He took her arm and walked out of the café with her.

"Here!" she said. "Not so damned fast!" He ignored her protest, his grip on her arm like steel. He glanced over his shoulder. Gestapo was right behind them. Paul turned into the Fasanenstrasse, and as Marianna opened her mouth to protest Paul bundled her into a doorway and pressed his mouth on hers. Her lips were slick with lipstick.

"God in Heaven, can't you wait?" she hissed, wrestling herself free, pushing him away. He pulled her closer with his left hand and put his right hand on the side of her neck, pressing. Her knees buckled and he let her slide into a sitting position just as Gestapo came around the corner at a brisk pace.

"Hello," Paul said, stepping out. The Gestapo man's eyes widened and his hand darted towards the pocket of his leather overcoat, but Paul was already moving. He hit the man across the side of the neck the same way he had hit the taxi driver. Gestapo folded forward with an agonised grunt, his forehead hitting the pavement with a strangely loud *glock*! Paul dragged the man across to the doorway, anxiously scanning the street. It was already after eleven. There were very few people on the side streets at this time of night; most of them stuck to the fleshpots on the Ku-damm. He looked back as he hurried towards the taxi up the street. The two bodies huddled in the doorway were quite invisible. He drove the taxi around the corner into the Fasanenstrasse, and in a couple of minutes more, he had manhandled Gestapo into the back of the car. He was halfway across the sidewalk with Marianna's arm around his shoulder, her feet dragging behind, when someone shone a torch in his face and demanded to know what he was doing. He looked up. Two *Schupos* had come up in a car. He hadn't even heard it.

"Girl friend's passed out," he said. "We were having it off, like. In the doorway."

"That your taxi?"

"I'm off duty," Paul said.

"Get her off the street," the policeman snapped. "Damned drunks."

"Yes, sir," Paul said, still using the working-class accent. "Thank you, sir."

"Damned drunks," the man said again. "Doing it in doorways." The window rolled up and the car slid away. Paul let out his breath in a long, long sigh of relief. He bundled the whore into the front seat of the taxi and got into the driving seat. Then he drove carefully south on Fasanenstrasse, heading for Uhlandstrasse. There was a huge warehouse there belonging to a removal contractor

21

named Franzkowiak, with an open car park between it and the adjacent Post Office. When he got there, Paul opened Marianna's purse. As he had expected, she was carrying a small gun. It was strictly illegal, but most of them did, anyway. The gun was a pearl-handled Walther PPK, ·22 calibre, with a seven-shot magazine. He reached into Gestapo's inside pocket and took out the man's wallet. Apart from the usual identity cards and snapshots, it contained about seventy Reichsmarks. He took out the notes and stuffed them into Marianna's purse. The car park was completely deserted. Gestapo groaned a little as Paul dragged him out of the car and propped him up against the wall of the Franzkowiak warehouse. He put the little automatic hard against the man's sternum and pulled the trigger. The gun made a noise like a muffled cough. Gestapo's eyes opened wide and then closed again. Paul felt for a pulse: there was none. Now he wrestled Marianna's body out of the car, sweating even though the wind was sub-zero. He laid Marianna across the dead man's legs. She would be unconscious for another ten or fifteen minutes, he reckoned.

Paul got back into the taxi and drove it to the Savignyplatz, making sure nobody was about before he got out of it. Then he walked down to the Ku-damm and went into Kranzler's for a *schnapps*. His mind went over every step he had taken. Had he covered everything? The taxi driver would tell the police he had been robbed. There would be nothing to connect that event with the discovery of the dead Gestapo agent in a Wilmersdorf car park. Alben Graumann, Paul thought. That was his name. There had been photographs of a smiling woman. He closed his mind to those thoughts. And Marianna? When she woke up and found herself lying alongside a dead man, she would run for cover. No chance of her going to the police: whores had no rights in Germany. She would never mention the matter to anyone, if she had any sense. Not that it would make any difference if she did, Paul thought. He called the waiter over and ordered another *Zwetschkewasser*. After a while, he stopped trembling.

Berlin, March 22, 1941

The headquarters of German Military Intelligence, or to give it its full name, *Amt Auslandsnachrichten und Abwehr*—the foreign intelligence and counter-intelligence arm of the German Army—was at Tirputzufer 72–76, a great, grey granite building which formed the southern end of the even enormous complex of buildings known as the huger "Bendlerblock" which housed the High Command.

The *Abwehr*—the word means 'defence'—was said to be one of the best clubs in Germany. Its functions, which ranged from sabotage through postal censorship, from the monitoring of diplomatic radio transmissions to the recruiting of spies, were handled by five main departments, known as Sections. *Abwehr* One, the secret information service, was commanded by a tall, dark, elegant Rhinelander, Hans Piekenbrock, who had been a lieutenant in the Eleventh Hussars before transferring to General Staff duties in 1927. It was he who had organised the disorganised Canaris, he who had divided the *Abwehr* map into areas of 'primary' and 'secondary' interest, he who had reorganised the *Abwehr's* focusses of activity abroad. The cheerful 'Pieki' was Canaris's deputy, confidant, and friend.

Abwehr Two, the sabotage and subversion section, was commanded by Lieutenant Colonel Erwin Lahousen, a Viennese-born nobleman of Franco-Polish origin. Section Three, counter-espionage, and Four, the foreign section, were commanded respectively by Colonel Franz-Eccard von Bentivegni and Rear-Admiral Leopold Burkner. Department Z, for 'Zentrale', the central administration section with its records of some 300,000 agents stretching back as long ago as 1914, was led by Major General Hans Oster. Brash and impulsive on the surface, serious-minded and simultaneously vain, Oster was temperamental, volatile, a womaniser. They said he was a fine example of the old adage that there is no sinner like the parson's son.

The *Abwehr* was not only the best club in Berlin, it was also the most exclusive: Most of its officers hailed from the same social background and all of them believed in the renaissance of Germany as a great power. None had ever shed a tear for the Republic, and—with a few notable exceptions—all believed Hitler would lead Germany to the position of leadership in world affairs to which she was entitled by right. There were no criteria for admission: one was selected, often by Canaris himself. He and his staff set the codes, the mores, the tone. *Abwehr* personnel worked with, but remained aloof from the principles and practises of 'the black ones', the SS. *Abwehr* officers were expected to adhere to a certain code of conduct in secret service matters, adjuring the deliberate jettisoning of all scruples which became *de rigueur*—when you donned the black uniform.

Paul Kramer sat in his office on the third floor of the *Fuchsbau*—*Abwehr* officers always called their offices 'the Fox's lair' as a little tribute to the silver-haired old fox who commanded it—and waited for his boss to return from the daily briefing, known as 'The Column', which was in progress in the conference room on the third floor. Paul was chief assistant to Lieutenant Colonel Joachim Rohleder, commanding *Abwehr* IIIF, the principal sub-section of all the other sections. It had begun as a *referat*, or 'desk' with a staff of some thirty-five officers. Its main task was counter-espionage, which, simply put, meant the recruitment of informers and spies, the defeat and/or penetration of enemy espionage services, the manufacture of 'play-back' material, or disinformation, the surveillance of suspected spies and agents. These days that meant mostly the Russians, although *Abwehr* penetration of *Razdevupr*, the Russian secret intelligence service, was minimal. After the Russians came the Swedes, the Swiss, and the Americans. Agents were placed in most of the foreign embassies still functioning in Berlin, their job to gauge the intentions of those countries towards the Reich. It was a lot easier in the old days, Paul thought, when everyone knew everyone. The British SIS had a listening-post in an apartment above the Maybach car showrooms, and the American Office of Naval Intelligence operated out of the Frigidaire place on the Lutzow-platz. At the Königin Bar, a rendezvous that was popular with tourists and foreign attachés, fifteen of the twenty hostesses had been in *Abwehr* pay. Paul smiled at the recollection. What a green young officer he had been when Canaris had accepted his application for *Abwehr* duties and given him the rank of *Erganzungsoffizier* in the newly-formed Section IIIF! There had been a lot to learn. Not just how espionage worked, but the jargon that went along with it. An enemy espionage circuit, was an 'orchestra'. Its leader was a 'conductor', a *kapellmeister*. Radio operators were 'pianists' and their transmitters 'pianos'. Informers were 'tipsters', in-house spy teams *'hauskapellen'*.

Intelligence work was, first and foremost, paperwork. The installation and upkeep of card indexes, the compiling of intelligence digests and situation reports, the systematic perusal and evaluation of periodicals, newspapers, specialised literature and official publications took priority over 'running' agents. Much as he preferred working in the open, Paul found himself daily more chained to his desk, reading files, analyses, operational reports, orchestrating the flow of information, reports and action papers which were daily generated inside and outside the section, and presenting them to Rohleder before he attended 'The Column'.

Paul picked up his clipboard as Rohleder came in, flanked by his secretaries. Rohleder inclined his head slightly to one side, and Paul rose and followed him into the office. There was a deep frown on Rohleder's face.

"Something wrong, Chief?" Paul asked. He thought he knew the answer. The bush telegraph in the *Fuchsbau* had been buzzing all morning, and, as usual, it was damnably well-informed.

"Pieki just told us that van der Osten is dead!" Rohleder said, anger in his voice. "Killed stone dead. In New York."

"I thought he was in Hawaii," Paul said, knowing otherwise. "Spying for our little Japanese friends."

"He was," Rohleder said, sitting down at his desk and lighting a cigarette. "But he went to Los Angeles and from there to New York. He was to take control of our orchestra there, expand it. He hadn't been there more than two days. Two days, and he's dead!"

"How did it happen?"

"He was run down in Times Square by one of those yellow tanks the Americans use for taxis. I doubt he knew what hit him, poor bastard!"

"You think the Amis killed him?"

"Americans?" Rohleder said, with a sour grin. "The damned Americans wouldn't recognise an agent if he walked into the White House carrying a bomb with the fuse lit! No." He drew reflectively on the cigarette, blowing smoke in a thin stream towards the cream-painted ceiling. "It was the British. I can feel it in my bones."

Ulrich van der Osten had been something of a legend at the *Fuchsbau*. The scion of a rich Junker family with a tradition of intelligence work, he had been one of the guiding hands behind Franco's rise to power in Spain. At the end of the civil war there, he stayed on in Madrid, living the life of a grand *hidalgo* and calling himself Don Julio Lopez Lido. He continued, however, to recruit agents and informers for *Abwehr* work, sometimes debriefing foreign agents whose cover could not be jeopardised by trips to Berlin.

"Does that mean the American operation is compromised?" Paul asked, knowing the answer. He listened to Rohleder's voice without really hearing what he was saying. Ulrich van der Osten had died, as no doubt other agents-in-place would either die or be imprisoned, because two weeks ago, Paul had passed full details of their mission to the American, Sam Gray. Two sheets of paper, he thought, that was all it took. Men who had been through the tough training course at Quenzsee, elaborately prepared for their mission with documents, maps, clothes, identity papers forged by the technicians in Berlin-Tegel, had been rendered helpless by two sheets of paper listing their names, their contacts, and even the location of the *Afu* transmitter at Centerport, Long Island. Paul Kramer had killed Ulrich van der Osten as surely as if he had actually been at the wheel of the Checker cab that mowed the man down in the street. He realised that Rohleder had stopped talking.

"What happens now?" he said. The 'dropping' of agents on foreign soil, their protection and management, was the province of *Abwehr* Two.

"Erwin says we ought to kill some of their people," Rohleder said. "In reprisal."

"He can't be serious!" Paul replied. "And even if he was, the Old Man would never sanction anything like that!" It was a *sine qua non* of the Service: no assassinations, no political murder. Everyone with clean hands. Leave that sort of thing to the 'Blacks' in the Prinz Albrechtstrasse. Erwin von Lahousen knew that as well as any man in the *Fuchsbau*.

"Of course, of course," Rohleder said, testily. "All the same, Erwin is angry enough to bite a piece out of a plank. He says he smells treachery, and I think he may be right."

"Treachery?" Paul said, feeling a thin flicker of apprehension touch the ends of his nerves. "There, or here?"

"God knows," Rohleder said, rubbing his eyes. "It sometimes seems it's everywhere." Paul knew he was referring to the *Palmenzweig* case of the preceding summer. Rohleder, a typical, straightforward soldier, could not conceive of any professional soldier committing treason. Apart from the dishonourable nature of the act, he saw it as stupid: no one but an amateur would think to carry out treasonable acts with the Gestapo and the *Forschungsamt* maintaining their ceaseless vigil. It had happened the preceding June. Word was received at the *Fuchsbau* that the date of the Western offensive had been betrayed, probably by a German officer. For two days, Paul had lived with the sick certainty that his cover had been blown. Then the "brown birds"—the buff-coloured sheets on which the *Forschungsamt* submitted the typewritten reports of its telephone and cable monitoring— revealed that the Belgian Ambassador in Rome had been given word of the impending invasion of the Low Countries by someone 'who derives his information from the General Staff'. The Führer sent for Canaris and Heydrich and ordered them to find the traitor at once. Amt IVE of the Reich Main Security Office—Bergmann's counterespionage group—worked in tandem with *Abwehr* IIIF, commanded by Rohleder. The news spread like brush fire throughout the Bendlerblock. Even the most resolute opponents of the Nazi regime despised treason. Opposition to Hitler and his satraps was justifiable, even in wartime. But to betray one's comrades to the enemy was unthinkable.

Rohleder had worked indefatigably, and his dossier, codenamed 'Palm Frond', soon indicated that the leak had come from Oster's Z Section. With the chill demeanour which some people ascribed to callousness, Rohleder presented his findings to the Admiral, who gazed stiffly into space as Rohleder implacably showed that the traitors were Oster and one of his staff, Lieutenant Josef Muller, known to everyone on the Tirpitzufer as 'Joe the Ox'. Like Oster, Muller was an out-and-out opponent of the Nazi

27

regime, and he had been in Rome at the appropriate time.

To Rohleder's lasting fury, Canaris had adjudged IIIF's evidence insufficient. He argued bitterly. "Colonel Oster's game is dangerous in the extreme," he protested. "The inquiries instituted by my Section could as easily—and as successfully, sir—been carried out by the Gestapo. With repercussions to this department and yourself that I am confident would have been most unpleasant!"

"Enough, enough!" Canaris said. And with that, and the fact that Canaris seemed no longer to have the same rapport with his Chief of Staff, Rohleder had to be content. The investigation into the Western offensive leak ground to a halt. Would the death of Ulrich van der Osten start another?

"Well, what have we got coming in?" Rohleder said, and his words gave Paul the answer to his unspoken question.

"Some stuff from the Greek desk on the kidnapping of Stoyadinovich," Paul reported. "And we're getting a stream of signals from Belgrade about a possible coup."

"Better give them all to me," Rohleder said. "I'll show them to the Old Man. What about the Ivans?"

"We've provided OKW with a full appreciation of the military situation, or as much of it as our people have been able to find out. They don't really want us to put too much into it, you know. Jodl has barred us from strategic espionage anyway. He says the Russian campaign will only take nine weeks."

"You sound as though you think he's wrong."

"I sound as though I think he's optimistic," Paul said. "I hope to God he isn't wrong."

"The Führer says the Russian Army is a joke. He says that Russia will collapse like a soap bubble."

"Who am I to argue with the Führer?" Paul said, sententiously.

"Who, indeed?" Rohleder said, his habitually stern expression relaxing into a smile. He was from Stettin. Career soldier through and through, Paul thought. Lichterfelde, then the élite 8th Grenadiers in the Great War. Rohleder had been running a business in Buenos Aires when Germany's rearmament had tempted him back into uniform. He was one of the few senior officers at the *Fuchsbau* who got on well with the Gestapo. The fact that he did made life a great deal more pleasant for Canaris and Piekenbrock and the rest.

"What about coming around for a drink tonight?" Rohleder said, putting out his cigarette. "Emmy was asking after you."

"Give her my love," Paul said. "I'll come another time. I've got a date tonight."

"Ah, youth!" Rohleder said, with a grin. "The girls these days!"

"You've had your moments," Paul said, wishing he could like the man more. He got up and went back to his own office, working until six. He was hardly aware of what he was signing, what reading, and what re-routing to other departments and *Abwehr* offices. His mind functioned automatically, handling the routine tasks while another part of his brain pondered the serpentine reach of death. In books, in films, death was reasoned, plotted, planned. In real life, death was random, irrational. He thought of Ulrich van der Osten hurrying all the way around the world to keep that fateful appointment in Times Square. The carelessness of a filing clerk in Piekenbrock's office had enabled Paul to pass to the Americans complete details of van der Osten's plans, contacts, destination. And there was Death, waiting beneath the glittering neon lights of Broadway.

Well, Paul told himself, it's a war. And this is my way of fighting it.

Berlin, March 28, 1941

"He's going to Russia for six weeks," Erika said. "With Heydrich."

She shifted her body to a more comfortable position, and

sighed with satisfaction. Her skin was soft and faintly damp with perspiration after their lovemaking. Not love, Paul thought, as he stroked her cascading golden hair, and wondered for the thousandth time why he kept coming back to her. The sex, of course. There was nothing else. They had never even talked about anything like that. It was as though they had agreed to it: no talk of love.

"Russia?" he said, languidly. "What's he going to do in Russia?" Anything happening in Kurt Bergmann's world was of interest to Paul. The machinations of Department IVE of the Reich Main Security Office were a major part of the puzzle which he was always trying to piece together.

"You know about the offensive," Erika said. "*Kriegsbereitschaft* is May 15."

"Yes," he said. "I know that." Battle readiness on the Russian front. The High Command was still deeply divided about the wisdom of going to war with Russia, but Hitler was driving them towards it like cattle to an abbatoir. A month earlier OKW Abteilung L had devised what General Keitel none too modestly described as 'the greatest diversionary manoeuvre in military history'. It was a double bluff, designed on the one hand to make the Russians think the troops massing on their borders were part of the projected invasion of Britain, while at the same time persuading the British that Germany planned to attack the Soviet Union instead. Lahousen was at Camp Zeppelin, the new headquarters of the Army General Staff in Zossen, south of Berlin. Bentivegni had already put everyone in *Abwehr* Three on overtime. IIID collaborated with OKW Abteilung L in preparing false reports which were fed by IIIF to the enemy. The neutral capitals of Europe were already buzzing with rumours of the subtle German plan to disguise the impending invasion of England. The Soviet military attaché in Berlin, Major General Tupikov, was 'disinformed' by means of false information passed to him by an *Abwehr* double agent working in the Soviet State Security Service. For the past two weeks, Paul had been working non-stop on an operation code-named *Shark*, simulating major troop movements from Scandinavia to Brittany.

"Quite a lot of our people are going East," he said to Erika. "What is Kurt going to do?"

"Heydrich has given him special responsibilities," Erika said. "He won't talk about it. Says Heydrich will be flying a fighter at the front and leaving him to do all the dirty work, something to do with the resettlement of the population. He's getting his *Standart*."

Quite a promotion, Paul thought, from the SS equivalent of Major to Colonel in one jump. Heydrich must have something very special in mind for *Standartenführer* Kurt Bergmann. He reached across Erika's naked body and got his cigarettes off the bedside table.

"When does he leave?"

"The end of April," she said. "Or the first week of May. It hasn't been decided. Give me one of those."

Paul lit the cigarette for her and watched as Erika threw her arms above her head and stretched like a cat. Her body was lean, soft, and lovely; she never failed to arouse him. There was a store on the corner of the Schillerstrasse where they kept wine chilled, ready to sell. Paul always stopped there on his way to the apartment and bought a bottle of champagne. Erika would be waiting and they would sit close together on the sofa and drink it. By the time he could feel the light pressure of the alcohol on his temples, Erika would look at him and smile.

"Let's go up," she always said.

There was no 'up'. The bedrooms were along a narrow hall, lined with framed pictures of old cities: Danzig, Nürnberg, Cracow. Erika would draw the curtains and then take off her clothes. He liked to watch her, not so much because it aroused him, but because there was something moving about watching a woman bare her body, cast aside all her defences. Then she would slide into the four poster alongside him, and they would just lie there, shoulders touching, until their body warmth spread beneath the sheets.

Erika was a squirmer. When she was naked in bed, her buttocks moved almost imperceptibly, like oiled pistons. Sometimes she would reach for him; others, he for her. There was no pattern. They had no habits. He could re-

31

member the first time as clearly as if it had happened an hour ago. A party at the Siemens place, too many drinks. He had seen the invitation in her eyes before. This night, he accepted it.

"Well?" she said, when they got back to the apartment. She sat on the sofa, her arms stretched along its back. "Do you want another drink? Or anything?"

"I want you in a bed with no clothes on," he said.

He kissed her. Her tongue was like darting fire. She moaned when he touched her breasts. And then she was naked on the bed with her arms stretched above her head and her eyes closed and he thought that perhaps she was apprehensive, or even a little ashamed. He was wrong: she had no shame, no taboos. She drew in a sharp little breath when he entered her, and sighed like a delighted child as he began to move. And then she was as hungry and eager as he, and matched his thrusts with her own, her head thrashing from side to side on the pillow in the utterness of their climax, until they collapsed together, panting, hearts thundering, limbs as powerless as string.

It was always explosive, always. He learned that the small inhalation of breath, the sigh, were the same each time. He learned that some nights she would want him only once, and others again, and sometimes even again. Each time was the same, each time was different. Sometimes he thought he could not, and she would smile that witch smile of hers, and her long, golden hair would fan across his body like a silken whip, while the blood sang in his ears as all the centre of him was drawn between her knowing lips.

Afterwards, too, the same thoughts in the silence. Both of them were that shade too smart to fall in love. Both of them knew that they could get along fine without the other—indeed, Paul felt sure he was not Erika's only lover. Yet still he came to her, taking the soft gift of her eager body with hungry pleasure. Sometimes he almost loved her; but never quite. Part of him always stayed detached, uninvolved and quite objective. At the moment, in the moment, he came close to loving. But not later, and never constantly. He could yearn for her without caring, want her without needing.

32

One evening, he arrived at the apartment to find that she had a visitor, a pert little brunette with saucer-wide eyes and splendid breasts which the V-neck sweater she was wearing did absolutely nothing to conceal. She had a wide, generous mouth and her hair was cut pudding-basin style, with a fringe.

"Paul, darling," Erika said. "This is my dear friend, Anni. Anni, this is Paul. There, now we're all friends." Her words were just a trifle slurred, and Paul frowned. Erika wasn't a drinker. He stifled a vague unidentified annoyance.

"Hello, Paul," Anni said. "I've heard a *lot* about *you*." She put too much cuteness into it, keeping her eyes wide and innocent, like a little girl being told a ghost story. I am not bad, they said. But I might be naughty.

"I brought champagne," Paul said. Erika was making no move to get rid of the woman, and he wondered why.

"Oooh," Anni said. "Real champagne."

"Open it, darling," Erika said. "I'm sure Anni would love some."

"Why not?" Paul said.

"Do you know," Anni said, as he tore off the foil and unfastened the wire cage. "I never took a drink until I was twenty-three."

"None of us did," Paul said. "It's the war." It was a well-worn catch phrase. Anni giggled.

"I think I'm going to like you," she said. She clapped her hands as Paul eased the cork out of the bottle. It made a sound like an exaggerated blown kiss.

"Where are you from, Anni?" Paul asked, feeling strangely exposed. Erika was watching him like a cat at a mousehole. There was a sexual tension in the air, and for a while he did not understand why.

"Moosburg," she said. "We moved to Berlin when I was nineteen."

"Ah", he said, thinking of wide-eyed little Anni being nineteen in prewar Berlin.

"We lived in Schoneberg, a nice little house on the Frankenstrasse. My father worked at the Post Office. Everyone knew him. And my mother, too. 'Good morning, Frau Deschke,' they'd say. All the shopkeepers, everyone. They all knew my parents." There was a wistful note in her voice, as if she was trying to remember the respect in the voices of the shopkeepers.

"You're not married, Anni?"

She did not reply. She turned to face him and what he saw in her eyes turned the key in Paul's mind. *Dummkopf*! he told himself. Now he knew, and he looked at Erika. She smiled that witch smile he knew so well.

"Anni," she said, softly. "What time is it?"

Anni was looking at Paul the way a woman looks at meat on a slab. She ran the pink tip of her tongue across the ripe lips.

"Bedtime", she said.

Paul kissed Erika's shoulder to make her move. "*Du,*" he said, "I'm hungry."

"There's stuff in the kitchen," she said, turning over. He padded into the kitchen, found the bread, cut enough for two sandwiches. Rubbish sandwiches, they called them. Ham, cheese, hot mustard, sausage, whatever she had, all piled on bread.

"Your heart attack is served," he grinned, as he put the food on the bedside table. Erika smiled back at him and sat up in the bed. She saw his eyes on her breasts.

"Eat your sandwich," she said.

"Later," he replied, taking the plate out of her hands. Her mouth tasted of mustard, and her body led him once again to red oblivion.

"What time is it?" she asked, lazily.

"After eleven," he said. "I'll have to leave soon. Where is Kurt tonight?"

Kurt rarely got home before one or two in the morning. Work was life to him. Nothing else was as interesting or exciting. And after work, most nights, Heydrich would want to go on the town. He needed company and Kurt provided it. Part of his job, he said; there was no choice in the matter. Once in a while, when Kurt went away, Erika would try to persuade Paul to stay overnight. He never did. It was stupid not to, and yet it was like a point of honour. Which, he reflected, was just as stupid.

"Some boring conference or other," she said, offhandedly.

"At the Hedemanstrasse, I think. What's there?"

"The Race and Resettlement Office," he said, turning the pages of the dossier in his mind, RUSHA was one of the five key branches of Himmler's SS. Was Kurt—and therefore, by definition Heydrich—becoming interested in what the 'Blacks' called 'the Jewish problem'? In 1940, Himmler's office had come up with a crazy plan to resettle all the Jews in Germany on the island of Madagascar, such 'resettlement' being financed by the expropriation of Jewish property. Madagascar would then become the new Jewish state. It was a typical product of Himmler's thinking—muddled, formless and impracticable. Outside of that varnished-jackboot brigade in the Prinz Albrechtstrasse, no one had ever taken the Madagascar plan seriously. It was dismissed as yet another of the little chicken-farmer's schemes, like his *ersatz* Camelot at Wewelsburg. But what had Erika said about Kurt's new job in Russia? *Something to do with the resettlement of the population. He won't talk about it.* Had 'the Jewish problem' been reviewed?

"I'll have to go," Paul said, swinging his legs out of the bed and standing up. Erika reached over and ran her fingers down his spine.

"I love your back," she said.

"Especially when it's going through the door, eh?" he grinned. "Tell me, what ever happened to Anni?"

"Anni?"

"That little girl from Moosburg. The one with the short hair and the long fingernails."

"Oh, Anni Deschke!" Erika said. "She went back to Munich. She was afraid of the bombing. Why, did you——?"

"No, no," Paul said, hastily. "Just a question. I'm not that eager to play three in a bed."

"Oh," Erika mock-pouted. "And I thought you enjoyed it."

No, he thought. I don't enjoy being used, and you used me that night. I was incidental, a piece of soft machinery you needed. You decided you wanted to try it, and you set it up, and you drank a little too much to quell your reluctance to share me. He wondered what other little games she had played with that lovely, lithe body. What marvels we all are,

35

he thought. Sin upon lie, betrayal upon perfidy, yet nothing shows. You would think the evil might erupt, like boils. He looked at Erika. Yes, he thought. She has done it all. She probably puts me out of her mind the moment the door closes behind me. The animal has been fed. The time we spend together is like the time spent on a ferry-boat, neither in one place nor in another. He put on his jacket and bent over to kiss her goodbye.

"You going to stay in bed?"

"Mmm," she said. "I'll probably read awhile."

"I'll call you."

"Kiss me again."

He kissed her and then went along the hall, letting himself out of the flat. The wind whipped down the Spandauerstrasse as if it was looking for prey. The clouds were low, heavy with snow. There would be no raid tonight, he thought, not even an alert. He decided to walk home. It wasn't far. The streets were empty, and the sound of his feet echoed off the walls. He thought about what Erika had told him. Life for Jews in the Reich was very hard now. They could no longer even leave their homes without a police permit, nor shop except between the hours of four and five, by which time most of the decent stuff had been sold. They were not permitted to buy clothes, smoke tobacco, use public telephones or transport, keep pets, have their hair cut, own electrical appliances or bicycles. If Heydrich was taking an interest in them, even worse lay ahead. Heydrich was said to be pathological about the Jews. There was a rumour it was because one of his grandparents had been Jewish.

As he turned into the Mommserstrasse, three *SS-Oberschütze* reeled past him, trailing alcohol behind them like cologne in the wake of a dowager. They were singing the obscene version of *Lili Marlene*.

> *Sie nahm ihn in ihr Zimmer,*
> *Es lag im ersten Stock*
> *Beim roten Lampenschimmer*
> *Sie tanzt im Unterrock . . .*

His apartment was in the Bleibtreustrasse, its frontage so mock-Baroque that it made him smile every time he turned the corner of the Ku-damm and saw it. He let himself in, promising himself as he went up the stairs that he would find out exactly what it was that Kurt Bergmann was involved in. One thing was for sure: if Heydrich had anything to do with it, it was bad.

Berlin, April 20, 1941

He got to his vantage point in the Tiergarten ten minutes before the American was due. He had selected the meeting-place carefully, a short distance from the main path nearest the Tiergartenstrasse where two benches looked out on to the water, willow branches trailing down, secluded from the bustle of the nearby avenue. The bare branches of the trees bore the faintest traceries of green: through them Paul could see the frontages of the embassies on the Tiergartenstrasse, the bulkier, imposing mass of Dr Ley's Labour Front building. He looked at this watch. Five minutes to go.

An old man and woman walked along the path, her arm through his. He saw Gray arrive punctually, a big, wide-shouldered man with sandy hair and the walk of a prizefighter. Gray sat down on one of the benches and began to read a newspaper. Paul moved out of the copse of trees in which he had been standing and walked towards the rendezvous, not hurrying.

"*Grüss Gott,*" he said, sitting down next to Gray.

"Karl," Gray said, without looking at him. The American knew him as Karl-André Rauth. It was the name of a friend of Paul's who lived in Königsbrunn. "I thought you preferred not to meet face to face."

"Usually," Paul said. When it had become apparent that he would have to go on using the American as his channel to British Intelligence, Paul had made several conditions, all of which the American had readily accepted. The most important one was that Gray would make no inquiries about

37

his identity, for they would be certain to attract *Abwehr* attention and hamper his activities. They would work through a series of "drops" and "cut-outs" which he, Paul, would set up. "But this was urgent. It couldn't wait."

"Go ahead," Gray said. He spoke slowly, as if picking each word carefully before he uttered it.

"We agreed that biographies would not be exchanged," Paul said.

"That's right."

"I have to change that rule. So that you will understand."

"All right."

"Prague," Paul said. "I'm being sent to Prague."

"Prague?" Gray frowned.

"I am in Military Intelligence."

"It had to be something like that."

"The department of which I am a part deals with counter-espionage."

"That's rather ironic," Gray remarked, smiling.

"This whole damned thing is ironic," Paul said. "The Czech underground has begun to be troublesome. To penetrate it is the job of the *Abwehr*. I have the most experience of that country. I speak the language. So I have been appointed to take charge of our operations in Prague."

"I see," Gray said. "Well, I guess there's not a hell of a lot we can do about it. Isn't there any way we can keep in touch with you, Karl? My people have been very impressed by the material you've given me."

"If it is possible, I will make contact," Paul said. "I can't know for sure how things will be until I get to Prague."

"I see that," Gray said. "Is there anything I can do for you? Money?"

"I don't do this for money, Mr Gray," Paul said.

"Why do you do it?"

"We don't all think of Hitler as Christ reborn, you know."

"A lot of Germans feel that way. They don't all . . . do what you do."

"Turn spy, were you going to say?"

"Something like that."

"I have my reasons," Paul said.

"Yes?" Gray said. Paul grinned. He had no intention of discussing his motivation with the American, but he admired Gray's disingenuous way of encouraging him to go on talking.

"Let's just say that I hate those black-shirted bastards," Paul said.

"Amen to that," Sam said.

"Let me ask you a question," Paul said. "How closely do your people work with British Intelligence?"

"We give them everything we get," Gray said. "We like to believe they do likewise." Paul sensed he was surprised by the question.

"Does the code name 'Jonathan' mean anything to you?"

"No."

Paul shrugged. There was an anti-Hitler group in operation in Berlin. They called themselves various things: the Resistance Circle, the Black Orchestra. Some of the senior generals were a part of it, *Abwehr* officers, like Oster and his assistant Dohnanyi. They were liberals, idealists, dreamers. They had no real conception of how to effect a coup, yet they talked constantly of doing so. They were up to something now, and the code-name he had heard was 'Jonathan'. Oster had been in touch with someone in Geneva who had a line to London. Something big was in the air, but Paul had not been able to find out yet what it was. He was not a part of Oster's group, nor any other resistance organisation. The only way to do what he knew must be done was for one man, and one man alone, to do it. No connections, no strings, no partners, no clever plans. Get the most sensitive information and place it where it will do the most good. Keep it simple, that was the trick. The more complex it was, the easier it was to leave tracks.

"When will you go to Prague?" Gray asked.

"At the end of the month, I think," Paul said. "Perhaps a week or so later, but not more. Why?"

"I need some information," Gray said, slowly. "About Hitler's security arrangements."

Paul grinned. "You know it's his birthday today?"

"Hard not to know," Gray said, sourly. "Your Army gave him a fine birthday present, didn't they?"

The news had come through that day: Greece had capitulated. The government in Athens had advised the British that further resistance was useless.

"You want information about his security arrangements."

"Can you get it?"

"I suppose it is no use telling you that access to such information is highly restricted?"

"No use at all," Gray said.

"I can tell you this much now," Paul said. "He drives his security people crazy, always changing his arrangements at the last minute. He's totally unpredictable, no doubt with good reason."

"Method in his madness, you mean?"

"He' not crazy, he does it on purpose. Nobody is more aware of the fact that there are a lot of people who would like to put a bullet in him than our beloved Führer."

"All the same," Gray said. "Anything would be useful."

"I'll see what I can do," Paul said. "When do you plan to kill him?"

"What?"

"Mr Gray, we are not children," Paul said. "The only reason you can want information on Hitler's security is so that you can penetrate it. Which means you plan to do so. When?"

"Karl," Gray said. "I'd tell you if I knew. I don't know a thing."

"Mr Gray, I risk my life regularly to get your people information," Paul said, slowly. "Do not fence with me, I beg you."

"I'm not fencing with you," Gray said. "I honestly don't know what they want the information for. They didn't tell me. But even if they had, I'm not sure I'd tell you."

"Because I might 'double', you mean?"

"Because you might get caught, I mean," Gray said flatly, and his words made a tiny shiver touch Paul's inner self, like a feather falling on fresh snow.

"I'll see what I can do," he said again. "Now listen. There is something else. Heydrich has been in Pretzsch. You know where that is?"

"No."

"Northwest of Leipzig, near Wittenberg. He has been

setting up special SS units called *Einsatzgrüppen*."

"Special task forces," Gray translated. "What for?"

"I saw a paper written by Himmler," Paul said. "He wrote it at the beginning of April and sent it to Hitler. It is *Strengste Geheim,* absolutely secret. Only about a dozen people were permitted to read it. No one was allowed to keep a copy. It had to do with the treatment of the foreign populations in the East."

"Russia?"

"Not just Russia," Paul said. "Poland, Latvia, Estonia, Lithuania. Everywhere. All Jews in those countries are to be exterminated."

"You mean sent somewhere else?"

"No," Paul said. "I mean exterminated. Destroyed. Wiped out."

"But . . . that's impossible!" Sam Gray said.

"Himmler doesn't think so."

"How many of these *Einsatzgrüppen* are there?"

Four, Paul told him. An *Einsatzgrüppe* consisted of about three thousand men, the equivalent of an Army battalion. Gestapo, Orpo, Kripo and foreign military police, together with Waffen-SS, formed three-quarters of the complement. The rest were clerks and technical personnel.

"Twelve thousand men," Gray said. "Twelve thousand men couldn't kill all the Jews in Poland, in Latvia."

"They're not in a hurry," Paul said.

"Can you get me some documentation?"

Paul shook his head. "No one signs documents authorising genocide. Not Heydrich, not Himmler, not even our beloved Führer."

"There must be something," Gray said.

"Maybe," Paul said "But I doubt it." He stood up and looked around. There was no one in sight. Birds flitted between the branches of the trees. A duck quacked on the water. Sam Gray stood up, too. He shrugged, as though it was a habit.

"Tell them," Paul said, urgently. "For God's sake make them understand."

"I'll try," Gray said. He held out his hand. Paul shook it, feeling awkward, but wanting to do it anyway.

"I must go," he said.

"You're a brave man, my friend," Sam Gray said, with a small smile. Paul said nothing. He stood watching as the American walked away briskly along the path towards the Hofjägerallee. I never thought of it like that before, he thought. Brave, cowardly: they were words for battlefields, not for the twilight war he was fighting. When he looked again, Sam Gray was no longer in sight. I wonder if we will ever meet again? Paul thought. Then he turned and hurried along the gravelled path beside the still water.

Prague, May 14, 1941

"We have a new refugee here," Masaryk's voice said from London. "*Herr* Rudolf Hess who, until Saturday, was the greatest man after Hitler in the Nazi Party and the second greatest man in the whole German Valhalla."

"Hess is in England?" Masin said, incredulously.

"*Zavreny!*" Morávec said "Shut up, man!"

The light from the radio lit his swarthy face. He bent closer to hear the voice of the Czech Minister of Foreign Affairs giving his weekly Wednesday broadcast over the BBC. Static occasionally obscured it, and once in a while the words faded away completely, but Morávec never once relaxed his attention.

". . . dictators are wrecked in the end," Masaryk was saying. "Each day they roar to the world: one Führer, one people, one Reich, unity—and all at once the deputy of this one Führer breaks away from them and flies to an enemy country. This is a great thing and soon we shall probably learn much more and important things".

He went on to talk about the raids, the damage to Westminster Abbey, the Houses of Parliament, the destruction of the Czech Red Cross premises. They were in West Dulwich, in a place called Rosendale Road. Morávec often wondered what they looked like. In his mind's eye he saw brick-built suburban villas with neat front gardens full of rose bushes. Typically English; prim, proper, polite.

Masaryk's broadcast was coming to an end. Morávec looked up at Masin and tapped his wristwatch. Masin nodded, and held up a sheaf of papers. The material was already encoded for transmission. Morávec nodded, *dobry,* good.

The apartment they were using was on the top floor of a house in Nusle, not far from the Kresomyslova railway bridge. Masin was the inside lookout tonight. The Novakova girl was on the street with a flashlight. Morávec would transmit.

". . . our splendid pilots brought down six German aircraft and with them thirty German murderers. One of these lads of ours knocked off three aeroplanes in one night. Excellent. Our congratulations and thanks. Good night."

The vital words were six and thirty, three and one. They meant that the Czech receivers at Woldingham would be standing by at thirty-one minutes past each hour from now until six-thirty a.m. Morávec glanced at the luminous dial of his watch.

"Not long," he said. He switched to *transmit,* and put on the headphones. His fingers touched the ebonite knob of the Morse tapper. For some reason he could not explain, he felt uneasy. Maybe it was because of Balaban. The Gestapo had captured him three weeks ago. That bastard Leiche, he thought. The picture of the ugly Gestapo chief appeared on the screen of Morávec's mind. He blotted it out. No use thinking about that, he told himself. No use thinking about beery, cheery Balaban in the cellars of the Petschek Bank. After three weeks, he would have told them everything.

He rubbed his eyes angrily, fighting his own fatigue. We've been on the run a long time, he thought, over two years. A hint of a smile touched the thin lips. They had called themselves 'The Three Kings'—Balaban, Masin, and himself. Between them they supervised and co-ordinated the work of the Czech resistance in Prague and Brno, their motto *I remain what I was.* They passed the word: we will hurt the Germans most by helping them as slowly as we can. Carelessness before care resulted in 'accidents' on the railways which delayed vital supplies. Mysterious fires destroyed petrol stores. Vital orders were 'mislaid' or filled incorrectly. Factories went on turning out obsolete goods months after they had been ordered to stop. Ammunition was sorted wrongly, boxes labelled incorrectly. Go slow, go slower, produce less. In factories, in stores, in signal boxes, in streetcars, patient, grim determined Czechs dragged their heels to slow down the mighty German war machine the only way they knew how. Production fell: at the Königinhoffer cement works, the Brno Waggon-und-Maschinen Fabrik, at the Sphinx enamelware-works, and in the Kbrojovka armament factory at Brno. Czechs boycotted the families of workers employed in Germany: women whose husbands had gone there were refused membership of the only permitted Czech political organisation, National Solidarity. In one village, the police were turned away by four midwives before they could find one who would attend a woman whose husband was working for the Third Reich.

If a German asked a Czech the way, he was more than likely to be sent in the opposite direction. If he ordered beefsteak in a restaurant, after a very long wait he might get fish. German officials had to be paid a higher rate of pay for working in the Protectorate than those in Germany, in spite of the fact that the cost of living was lower. Landlords refused to let their flats to Germans, shop-girls failed to notice them waiting to be served. In restaurants, they found the wine lists printed only in Czech, the prices on the menu only in Czech currency. The radios had a strange penchant for switching to other stations at ten o'clock, when the German news was being broadcast.

We fight the war of the flea, Morávec told his people. We can live on the body of our so-called masters, safely hidden until we choose to bite. Having bitten, we move to another part of the body and bite again. And again and again. And all our masters can do about it is to scratch! A tumblerful of water mixed with corn seed will ferment and ruin what might have been acres of corn. Break off the shoots from seed potatoes and they will not grow. Put a spoonful of sugar into a drum of petrol and it is useless. And one thing remember above all others: to every German question and

44

every German order, reply *Nerozumím nemečky*. I do not understand German.

Even so, they were losing ground. The old organisation, *Obrana Naroda,* the Defence of the Nation, had been completely infiltrated and rendered harmless by the Gestapo. The men who had run it, old soldiers who stayed behind when the Nazis marched in, could not think in the new ways. You could not run a resistance movement like the Army. You could not recruit spies simply on the basis of their being Czechs. It had been a not-altogether unexpected blow when they arrested General Josef Bily in the spring. But Balaban, whom the Gestapo had captured on 22 April, was a serious loss. Losing Balaban was like losing an arm.

He sighed. It was time to begin. "All clear?" he said to Masin.

Masin edged back the blackout curtain and looked out into the street. He pressed the button of his torch once. Almost immediately a light blinked back below, Antonie Novakova indicating that the street was empty.

"All right," Masin said.

Morávec began sending. The headphones hissed softly, and he tried to visualise all the miles between his transmitter and the receiver in England. Then the call came through, startlingly clear: *go ahead*. He began sending. There was a lot tonight. Military aircraft production. Figures from the Skoda works, from Kbrojovka. Construction of new factories. Cuts in rations. Shipments of ore. Rail movements.

"*Pozor!*" Masin hissed. "Gestapo!"

Antonie Novakova had seen the car and given the signal, three quick blips of light. Nobody else would come up the street like that, crawling, the black Citroen moving like a squat prowling animal up the cobbled hill. The car had a direction finder on its roof, turning, turning. Four men inside, or five? It didn't matter. She knew what she had to do. She ran across the street and took up her position in a dark doorway. Her hands were trembling and she felt cold. She huddled back out of sight as the Citroen slid to a silent stop outside the house. She heard the *grrrackk* of the handbrake. A man got out, looking up at the building. He was huge and ugly. Someone had once said that he looked like an avalanche with a gargoyle set on top of it. His name was Gerhard Leiche, and he was a *Kriminalkommissar* in the Gestapo. He pulled a Mauser 9mm pistol from the pocket of his long, leather overcoat, and aimed it at the lock on the door. He fired the gun and kicked the door open. The other men who had got out of the car surged in after him. Antonie heard the thunder of their feet on the stairway, shouts, a woman's scream. Then shots: one, three, followed by the fast *brrrrraaaaappp!* of a machine pistol.

The driver of the Citroen got out of the car and stood on the sidewalk, looking up towards the windows on the second floor. More shots rang out inside the house. Antonie could hear the hoarse shouts of the Gestapo men. The street remained in darkness; nobody came out to investigate what was going on. It was better not to know.

Something snaked down from one of the windows above, a long, thin wire. The Gestapo man grunted and reached into his pocket. Up above him, a man was climbing out of the window. The Gestapo man had a gun in his hand now. Antonie stepped out of her dark hiding place, holding her pistol in her right hand. Gripping her right wrist with her left hand she aimed the gun, emptying her mind. The pistol barked and the Gestapo man was slammed against the wall by the force of the bullet. He fell face down, groaning. Antonie ran across to where he lay and put the gun behind his ear, pulling the trigger. The sound of the report was not very loud. She turned away quickly from the splattered mess oozing from beneath the man's face.

Morávec came sliding down the wire, the transmitter slung over his shoulder. He was sweating: she could smell him. He looked at the dead man on the sidewalk and then at the girl. Antonie nodded at the car and then ran to the doorway of the house. The thunder of boots coming down the stairs filled the hallway. She emptied the pistol into the darkness. There was a shout: pain, anger, surprise? She ran across to the Citroen, which Morávec had already started. He jammed it into gear and they roared up the deserted street, skidding around a corner. He did not drive very far. As soon as they got into the Vysehradska he turned into a side street and stopped. Antonie saw that the steering wheel was slick with blood.

"Vaslav, you're hurt!"

"Damned wire!" he hissed. "Look at that, will you? Christ's nightshirt!" He held out his left hand. The little finger hung by a thread of sinew. Blood was pumping from the stump.

"You've got to get to a doctor," she whispered.

"I will," he said. "Tie something round it."

She took a handkerchief from her pocket and bound the hand best as she could. Blood immediately stained the white fabric.

"That will have to do for now," Morávec said, roughly. "We've got to get away from this car. Will you be all right?"

"Yes," she said. "What about Masin?"

"He's finished," Morávec said, savagely. "That bastard Leiche has got him!"

There was nothing more to be said. He embraced her roughly and hurried off. Antonie watched until his sturdy figure disappeared into the darkness. Then she turned and walked away in the opposite direction. I'll have to hurry, she thought. Papa worries when I'm late.

Berlin, May 15, 1941

Kriminalrat Walter Abendschon pushed the typewritten report on the death of Alben Graumann away from him with an expression of acute distaste. What the hell did they expect him to do with it? he wondered. Gestapo agent Alben Graumann, 48, found dead in the car park of a removals warehouse in Wilmersdorf. A ·22 bullet, probably from a Walther PPK, had been fired directly into his heart with the muzzle of the gun pressed against his body. The autopsy report listed two other injuries: a contusion below the left ear, and another high on the dead man's forehead. Had Graumann been in a fight, got laid out and then shot? By whom, and for what reason? Was it some kind of execution? Revenge? Fooling around with someone's woman? There had been traces of a woman's face powder on Graumann's overcoat, cheap stuff that could be bought in any large store. And that was it: dead end. Abendschon shook his head vexedly, thinking of the options available to him.

One, he could do nothing. Graumann wasn't the first Gestapo agent to have been murdered, and he wouldn't be the last. He could think of one or two he wouldn't mind murdering himself. So: he could go through the motions, and at the end of them, report that no new leads had been uncovered. Then the buck would be passed back to where it belonged, to Heini Müller and his gang at *Nummer Acht*.

Two, he could try to solve the mystery of Graumann's murder. Come up with a suspect, make an arrest, haul in the poor, frightened bastard who'd done the job, and hand him over to Gestapo Müller. Might as well shoot him myself, Abendschon thought. It would save wasting the energy of the Prinz Albrechtstrasse sadists and the time of the People's Court.

Not much of a choice, he thought. Well, there aren't all that many choices any more. Not like the old days. He grimaced: the old days were dead and gone, and they were never coming back. He had a theory: Walter's First Theory of Diminishing Expectations, he called it. Its basic premise was, if you want the best there is, you've already had it. The future held only imitations of inferior quality. The theory applied to the service you received in stores and restaurants, the quality of the goods your steadily inflating Reichsmarks bought, the progress of the war, and the men who had come to power in Germany. It applied to superior officers, to sausages; it applied to police force recruits and sex. It was, Abendschon readily admitted, a profoundly pessimistic way to look at life, but after more than twenty years in the service of the *Kriminalpolizei*, twenty years in which he had seen every facet of his fellow man's darker side, Walter Abendschon rarely felt any reason for optimism. There had been a lot of changes since he had joined the police force in 1920. And none of them for the good, either.

He pulled the Gestapo report towards him again, pushing

his glasses back up on his nose as he did. Another damned imposition visited on him by time. He had resisted buying glasses because he was convinced that the minute you let yourself believe you needed them, then it became a fact. So what if he had to hold small print at arm's length to read it, and what if he couldn't even see the numbers in a a a telephone directory any more? A man could manage. In the end, he'd given in. He could see the smallest print now, but it didn't make him any happier. The glasses were further proof of his theory, that was all.

So: Graumann had been on a routine surveillance detail. Reason: not given. Subject: *Oberst* Paul Kramer, *Abwehr* IIIF. Abendschon shook his head. Damned Gestapo, he thought, shadowing senior Military Intelligence officers. *Reason: not given!* No one was ever told more than it was felt it was necessary he should know. Graumann might have been shadowing Kramer for fiddling his expenses or for plotting to overthrow the government. It might simply be because someone had forgotten to tell Graumann that the surveillance was called off. You were not permitted to know, and not invited to ask. That was how they worked now, the stupid, methodical, idiotic Gestapo, run in turn, as was the Criminal Police Division, by the over-compartmentalised, over-organised, over-staffed Reich Main Security Office. You had to be a damned cipher expert to work out which office did what. Nobody took responsibility for anything. Except at the top, of course. Everyone knew who was at the top of the RSHA: nobody but "Mr Suspicion" himself, Heydrich. And coordinating the work of Gestapo, Security Police, and all the other law-enforcement branches of the Reich, as well as his own counter-espionage group, was Heydrich's aide and confidant, *Standartenführer* Kurt Alfred Bergmann, newly returned from the Russian front. It was difficult to decide which of them was the bigger shit.

Abendschon got up heavily from his chair. He was a big man, about fourteen pounds overweight for his height, which was slightly under six feet. He was as broad as an ox across the shoulders, his once-abundant hair now thinning and flecked with grey. As a young man he had been an athlete. Before the Great War, before he had been shot out of the sky over Amiens in the little Pfalz. All but a quarter of a century ago, he thought, my God, where do the years go?

He picked up the telephone and dialled an extension at Gestapo headquarters: *Nummer Acht*, everyone called it, number eight Prinz Albrechtstrasse. Half an hour later he put the phone down again, frowning. Graumann had been assigned to Amt IVE, counter-espionage. Bergmann's little empire, he thought. Not your normal surveillance at all. Why would Gestapo counter-espionage be watching an *Abwehr* counter-espionage agent?

He knew the answer he would get if he asked, so he did not bother to ask. He sighed. They had a saying at the *Kriminalpolizei* building in the Werderschermarkt: the Gestapo allow you to be the donkey; they supply the saddle and the rider. Well, he wasn't about to find their man and watch some jumped-up Gestapo *Kriminalassistant* take the credit.

It was the crime itself that insulted him. Berlin was his city, and nobody killed people on its streets and got away with it. In all the years he had been a policeman, they'd only had about half a dozen unsolved murder cases; and not one of them was mine, he thought. He had a good record. He was a good policeman and he was proud of that.

He joined the *Kriminalpolizei* in the same year as sallow, careful Arthur Nebe. They both went into the drugs and theft section. By the time Hitler came to power fourteen years later Nebe, his old comrade in fighting the Russian *T-Apparaten* and later *Z-Apparaten*, had become head of the Criminal Police. Abendschon, his ambition not so naked, had risen less rapidly, acquiring on the way a wife, two sons, and a little villa near the Weissensee. It was Eva and the boys, more than anything else, which had kept him on the force. There had been a hundred times he had wanted to get out, and never more than in September, 1939, when Germany had gone to war with England, and that black-hearted bastard Heydrich had been appointed head of the Reich Main Security Office, and chief of all Germany's police functions. You can see where it's all going, Abendschon had told his wife. And that was exactly where it had gone.

He sighed again and looked out of the window. Heydrich and his cohorts were all running around in small circles trying to find someone to blame for the flight to Britain of the deputy-Führer, Rudolf Hess. Goebbels—'Mahatma Propagandi,' as he was known—was telling the German people that Hess was crazy. Deputy-Führer, but crazy! What did that make the rest of them?

It was a nice day. If the lime trees were still standing in the Unter den Linden, it would be nice to go for a walk, he thought. But there were no trees there any more. They had been cut down and replaced with great ugly marble pillars crowned with eagles, as charming as a fist. All the pleasure of sitting at a pavement table, the leisurely feeling of boulevard life, had been destroyed at a stroke. The Unter den Linden was a place for goose-stepping Waffen-SS now. There were no boulevardiers in Berlin any more.

Come on, Walter, he chided himself. No use pining for the old days. They are gone. Everything that ever mattered is gone. Eva, the boys . . . well, he wouldn't think about that today, thank you. He looked at the photograph of Alben Graumann on the Gestapo personnel record, turned the pages. A wife, Karin. An address in Schmargendorf. No children, by the look of it. Start with the wife, he thought. Then Kramer? He could look up his record easily enough. It might not tell him anything. You never knew. After twenty years, you learned that damned few cases were ever solved by brilliant deductive work on the part of a detective. Plodding, boring, routine police work was what usually did it. All right. The wife, then Kramer. Then what? A vehicle and pedestrian survey, perhaps, at the scene of the murder. What you did was to interview everyone who had passed the place where the body was found between the hours of eleven p.m. and three a.m., the parameters set by the police doctor's autopsy. You kept it up for ten days or so. People do things out of habit, every day more or less the same. They get up, they shave, they eat breakfast, they catch a tram at the same spot, meet a friend, buy a newspaper at the kiosk. It was surprising how often a VPS produced results. The trouble was the paperwork.

Walter Abendschon hated paperwork. He saw his job as the prevention of crime, not the writing of reports. That was how they'd done it in the old days. Now it was the other way around: if you could write good reports, you could go straight to the top. That was why none of the men Abendschon respected as investigators were at the top. Why he himself had risen as high as he ever would in the ranks of the *Kriminalpolizei*. It didn't bother him. He was nearly fifty now; and there was a decent pension.

He watched a girl in a pretty print frock walk down the street below. The breeze moulded the dress to her body and he felt a faint pulse of lust. Dirty old man, he thought. He tapped his desk twice, making a decision. He would go and see Graumann's wife tomorrow.

Washington, June 30, 1941

Grainy-eyed from lack of sleep on the twenty-six-hour Clipper flight from Lisbon, Sam Gray matched the brisk pace set by his Marine escort along the busy corridors which linked the State, War and Navy Building with the White House. *Report to General William Donovan*: that was all Landis had told him before he was bundled into his priority seat on Pan American's Boeing 314. As he hurried after the Marine, secretaries bustled past them, sheaves of paper under their arms. The whole place hummed with an air of urgency. The Marine steered Sam left and down a corridor at the end of which were double doors bearing the Presidential seal. The Marine knocked and stood respectfully aside. The door was opened by invisible hands, and Sam found himself in an airy room dominated by a long, shining table. At the head of the table, cigarette holder cocked at a jaunty angle, sat the President of the United States.

"Well, son, we're glad you could make it," Roosevelt said. The familiar, aristocratic voice was warm. His heavy head was tilted to one side, and there was a smile on the thin lips. The sunken eyes were sharp and inquiring. He looked as tired as Sam felt.

"Mr President," Sam said, concealing his surprise.

"Mr Gray—Sam, isn't it? I want you to meet General

Donovan," Roosevelt said. He gestured towards a silver haired, dumpy-looking man in a rumpled uniform. Donovan, still standing by the door he had so silently opened, surveyed Sam with mild blue eyes. He nodded, as though Sam was about what he had expected, and came across to sit at the table on Roosevelt's left.

"Sit down, Sam," he said, pointing at a chair with his chin.

"Thank you, General," Sam said. He'd done his homework before he left Berlin. This was the famous 'Wild Bill' Donovan, the most decorated American soldier of the Great War, a successful corporation lawyer who had become Roosevelt's special adviser. Among, Sam reminded himself, a lot of other things.

"What you are about to hear now is ultra secret, Sam," Donovan said. "You realise that, of course."

"I understand, sir."

"All right. In January of this year, a top level policy conference was convened here in Washington. It was code-named ABC-1, and its main purpose was to define British and American joint policy in the event of war between this country and Germany. A number of matters arising out of that conference were of an intelligence nature. Which put us at something of a disadvantage."

"We suffer from never having had a secret intelligence service like the British, or even the Germans, have," Roosevelt said. "The FBI, or course, is perfectly capable of handling internal security. But when it comes to operating outside of the United States, we are babes in arms. So I have decided, and the Joint Chiefs concur, that it's time America had such an organisation. General Donovan is going to head it up, with the title of Coordinator of Information."

"So all we need now," Sam said slowly, "is some information."

Roosevelt's eyes widened a fraction, and the cigarette holder rose to an even jauntier angle. Then he smiled, the warm smile which had won millions of hearts, as genuine as sunshine. Sam smiled back; it was impossible not to. Roosevelt could make you like him just by smiling. That was a hell of a gift to have if you were a politician, Sam thought.

"I like this one, Bill," Roosevelt said.

"So do I, Mr President," Donovan said. "That's why I want him on my staff."

"You want me to be a spy?" Sam said.

"Not exactly," Donovan replied. "Although you're close. I want you to head up our German section."

"I'm flattered, General," Sam said. "But why me?"

"You've got the right profile, Sam," Donovan said. "You were born in Germany, weren't you?"

"Yes, sir. I took out citizenship papers in—"

"We know all that," Donovan said, waving an arm. "What's more important is that Landis says you have a natural aptitude for intelligence work, and after studying your reports and your personal dossier, I can see why he does. You probably know more about Hitler's Germany than any man we have. And that's why we want you on the team."

"Starting when, General?"

"Now," Donovan said. His voice was as mild as milk, but one look at the pale blue eyes told Sam that Donovan was not a man who often took 'no' for an answer. He shrugged.

"Take it you're agreeable?" Roosevelt said. "Jim-dandy! Bill has a lot of questions for you."

"Sir," Sam said, waiting.

"This Berlin contact of yours," Donovan said. "Is he reliable?"

"He gave us the Hitler directive on the invasion of Russia, General," Sam said. "And he confirmed the date of the attack."

"That's right, he did," Donovan muttered. "And the damned Russians wouldn't believe it. Well, they know better now, the poor bastards." There was a little silence. Hitler had launched his blitzkrieg exactly on schedule, dawn of June 22. All along an eighteen hundred-mile front, three million soldiers of the *Wehrmacht* had fallen upon the unsuspecting Soviet army and swept it contemptuously aside, spearing towards Lvov, Minsk, Brest-Litovsk. German units were at the gates of Riga, across the Berezina River, heading for Kiev, heading for Moscow, heading for Leningrad.

"What's the man's name again, Bill?" Roosevelt asked.

"He calls himself Karl-André Rauth," Sam offered. "That's not his real name. He is an officer in German Military Intelligence."

"Has he ever said anything about a plot to depose Hitler?"

"No, sir."

"Yet you have reported that there is a strong anti-Hitler faction in German High Command."

"General," Sam said. "Let me try to explain the dichotomy which exists at the Bendlerstrasse. A great many of the senior generals of the German Army loathe Hitler. They loathe the Nazis collectively and individually. They will not socialise with them, they will not—because it is part of their code, and because they have the right not to—join the Party. They actively opposed Hitler's plans for war. They did not want to invade Poland, or the Low Countries. They did not want to go to war with Britain. But they did it because it was their duty. Duty first, because the State comes first. The fact that the State is led by someone they hate makes no difference. As for Hitler, I imagine he feels much the same way about them. He's had his collisions with the Army, and so far he's won all of them. They might talk about deposing him, but I doubt they would go any further."

"Why not?" Donovan rasped.

"I'm not sure I could explain it," Sam said. "It has to do with the way a German Junker would see the act of treason."

"Try us," Roosevelt said, leaning forward.

"Men like these," Sam began, choosing his words carefully, "do not contemplate treason lightly. And when they do, they carefully define what they mean. To do what Karl does, to betray their country's secrets to a foreign power, would be unthinkable. It would place a man beyond the pale. That would be what they call *Landesverrat*, treason against the state and one's own comrades. But to attempt to overthrow the government, or to change the constitution by force, which is also treason, they see differently. It is still treason, but perhaps a permissible kind."

"Damned if I see the difference," Roosevelt said.

"If the government is leading the country into ill-considered hostilities, against a foreign power, the Army might see it as its duty to prevent that government from doing so. If the only way to do so was to depose the head of state, it

would do it. That would be what they call *Hochverrat,*
which is quite a different thing to treasonable betrayal, or
Landesverrat. The one is honourable, the other unthinkable."

"It's a damned fine point," Donovan said.

"Yes, sir," Sam said, wondering whether the words ex-
isted by means of which he could make men with the background of Donovan and the President understand the
thought-processes of an aristocratic German Junker.

"Interesting," Roosevelt said. He gave Sam his big smile
again. It was like trying to ignore sunrise, Sam thought.

"How much do you know about British Intelligence,
Sam?" Donovan asked, abruptly.

"Only what I've picked up these last few months, sir,"
Sam said. "Not a great deal. MI5, MI6, that sort of thing."

"I'll break it down for you," Donovan said. "All military
intelligence breaks down into two or three areas. Espionage
against your country's enemies; counter-espionage on your
own ground; and overt action, such as sabotage on enemy
territory. In Britain, the foreign espionage is handled by
MI6, also called the Secret Intelligence Service. MI5 handles
counter-espionage, and overt action is the province of a new
group they have, called Special Operations Executive."

"That the one in Baker Street?" Roosevelt said.

"That's it, Mr President," Donovan said. "Norgeby
House."

"I used to read Sherlock Holmes stories."

"Maybe they did, too, sir," Donovan grinned, rubbing his
eyes tiredly. "You got all that, Sam?"

"MI6, MI5 and SOE," Sam said. "Yes, sir."

"In April, the British Joint Chiefs of Staff created an
overall agency to control all espionage, subversion and de-
ception. Officially, it does not exist. It is known as the
London Controlling Section. All other security agencies report to its head, a man called Oliver Stanley."

"I see," Sam said, wondering where the hell all this was
supposed to lead him.

"I want you to be our liaison with LCS in London,"
Donovan said.

Sam shrugged. "Yes, sir," he said, waiting.

"You're wondering what the hell this is all about, aren't
you, Sam?" Roosevelt said. He stubbed out his cigarette and

inserted another into the holder. "Go ahead, Bill. Tell him."

"One of the things the British mooted at ABC-1 last January was an assassination attempt on Adolf Hitler," Donovan said. There was a long silence. Roosevelt looked at Sam expectantly, then grinned.

"Bill," he said. "He doesn't believe you."

"Oh, I believe him, Mr President," Sam said.

"You don't think it's feasible?"

"May I speak frankly, sir?"

"Of course."

"I think it's lunatic," Sam said, flatly. "Nobody could get near enough to Hitler to kill him, except maybe one of his own people."

"The British think they can do it. They say there is reason to believe that the German general staff is ready to mount a coup d'état."

"What makes them think so?"

"LCS says approaches have been made through Professor Karl Burckhardt, head of the International Red Cross in Geneva."

"By whom?"

"A man named Haushofer. LCS will tell you more."

Sam shook his head. There was vexation as much as doubt in his gesture. It was possible, he supposed. Anything was possible in the slimy labyrinth that was Hitler's Germany.

"What do you know about the Hess affair, Sam?" Donovan asked. The question was abrupt and unexpected. Sam shrugged. He was getting used to being asked unexpected questions.

"Only what the British have told us, General," Sam said. "He flew to England early in May. Landed in Scotland, gave his identity as Alfred Horn, a Luftwaffe *Oberleutnant,* and asked to be taken to some Duke or other."

"The Duke of Hamilton," Donovan supplied. "Go on."

"He was taken to meet Hamilton, and told him he was Rudolf Hess. He had a peace plan with him, a mission to save mankind. If the British were prepared to talk armistice, he was sure he could get Hitler to listen. If not, she would be subjugated. That's pretty well all the news we've had."

"It's a lot more than they've told their own people," Donovan remarked. "The newspapers have been having a Roman holiday with the story."

"I read some of them," Sam said. "What was that line? 'What is the deputy Führer of Germany doing in England? Your Hess is as good as mine!'"

"Churchill sent me a note," Roosevelt said. "He said they were letting the Press have a good run for a bit, to keep the Germans guessing."

"Hmm," Donovan said, and Roosevelt smiled.

"Yes, Bill," he said. "Hmm, indeed. I wonder what really is behind this story?"

"Maybe Sam here can find out for us, Mr President," Donovan said. "I can't escape the feeling that there's some connection between the Hess thing and their plans to kill Hitler."

"Hess is one of Hitler's most devoted followers, General," Sam said. "He has been with him right from the start, even went to prison with him after the Munich *putsch*. I can't see him having anything to do with a plot to kill the man he worships."

There was another lengthy silence. Donovan stuck out his lower lip and frowned at the folders on the table in front of him. Roosevelt blew smoke into the air and said nothing.

"Mr President?" Donovan said, finally. Roosevelt sighed and nodded.

"Tell him the rest of it," he said.

"Churchill is desperate, Sam," Donovan said. "The British need a morale-booster, breathing space, anything. Their attitude to this whole thing is that it doesn't matter a wholesome goddamn who does what to whom, just so they can throw a spanner into the works. Churchill wants the thing to go ahead. In fact, the wheels have already begun to turn. Look."

He pushed a buff-coloured memorandum across the table. It bore the printed heading of the British Ministry of Defence, and the serial number 1229. It was rubber-stamped VERY URGENT and CONFIDENTIAL. The memorandum was dated May 19, 1941. It stated that War Office authorisation had been granted for the immediate parachute training of five officers and five other ranks, team purpose unspecified.

"Parachutists?" Sam and incredulously. "They think they could drop parachutists into Germany to kill Hitler?"

"They haven't decided anything, Sam," Donovan said. "They're waiting to talk to you."

"Me?"

"That was why we asked you to get details of Hitler's security arrangements." Sam thought of Karl Rauth sitting beside him on the bench in the Tiergarten. *The only reason you can want information on Hitler's security is so you can penetrate it.* Sam had thought then, when Karl said it, that the whole idea was crazy. He had not changed his mind. It was still crazy, and he said so.

"You may be right," Donovan said. "But it's not our decision. We'll find out more when you get to Canada."

"Canada?" Sam said.

"The British have a special training camp at Oshawa," Roosevelt said. "Just outside Toronto. They call it Camp X. If the Hitler thing goes ahead, that's where it will be planned."

"When do I leave, sir?" Sam asked.

"You've got a seat on tonight's flight to Toronto," Roosevelt said. He didn't say it like a man who was expecting an argument.

Berlin, July 10, 1941

Marianna Gris was frightened. You could end up in a KZ servicing fifty Poles a day if you were convicted for prostitution, and the *Schupos* had caught her red-handed, propositioning a 'Fritz' on the corner of the Bleibtreustrasse. As if that wasn't bad enough, they hadn't taken her and the other half dozen girls they'd picked up to the usual place, the *polizeirevier* on Nestorstrasse. They had all been brought in the black van to the main police building at Sophie Charlottenburg-platz.

Officially, there was no prostitution in the Third Reich.

Working the streets was *verboten,* so most of the girls used the hotels, bars and cafés. The alternative was a brothel. Marianna considered herself a cut above that breed. More exclusive, like. She knew most of the *Schupos,* just as the policemen knew most of the girls. They took their bribes from the *Kotzen,* the pimps, and turned a blind eye. Once in a while they'd pull one of the girls in, just to show they were on the job. The girls accepted that as an occasional hazard. They fined you and let you go: anti-social behaviour, it was called. All part of the overheads. But this time was different, and Marianna knew instinctively that something was wrong.

Two men came into the cell and tapped one of the girls on the shoulder. One of them was a big, burly fellow wearing a dark stubble. His eyes were bloodshot and he was smoking a foul, wet-ended cigar. The second man was thinner, sandy-haired, going bald at the front. He had a resigned look, as though he had given up hoping ever to hear the truth spoken. The girl got up off the bench and went out of the cell with them.

"*Kripo,*" one of the girls whispered to Marianna, and her heart sank still further. Detectives normally took no notice at all of prostitutes. As long as a girl was discreet and not too obviously on the game, they left you alone. Especially if, like Marianna, the girl was French-born. Thanks to *Reichsführer* Himmler's racial edicts, it was a damned sight safer for an SS-man to pick up a foreign born tart than a German woman, who was supposed to save herself for the production of fine Aryan sons to serve the Führer.

One by one the girls were taken out. None of them came back. Were they being released after questioning? Or worse, taken somewhere else? Marianna fought hard to keep the fearful word out of her mind, but it kept drifting back in, like a black cloud: *Gestapo.* After about two hours, the fat detective with the bloodshot eyes came in, and jerked a thumb at Marianna. She followed him out of the cell and along a brightly-lit corridor. She looked through the windows of the offices as she walked past. Inside, women were typing, men sitting at desks frowned over piles of paper. The fat man pushed her into a room. It contained a table, a chair, a bench along one wall, a grey filing cabinet and an unshaded electric light. There was no window. The floor was gritty with dirt and littered with cigarette butts. A broken cup lay in one corner. On the table was a lid from an Ovo tin, full of cigarette ash and more butts.

"Sit down," the fat man told her. His voice was harsh, as if anger was his natural state. The door opened as Marianna sat down, and the other man she had seen before came in. His face bore no expression whatsoever. He looked at Marianna as if she were a pair of shoes.

"You are Marianna Hermione Gris?"

"Yes."

"Yes, *sir*."

"I'm sorry. Yes, sir."

"French, eh?" the fat man said. "You're in trouble, Frenchie."

"What for?" Marianna said, acting indignant. "I haven't done nothing."

"You're a whore, aren't you?"

"Albert," the sandy-haired one said, mildly. "Go easy."

"Hold your mouth, Rauch!" the one called Albert snapped. "This is my interrogation. Now, you!" He glared at Marianna again.

"Please," Marianna said. "I wasn't doing nothing. This fellow stopped me. Asked me the way. I was only being polite."

"Being polite, eh?" Albert sneered. "You stand on that corner seven days a week, noon till midnight, being polite, do you? Think I'm a damned idiot, do you?"

"Albert," the one called Rauch said, again. The fat man ignored him. He hitched a heavy ham on to the corner of the table and blew smoke into Marianna's face.

"All right, Frenchie. Answer some questions."

"Anything," she said. "You just ask."

"Don't lie to me, Frenchie," he warned her. "You know what'll happen if we send you up, don't you?"

Marianna shivered. Everybody knew about the camps. They said you never came out alive. She watched as Albert took a photograph out of his pocket and laid it on the table. Oh, Mary Mother of God! she thought, it's *him*! Her mind emptied all at once. She could not think. It was as though someone had struck a mighty gong in her head, and simultaneously stuffed her ears with cotton wool. They couldn't know! How could they know? They must know! How did they know?

"Well?" Albert said, "You know this fellow?"

"Look at her face," Rauch said.

"You *do* know him," Albert said, his voice thickening with interest. He slid his haunch off the table and bent over Marianna, lifting her head with his stubby forefinger. His breath smelled.

"No," Marianna whispered. "No."

"Maybe we ought to take her downstairs, and see if we can't jog her memory, eh, Rauch?" the fat one said. He clenched his fist and stared at it ruminatively, as if trying to remember the last time he had used it.

"You'd better tell us, Marianna," Rauch said, softly.

She looked at him and then at the fat detective. Rauch caught the glance and jerked his head. Albert, the fat man, hesitated for a moment, as though intending to argue. Then he got up and went out of the room, shutting the door with an angry bang. Rauch turned to face Marianna. He and Albert had worked out their technique a long time ago. Albert was the bully; he was the nice guy. It wasn't foolproof, but it usually worked. He offered Marianna a cigarette and lit it for her. She inhaled the smoke greedily and smiled back at Rauch. He had a nice smile, she thought. It completely banished the fed-up look he had been wearing.

"I never done it," she said, anxiously. "I swear I never."

"Tell me what happened," he said.

"I don't even know who he is. Was."

"That's not important. How was he killed?"

"I don't know. I mean, I know he was shot. But I don't know how," Marianna said. "I never done it! You've got to believe me!"

"All right," he said. "Let's say I believe you. Tell me the rest."

"The . . . it was my gun."

"What was?"

"He was killed with my gun."

"But you didn't do it."

"I told you that."

"How did someone else get your gun and kill him?"

"I don't know," she wailed.

"Where is the gun now?"

"I threw it into the lake in the Hindenburg Park."

"Why?"

"I was afraid," she said. "I was scared I'd get the blame."

"Whereabouts in the lake did you throw the gun?"

"Off the bridge. The Bar-brüke."

"Wait there," he said. He went out of the room, not closing the door. She heard him speaking rapidly to someone, and caught a few words. "*Pistole . . . Fennsee . . . dringend.*" They're going to search for the gun, she thought. Rauch came back into the room. He looked at her for a long time, as if trying to decide how angry to be. When he spoke, his voice was patient, as if he were speaking to a wayward child.

"Listen to me now, *Liebchen,*" he said. "Listen carefully. I want the whole story. Understand me? Everything. Not a word missing. Otherwise, you're going to be in more trouble than you know what to do with."

Marianna shivered. there was no trace of the nice smile now.

"I never done it," she whispered.

"We've been looking for you for a long time, Marianna," Rauch said. "You don't think we've been pulling you tarts in by accident, do you?"

"I didn't know."

"We're not interested in you. We want whoever it was that killed Graumann."

"Who?"

"The dead man."

"Was that his name?"

"You didn't know him?"

"No!" Marianna said, shaking her head violently. "I never seen him until I woke up in that car park. And there he was." She was silent for a moment. "What's going to happen to me?"

"If you had nothing to do with Graumann's death, nothing will happen to you."

"I'll bet," she said.

"Don't you trust me, Marianna?" Rauch said, and he grinned.

"Fucking coppers!" she said, and started to talk. The sandy-haired Rauch listened without interrupting until she was finished. Then he went out of the room and placed a call to *Kriminalpolizei* headquarters on the Werderscher-markt. Twenty minutes later, Marianna Gris looked up to see a big man in a black overcoat and a wide-brimmed felt hat come into the room. He had a thin-lipped, uncom-promising mouth, turned down at both ends, and his heavy eyebrows were joined in what appeared to be an habitual frown. It was his eyes which took the harshness from his face. They were the brightest blue that Marianna had ever seen. He showed her a *Kripo* warrant disc.

"My name is Abendschon," he said. "*Kriminaloberassistant* Rauch has given me a short version of what you told him. I would like to hear it in full from you, if you please."

Marianna swallowed noisily and nodded. He looked all right, even if he was *Kripo*. Sooner them than the Gestapo, any day of the week, she thought, with a shudder.

"Got a cigarette?" she said. "Have you?"

Abendschon nodded and gave her a cigarette, lighting it. He didn't smoke himself, but he always carried a pack. Giv-ing a suspect a cigarette forged a bond between him and the interrogator. Often no more was needed.

"I was on the Ku-damm," Marianna said. "In the Café Dobren."

"What time was it?"

"When he came in, you mean? About ten-thirty. Maybe a little later. He asked me if he could sit down and started talking to me. Asked me if I'd like some wine. I thought, that's a bit of luck. He said he was from Hamburg."

"Did he have a Hamburg accent?"

"I wouldn't know," Marianna said. "I'm from Alsace."

"What did he look like?"

"Tall," she said, frowning to remember. "Good looking. He had a good body. Like a ski instructor."

"How old?"

"Thirty-five. Give or take a year or two."

"Well dressed?"

"Not specially."

She told him how the man had sat with her for a few

minutes, then excused himself to go to the men's room.

"Gave me fifty Marks," she said. "Left the wine. He was gone for ages. Then he came back in and got his coat, in a hurry all of a sudden. 'Come on,' he says, and grabs my arm. Off we go, damned near galloping. I thought at the time it was funny. You get some that can't wait, but he didn't look like one of those. You can usually tell."

"Where did you go?"

"We walked down the Ku-damm, and turned into a side street. Fasanenstrasse, I think. Then he pushed me into a doorway. I thought he was going to do it right then and there, get us both arrested. I mean, I'm not one of those Giesebrechtstrasse alleycats, you know, and I said to him, I said—"

"The man, the man!" Abendschon said, impatiently. "What happened then?"

"I don't know," Marianna said. "Honest, mister. I thought afterwards, he must have put something in my drink. I remember him pushing me into the doorway, and then everything went black. And I woke up in that damned car park, bloody frozen!" She shivered, as if remembering the icy numbness of her body on the unyielding concrete, the biting wind. "I felt as if someone had cut my legs off. Then I seen why. That man. He was lying on my legs. I could see he was dead. One look and I knew. All I could think of was, what will I do? Supposing someone come along and found me there, lying on the ground next to a dead man I'd never seen in my life?"

"What did you do then?"

"I seen the gun, my gun. It was lying on the ground. I never did like the damned thing. Well, it had been fired. I put it in my purse. I couldn't hardly stand up, let alone walk. I kept banging on my legs with my fists, trying to get the circulation going. And then when it started, I thought I'd scream!"

"What time was this?"

"It must have been nearly three in the morning. Christ, it was cold!" she said. "It was half-past when I got home, I remember that."

"Where do you live?"

"Leibnizstrasse," she said. "By the Post Office."

"Very nice," Abendschon said, mildly. "Live alone, do you?"

"No, my boyf—." Her hand flew to her mouth.

"Was he in on it, Marianna?" Abendschon said. "Was it him that took the money, or you?"

"I never touched him!" Marianna shrilled. "I never went near him. He was all covered in blood. Covered!"

"His wallet was empty," Abendschon insisted. He saw the look on her face and waited.

"I found it!" Marianna said, the shade of defiance that had been in her voice turning to wheedling. "It was in my purse. I found it when I got home. I wasn't going back there."

The big detective got off his chair. "What number Leibnizstrasse?" he said. There was no trace of friendliness in his voice any more.

"Twenty-eight," she muttered. "Top floor."

She told him the name: Jurgen Schiel. He went out, closing the door. After about ten minutes, Marianna got up and went across the room. She opened the door a crack and looked out. The fat detective, Albert, stared at her from a bench in the corridor. There was still no expression on his face. Marianna closed the door hastily and sat down again.

Abendschon was back within an hour, although to Marianna it seemed that he had been gone a week. His coat was wet. It must be raining, she thought.

"Well, Marianna," he said. "So far so good."

"What do you mean?"

"We found your gun where you said it would be. And your—friend, Jurgen, confirms your story. As far as it goes."

"I'm telling you the truth!" she said. "I swear it."

"We still haven't cleared up just who your mysterious client was. The ski instructor."

"He never told me his name," Marianna said, agonisedly. "I thought he was just another Fritz."

Walter Abendschon took a photograph out of his inside pocket and laid it on the table alongside the photograph of Alben Graumann. Marianna looked at it. She thought she was going to faint.

"Is . . . that him?"

"You tell me, Marianna," Abendschon said.

"It looks like him. Only younger."

"It's not a recent photograph."

"I *think* it's him," she said. "Do you want me to say it is?"

Abendschon didn't answer and Marianna lapsed into glum silence, thinking her answer had somehow displeased him. In fact, the opposite was true: Abendschon was pleased. Once again, the old methods had proven to be the best. No flashy tricks. Just persistence and patience.

The vehicle and pedestrian survey he had set up brought in seventy-six reports, most of them useless. The vital one was the statement of an old cleaning lady who had seen a woman coming out of the Franzkowiak car park around three o'clock on the morning that Graumann's body had been found. The old lady said the woman was walking very erratically, and that she looked like a tart. You didn't see many of them so far from the main boulevards: that was what had made her remember. And that was all Abendschon needed. Word was passed down to the uniformed police. About two thousand tarts had been shown Graumann's photograph before his hunch paid off. Abendschon felt no triumph. Solving the problem had left him with an even bigger one. It began to look very much as if Paul Kramer, deputy head of *Abwehr* Section IIIF, had murdered Gestapo agent Alben Graumann.

The next question was: *why?*

Oshawa, July 14, 1941

The big black Ford sedan moved smoothly out of the airport and on to 401, going east along Lake Ontario. There were sailboats on the water. It was a pretty day. The driver, a dark-haired girl in WRAC uniform, had met Sam at the airport and given him an ID card and a chain bracelet which carried a disc bearing the legend S25-1-1. She told him her name was Jennifer Moffatt. She hadn't spoken since.

Sam looked out of the window. A road sign went by. *Oshawa. Elevation 325 feet*, it said. The car turned off the main road and on to a narrow track between close growing trees. Ahead of them was a striped pole barrier. The driver stopped, and three men in battledress materialised from among the trees. They all carried Sten guns. The leader came light-footedly across towards the car as Corporal Moffatt rolled down the window and handed him the ID cards. He was a young, tough-looking fellow about an inch above six feet in height. There were no insignia on his uniform. He checked Sam's face against the picture in the ID card and snapped to a salute.

"*Eveninsah!*" he said, without visibly moving his jaw. Then he rapped out a command to the other two, who ran to raise the barrier. The car bumped down a dirt road and around a long, right-hand turn. Through the trees ahead Sam could see a scatter of wooden buildings. The place seemed familiar and it took him a few moments to realise why: it looked almost exactly like the summer camps for kids he had seen in upstate New York. The same wooden huts, the same dirt paths, the same glint of lake through the pines. The car pulled up outside one of the larger buildings, and Sam got out of the car. As he did, a tall, stooped man in the uniform of a British Army captain came down the steps towards him.

"You must be Sam Gray," he said, smiling. "I'm Nöel Mason-Morley. Glad you could come. Welcome to Glenrath." The staccato speech, Sam was to learn, was typical. Mason-Morley was a thin man with a long face and a cavalry moustache that concealed a thin-lipped mouth. His handshake was firm and strong, the brown eyes keen and direct.

"Glenrath?" Sam said.

"Oh, sorry. Name of this place before we took it over. Big estate. Belonged to a family called Sinclair till BSC acquired it."

BSC was British Security Coordination, which had offices in Rockefeller Center. Its head was the millionaire Canadian

William Stephenson, who had purchased Glenrath and then transferred the title to the Crown, Mason-Morley told Sam, as he showed him into what he apologetically referred to as the Officers' Mess.

"Can I get you anything?" he asked.

"Nothing, thank you," Sam said. "Let's get down to business, shall we?"

"Splendid!" Mason-Morley said. "My chaps are all agog to meet you."

"You've decided to go ahead, then?"

Mason-Morley frowned slightly, as though puzzled by the question. "Of course," he said. "It's never been a question of whether. Only how."

"I see," Sam said. "And that's why I'm here?"

"To brief my boffins on Hitler's security," Mason-Morley said. "They'll come up with the ways and means."

"All right," Sam said. "When do we begin?"

"As soon as you are ready."

"I'm ready now," Sam said.

"Splendid!" Mason-Morley said again. "Let's go over and meet the chaps, shall we?"

Mason-Morley's 'boffins'—a catch-all word to describe the men who worked in specialist fields: scientists, camouflage experts, weaponry designers—were a ragbag of nationalities. A couple of Scots, a Czech, two Hungarians, some Canadians, and, of course, Englishmen. All of them had one thing in common apart from their work: the marks of stress, dark smudges under the eyes, fingers stained with nicotine. Mason-Morley introduced them, one by one. Elder Wills, former scenic artist at London's Drury Lane Theatre, a survivor of Dunkirk, master of camouflage. The Korda brothers, Zoltan and Alex, who reproduced 'sets' identical with the actual locales in which agents might have to work. Aram Bojac, the Polish-born mine worker who had become Camp X's demolition expert. Ernie Bavin, Bill Deakin, a tall, languid fellow from Naval Intelligence called Fleming, Harvey Wells, Angus Laurence, John James, the names ran into a muddled mess in Sam's brain. He made no attempt to memorise them at this first meeting. They would get to know each other well enough over the next week or two.

Living at Camp X, he learned, was very much like being

tossed into the middle of a large, noisy and argumentative family. They quarrelled and got drunk, they criticised each other with vitriolic fury, worked incessantly—almost angrily, Sam thought—and generated an *esprit de corps* that would have done credit to the Brigade of Guards.

"The rule here is simple," Harvey Wells told Sam. "We can call any sonofabitch in the camp a sonofabitch any time we want to. But God help any other sonofabitch if he calls our sonofabitch a sonofabitch!"

Their pastimes were as varied as their backgrounds. Chess was the most favoured game, as well as the most hotly argued-over one. Table tennis was played with formidable fury, crosswords completed on a competitive basis. More than fifteen minutes on the London *Times* was considered pathetic; anyone who sneaked a look over someone else's shoulder was called names that would have made a Turkish brothelkeeper blush. Their most lordly contempt was reserved for Canadians. According to the Camp X team, the greatest thrill of a Canuck's life was when the snow didn't stick to his shovel. They pulled no punches, especially among themselves. Sam liked them all tremendously.

Life at Camp X had a rhythm which Sam fell readily into. Rise at seven, shower and shave, breakfast in the Team Mess. Project teams at Oshawa worked and ate separately. What each team was doing, members of another, as if by some unwritten rule, did not ask. They walked from Mess to lecture hall, usually arguing or making bets. They would bet on which of two birds would fly off a fence first. They also told awful schoolboy jokes, the lousier the better.

"What's the difference between a drainpipe and a dumb Dutchman?"

"I give up."

"One's a hollow cylinder and the other's a silly Hollander." (Groan.)

As for Captain Nöel Mason-Morley, Sam found that all his attempts to establish friendly rapport were gently but firmly fended off. He realised quite quickly that Mason-Morley would tell him the answer to any question he asked, but not a syllable more. He learned all the salient facts of the man's life: Eton and Balliol, a first in history followed by law school, the Bar, and the Foreign Office. Service in the Balkans and Czechoslovakia until the outbreak of war, followed by secondment to the Political Intelligence Division and then to LCS. Forty-two, married to the former Lady Lavinia Devon, two sons, a good country address—Sam knew all that, yet still knew nothing about the man. It was irritating, like an unscratchable itch, to conclude that Mason-Morley would never tell him anything he did not need to know, nor let him see anything other than what it was strictly necessary for him to see. Was it clumsy, or did Mason-Morley intend him to understand that he was being kept on a leash? The latter, Sam decided. Well, maybe that was how the British saw Anglo-US cooperation. If Nöel Mason-Morley was determined to keep him at arms' length, there wasn't a hell of a lot he could do about it. After a while, he accepted the status quo, while remaining irritated by the knowledge that it had been imposed on him: a defeat of sorts for him, a victory of a kind for Mason-Morley.

Well, say what you will, Sam thought, Mason-Morley knew what he was about. He laid it right on the line from the very first time they assembled in the so-called lecture hall. In fact it was a long wooden hut with a raised dais at one end. A blackboard and easel stood to one side. A desk and several upright chairs, canvas and steel like the ones set out in rows before the dais, gave the whole place the atmosphere of a makeshift school. Which was exactly, Sam thought, what it was.

"Gentlemen," Mason-Morley said. "To business."

The silence became different. It had an intensity that Sam could feel. He became aware that several of the assembled team were watching him, not Mason-Morley.

"The code name of this project is 'Wolf Trap'," Mason-Morley began. "Its objective is to achieve, by means of an assassination attempt upon Hitler, the possible overthrow of the Nazi dictatorship and the creation of armed resistance throughtout Europe to the German rule. It is part of an overall policy formulated by LCS, whose principal objective is to make the Nazis—or 'Nartzies', as Mr Churchill calls them—run around like the proverbial blue-arsed fly." He waited for the laugh and then moved on, his timing as perfect as Jack Benny's. "To that end, agents will be put in place wherever they can be landed. All of them will be given specific tasks. Sabotage, indoctrination, recruitment and so on. Over and above these tasks, it will be their job to spread word throughout Occupied Europe that we are about to invade and open a second front."

"Even though we know that's impossible, sir?" said someone in the audience.

"Precisely *because* we know it is impossible, Ian," Mason-Morley replied grimly. Eighteen missions had been flown this year so far, he added. That figure would be doubled by December. Liaison with the Polish government-in-exile's Deuxième Bureau was working well, he reported. The Dutch were also co-operating, as were the Belgians. The MI network in Denmark was operational again, and producing excellent intelligence via a link in Sweden.

"The assassination of Hitler will be the signal for all these networks and agents to act in unison, to create or encourage armed local insurrection, which in turn would bring pressure to bear upon the Army to stage a coup d'état. So our first question must be: given that we want to kill Hitler, where is the best place to do it? There are only two or three: at his residence on the Obersalzberg near Berchtesgaden; in Berlin; or in Munich. Our intelligence sources say he spent most of May in Berchtesgaden, but will not return there this year. That leaves either Berlin or Munich. I don't think I need state the obvious by saying it would be damned difficult to get paras into Berlin. That leaves Munich. Hitler goes there every year to celebrate the anniversary of his attempt to seize power in 1923. He's never missed yet, and we don't think he will this year. So we have a place: Munich. And a date: November 9."

There was complete, rapt silence. A place and a date took Operation Wolf Trap out of the realm of fantasy and made it hard reality. On November 9 in Munich, determined men would try to kill Adolf Hitler, Führer of the Third Reich. My God, Sam thought, that's less than four months away.

"We have a secondary reason for preferring Munich," Mason-Morley went on. "And that is its proximity to the Czechoslovakian border. Our most valuable source of information inside Nazi-occupied Europe is in that country, together with an armed and active resistance organisation. It is called *Obrana Naroda*, the Defence of the Nation. According to the Czech chief of intelligence in London, Colonel Morávec, it had a strength of several divisions, commanded by Regular Army officers who all went underground when Germany invaded the country in 1939. Morávec says that they have about 100,000 rifles and 10,000 machine guns, a sabotage section, and links with the puppet government. The existence of *Obrana Naroda* is a significant factor in the choice of Munich, because it can provide assistance and back-up for our paratroops." He paused, as if for effect. Then he turned to Sam and smiled. It was as if he sensed the objections forming in Sam's mind.

"Now I'm going to hand you over to our American friend, Sam Gray," he said. "And he can tell you why Operation Wolf Trap is impossible."

He sat down, and every eye in the room turned to Sam as he stood and faced the assembly. Do I sugar the pill or give it to them straight? he wondered. Straight, he decided. No point in minimising the problems.

He began by telling them a little about the man who was their target. Adolf Hitler, born April 20, 1889 in Braunau, a small village on the Inn River between Austria and Germany. The Führer and Chancellor of the Third Reich was in good shape for a man of fifty-one who rarely took any exercise more strenuous than a short walk. Medium height, dark, lank hair and pale blue eyes, a strutting walk in public that changed to a strange, almost womanish gait in private.

"He is shrewd, arrogant, biased, a self-educated man whose opinions exactly match the prejudices of the average German," Sam told them. "He is neither the figure of fun your radio comedians try to make him, nor does he foam at the mouth and chew the carpets the way the propaganda people would have you believe. And one thing I can tell you about him for certain is that he is not an easy target."

Hitler made a point, he told them, of rarely being where he was expected to be. He had survived a dozen assassination attempts and was fully aware that another was always a possibility. And he had done so by a carefully planned lack of pre-planning, deciding at the very last moment by which means he would travel, where to appear to the crowds.

"He hardly ever announces his plans or destinations,"

Sam said. "He often makes his decision on the basis of a tossed coin. And even as he is about to step into his plane or his car or his train, he may call off the whole trip. You could call it intuition, or cunning, or fear, and all three would be correct."

Thirty or forty specially-selected SS and SD officers hugged the huge armour-plated Mercedes 770-K in which he travelled, each armed with two 9mm pistols and fifty rounds of ammunition. Hitler himself was always armed— he was a proficient shot—and on public appearances wore a bulletproof vest and a steel-lined cap that weighed three and a half pounds. Escort cars formed a flying wedge before and behind the Führer's vehicle, each carrying six more pistols and as many Schmeisser machine-pistols, plus a machine-gun.

"It's a standard joke that the Germans are a thorough race," he went on. "It is also true, and nowhere more evident than in the arrangements to protect Hitler. Let me give you an example of how the system works. Suppose Hitler has to go somewhere: to Munich, say, from Berlin. The first thing that happens is that those responsible for the three alternative modes of travel—road, rail, or air—are alerted. None knows for certain what Hitler's choice will be. So schedules are drawn up for the special train, the *Führersonderzug*, and catering is ordered, refuelling stops plotted, and so on. Meanwhile, Hans Baur, his personal pilot, works out flight plans and gets weather reports, and all civil and military flights are informed of the flight plan. Erich Kempka, Hitler's chief driver, decides whether open or closed cars will be needed, and how many. All go on immediate standby. Then, at the very last moment, Hitler decides whether to fly or go by car or what. Nobody, and I repeat, nobody knows until that moment. If he goes by train, the route is a *Geheime Reichssache*, a state secret. The special planes and the cars make their own way to Munich, to be available there at a moment's notice. Then all the protection squads have to be organised, plus his two secretaries, the press chief, the doctors, the photographer, radio operators, valets and God alone knows who else. The logistics of the most simple journey can be enormous, but they rarely get fouled up. And that, gentlemen, is what I mean by thorough."

If that had discouraged them, Sam thought, it didn't show. Well, that was the good news. Now he was going to give them the bad news.

Getting a man or men into any position where they might get a clear shot at Hitler was not going to be at all easy, he told them. Security surrounding any regularly recurring event starring Hitler was intense and stringent. An 'A-file' on all enemies of the state living in the wider vicinity of such places as the November march route was kept constantly under review.

"For your purposes, you may think of an enemy of the state as anyone who has been heard to say he does not necessarily agree with everything Adolf Hitler has ever said or done," Sam said. "The criminal police also check their files on all known criminals, and the security services check out all foreigners. Further files are kept on all persons living or working within 500 metres of the site of such events, and on people who have storage areas near them, or garages, or offices, or make deliveries in the area."

Every one of these persons would be checked for political, moral or criminal activity, and either cleared or placed in preventive detention. Every new arrival and every departure from the area must be recorded, he told them. At least three months before every Führer appearance, checks on foreigners and all others entering or leaving Germany were intensified. No exceptions were permitted.

"We managed to get hold of a *Sicherheitsdienst* memorandum," Sam said, thinking, as he spoke, of the man he had known as Karl Rauth. *You're a brave man, my friend.* "I'll read it to you. You may find it instructive. I quote: 'A complete review of all advance security will be effected in secrecy in the period four weeks before an event, and ending one week before it. If possible, the area under examination will be closed while it is given renewed examination of an unsurpassed thoroughness. This survey will extend to basements, attics, side and secondary rooms of all kinds, sewage systems, sanitary installations, floors, walls, pillars, ceilings, furniture and decorations, platforms, stands and other tem-

75

porary structures, cables, transformer stations, underpasses, bridges, lamp-posts, monuments, advertising pillars, sand-boxes, telephone booths, mailboxes, scaffolding, garages, power lines, pylons, flagpoles and so forth. All screening will be effected with the most sophisticated available scientific and technical equipment, such as sensing, listening and screening devices. spotlights, metal-detectors and electro-magnets. Explosives experts must be consulted to indicate on the basis of their experience those places especially suited for assassination attempts with explosives'."

He stopped and looked up, hoping that what came next would not be overkill. Nobody spoke. "Not very encouraging? Well, I'm afraid there's worse to come. There's even tighter surveillance in the last few days and hours before the event. No one is allowed through the security cordon without a pass, issued and approved by the Gestapo. And all passes are collected after the event."

He turned to Mason-Morley. "That's about it, Captain," he said.

"Certainly seems like it, Mr Gray," Mason-Morley said. "Well, gentlemen, there is your problem. It's your job to solve it. Questions?"

"How many men can we put in, sir?" someone asked.

"Up to you," Mason-Morley replied. "We have well over a hundred volunteers from the 1st Czech Army Brigade at Cholmondely Castle. They begin training at Camusdarach next month."

Camusdarach was in the Scottish highlands above Mallaig on the Sound of Sleat. It was one of the most rugged of Britain's Commando training courses. It was to be set aside for the sole purpose of training the Wolf Trap team, he explained.

"What about Hitler's residences, sir?" Laurence asked. "Any chance of getting to him there?"

"We'll be covering the residences in the coming days," Mason-Morley replied. "But I think it wouldn't be anticipating Mr Gray to say they'd be a hard nut to crack."

"And then some," Sam added.

After another hour or so, in which the questions came thick and fast, Mason-Morley called a halt for the day. "I shouldn't be surprised if you chaps could use a drink," he said, with a thin smile. That got a raucous cheer, and he held up a hand. "Very good, then. See you at dinner!"

They went out of the lecture hall. As the sergeant closed the door behind them, they heard the arguments begin. Noël Mason-Morley smiled and led the way across a clearing to the Mess. There were no signposts at Camp X. Armed soldiers patrolled the intersections of the paths between the trees. Inside the Officers' Mess, Mason-Morley ordered drinks and they sat in battered but comfortable wicker chairs by the empty fireplace.

"How long do you think this is going to take, Noël?" Sam asked, sipping the Glenlivet.

"A week," Mason-Morley said. "Two at the outside. There aren't all that many options, after all."

"I hope I didn't make it all sound too hopeless."

"No," the Englishman said. He was quiet for a long moment, staring into his gin and tonic as though it were a crystal ball and he a fortune teller. "I say, you'll come over to London, won't you?" he said at last. "Help me put it to the Chief?"

"Sure," Sam said. "What's he like?"

"Damned tartar," Mason-Morley said.

The rest of Sam's stay at Camp X was one of intensive, mind-numbing work. Plan after plan after plan was mooted, picked apart, stitched together again, demolished. Tempers frayed, patience vanished, as earnest, dedicated men weighed the effects upon the human head of a tracer bullet fired from a high-powered rifle, the efficacy of the limpet mine compared to the poisoned grenade. What if someone could get into Hitler's first-floor apartment at Prinzregentenplatz 16 in Munich and plant a bomb? Send for Sam Gray. He told them about the system of passes used there and at the *Führerbau* in the Arcisstrasse. Whether Hitler was there or not, fourteen *Sicherheitsdienst* officers were assigned to the apartment. All passes were regularly inspected and revalidated. Strike the apartment. What about the cars? How well protected were they? Sam told them.

"There are forty cars altogether," he said. "In practice, Hitler uses only three or four. The one he prefers is a 7·7 litre Mercedes-Benz tourer, registration number 1A-14845.

It has 30mm bulletproof glass all round, 8mm steel plate in the doors, and to head height behind the passenger seats. The driver's compartment is steel-lined. Top speed is over a hundred miles an hour, even though the car weighs more than ten thousand pounds."

"No use thinkin' in terms of a road-block, then?"

"Kempa's instructions are to ram any obstacle at full speed," Sam said. "I don't think the roadblock's been built that could stop a 4½-ton vehicle moving at nearly six hundred feet a second."

"Scratch that one, then. What about the train?"

So it went, day after day, until finally, they ran out of ideas and came back to the point from which they had started. There was only one chance of killing Hitler in Munich. A sniper in a high place with a rifle loaded with tracer.

"We've tried every damned trick in the book except possibly persuading the bastard to kill himself," Gus Laurence said, wearily. "So this has got to be it."

The team was assembled for the last time in the big hut. Sam surveyed the now-familiar faces of the Wolf Trap team while Mason-Morley spoke. Now that it was almost over, he could see the way that strain had marked them all. He felt damnably tired himself, although beneath the weariness stirred an elation he was sure the men listening to Mason-Morley shared. Time, as the British were fond of saying, to let the dog see the rabbit.

"I want to thank you all for your untiring energy," Mason-Morley said. "I'm sure the Chief will approve your plan. You'll be advised if the operation is successful. That's all. Take the rest of the day off."

It was a well-worn joke. They rarely finished before nine or ten in the evening. Tonight was no exception: the time was nine forty-five. One by one they came up to shake hands, the Kordas, Bojac, Gus Laurence, everyone.

"Don't forget the old camp motto, Sam," Harvey Wells grinned.

"BBB," Sam said. "Bullshit baffles brains."

"Every time," Wells said. "Every time."

In New York, Noël Mason-Morley insisted on buying

Sam a slap-up dinner at Sardi's, squelching all Sam's objections. He was a horse-player, and he had won a lot of money on the Kentucky Derby in May.

"First chance I've had to spend it," he told Sam. "So this is on Whirlaway. And no more arguments."

Throughout dinner he rattled on about Royal Ascot, the champagne buffets in the sunlit marquees, the smart crowds in the Royal Enclosure, the King and Queen coming up the course in their open landau. Sam found it hard to concentrate on what the Englishman was saying. His mind was full of what lay ahead. Now, as throughout his time at Camp X, he was plagued by the feeling that the project lacked a core, that it was being done for the sake of being done. He said as much when he talked to General Donovan in BSC headquarters at 3603 Rockefeller Center.

"I don't want to sound paranoid, General," he said, "but I can't escape the feeling there's more to Wolf Trap than we're being told."

"Could be," Donovan replied. "The Brits don't altogether trust us yet. They see themselves as old pros in the intelligence game, and us very much as tyros. They're working on the 'need to know' principle. Don't let it throw you. Keep your eyes and ears open, and keep me informed."

So Sam shrugged away his misgivings, and had his prime rib with Mason-Morley. After dinner, the two men walked along 44th Street to Times Square. The theatre marquees were ablaze with neon, heartbreakingly cheerful. Pretty girls giggled past, legs agleam in nylon, pursued by the wolf whistles of American sailors in summer whites. Kids bought hot-dogs from sidewalk vendors. There was a long line of people waiting to buy tickets for *Gone with the Wind*. Americans obviously preferred Scarlett O'Hara's war to Hitler's, Sam thought. How could you make them realise what it was like in Berlin, in Prague, in London? War would never be real to the mass of Americans until they heard bombs falling, or saw an armed enemy in the streets of their cities. It was Europe's war, and in a perverse way, Sam was glad he was going back to it. Grim and embattled places though they might be, the blacked-out streets of London were infinitely preferable to the raucously-lit ones of Manhattan.

Give it back to the Indians, he thought sourly, as the Pan American clipper surged into the air the following day and banked over the teeming city. He felt no regret. In fact, he felt as if he was going home.

Prague, July 17, 1941

Heat haze shimmered on the Vltava. The spires of the cathedral soared above the roofs of the houses clustered below the castle. In the Old Town Square, a knot of soldiers and civilians was gazing up at the great clock, waiting for the hourly procession of Apostles, Christ, Death tolling his little bell. A galleried curve led past shops with displays of Bohemian crystal and a sign for a restaurant, *U Radnice*. Paul's feet echoed on the cobbled stones, bouncing off the anonymous walls. A dog barked in an apartment. He smelled fish frying.

Prague.

It was good to be back, even though the whole atmosphere of the city had changed with two years of German occupation. The overt hatred that he had seen in 1939 was gone now, replaced by sullenness and apathy. The Czechs would never love their German conquerors, but they had become accustomed to their presence. Not like before the Occupation. They had been ready to fight: the Army, the people, everyone. They cut the telephones, distributed gas masks, organised a blackout. In the shops, apart from food, the most popular item for sale was a gramophone record of a war song called 'Come on. Adolf!'

Then the sell-out: Munich. Nobody could believe it. Hitler demanded Czechoslovakia, and France and England gave it to him. On a plate: no conditions. The Army was not even to be allowed to contest his occupation of its homeland. He remembered the shouting crowds in the KLM offices, as refugees and emigrés wanted by the Gestapo frantically jostled to buy airplane tickets, on any plane, to any destination. And Unity Mitford, dressed in a grey tweed suit with a swastika lapel badge, golden hair falling to her shoulders, drinking tea at the Esplanade Hotel.

Paul walked beneath the old Powder Tower and turned right towards Wenzelplatz. He remembered the phalanxes of troops from the 3rd and 5th *Heeresgruppenkommando* marching along this street, arms swinging, faces rigid. And the Czechs lining the streets, hatred naked on their faces as the tanks rumbled and clattered past. And the poor Jews and the other desperate ones, unable to escape the spreading stain of Gestapo pursuit, who hanged themselves in hundreds.

He had watched the 'Germanisation' of the new Reich Protectorate, of which Prague was now the capital, and watched how the Czechs smouldered as it was imposed upon them. Their new master was the *Reichsprotector*, Baron von Neurath. The man who would enforce the Führer's will was not the old diplomat; everyone knew that. It was the fanatical Sudeten Nazi, Karl Hermann Frank, a former publisher from Karlovy Vary, a tall, lean man with a small head and a blind eye. The choice before the Czechs, Frank announced in his newspaper *Der Neue Tag*, was simple: collaborate and have peace, or resist and invite reprisal. Henceforth, Czech officials would be dismissed if they did not know German within a certain time. Streets would be renamed to commemorate German heroes. Czech national monuments would be taken down and used as a contribution to the wartime metal collection. Every town must use its new German and not its former Czech name. Telephone directories, theatre tickets, tram signs, street names must all be in German. All law courts would function only in German. Teachers would be held personally responsible that all their pupils properly understood the place of the Czech nation inside the German Reich, the necessity to collaborate with the Germans, and to respect the Führer, Adolf Hitler. "Where the swastika has once waved," Frank declared, "it waves forever!"

It was clumsy, Paul protested, and what was worse it had the reverse effect to what they were trying to achieve. His reports then were full of warnings: trouble brewing. When it came it was almost like spontaneous combustion: October

28, Czech National Day, the anniversary of the day on which Austrian rule had given way to Czech in 1918.

At first, people just gathered in crowds in the centre of town, walking together quietly through the streets, wearing Czech national colours and Masaryk caps. Germans in uniform mingled with them; there was no overt hostility. Even the weekly parade of the SS through the main streets caused no more than the usual muttered curses, the conspicuous turning away of heads. Then someone, somewhere, made one of the Czechs take off his colours, or his cap: it made no difference. The mob was aroused, the flame lit. Troops were called out to maintain order, first firing blank and then live ammunition. And then the crowd went mad.

German street signs were torn down, notices ripped to pieces. Shops known to be pro-German had their windows kicked in, German schools were broken into and the hated books burned, Germans who had mistreated Czechs were beaten by phalanxes of angry Czechs shouting 'Long live Beneš!' The riots were brutally suppressed. How many people were killed, how many wounded nobody knew.

Among the wounded that day was a student named Jan Opletal. He was taken to the new Gestapo headquarters, the ugly blackened Petschek Bank, abandoned by the Jewish financier who had owned it; and there, a fortnight later, Opletal died.

Every student in Prague was on the street for his funeral on November 15. Again there was stupid provocation; again, rioting. The students marched through the streets with banners, singing Czech anthems. When he heard what had happened, Hitler swore to reduce Prague to ashes if the demonstrations went on. Old von Neurath quailed; but Frank knew what was wanted, and he set to work with typical zeal. On the night of November 16 the SS fell upon the student hostels, dragging the students from their beds, out into the freezing streets, boys and girls alike. They beat the boys mercilessly, and did unspeakable things to the girls. Nine of the students were executed in front of their comrades at Ruzyn aerodrome. Hundreds more were kicked and cursed into lorries and driven off into the night to the KZs. All the Universities were closed forthwith. It was apparent that kindness did not work, Frank said. The mailed fist would henceforth be used instead.

Paul turned into the Wenzelplatz. Sunlight gleamed on the gilded domes of the National Museum. The pavement cafés were crowded. Here and there, Czech girls sat with German soldiers, laughing. Not all Czechs hated the Germans. Many now accepted the Occupation. Pragmatists, he thought: a job was still a job, families had to be fed, rent paid, and life, for all its lacks, still had to be lived.

Entirely on impulse, Paul went into a telephone cabin and called the Novak house. Maria answered.

"Dobry den, Pani Novakova!" he said, cheerfully. *"Mluvite nemečky?"*

"My God, I don't believe it!" she said. He had always called the same way, asking if she spoke German. "Paul, is it really you?"

"Thought you'd got rid of me for good, did you?"

"How long are you here for? What are you doing now? Oh, Jan will be so happy to see you! Where are you staying? When—?"

"Hey, hey!" he said, gently interrupting her. "One question at a time!"

"Oh, I'm sorry, I'm so excited," she said. There was a smile in her voice. "Answer me this, then. Can you be here by seven-thirty?"

"Easily," he said.

"Good. We'll eat at eight."

"I'll bring some wine," Paul said, and hung up. He was still smiling, hours later, as he walked out of the 'Glass House' in Dejvice and got into his car. His offices were in one of the complex of military buildings which had formerly housed the Czechoslovak General Staff. The SS had made their headquarters in the one-time Staff College. With typical finesse they had renamed it 'Adolf Hitler Caserne'. As he drove towards Bubenec, Paul thought back to the old days, when he had first come to Prague.

Jan Novak had been a lecturer at Charles University then, his wife a plump, bustling woman with a pretty face. There were two children, Frantisek and Antonie. Franta was eighteen and Paul had become his hero. Tonie was a grave, dark-eyed twenty-year-old studying law at the University. 1938, he thought, where do the years go? She would be an old married woman now. What was the name of the boy she married? Josef, that was it. Josef Branik.

In those days the Novaks lived in a rambling old house near Bubny Station, a place full of books. Jan read everything he could lay his hands on: papers, magazines, books, trash or the classics, it made no difference. He'd read the labels on the jam pot if there was nothing else, Maria said. He was also an amateur painter. He took a tree from this magazine illustration, a farmhouse from that, a sky from yet another. Turpentine, Paul thought. There was always a smell of turpentine.

Prague.

For all the sour apathy of her citizens towards the Germans, the city was still the setting for a fairy tale. The old spires, the riotous mixture of architecture, the unchanged cobblestoned streets with their arcaded shops were a warm and welcome change from the tensions of Berlin. He stopped for a traffic light. A tram trundled up, bell clanking. A flock of pigeons soared up and around the trees, like grey-white leaves blown in a gale. Sturdy peasant women in blue-checked frocks with white halters and aprons, their hair covered by lace scarves, stood gossiping on the sidewalk. There was a summery lassitude in the air. Geraniums blazed on balconies, and old men nodded on wooden benches beneath the elms. It was almost possible to believe that there was no war.

He parked the car and walked down to the little square where the Novaks lived. Old people sat beneath the trees, watching the children play. An old woman in a black dress was feeding a chirrup of sparrows. A yellow gravel path bisected the square diagonally. An old stone fountain stood in the middle of the square. He had never seen it working.

He knew how things were with most Czech families: rationing was strict, everything was in short supply. So he had brought coffee, sugar, soap, salt, cotton, butter, flour and some sausages from the commissary in Dejvice, and picked up two bottles of *Tri Gracie*. He remembered that there was a flower shop around the corner, and bought a bunch of chrysanthemums for Maria. Then he walked back to the square and knocked on the door of the Novak house. Maria opened the door. She looked at him for a moment, her eyes full of tears. Then she threw her arms around him, laughing and crying all at the same time.

It was a noisy, joyous reunion. Maria looked exactly as she had done the last time he saw her, but Paul told her that he was sure that she had lost weight. She hugged him and kissed him and said that he was a liar.

"Too many *knidliky,* that's her problem!" Jan boomed. "Mine, too, if the truth be told!" He slapped himself on the belly. "Well, a man's got to fill his belly somehow!" He was a huge, broad-shouldered man who looked more like a farmer than a teacher. He had a strong, deep voice. His face looked fuller than Paul remembered, and his body thicker around the middle. He must be over fifty now, he thought.

"Well, Maria," he said, "are we having some of those famous dumplings of yours tonight?"

"We'd better be!" Jan growled. "Hear me, woman?"

"I hear you," she said. "Open the wine."

They ate everything. Maria had bought a small duck on the black market, and queued for some cabbage to make *sauerkraut.* She cooked the sausages Paul had brought: they were a rare treat, she said, with real meat in them, not the things they were passing off as sausages in butcher shops these days.

"We starve so the damned Germans can eat well!" Jan said. "They take everything!"

"We didn't do too badly tonight," Maria said. "Thanks to this 'damned' German!"

"Paul's not a *German,*" Jan said, scornfully. "His mother was Czech!" As far as Jan was concerned, Paul was as Czech as he. He knew Paul would not be insulted by anything he said about the Germans. They had left all that behind them years ago.

"That's what you always say," Maria said.

"Well, it's true, isn't it?" Jan looked at Paul.

"If you say I'm a Czech, Jan, who am I to argue?" Paul smiled. They took the dishes out to the kitchen. Paul washed, while Maria and Jan dried.

"Never hear any good news any more," Jan grumbled. "Every time you open the damned paper or turn on the radio they're there, shouting at you, giving you new orders. Every day something bad, every new thing always worse. You can't spend your life wondering what the swine are going to do to you next, yet you have to. There's no alternative. You can't protest, you are not permitted to argue. You can do nothing except wait and hope, wait and hope, knowing it is futile to wait and pointless to hope."

"That doesn't sound like you, Jan," Paul said.

"You think that's what he does, sits around waiting and hoping?" Maria said. "This one? That will be the day!"

"A man has to do something," Jan rumbled.

"What can you do, Jan?" Paul said.

"We can fight," Jan said. "We can hate them. That's fighting in a way. We can avoid helping them. That's fighting, too."

"You think that will make any difference to them?" she sniffed, putting coffee cups on a tray. "You think your dragging your heels will stop the Wehrmacht from marching into Moscow?"

"We've got to do something," Jan said. "Anything is better than nothing."

"Until they come and take you to the Petschkarna!" Maria said. Czechs referred to Gestapo headquarters with grave-digger humour. The huge whitewashed room in which all suspects were detained was known as the "cinema" because of the rows of benches, always full of people staring rigidly ahead at the white walls.

"Ach!" Jan said, exasperatedly, "they'll never get me into that damned place. What about a *schnapps*, Paul?" He opened the sideboard cupboard and brought out a bottle of Asbach. "I've been saving this for a special occasion."

"Well," Paul said. "This certainly qualifies."

Maria brought the coffee and they made a fuss over drinking it: it was a long time since they had drunk good strong coffee, Maria said. Paul noticed that she had brought out her best china, and that Jan was pouring the brandy into the fine crystal glasses which had been his mother's wedding gift to them. It was their way of telling Paul that he was a very special guest and he was touched by it. He thought of the first time he had visited them. God, I was sorry for myself then, he thought. Wallowing in a sea of self-pity. He allowed himself a wry grin. It was a long time since he had thought about Brigit.

"What are you smiling at?" Maria asked.

"I was thinking about Brigit," Paul said.

"Do you ever see her?"

"No," Paul said. "She's married again. Some fellow who works in the Child Welfare Department."

He remembered how alone he had felt at first. The transfer to Prague came almost simultaneously with finding out about Brigit. Well, it had been stupid to expect anything else of her, he supposed. She was far more in love with the idea of being a *hausfrau* than actually being one, especially one who was the wife of a soldier. Army pay was little enough, and ends often did not meet. He was away a lot, too; perhaps, in the end, not always because he had to be. He sent her as much as he could afford, keeping only enough for a very modest mess bill and a few Marks to buy a train ticket home. He planned to surprise her on her birthday. Surprise was right, he thought. He was stationed at Königsberg when the news came through from Berlin that he was to be posted to Prague as aide to the Military Attaché. He got leave, rushed back to Königsbrunn, bubbling to tell her the good news. The apartment was cold and unlived-in, and there was dust on the furniture. He telephoned Brigit's parents; they sounded uneasy and he could not imagine why. What possessed him to rummage in the bureau he never knew. But that was where he found the letters, a small bundle of them tied with ribbon, and altogether too specific for there to be any doubt. Rage burned through him. Self-pity extinguished it.

He waited all weekend for her to come home, but she never did. Much later he learned that she had been at Starnberg with her lover. He went to the station late on Sunday night and put his bag on the train. Almost as an afterthought he telephoned his mother to tell her what had happened. She sounded almost glad. She had never liked Brigit, she said; she was not at all surprised to hear this. Her voice was cold and unfeeling; serves you right, it said.

"I remember coming here that first time," he said to Maria. "It seemed so . . . warm. So noisy. Everyone seemed to like each other. I'd never known that."

"You looked lost," Maria said. "You remember, Jan, I said to you, 'that boy has such sad eyes'."

"I remember Franta thought he was splendid," Jan smiled. "Must have been the uniform."

"How is he?" Paul asked.

"He got out," Jan said, with evident satisfaction. "He made his way to England and joined the Royal Air Force."

"An Observer," Maria said. "A sergeant, too."

"And Antonie?"

The smiles disappeared. Maria looked at Jan, and he cleared his throat.

"You remember she married that boy?" he said.

"Josef," Paul said. "I always thought it was a mistake, that they were too young."

"He's dead," Jan said flatly. "The Gestapo killed him."

"When was this?"

"January. He was going to be a teacher, you know."

"What happened?"

"He was mixed up with a resistance group," Jan said. "one night he didn't come home. They had him down at the Petschkarna. They tortured him to death."

"I'm sorry," Paul said.

"We've come to terms with it now," Jan said. "He was a fine boy."

"And Antonie?"

Maria shook her head and Jan shrugged. "Another?" he said, raising his eyebrows and picking up the bottle. Paul nodded and let the silence extend as Jan poured the brandy.

"She hates them more than I do," Jan said. "And that's something."

"Too much," Maria said. "She hates them too much. I sometimes think, Paul, it's unhealthy for a young girl to hate that way."

"She has a job?"

"She works for Lufthansa, in the express freight department."

"She hates Germans, and yet works for Lufthansa?"

Jan said nothing. He looked at Paul levelly, and Paul knew what he was saying by saying nothing. Antonie was using her job as a means of getting information for the resistance.

"If. . . " Maria began to say something and then stopped, as if deciding better.

"Go on," Paul said. "You'd better tell me."

"If she . . . behaves badly, Paul, when she comes home. Please don't be angry. Don't take it personally. She has been so terribly wounded."

"I understand," Paul said. He remembered Antonie's face: grave, and shy, framed by dark hair.

"She hates them," Maria said. "She hates everything German."

"She may say things she will . . . regret, later," Jan said.

"It's all right, Jan," Paul said. "You know my feelings about the Master Race."

Jan's face lit up. "You've not changed, then?"

"Of course not."

"See?" Jan said, clapping him on the back. He was looking at Maria. "I told you!" They talked about it before I came, Paul thought. They wondered whether I might be coming to their house to spy on them. Maybe they still do.

"I hate them as much as any man alive," he told his friend. "As much, perhaps more, than you or your daughter ever could, Jan."

Maria frowned and shushed him. "It's not only foolish to talk that way. It's dangerous!" she scolded.

"No Gestapo here, are there?" Paul grinned, lifting up the tablecloth and making a show of looking under the table. "You haven't gone and joined the damned Gestapo, have you, Jan?"

"I'm just a teacher in a boy's school," Jan smiled. And head of a resistance group called *Jindra,* Paul thought. There was a dossier on Jan Novak at the Glass House compiled by Paul's predecessor; doubtless there was an even bulkier one at the Petschek. Well, Jan knew the risks; and he would certainly know that. He wondered whether Maria knew, and if so, how much.

"And I'm just a civil servant," Paul replied, putting enough double meaning in it for Jan to understand that he knew. Jan looked up sharply, and his eyes sparkled like a man who has just found a worthy adversary in a chess game. "Here, are you going to drink all that brandy on your own?"

"Take, take!" Jan said, waving expansively. "Nothing too good for a civil servant, I always say!"

"You haven't told us anything about yourself, Paul," Maria said. "What have you been doing in Berlin? And how long will you be here in Prague?"

"Answering the last question first, I don't know. But at least a year. There are going to be a lot of changes here."

"You'll have to tell us all about them," Jan said, putting a shade of emphasis on the words that gave them a much wider meaning.

"I will," Paul said. "As for Berlin, I was attached to General Staff. Just another Berlin partygoer."

"Have you got a girl friend?" Maria asked.

He thought of Erika's perfumed body twisting in the tangled bed. "No," he said. "I haven't had the time to run after girls."

"Maybe you'll find one here," Jan grinned. "Where are you staying?"

"I've got an apartment in Smichov. Very comfortable."

In fact, he had two apartments. That was a routine precaution. The one in Smichov was in his own name. His "cover" apartment, the one he used for clandestine work, was in the suburb of Brevnov. He had rented it in the name of Bergmann. His little joke rather amused him.

"Well, Mother, what about some more of that coffee?" Jan said.

"Don't call me Mother!" Maria said, without rancour. "And don't you go and get drunk, either!"

"Me?" Jan said, with a huge grin. "Get drunk?"

He sloshed some more *schnapps* into the glasses, while Maria tutted in fond disapproval. Paul told them something about the changes which Berlin planned for Prague. Thousands of new civil servants were already streaming into the city.

"They are going to make this country German," Paul told his friend. "Whether you Czechs like it or not!"

"They'll find they have a fight on their hands if they try!" Jan growled.

"You can't fight tied up in red tape!" Paul told him. "Listen to me, Jan! Do you know they've set up an Administrative Academy in the Czernin Palace whose sole purpose is to train German officials? Every time one of them becomes qualified, a Czech somewhere will lose his job. A judge, a railway official, a clerk in a town hall will be arrested and his place will be taken by a German."

"They can't arrest us all," Jan protested. "Nor ship us all off to Mauthausen or Terezin."

"They don't want to," Paul said. "They'll *permit* you to remain Czech. So long as you understand and obey German orders, you can be as Czech as you like, and the more blindly, provincially Czech you are the better. A picturesque feature of the countryside, something quaint for the tourists."

"You sound as if you think the Nazis are going to win this war."

"I don't think that at all," Paul said. "But there will be hard times before we see them beaten, my friend. And those hard times will come soon."

Jan nodded, a faraway look in his eyes. Just for a moment, he looked old and tired. Then the smile came back.

"All the more reason to live dangerously while we can!" he said. "Some more brandy!"

"You've had enough, Jan!" Maria said. "You know it upsets your stomach!"

"My darling wife, listen to her!" Jan growled. "If she had her way I'd be the most miserable man in Prague."

"You *are* the most miserable man in Prague!" she retorted tartly. Jan started to say something, but just at that moment, they heard a key in the door, and then Antonie came into the room.

My God, Paul thought, she's beautiful!

London, July 29, 1941

The light breeze carried the tainted stinks of burned wood, chemicals, brick dust. St Paul's stood in solitary, soot-streaked splendour above a wilderness of destruction. There was nothing left of Cheapside but a surreal nightmare of twisted, tangled girders and mountainous piles of rubble and brick. Stepney was all but gone, they said. Whitechapel, Poplar, Shoreditch, Bermondsey flattened. They were training troops for house-to-house fighting in what had once been West Ham.

Everywhere, ruins. Houses with sheared-off fronts. Gutted stores and blackened girders and the shells of churches whose God had been unable to protect them. In the wilderness of devastation, figures moved on the dead grey peaks, salvaging such pitiful remnants of their homes as they could find. The streets were thronged with purposeful-looking people, men in shabby coats and trilby hats carrying briefcases. Where were they going so eagerly? What did they plan to do when they arrived? It was as if, by activity, they could banish the ubiquitous evidence that their city was being systematically wiped out.

'London Can Take It!' someone had defiantly daubed on the walls of an EWS tank. And it has, Sam thought, as he walked down Whitehall. There had been a hiatus in the German raids since May. They needed all their planes for the Russian offensive. Now, with the 'bomber's moon' lighting up the skies, the familiar *vurr-vmm, vurr-vmm* of the German planes filled the night once more.

A queue of drably-clad people stood patiently at the bus stop on the corner of Whitehall Place. Sixty, seventy people, waiting for a bus that might arrive in two minutes, or two hours, or not at all.

"See yer termorrer, Maggie!" he heard a woman shout.

"If yer don't they'll be diggin' me aht!" her friend called back. Cockneys, Sam thought. They'd crack jokes on the doorstep of Hell. And from all he'd heard, the "blitz" was just that: hell. Not only in London, but in the provincial cities, too: Liverpool, Coventry, Southampton. Two million homes destroyed, they said. Direct hits on Westminster Abbey, the Houses of Parliament, the Mint, the Strand Law Courts, the War Office, the Tower of London. A million dollars's worth of books burned to drifting ash in the British Museum. Thousands killed, maimed.

Now the bombers were back. The radio comedians sang jokey songs. 'Got your gasmask, got your flashlight, all right, good night.' The British needed a laugh. The news was all bad. Hitler's *blitzkrieg* in the East had so far been a complete success. The major Russian cities were falling as if by timetable: Minsk, June 28, Lvov the next day, Riga July first, and a week later the Panzers were across the Dnieper. The Luftwaffe had bombed Moscow. Stalin was calling desperately upon the British to open a 'second front' by invading Europe. One look at London told you how remote a possibility that was.

Sam looked at his watch. The meeting was scheduled for ten-fifteen, and he liked to be punctual. He turned into Great George Street, past a sandbagged pillbox. Barbed wire strung on pole and X-frames stretched all along the frontage of the Ministry in Storey's Gate. Sam presented his pass to the armed soldiers at the wire, and again to the armed Marine guarding the door. He was passed from the street into a tiled hall, in which stood another sandbagged machine-gun emplacement. The floor was gritty. On the far side of the hall stood a commissionaire's desk. Opposite were elevator doors, flanked by two armed Marines.

Sam gave his pass to the commissionaire. He looked very young and very fit. Commando, Sam thought, noting that the glass of the booth had the faint discoloration of bullet-proofing. The commissionaire handed back the pass and saluted.

"Know the way, sir?" he asked. Sam shook his head. "Righto," the commissionaire said, cheerily. "I'll take you down." He turned and spoke to someone Sam could not see. "'old the fort, Charlie."

"Aye-aye," said the unseen man.

The commissionaire led Sam across to the elevator and took him down to the annexe which housed the Cabinet war rooms, nerve-centre of the British High Command. It was a sprawling complex thirty-five feet beneath the city streets, roofed with fifteen feet of concrete reinforced with torn-up trolley lines. Sam looked about him with keen interest: very few Americans had ever been admitted to this holiest of holies. The walls were painted standard British government cream and green. Huge air ducts, the drone of fans, condensation: it reminded Sam of nothing so much as being below decks on a battleship.

"Follow me, please, sir," the young Commando said, leading the way along a corridor. Through an open door, Sam caught a glimpse of a big room with huge maps on the wall, speckled with coloured pins. Two kinds of telephone, green and red, clocks showing the time in Berlin, Rome, Sydney, Tokyo and Washington.

Sam's guide stopped at a door and knocked. After a moment's wait, he swung open the door, stepping back to allow Sam to enter. Once again, the nautical idiom was reinforced. Sam found himself in a room about the size of a warship's wardroom. There was a print of old London Bridge on one wall, a portrait of King George VI on the other. A round conference table and some chairs completed the furnishings.

Sam recognised only one of the men in the room. He smiled and stuck out his hand as General Donovan came across to welcome him. The other two men continued talking quietly. Apart from an apparently incurious glance, they took no notice of Sam's arrival.

"Well, Sam," Donovan said. "Welcome to the Hole in the Ground. How was Oshawa?"

"Pretty damned unbelievable," Sam said.

Ever since he had been there, a song called "I'll never smile again", close-harmonised by a group called The Pied Pipers, had stuck inside Sam's head as if it had been implanted there by a brain surgeon. He would never hear the song again without remembering those furious arguments, those endless questions, intensive, demanding weeks in which plan after plan to kill or maim Adolf Hitler was proposed, dissected, and discarded.

"Is Churchill going to be here?" he asked Donovan.

"He's at Ditchley Park," Donovan said, dashing Sam's hopes of meeting the legendary British Prime Minister.

"Anything new on Hess?"

"They've got him locked away someplace in Surrey," Donovan said. "Nobody gets to see him, and I mean nobody. Everytime I ask, I get the old hocus-pocus. Maybe your friend Mason-Morley will enlighten us."

Don't bet on it, General, Sam thought, as Mason-Morley came towards them. "Hello, sir," the Englishman said. "Sam. Good to see you both again."

"We were just talking about Hess," Sam said.

Mason-Morley made a face. "Damned nonsense," he said, disgustedly. "Bloody fellow doesn't make any sense. Damned embarrassment, the whole thing."

He went past them before they could ask anything else, and shook hands with the nearer of the two men sitting at the table, a grey-haired, distinguished-looking figure with an acquiline nose and penetrating eyes.

"Good to see you, sir," Mason-Morley said. "And you, Chief."

So the other one was Stanley, Sam thought. The head of the London Controlling Section was an almost ordinary-looking man, with a bland, moon face, and heavy horn-rimmed glasses. He wore the uniform of a Colonel in the Royal Field Artillery. He was said to have a temper for two. Still waters, Sam decided.

"Gentlemen," Mason-Morley said, "let me introduce you to Sam Gray of General Donovan's staff. Sam, this is Lord Swinton, Chairman of the National Security Executive." He turned towards Stanley. "And this is my Chief. Colonel the Honorable Oliver Stanley, head of LCS."

"A pleasure to meet you, sir," Sam said. "I've heard a lot about you."

"Really?" Stanley said, without the slightest degree of interest. Loves Americans, Sam decided, the way some of the upper class British do. And no question that Stanley was upper class. Son of the Earl of Derby, he had been a Minister of War and a member of Churchill's cabinet. They said he and Churchill didn't get along. Stanley looked like a man it would be very easy not to get along with, he decided. As for Swinton, he had no idea who he was or what the National Security Agency was. Maybe one of these days they'll tell us, Sam thought. About the same time we start having to shoot down our bacon. He watched as Mason-Morley lifted back the cloth covering the blackboard to reveal a large-scale street map of Munich.

"After much deliberation, gentlemen," he began, "We have decided upon Munich as the location for our attempt on Hitler, and November 9 as the date." He laid the tip of his pointer on the map at a place where six streets formed a junction.

"Rosenheimerplatz," he said.

On the northern side of this junction, he told them, stood the beer-cellar restaurant in which, in 1923, the young Hitler had tried to start the insurrection he hoped would topple the government.

"Every November, Hitler celebrates the anniversary by marching from there with all the top Nazis. He comes down the hill here, across the Ludwigsbrücke, up past the Town Hall, then along here, to the Odeonsplatz in front of the Feldherrnhalle. Now. . . ." Again the pointer tapped the map. "Here is the Ludwig Bridge. Just north of it is the municipal swimming baths. Thanks to our American colleagues, we have a photo of that building."

Donovan had asked for a call to be put out in America. Anyone who had holiday snaps taken in Europe, or family photos showing buildings or monuments, was asked to send them to Washington. Millions had poured in, to be classified by country, then city, then area. Mason-Morley passed around the photograph of the smiling group standing on the Ludwig Bridge, the squat ochre-painted three-storey building behind them, crowned by a high square white tower with a clock on each face. Above the tower was a cupola.

"Looks more like a church than a swimming baths," Swinton observed.

"Wouldn't make any difference if it was. If we get someone up there, he'll have a beautiful clear shot at Hitler," He looked at Sam as if to say, all right, I'll tell them.

"From what we now know of the arrangements for Hitler's security, we know it's going to be very difficult to put a team in place," he said. "But I'm convinced it's worth the try."

"Let's suppose you can pull it off," Stanley said. "How do you rate the chances of success?"

"Success, in this instance, would not be the sole object, sir," Mason-Morley said. "We will succeed by its being seen that the attempt was made."

He lifted the map of Munich and revealed beneath it a large-scale topographical map of the area between Munich, which was in the bottom left-hand corner, and the Czech city of Pilsen, near the top right. The former border snakingly bisected the chart from top to bottom, north to south.

"We plan to put in two teams of three men, by parachute," he said. "This area, near the German-Czech border, will be the drop zone. A provisional drop date of October 10 has already been set, subject to your approval." He looked at Stanley who looked at Swinton.

"Well, Philip?" Stanley said.

"I enter only one demurrer, Oliver," Swinton said. "This Wolf Trap business might blow up in our faces if, in doing away with Herr Schickelgruber, we unite Germany by giving her a martyr."

"I see your point," Stanley said. "I think the risk is acceptable. If taking Hitler out of the picture creates confusion, or might precipitate an Army seizure of power, we can't afford to ignore the chance."

"I suppose you're right," Swinton said, although it was plain he found the whole proposition distasteful. There was silence for a moment. "Winston doesn't want any of this on the record, Oliver," he said. "Send the weeders in, the moment it's over."

"Of course," Stanley said, stiffly, as though annoyed that Swinton felt he needed to be told. "We go ahead, then?"

"I think so," Swinton said. "Yes."

That was it, Sam thought. Nothing dramatic. Stiff upper lip, chin-chin, and all that. The heads of Britain's most secret services had just given their imprimatur to a mission which could alter history, and nobody even looked excited. Swinton stood up.

"I'll go and see Winston," he said. "And tell him Wolf Trap is activated."

Prague, August 9, 1941

He knocked on the door and Antonie opened it. She was wearing a dark sweater and skirt. There were dark shadows under her eyes.

"Oh," she said, without enthusiasm. "It's you."

"Your father isn't here?"

"He'll be back soon, He left something at the school and went to fetch it."

"May I wait?"

"I suppose so."

He followed her into the sitting room. A half-completed oil painting stood on Jan's easel. It was a picture of a farmer ploughing with a pair of sturdy horses. A photograph of an oak, torn from a magazine, was pinned to the board with a thumb tack. Jan had already begun to copy it into the background of the painting. Paul smiled. He could smell the turpentine. It reminded him of the old days.

"I bought some coffee," he said.

"Thank you," Antonie replied. She put the coffee on the sideboard and sat down at the table. Paul saw that she had been reading the authorised Czech-language newspaper, *Narodni Politicka*. She made no attempt to pretend a welcome.

"What ever happened to that photograph of you that used to stand on the sideboard?" he asked her. "You were wearing a blue suit with a white straw hat. I used to think how pretty you looked."

"It's gone," she said. "And so has the girl who wore it." He felt the chill of her dislike.

"Did I say something wrong?" he asked.

"Nothing," she said, without looking up. It was as if nothing he could say interested her.

"Tonie, we've known each other a long time," he said. "As far as I am aware, I have never done anything to make you dislike me. Yet you obviously do. Would you tell me why?"

"You wouldn't understand,"

"Try me."

"I don't wish to discuss it."

"I do."

"Do you think I give a damn about that?" she snapped. "I don't give a snap of the fingers what you or any other Nazi wants!"

"Nazi?" he said. "You think I'm one of them? I hate them as much as you do!"

"Of course," she said, sweetly. "That's why you're an officer in the Wehrmacht."

"That's exactly right," he said. Tonie frowned, because his words made no sense to her. That was what he wanted, to put her a little off balance. Jan had told him she had gone through hatred into prejudice. All Nazis were bad Nazis. There was no such thing as a good German, unless it be a dead German. It was not even anger which drove her any more: just cold, unrelenting hatred. So he told her the truth: it was because he, too, hated the Nazis that he had become an officer in the Wehrmacht. She did not know that yet, and so the truth confused her a little. He did not elaborate.

"I don't know why I'm listening to you," she said into the silence. "You're all liars. Every one of you."

"No," he said. "That's not the truth."

"Truth!" she spat, eyes flashing again. "I've heard your Nazi truth, *Oberst* Kramer, and it isn't worth what cats do in dark corners!"

"If I were what you think I am, do you think I'd allow you to say such things to me?"

"What would you do?" she said, tossing back the dark hair. "Have me taken down to the Petschkarna? Give me a little of their special treatment? Do you think I care what happens to me?"

"Tell me why you feel this way," he said. "Is it . . . because of Josef?"

"Don't talk about him!" she blazed. "Don't foul his name with your filthy German tongue!"

"Tonie, listen—."

"Understand me, *Oberst*," Tonie said, her voice poisonously controlled. "I loathe and despise you and everything you stand for. I suffer your presence only because of my parents. If this were my house, I wouldn't allow you across the threshold!"

"Do you have any idea why I come here?" he asked.

"To spy on us, I expect. That's what you people do, isn't

it? Inveigle yourselves into someone's home, and then when they've incriminated themselves, send in your damned Gestapo!"

"You can't believe that, Tonie," he said.

"I'll tell you what I believe," she said. "I hate your kind and I believe I always will."

"Because of Josef."

"Yes!" she hissed. "Because of Josef!"

"Tell me what happened."

"Why do you want to know?"

"Because I care about you, Tonie."

She looked at him in that direct way she had always had. There was doubt in her eyes for the first time, and perhaps, he thought, a question she would not permit herself to ask.

"Why should you care about me?" she said.

"I always have," he said. "Since you were just a kid."

She looked at him again, but her eyes were flooded with contempt now. She shook her head from side to side.

"Well, well, *Oberst*," she sneered. "You're like all the rest of them. You want to fuck me. Well, you can if you want to. My body means nothing to me. I've used it before. One more time won't make any difference."

"Don't talk like that!" he said, perhaps more sharply than he had intended. Again she looked at him, that uncertainty behind the anger in her eyes. "Don't try to make yourself sound worthless!"

"You think that's what I'm trying to do?" she said. "I'm trying to tell you how much I hate your kind, *Oberst*. I'm trying to tell you that I'll sleep with them if they want me to. And slit their throats when they've done with me. And laugh at the thought that they died thinking they'd had another Czech whore without paying!"

He thought of her in bed, the lissome body and the knowing lips used as weapons, and inside the head, behind that madonna face, the knowledge of what she was going to do burning, burning. Jan said she had a will of iron. Nothing could deflect her from her purpose, he said. She was part of Morávec's Sparta group. She had started as a courier, and slowly become involved in the more dangerous activities of the resistance leader. Jan said she had killed a Gestapo agent the night Morávec escaped from the house in Nusle.

100

Paul wondered whether his friend knew the other things Antonie did, and decided he could not possibly know. Such knowledge would break a man like Jan Novak.

"I asked you to tell me what happened to Josef," he said.

"Look in the files," she said. "Don't you Nazis have files for that sort of thing? All the little details lovingly preserved?"

"I'd rather hear it from you."

"That how you get your thrills, is it, *Oberst*? Listening to the widow's story of how they tortured her husband to death?"

"It seems a shame," he said, "For so much love to have turned to so much hate."

Her eyes widened, and for a moment, he thought she might leap out of the chair and throw herself at him, squalling like a cat. Then the flame of anger faded, although the bright glow of dislike remained.

"All right," she said. "All right, *Oberst*. You asked, I'll tell you. Perhaps it's time you knew what wearing that golden Nazi Party badge makes you accomplice to!"

His name, she said, was Josef Branik, fair-haired Josef with the clear blue eyes and the straw-blond hair. They had been students at Charles University. He asked her for a date one day, quite suddenly. It was after a class in vacuum physics, she would remember that all her life, snow falling although it was nearly the end of March, unseasonal cold, and the way Josef had smiled and nodded like a fool when she said yes.

"We used to save seats for each other in the student's cafeteria," she said. Her eyes were unfocussed, her mind far away. The room was full of silence and memory. "We would walk back slowly to class together. At weekends, we would go out into the country by coach. Josef and I never heard the driver calling us back after the picnics. The other students used to call him *Pan Roztrzity*, 'Mr Absent-Minded'."

Josef was going to be a teacher: he loved children. They asked their parents for permission to marry. No, everyone said, they were too young. When you have completed your studies, when you have your degree, then, perhaps. But Josef said that 1938 was not a time for waiting. The world could go to war at any moment. If Hitler invaded Czechoslovakia, the way he was always threatening he would do, then every Czech would rally to the call to arms. Josef was a true Czech, a patriot. If the Nazis come, we will fight them, he used to say. I will fight them if I have to stand on the border alone to do it.

"We had a little flat above a shop," she said. "Oh, how much of my life was bounded by the walls of those two rooms!" She remembered the sound of the cobbler's hammer in the shop below, and the flowered wallpaper that they bought. Josef's friend, Arnost Perek, came to help them hang it. They bought some pictures: seascapes. Like many Czechs, neither of them had ever seen the sea.

"Even when the Germans came, it didn't disturb our little world. Josef said the British and the French had let us down, and that there was only one way to fight the Germans now. I didn't know what he meant. Not then. Not for a long time."

"Tonie," Paul said softly. "You were so young. Just a child."

"No," she said, her voice as soft as his. "I was a woman. I was so very much in love. All my days and all my nights were one thing: Josef."

The summer passed. Their days were bright with hope. Maybe it would not be as bad as they had feared. They knew a lot of German people. Not all of them strutted around in steel helmets and musical-comedy uniforms. Then the *Reichsprotector*'s office gave orders that Czech National Day, October 28, was not to be observed. Nobody took any notice. People dressed in their best clothes, and wore red, white and blue 'freedom' ribbons. Crowds gathered outside the Petschek Bank and the Nazi Party building. The police came, and told the crowds to disperse. Nobody moved. The police fired over the heads of the people and still nobody moved.

"Then they fired into the crowd," Antonie said, speaking the words like a litany. "They killed one man, and wounded a dozen, fifteen more. One of them was a friend of Josef's, a student named Jan Opletal. He was taken to the Petschkarna, and died there a fortnight later. There were demonstrations again. And then we found out what the Nazis were really like. Yes, they showed us their true colours then."

On the night of November 16, all Czech universities were occupied by the SS. Everyone living in the student homes in Prague and Brno was arrested.

He saw the soft glint of tears in her eyes, but he did not speak. This was her own exorcism, her own need. Her face was sombre and still, her voice little more now than a monotone.

Hearing all this from Josef still did not strike fear into her heart the way perhaps it should have done, she said. The execution of someone you did not know, and had never heard of, in a place you have never seen, is by definition real and unreal at the same time. Antonie did not notice, as the days went by, that her husband's anger was growing into hatred, or that he came home later each night. He always had a good reason. She was too much in love to question him.

"Then one day, he didn't come home at all," she said. "I thought, perhaps he's stayed out too late, and doesn't want to risk breaking the curfew. But it wasn't that at all. Arnost came to the apartment. He said Josef had been arrested. I could hear the cobbler downstairs, banging with his hammer. It didn't seem possible he could go on mending shoes while Arnost was telling me that Josef was in the Petschkarna. 'Don't you worry, little sister,' he told me. 'He'll be all right.' He said Josef had been mixed up with some resistance organisation, and that he might even have to go to prison for a little while. 'He's been foolish,' Arnost said. 'But you mustn't worry. He hasn't done anything serious.'"

There was no more news for a week, two weeks, three weeks. She went to the Petschkarna and was coldly told that her husband's case was being considered and that there was no further information. A few days later the postman came to the door with a parcel. It was covered with the circular franking stamps of the Gestapo.

"What is it?" she asked him, a great fear swelling inside her, a fear so enormous she thought it must surely still her heart. The postman shook his head and hurried away, his face grey and sad. She closed the door and went inside, tearing the paper off the package. Inside it was a small urn full of ashes with her husband's name stencilled on the side, together with the place and date of his execution. She stared at it uncomprehendingly. The enormity of such unspeakable savagery numbed her mind.

"It was such a little thing, our happiness," she whispered. "Yet they took it from us without mercy." Her eyes filled with life and anger as she said the words. "Now you know why I hate you, *Oberst*. You and all your carrion kind!"

"I wish there was something I could say to you," Paul said. "To make you believe that this is not what your Josef would have wanted."

"Josef was a brave and honest man, *Oberst*," she said. "You can't have any idea what he would have wanted!"

"I know this," Paul said. "He would not have wanted you to be alone."

She frowned. "I'm not alone. There are many of us. We are strong. One day we will win. You can't stop us."

"Tonie," he said, softly. "Listen to me. You are with them. You are one of them. But you are alone. You don't belong to anyone. Believe me, I know what I'm talking about."

"I don't need anyone," she said. "No one!"

"That's not true," he told her. "One person alone is no damned good for anything."

"You believe that, don't you?" she said, wonderingly. "Imagine that! A romantic Nazi! What will they come up with next?"

"No," he said. "You don't believe that, Tonie. You know what I'm saying is true. But that hatred you have in your heart blinds you."

"Why are you telling me these things?" she said.

"Because I know that for me—and for you, Tonie—it could end any moment. Like that!" He snapped his fingers and she flinched. "A mistake, a misplaced word, carelessness, and they would have us. And what would we have had as a reward? Honour, duty, glory, pride? Would that be enough?"

"I belonged to someone . . . once," she said. "That will be enough."

"Perhaps," Paul said.

"Papa says you . . . help. Is it true? That you . . . tell him things?"

Paul said nothing. She continued looking at him for a long time. Her dark eyes looked huge in the encroaching dusk. She made no attempt to put on a light. He sensed a change in her.

"I'm confused," she said. "Frightened."

"Everybody is, Tonie."

"I was sure I hated you."

"Maybe you do."

"No," she said, slowly.

"That's good."

He went across to her. He took her hand. It was cool. She looked up at him, her eyes unreadable. "He's dead, Tonie," he said to her. "Let go."

"I . . . can't," she said.

"Yes, you can."

"I don't know how. I don't know what to do."

"Hold on to me," he said, drawing her to her feet. He took her into the strong circle of his arms. She sighed and laid her head on his shoulder. He did not kiss her. They stood like that for what seemed like a long time. Then, almost as if she was embarrassed by having revealed herself to him, she pulled out of his arms, turning away.

"Listen to me, Tonie," he said. "I've spent all my life steering clear of deep attachments. I never let anyone get really close to me, see inside my mind. I always believed relationships like that could tear you apart."

"And now?"

"Now I know what I told you is true. Nobody's any good alone."

She half turned; her eyes were full of tears again. They searched his face as if for some special meaning only he could impart.

"I . . . are you saying what I think you are saying to me, Paul?"

"Yes," he said, taking her into his arms again. She did not resist. Nor did she speak. Surrender itself was enough.

Berlin, September 8, 1941

Walter Abendschon was not a swearing man. It was his opinion that cursing was a mark of insecurity, and betrayed a person's inability to express himself properly. There were perfectly good words to cover every conceivable human situation, without resorting to curses. Nevertheless, there was only one word which expressed how he felt today, so he said it.

"*Scheisse!*" he growled, banging his fist on the desk. He stalked across to the window and looked down at the square below. Ministry typists and clerks from the Reichsbank sat on the benches, eating their sandwiches. The girls wore summery frocks; the men were in shirtsleeves. The sky was cornflower blue, not a cloud anywhere. It would be nice to go to the mountains, Abendschon thought. Walchensee, perhaps. Eva and he had honeymooned in the Hotel Post at Walchensee. They had walked all the way up to the top of the Herzogstand; there was no chairlift in those days. Below them the lake looked like a picture taken from an airplane. A long way away, over the top of the Steinriegel, they could see Mittenwald nestled in its valley at the foot of the Karwendeln.

"*Scheisse!*" he said again. He wished he could be in Walchensee now. Anything rather than put on his jacket and obey the summons to appear before *Standartenführer* Kurt Bergmann in the RSHA executive office at Wilhelmstrasse 102. What the devil am I going to tell him if he asks me about Kramer? he thought. You never knew which way Bergmann would jump. He was a cold fish, and no mistake. They said that when he pissed, ice came out.

"Have you any evidence other than the word of this woman, Gris?" he would ask in that soft, reasonable voice. "*Evidence*, not gossip?"

"No, *Standartenführer*," Abendschon would be forced to admit.

"Can you give me any plausible motive for Kramer's killing Graumann?"

"No," again. There was nothing in the book about telling someone with Bergmann's temperament and position that there was, indeed, a motive; that Kramer might well have killed Graumann because Graumann had tailed him to Erika Bergmann's apartment and realised, as Abendschon had done after three or four times, that Kramer's visits there could hardly be courtesy calls. Kramer was hardly likely to want that on a report which Bergmann would see as surely as the fact that there was a Sunday in the week. The question was: would he have killed to cover himself?

There was nothing in the man's dossier to support the proposition. Born in Königsbrunn, near Augsburg, March 7, 1908, father German, mother Czech. Only child. *Primarschule* followed by gymnasium. Maturation, law: then the Army. Married Brigit Schafer 1930. Recommended as assistant to the Military Attaché in Dresden in 1933. Divorced that year: the wife had not contested it, there were no children. In 1937, seconded to *Abwehr* duties. Transferred to Prague 1938, back to Berlin in May, 1939, then Prague again the following Spring, as head of the IIIF Desk there. Back to staff duties Berlin in November 1940, and that was it. Gold Party badge: one of the first hundred thousand. Well connected, highly thought of at the Bendlerstrasse. Abendschon had been discreet, but thorough. He knew all there was to know about Paul Kramer, and none of it told him a thing. He went to the places an officer with his rank and responsibilities would be expected to go to: Horcher's, the Adlon bar, Ciro's, Reich's restaurant in the Behrenstrasse. Cocktail parties at Fritz von Opel's or the Siemens house in Berlinerstrasse, friendly visits to the Embassies of the neutral countries: Switzerland, Spain, the United States, Sweden. Kramer seemed to be well-liked by the foreign diplomats with whom he lunched. The one he seemed to see the most of was the commercial attaché at the American Embassy, a man named Samuel Gray. There could be no sinister connotation there, either: Gray had left Berlin at the end of June and not returned.

So what had he got? Suspicion, and not much else. No witnesses, no evidence, nothing except the inconclusive testimony of Marianna Gris. Nothing: the very work seemed to mock him. Yet somehow, Abendschon knew he was right. Twenty years of police work had taught him never to disregard his intuition.

He rehearsed what he might say to Bergmann as he left

his office and walked along the Französischerstrasse in the bright September sunshine. There had been an RAF raid the night before, two hundred bombers. They said the Eden Hotel had been hit, and a bomb had fallen in the Hochmeisterplatz, damaging the church. Not exactly precision bombing, he thought. And hardly military targets. The raids were more of a nuisance than anything. One made a joke of them: noisy tonight, isn't it?

He thought of Karin Graumann. She was a small woman, with high cheekbones and green eyes with the slightest hint of an Oriental slant in them. The house in Schmargendorf was neat and warm. No, she told him, Alben had no enemies. He was a good man, kind, thoughtful. He let her talk: she seemed to want to. She showed him photographs of the two of them on holiday in Salzburg. She cried a little; Abendschon let her do that, too. He had learned long ago that it was better to allow people to cry. Patting them on the shoulder and making consoling noises didn't help at all, any more than saying 'Don't cry'. Better to say, go ahead, let it out. She talked freely about her husband, and it was clear that she had loved him. You only had to listen to her to know there was no likelihood of infidelity, either on her part or on Graumann's. His Gestapo record was as clean as a whistle. It was quite out of character for such a man to have abandoned a surveillance detail. Which meant he had still been tailing Kramer when he was killed, and which in turn meant that Kramer had been the only one with opportunity and motive, albeit one Abendschon did not find convincing, to kill him.

And if it wasn't Kramer, who else *could* it have been? The only other remote possibility was the whore, and that didn't make sense at all. Marianna Gris had been frightened, but nothing like as frightened as she would have been if she'd actually killed a Gestapo agent. No, he thought. Kramer was the only suspect they had, so he'd have to make the most of it.

He turned into the Wilhelmstrasse and walked down past the Ministry of Justice. He showed his warrant disc to the sleepy-looking SS corporal guarding the entrance to the Main Security Office. He went up to the third floor in the elevator, where he was again required to produce his warrant disc. The *Oberscharführer-SS* who inspected it looked anything but sleepy, and neither did the SS men with machine-pistols flanking his desk. Abendschon walked along the corridor until he came to a pair of doors alongside which was a slotted plaque. In the slot was a wooden plate on which was painted in neat letters the legend:

Standartenführer-SS Kurt Bergmann,
Reichskriminalrat Amt IVE

Abendschon pushed open one of the doors and went in. The room was square and well-lit, painted in cream and grey and furnished, as so many official rooms in Berlin seemed to be furnished, like the inside of a carriage on the Trans-Europe Express. There was a good view of the street: nice for watching the parades, he thought. Typewriters clattered, phones shrilled. Men in uniform hurried through. There were perhaps forty or fifty people working at the desks set in four neat rows between the door and the rear of the room, where another closed pair of doors was set in the centre of the wall. Bergmann's adjutant, *Scharführer-SS* Peter Eckhardt, looked up and gave him a mock salute. Abendschon nodded as the secretary in the reception area wrote down his name in the visitor record book and logged the time of his arrival, as she would later log his departure. She spoke into an intercom.

"Please go straight in," she said. "The *Standartenführer* is expecting you."

Abendschon patted Eckhardt on the shoulder as he passed his desk, and knocked on Bergmann's polished mahogany door. He heard Bergmann call "*Komm!*" and went in. A huge portrait of Adolf Hitler frowned down from the wall. A tattered Nazi Party flag hung beneath it. Bergmann's desk, an antique table, some armchairs, a carpet. Everything was neat, uncluttered. Like the man himself, Abendschon thought. Bergmann looked up as he came across the room. "Sit down," he said, waving at a chair.

The new rank badges were brilliantly silver on the

freshly-pressed black uniform. Abendschon catalogued the varnished jackboots, the silver eagle of the *Eisenkreuz 1st Klasse*, the gold Party badge, the manicured hands. A perfect specimen of the New Man, he thought, with that well-proportioned frame, those chilly but perceptive eyes, and that agile mind. 'Mr Indispensable,' they were calling him. Yes, a perfect specimen, Abendschon thought, all bullshit and cunning. He had little enough time for any of them, and even less for this one. There were too damned many of them altogether, all working for their own greater glory.

"You have been investigating the murder of Gestapo agent 6l.577 Alben Graumann, of this Department," Bergmann said, without preamble.

"Yes. I—"

"You will cease all further inquiries."

"May I ask why?"

Bergmann looked at him for a long, silent moment, eyebrows raised just enough to let Abendschon know he had been impertinent but that it was going to be overlooked. Abendschon felt a surge of anger at the man's arrogance. Damned upstart, he thought. I was catching murderers when you were a schoolboy.

"*Obergruppenführer* Heydrich has taken a personal interest in the matter," Bergmann said, eventually.

"Ah," Abendschon said. "*Obergruppenführer* Heydrich."

Bergmann looked up again, more sharply this time, his eyes narrowed. Abendschon's face was bland. He chose to decide that Abendschon had intended no disrespect. He could not have been more wrong.

"You will surrender all documents on the matter to this office immediately," he said. "Meanwhile I will accept your verbal report."

Abendschon told him the little he knew: Graumann's death, the vehicle and pedestrian survey, the testimony of the tart, her identification of the man she had met that night in the Café Dobren.

"Major Paul Kramer," Bergmann anticipated, with a self-satisfied smile. "*Abwehr* IIIF". He said it "ah-bay-vay," the way insiders did.

"You knew?"

"He was under surveillance on my orders."

Then he must know about Kramer and his wife, Abendschon thought. "Would the *Standartenführer* care to tell me why?"

"We are on to something big, Abendschon," Bergmann said, leaning forward, a wicked light kindling in his eyes. "We suspect he may be involved in anti-Reich activities."

Abendschon waited. 'Anti-Reich activities' was one of those sweeping Gestapo phrases that made it possible to arrest anybody for anything. It was an anti-Reich activity to chalk a slogan on a wall and it was an anti-Reich activity to blow up the Wilhelmstrasse.

"The *Obergruppenführer* and I are compiling a series of dossiers on certain officers in the *Abwehr*," Bergmann went on. "Some of them have been on our blacklist since 1936. I haven't yet decided exactly what part Kramer is playing, but it makes no difference. His name is going into the ammunition pack with all the rest!"

"Ammunition pack?" Abendschon managed.

"We'll bring them all down one day," Bergmann said. "And when we do, it will be the dossiers in the ammunition pack we'll do it with. We're watching them all, Abendschon, all of them. Every member of that damned 'gentlemen's club'. One day we will prove to the *Reichsführer* and the Führer himself that the whole damned *Abwehr* is a cooking pot for treason!"

"Then this Graumann thing—?"

"Graumann is unimportant," Bergmann said, waving a dismissive hand. "This matter takes precedence over the murder of one man, even a dozen."

You had to have a special point of view to look at it like that, Abendschon thought, quelling his disgust. But that was the way the New Men worked. One murder or a dozen, it made no difference to them, as long as the desired end result was obtained.

"Kramer has gone to Prague, as you know," Bergmann went on. "We don't know what that means, but there has to be some reason for it." That was another facet of the New Men's thinking: always conspiring, they automatically assumed conspiracy in even the simplest things. *Abwehr* could have sent Kramer to Prague for any one of a dozen reasons, none of them remotely to do with Bergmann's anti-Reich conspiracy.

"What could he do in Prague that he can't do in Berlin?" he asked.

Bergmann smiled. "That's what you are going to find out."

"I beg your pardon?"

"I'm sending you to Prague, Abendschon. I want you to watch Kramer. Find out what he is up to."

"I don't speak Czech."

"You don't need to," Bergmann said, impatiently. "The Protectorate has been completely Germanised."

I'll bet, Abendschon thought, but he did not say it. Everyone knew that the Czechs were Germany's biggest headache. Hitler was always ranting about wiping them off the face of the earth if they didn't come to heel. So far his threats did not seem to have had much effect.

"Prague is the biggest hotbed of treasonable activity in the Reich!" Bergmann said, as if reading Abendschon's thoughts. "We at the RSHA have been charged with quelling it, once and for all. I'll tell you something not a lot of people know, Abendschon. The Führer is very unhappy with old von Neurath. He's going to replace him, appoint a new *Reichsprotector*. The *Obergruppenführer* intends to obtain that appointment."

"But how?"

"How can he run Czechoslovakia and maintain control of the Main Security Office?" Bergmann said. "The *Obergruppenführer* is no ordinary man, Abendschon!"

"That's certainly true," Abendschon said. Bergmann gave him the sharp glance again, but Abendschon kept his face expressionless.

"Three thousand extra officials are being sent to Prague to set up a new administrative organisation. More will follow. If the *Obergruppenführer* is appointed, I, too, will be transferred to the Protectorate."

"I see," Abendschon said.

"I want you in place by the time I get there. Offices will be placed at your disposal, staff, anything you need. You will operate independently of all the other police organisations, reporting only to me. The Kramer case will be your responsibility."

"Why me?"

"Your knowledge of Kramer makes you perfect for the job," Bergmann said. "He doesn't know you exist, whereas I am sure he has already fully informed himself about the Prague Gestapo and *Sicherheitspolizei*."

"And what am I to do?"

"Watch him. Report his every move to me. I want to know everything he does, every address he goes to, the name of every person he meets. Everything, do you understand me? Let him believe he got away with the murder of Graumann. Lull him into a false sense of security. We'll go on watching and waiting. And then—." He held up his hand and closed the fist.

"I'll have to clear this with Arthur Nebe," Abendschon said. Nebe was his Chief, head of the *Kripo*.

"I've already taken care of that," Bergmann said, with a negligent wave of the hand. "You'll leave immediately. Have you any questions?"

Yes, Abendschon thought, what about Karin Graumann? Who's going to tell her that her husband's death was just an unfortunate incident, that Bergmann's plan and Heydrich's ammunition pack were far more important than the life of Alben Graumann? He shook his head and got up to go, masking his rising anger. He made a silent promise to himself. I'll get him for you, Karin, he thought. He walked to the door. Bergmann did not rise; he was already engrossed in some papers on his desk. Thank you, Abendschon, the detective thought. He turned and asked a final question.

"Tell me," he said. "Why does *Obergruppenführer* Heydrich want more power? Hasn't he got enough?"

Bergmann looked at him coldly. "No," he said.

Prague, September 27, 1941

On the last Sunday in September, a warm sunny day, *Obergruppenführer* Reinhard Tristan Eugen Heydrich and sixty-two members of his personal staff arrived in Prague. The SS flag, harbinger of terror, was hoisted for the first time on the huge flagpoles in the Cour d'Honneur in front of the Matthias Gate of Hradcany Castle—Hradschin, the Germans called it. Heydrich, a tall man with the face of a Medici, was welcomed by State Secretary Karl-Hermann Frank, himself an SS General, but more than willing to be outranked by Himmler's deputy and, or so it was rumoured, the Führer's favourite. Frank was content to be Heydrich's adviser and cohort. Heydrich was on the way up. He would not forget the ones who helped him, and Karl-Hermann Frank counted himself personally responsible for Heydrich's appointment.

Old Baron von Neurath simply hadn't been the right calibre at all. He had no nose for the beginnings of a 'situation', and it was as plain as a pikestaff that a situation was developing in the Protectorate which, if not stamped on, was going to blow up in their faces. From June to September, armament production had fallen by eighteen per cent, in some factories by twice that much. The first signs of an incipient strike movement were noted. The slogans of the resistance and the BBC—*pomalu pracuj,* 'work slowly'— were meeting widespread public sympathy. Sabotage increased to a totally unpermissible level: telephone wires cut, trains derailed, machinery in factories damaged, supply dumps and buildings set on fire, a hundred thousand litres of petrol burned. Then, during the second week of September, the government-in-exile, led by the traitor Beneš in London, had appealed to the population to demonstrate its solidarity by boycotting the Protectorate's Nazi-controlled newspapers. The response was so alarming that Frank demanded draconian measures be taken against the local resistance. Von Neurath demurred, and his refusal to act gave Heydrich the opportunity for which he had been waiting. Citing a report from the *Reichsprotector* which contained talk of preparation for rebellion and a general strike on Czech National Day, October 28, Heydrich asked for an audience with the Führer. It was fixed for September 22 at *Wolfschanze,* the *Führerhauptquartier* near Rastenburg.

Heydrich used the intervening time to fully brief himself, not only on the Prague conference convened by Frank on September 17, but on all aspects of resistance, summoning the chief of the Gestapo *Leitstelle* in Prague, *Sturmbannführer und Regierungsrat* Dr Hans Ulrich Geschke, to Berlin for the purpose. Geschke was able to provide Heydrich with proof positive of the collaboration between the Czech government in Prague led by General Alois Elias, and Beneš' government in London, which had been going on for years under the nose of Baron von Neurath.

When he reached *Wolfschanze* on the afternoon of September 21, Heydrich, together with Himmler and Frank, explained to Hitler the causes for and the structure of the Czech resistance. And most importantly of all, how to break its back. Hitler was fascinated, impressed. There was no doubt about it, Frank thought, as he watched Heydrich at work, the man's command was phenomenal, his memory incredible.

By the time von Neurath arrived at Rastenburg, he was finished. Hitler had already decided to take 'drastic action'. He had less need now, he said, for the expedience of diplomatic means. He would assume the office of *Reichsprotector* himself. As his personal deputy in Bohemia and Moravia he would appoint Heydrich.

"May I say that I am impressed and honoured that the Deputy *Reichsprotector* has asked me to stay on as Secretary of State?" Frank said. "And that we are all delighted he is to command us?"

"*Danke,*" Heydrich said. Flattery meant nothing to him. Neither did praise. "I have drawn up a timetable. You will assist me in its execution."

"At your command," Frank said. "When do we begin?"

Heydrich looked at him, his eyes as cold as a lizard's. "Now," he said.

He was as good as his word. An immediate State of Emergency was proclaimed in the political centres of the Protectorate: Prague, Brno, Ostrava, Kladno. The news was broadcast hourly by the radio to astonished Czechs returning from picnics, visiting friends. It was flashed on the screens in cinemas, where they were showing a film called *Moods of Love*. It appeared the following day in the press and on posters in the streets.

ALL ACTS AGAINST PUBLIC ORDER, ECONOMIC LIFE,
AS WELL AS LABOUR PEACE, TOGETHER WITH THE
UNLAWFUL POSSESSION OF FIREARMS, EXPLOSIVES,
OR AMMUNITION, WILL BE JUDGED UNDER THIS
LAW. ALL ASSEMBLIES IN PRIVATE ROOMS OR PUBLIC
HIGHWAYS ARE FORBIDDEN. THERE WILL BE NO
APPEAL AGAINST THE SENTENCES OF THESE COURT
MARTIALS. SENTENCES WILL BE CARRIED OUT
IMMEDIATELY BY SHOOTING OR HANGING.

The summary courts were permitted to bring in one of only three verdicts: not guilty, referred to the Gestapo, or death. Six death sentences were pronounced on September 28, twenty the next day, and fifty-eight the day after. The terror had commenced.

'Suspects' were rounded up, taken in manacles to Gestapo headquarters or directly to Pankrac prison. One hundred and forty-two Czechs were executed on the day after Heydrich's arrival, among them twenty-one officers of the former Czech Army, including six generals and ten colonels accused of participating in the London-directed resistance organisation. More than five hundred men were sent to the Mauthausen concentration camp. Day after day, the terrible red posters were posted in streets and squares by stone-faced SS. Firing squads worked like automatons at the Kobylisy shooting range. Hangings and beheadings were carried out around the clock at Pankrac. Fear stalked the streets like an animal.

On October 1, Heydrich summoned all Nazi authorities in the Protectorate to a conference at the Czernin Palace. There was no food, no drinks. Heydrich was not in Prague to give parties.

"I am interested in one goal only," he told them. "That this area should exploit its full economic potential. Anything which stands in the way of my achieving that goal I will suppress without mercy, whatever its origin or cause. Anything which helps me, I will support. The basis of my ap-

116

proach may be summed up in the phrase 'Less provocation, together with less tolerance'."

His demeanour was cold and precise, and with his strange, high-pitched voice and lynx eyes he looked, Paul thought, like a man who knew to a fraction of a millimetre what he could and could not do.

"This area is the heart of the Reich!" Heydrich went on tonelessly. "One day, it will be completely, definitively German. Those of its people found worthy of Germanisation will have my friendship, and my help. The rest, you may be assured, will be sterilised or simply stood against a wall and shot!"

A ruthless, cold-blooded machine of a man who knew exactly what he wanted and how to get it, Paul concluded. No wonder Kurt Bergmann got along so well with him. Look at the way they had handled the arrest of old General Elias. He was arrested that first Monday; the decision had obviously been taken in Berlin even before Heydrich arrived. Two days later, the First Senate of the People's Court, led by its President, Otto Thierack, arrived in Prague; and the following day, October 1, Elias was tried for high treason, sentenced to death, stripped of his civil honours. But he was neither executed nor pardoned, and Paul knew why. Elias was much too useful as a source to exert pressure on the Czechs. Heydrich knew, for instance, that the Minister of the interior, Jezek, knew all about the resistance, who worked for it, who had escaped, but Jezek had not even been arrested. Heydrich did not want to make a clean sweep; that would leave him no one to work with.

The terror continued.

A hundred men a week executed in Prague, two or three hundred more shipped off like animals to . . . where? A new word was whispered among the hunted: *vernichtungslager*, extermination camp. Daily, Heydrich reported his victories to the Führer, praising the good work of his minions. The two thousand Gestapo and twenty-two hundred police officers under his command were working a fourteen-hour day, seven days a week.

As soon as he was able, Paul got in touch with Jan Novak. They met in the Vitkov Park, by the National Monument. There was a breathtaking view of the city from the western end of the hill, but neither of them had eyes for it. They walked beneath the trees. Paul had bought some plums at a shop in the Husstrasse. They tasted of autumn.

"Things are going to be very bad, Jan," he told his friend. "They'll kill a Czech if he spits in the street. Tell your people to stop radio transmissions for a while. Lie low till this is over, till the state of emergency ends."

Jan was silent for a long time. He spat out the plum stone, and wiped his lips with the back of his hand. "The thing is," he said, heavily, "there's something on."

"What?"

"Do you want me to tell you?"

"No," Paul said. "Never mind."

"Morávec has to stay in touch with London" Jan said. "Until October 10."

Paul shook his head. "It's too damned risky, Jan!" he said. "The Gestapo is pulling everyone in. They know where all the transmitters are—I've seen their reports."

"All the same," Jan said stubbornly.

"Will you listen to me!" Paul said. "They know roughly where he is. If he transmits, they'll come and pick him up."

"Morávec isn't with the transmitter."

"Whoever it is," Paul said. "Get them out of there."

"All right, my friend," Jan said. "Thank you. I'll do what I can." They shook hands and he lumbered off down the hill. Paul watched him affectionately. Jan acted as the courier between Paul and the Czech resistance. He had declined to meet any of them, even Vaslav Morávec, the last of the famous 'Three Kings'. Only one person connected with the resistance knew Paul by sight, and that person was Jan Novak. He knew no one he would rather trust with his life. He went across to a trash basket and dropped the paper bag into it. Then he walked down the hill to the Husstrasse, and under the railway viaduct, turning left into the little park fronting the *Hauptbahnhof*. Up ahead, on the right, on the corner of Bredauergasse, sat the squat, unlovely Petschek Bank, Gestapo headquarters. Masin, Morávec's right hand man, was still in there: he was undergoing what they called 'sharpened interrogation'. Poor bastard, Paul thought. There was nothing anybody could do for Masin.

* * *

On the night of October 2, the intersecting beams of the Gestapo radio-detector vans did their work accurately. An excited operator whispered the information to the waiting Gerhard Leiche. The gargoyle face broke into a snarling smile.

"*Ausgezeichnet!*" he said, eyes alight with hellfire. He got out of the van and went around to the front. He drew a finger across his throat. The driver nodded and released the brake, coasting silently down the cobblestoned street. The street was empty, silent. The Gestapo team were well hidden, in doorways, street courtyards. Sending the van away was all part of the technique. There would be a lookout. He would see the van go and signal, all clear. The radio operators would resume transmission. And they would have them.

Leiche knew from police records that there were three apartments in the pinpointed building, one on each floor. The ground floor flat was occupied by a retired railway worker and his wife. The apartment above his was shared by three secretaries who worked at the Ministry of Labour. The top floor apartment, two rooms, really, was the home of two brothers, Pavel and Ata Stepanek, who worked at the Smichov brewery. Leiche had already concluded that it was from this apartment that the transmission was being made. But where was the damned lookout? He wasn't going to let the bastards trick him like that second time. As if reading Leiche's thoughts, his assistant, Ludwig Herschelmann, gently touched his arm. Leiche did not jump. He was not that sort of man.

"*Dort drüben,*" Herschelmann whispered, pointing with his chin. Over there. Leiche saw the pinpoint red glow of a cigarette and made a movement with his head. One of the Gestapo agents nodded, and slid soundlessly along the wall, disappearing into the darkness. They heard the lookout clear his throat and stamp his feet to warm them: there was a sharp edge on the night air. Ten minutes passed. They heard a scuffling noise, a muffled thud. There was no outcry and Leiche nodded again, satisfied. The Czech swine hadn't expected anyone to come out of the door behind him. Leiche's man had gone around the back of the house, used his skeleton keys. The rest was easy.

"So," Leiche said. He took his pistol from his pocket and cocked it. Without looking at him, he asked Herschelmann if everyone was in place.

"Jawohl, Herr Kriminalkommissar!"

"One outside," Leiche said, remembering how Morávec had slid down the aerial. "Three around the back."

He waited two minutes to give them time to get into position. Then he shot the lock off the door and ran up the stairs, his men close behind him. On the top landing there were two doors, facing each other. Herschelmann kicked one open, Leiche the other. A man behind his door tried to shove it shut and Leiche gave a great shout. His men slammed into the door and the shock team swarmed into the room, their guns ready.

There were only a few sticks of furniture in the room, a pine table, some wooden chairs, dark blue blackout curtains, the compulsory sandbox, and the transmitter in the corner. One of the two men in the apartment was lying on the linoleum-covered floor, his eyes bulging, face blue. Two Gestapo agents were wrestling with the other one, a dark-haired man of perhaps twenty-four in a leather jacket and blue pants. He had a round face and there was panic in his eyes. Herschelmann handed his chief a tiny metal cylinder with a glass top, and Leiche smiled his brutish smile.

"Well done, Ludwig," he said. He went across the room and lifted the arm of the man on the floor with the toe of his boot. "Dead, I suppose?"

"Yes, sir," Herschelmann said. "We couldn't get to him quickly enough. This one got in the way." He jerked his head at the captive boy.

"Scheisse!" Leiche said, and kicked the body. He saw the anger flare in the eyes of the captive youth, and nodded. "Well, at least we've got you, sonny. What's your name, eh?" He grabbed the young man's chin, roughly pulling his head around. The boy looked Leiche in the eye but he did not speak.

"A tough one, eh?" Leiche said, softly. "Well, you'll have your chance to prove it. All right, get him out of here!" He raised his voice so that everyone could hear him now. "I want everyone in this house arrested on suspicion. Everyone in the houses next door, both sides. Detailed statements from everyone else in the street. And I want them yesterday! *Verstanden?*"

His men nodded wearily. Mr Charm, they called him. They would be up all night, and working most of tomorrow without a break. Nobody complained, not about Gerhard Leiche. He stood with his hands on his hips, a craggy, ugly hulk of a man with a jutting forehead and a thick neck, dressed in a leather overcoat and a Tyrolean hat. He was disappointed, but he did not allow the disappointment to show. He had hoped he would catch the big fish, Morávec, not these little minnows. You Czech swine, he thought, I can *smell* you've been here. His hands clenched into fists.

"And get this filth out of here!" he roared, kicking the dead boy's body again. His men flinched and hastened to do his bidding as Leiche turned on his heel and stormed out of the apartment.

"Miserable bastard," one of the men muttered.

"Put it in your report," said another. "He likes constructive criticism."

Dorking, October 3, 1941

Automobiles reached Bellasis House by leaving the A24 and climbing up the road locals called 'the Zig-zag'. Just before the 'Hand in Hand' pub, a lane led off to the left through the dripping heath. At the end of the unpaved lane was a pole barrier, manned by armed guards. A few hundred yards beyond the barrier, Bellasis stood imposingly by the side of the lane.

Sam watched from a window as the big black Humbers disgorged their passengers in the gravelled forecourt. So these were the top brass of Czech Intelligence, he thought. Noël Mason-Morley identified them for him.

"The six-footer in the Colonel's uniform is Frantisek Morávec, head of intelligence," the Englishman said. "The one standing next to him is Major Karel Palecek, their forgery and espionage man. The one with the limp is Lieutenant Colonel Alfred Bartik, in charge of counter-espionage. He's also Morávec's deputy."

Sam watched as the Czechs were admitted to the house through the great panelled oaken double doors. Over the lintel was a scrollwork of stone, in the centre of which was the head of a lion. One of the paras had said it looked like the lion in *The Wizard of Oz*.

"Bert Lahr," Sam supplied. And Bert the stone lion became, a sort of mascot. They had come to Dorking for final indoctrination, after six gruelling weeks in Camusdarach. Twenty-two of them from the original hundred and sixty volunteers, trained now to kill, to live off hostile terrain, to elude the most persistent pursuer. They were schooled in the theory and practice of sabotage, and tried out their new skills in the railway tunnel above Arisaig House and the cuttings and embankments between there and Morar. From Mallaig they were taken to Manchester's Ringway aerodrome for parachute training, followed by some real jumps over Salisbury Plain. At the end of September they came to Bellasis for their final, intensive briefing.

They were just kids, Sam discovered, not even old enough to question the use that was being made of their idealism. Instant obedience, complete dedication, unquestioning patriotism. Well, Sam thought, maybe it was easier that way. As he got to know them, so he grew to like them. He did not keep them at a formal distance, the way Noël Mason-Morley did. Their lives had dimensions beyond this present task. They taught him a few phrases in Czech: *Ano*, yes. *Dekuji*, thank you. *Nemluvin Tchesky*, I don't speak Czech. And they would roar with laughter: you suu-u-re don't, Yank!

A cobbler's son, a joiner's son, a fitter, a farmer's son, a locksmith. Most of them had fled to Poland ten feet ahead of the Gestapo in March, 1939, when Hitler baldly told the world that Czechoslovakia had ceased to exist. Some, like the shy Kubis, had been in Gestapo hands and escaped. But not before they had branded him with swastikas.

Sam watched them as Staff Sergeant Krcek marched them into the high-ceilinged library which was being used for the staff meeting. Just kids, he thought. 'Freda' Bartos from Pardubice, the serious, determined Adolf Opalka. Karel Curda, at thirty, one of the oldest in the group, happy-go-lucky Josef Valcik, just turned twenty-seven. Vladimir Skacha, who had nearly come to blows with him when Curda suggested that perhaps Hitler had his good points. Arnost Miks, with the broad-planed boxer's face and heavy-weight shamble, Joef Gabcik, holder of the French Croix de Guerre, twenty-nine this year, dark haired and swarthy. Which of them would be chosen? How many of them would come out of Wolf Trap alive?

"Thank you, Staff Sergeant," Noël Mason-Morley said. "Sit down, please, men." He waited until the chairs stopped scraping and he had their full attention.

"You have been brought here today to hear serious news," he said. "I imagine most of you heard Mr Masaryk's speech last night. Let me say only this: events in Czechoslovakia are a great deal worse than what he said may have led you to believe. Just how much worse, I will let Colonel Bartik tell you."

"I begin by telling you *Obrana Naroda,* the National Defence Committee, has been completely penetrated by the Nazis," Bartik said. "The organisation upon which we had counted to lead the national uprising no longer exists. Forty-one radio monitors of the UVOD group captured, along with its leader, Colonel Churavy. Our most valuable intelligences came through the groups Sparta One and Sparta Two, controlled by our compatriot Captain Morávec. The first of these was located by the Gestapo in April. In May, we nearly lost Sparta Two, but we had luck. It was relocated and has been transmitting regularly. That is to say, it was doing so—until last night. Last night Sparta Two stopped sending. In the middle of transmission."

There was absolute silence. They all knew what his words meant. If Sparta Two had stopped sending in the middle of transmission the Gestapo had taken it. And its operators.

"Whether they have captured Captain Morávec we cannot ascertain," Bartik went on "Communication with the homeland is completely severed. How this affects your mission Captain Mason-Morley will inform you."

123

"As you men know," Mason-Morley said, getting to his feet slowly, like a jack-knife opening, "Operation Wolf Trap was predicated upon the conjunctive cooperation of the Czech underground. In particular, one source was to advise us of Hitler's movements. Without that information we would be working completely in the dark. Our priority now, therefore, is to get a radio into Prague with new encoding keys. Until we can do so, the mission is postponed. You will return to training and await instructions. That is all."

"Well?" Noël Mason-Morley asked Sam. "How do you think they took it?"

"Badly, I'd say," Sam replied. They were sitting in the drawing room. A big log fire crackled in the huge fireplace. Outside, rain was falling, giving the sunken lawn with its stone statues and urns and carefully clipped topiary a sad, neglected look. At the foot of the garden the ground fell steeply away into a gully, rising as sharply on the other side. With its great Georgian windows, its bell tower, stable blocks, and magnificent isolation, Bellasis was imposing evidence of how the wealthy Ridley family who owned it must have lived before the war. It was one of those houses that gave you the feeling the British would last forever.

While they were waiting for the Czech officers to join them, Sam asked Mason-Morley to fill him in on their background.

"We've always had close links with the Czechs," Mason-Morley said. "Best place in the world for keeping an eye on old Adolf, not to mention the Balkans."

"Were you out there?"

"Just for a while," Mason-Morley said. He did not elaborate. He never did. Sam had asked Donovan about him. Mason-Morley had been seconded to LCS from the Political Intelligence Division of the Foreign Office, Donovan said. They were the faceless, nameless ones, the ones who never got into the papers, who got their knighthoods without fanfare, who listed their occupation in *Who's Who* as 'civil servant, on attachment to the War Office'. Ask them what they did, and they would tell you they had a dull desk job, no worth talking about, old boy. They were the ones, Donovan said, who ran the ones who run things.

"How did they get to England?"

"We had a chap in Prague called Harry Gibson. He chartered a Dutch plane for them, got them out just before Hitler marched in. Gibson told Morávec he could only bring eleven people. He brought his staff, left his wife and children behind. He's that kind of man."

Like a great many Czechs of his generation, Mason-Morley said, Morávec had been born an Austrian, and fought on the Austro-Hungarian side through the Great War. He was on the Russian front with a Serbian regiment when he was shot through the ankle by a Bulgarian soldier.

"Wouldn't let them give him an anaesthetic," Mason-Morley said, shaking his head. "He was afraid they'd amputate while he was out. Sat through the operation wide awake. Can you credit it?"

"He must have been just a kid."

"Twenty-three." Like the Wolf Trap team whom Morávec and his officers were talking to now, Sam thought. Just kids, but with iron in their hearts. He'd had iron in his own heart at that age, too. He half listened as Mason-Morley told him how Morávec had graduated from the Staff College in Prague, the capital of the new Czechoslovak state founded after the war by Masaryk and Beneš. At thirty-three, he was promoted to the rank of Major, and the following year joined the Intelligence Section of the 1st Army. In 1934, he joined the General Staff and soon afterwards took control of all activities of the Second Department.

"Bartik joined him around that time, I believe," Mason-Morley continued. "He'd just got back from Austria, where he'd been in prison for spying. Apparently the Austrians spotted him because of that limp of his. Bit of a giveaway for an undercover man, I would have thought. Still, he's a good man for all that. Anyway, Bartik was one of the 'Eleven' who got out. Six or seven of them are here in London. The others are abroad: Stockholm, Zürich, Istanbul and so on."

"What about his wife?" Sam asked. "Is she still in Prague?"

"No, she got out later," Mason-Morley said. "Ah, here they are now! Hello, Bartik. Come and sit down. You know Sam Gray, of course."

"Indeed."

"How do your boys feel?" Sam asked him.

"They are despondent, I think," Bartik said. "*To se rozumi,* it goes without saying."

"I suppose so," Sam said. "Have you decided anything?"

"Our first concern is to discover whether Gestapo has completely penetrated all Prague resistance groups," Colonel Morávec said. He spoke slightly stilted English, but Sam was impressed once again by his command of the language. A tall, assured man with receding blond hair brushed straight back, Morávec had the forehead of an intellectual and the dark eyes of a dreamer. He was a commanding personality, one of the 'strong men' of the Czech government-in-exile.

"How soon can we get a bomber to go to Prague?" Bartik asked.

"I've talked to Dusty Miller at Tangmere," Mason-Morley said. "He can have a plane ready tomorrow. Have you got someone in mind?"

"One man, we think."

"Only one?"

"Less risk," Morávec said. "We send Pavelka. Major Edwards says he is most accomplished parachutist."

Frantisek Pavelka was a dark-haired boy who had celebrated his twenty-first birthday at Camusdarach. Bartik said the plan was to drop Pavelka near Caslav, about thirty miles east of Prague, where the boy had relatives. He would try to work his way into Prague and get in touch with the resistance there, and through them find Morávec, if he was still at liberty.

"The real problem is losing contact with Karl," Morávec said. "He is key to this operation."

"Who's Karl?" Sam said.

"Captain Morávec receives information from a highly-placed German spy in Prague. His code name is Karl. He is our most valuable agent."

"This man Karl," Sam said, slowly. "Has he worked for you for a long time?"

Morávec glanced at Mason-Morley, and Sam saw the infinitesimal nod. Tell him, if you want to. It was nice to know you were trusted.

"Since before the war," Morávec said. "1937. The summer."

The man they called Karl had first contacted them by letter. He offered his services to Czech Intelligence, claiming to have detailed information on German military and political plans. He made a number of conditions. He would give no name, nor consent to being 'run'. He would work at his own pace, and meet only one person from their side. They were not to ask his reasons, nor to investigate his background. They would work through a system of drops and cutouts which he would designate. He signed the letter 'Karl'. It all sounded very familiar, Sam thought. He might have a surprise for the smooth-skinned Colonel Morávec.

"He used a post-restante box," Bartik said. "We had it watched, of course. And soon learned that we were dealing with a professional. He had a cut-out system which was impossible to break without his knowing."

A 'cut-out system' was used by agents to avoid being traced. A letter was left in a specified place, a 'drop'. A man was briefed to pick it up. He was a courier. He took the letter to another drop, where it was picked up by another courier. Eventually, depending upon how many cut-outs were being used, it reached the person for whom it was intended. None of the couriers knew any of the other couriers. None of them knew the agents at either end. If any courier was arrested, he could implicate no one because he knew no one.

"We set up drops by letter," Morávec continued, picking up the story. "We asked him for *bona-fides*. He replied by giving us complete breakdown Gestapo and *Abwehr* plans in the event war. We were . . ."

"Wary?"

"Yes, wary," Morávec nodded. "But he was genuine. He gave us much important information. Then in February, 1939, he asked for a meeting. Colonel Fryc, our expert on German matters, met him at Turnau in Austria. He told Fryc that Czechoslovakia was to be annexed. We were able to get out of country with all our files before the Germans took over. It was a coup. Everything in that little plane. There was a great snowstorm bearing down on Prague. 'God's wrath', they called it, later."

"And Karl?" Sam asked. "Did you ever meet him, Colonel?"

"He was very much opposed to meeting anyone," Morávec said. "He believed the fewer people who could identify him, the better. But he agreed to *treff* in the Hague. I met him there with two of British Intelligence."

"Stevens and Best," Mason-Morley explained. "The two who were kidnapped by the Nazis a few months later."

"Karl said he did not mind to meet, because he knew we must leave and go to Britain. No danger there of Gestapo interrogation, he said. He laughed as he said it, but not as if it was funny. He had brought with him complete German plans for the invasion of France."

"Damned French wouldn't believe it!" Mason-Morley said, with a short, sharp bark of a laugh. "Thought their damned Maginot Line was impregnable. The last word we had from Karl was a breakdown on Operation Sea Lion."

"That was the projected invasion of Britain, wasn't it?"

"Spot on," Mason-Morley said. "Karl sent us everything: the military strength of the units involved, targets of the *Einsatzgruppen,* names of people expected to collaborate, lists of those who would be shot."

"Then nothing," Morávec said. "It did not come as surprise. He had always said, do not expect me to keep on. The Gestapo is not stupid, he told us. If there was anything truly important, he would try always to contact us."

"Do you know his real name?" Sam asked. Morávec did not reply. His dark eyes studied Sam, and the silence lengthened. Then he spoke.

"Why do you ask me?"

"You say he stopped providing information in the summer of 1940?"

"Yes."

"And he contacted you through Morávec in Prague?"

"In June," Morávec nodded, glancing at Bartik. His deputy shrugged.

"He was in Berlin," Sam said, watching Mason-Morley's

face. "It must be the same man. He even used the same name: Karl."

"I am afraid I do not understand, Mr Gray," Morávec said, leaning forward in his chair. Bartik, too, was watching intently.

"I was contacted in Berlin last January," Sam said. He told Morávec about the rendezvous that icy January night in the Berlin cinema. He told them about the documents that had been in the envelope, a copy of an actual *Führerrichtungweisend* outlining the German attack on Russia.

"He told you he'd find a way" Sam said. "And he did, through me. It was the only channel he had to the Allies."

"This does not mean it was the same person."

"I met him in the Tiergarten," Sam said. "He told me he was being sent to Prague."

"You met him?" Bartik said. "In a park?"

"He is a man of between thirty and thirty-five years of age," Sam said. "Blond hair, blue eyes, tall, good-looking. He used the name Karl-André Rauth. He signed all his notes 'Karl'. It must be the same man."

Morávec looked at Bartik, whose face was unreadable. He smiled at Sam, but it was not a warm smile. Sam thought he knew why: British Intelligence had not seen fit to pass the material Karl had given him to the Czechs. Spymasters were always jealously protective about 'their' agents.

"So," Morávec said. "Now he is back in Prague. Of course, you will leave him now to us, Noël?" The request was politely framed, but Sam was not misled. Morávec was telling the Englishman to stay away from Karl.

"Of course," Mason-Morley said, urbanely. There were two spots of colour high on his cheekbones.

"Good," Morávec said, as if to say, this matter will not be discussed again. "Now we must make our plans to get a radio into Prague." He turned to Bartik. "Pavelka is ready?"

"Yes, sir."

"Good," Morávec said. "If he can contact Dr Vanek, the *Jindra* group will take him to Captain Morávec. Once he has a radio and new codes, we will begin again to receive information."

"You're not related?" Sam asked. "You and Captain Morávec?"

"Not at all" Morávec said, getting up from his chair like a very tired old man. "It is a common name in Czechoslovakia. We must go, I am afraid." He shook hands with Noël Mason-Morley and then with Sam. "*Ved klidny zivot,*" he said. "Lead a peaceful life."

Sam grinned. "That'll be the day," he said.

Prague, October 27, 1941

Cities, Walter Abendschon had decided, were a bit like women. When they were gay and charming, they were a delight. Munich was charming, *gemütlich* and smiling. Berlin was daring, confident. Vienna, Paris, they were gay and charming cities. And charming cities, like charming women, never lost their attraction and never grew old. There were cities without charm, of course. He had never liked Hamburg or Frankfurt much. He had been in Metz once. All he could remember about Metz was that the water was hard. As for Brussels the less said the better. However, even Brussels was preferable to Prague. It was as plain as the nose on your face that no matter how many swastika banners were draped over her balconies, no matter how many of her street names were Germanised, no matter how many times that deputy-*Reichsprotector* Heydrich shouted that she was irrevocably part of the Greater German Reich, the River Moldau would remain the Vltava, the Dienzenhoferbrucke would remain Jiraskuv Most, and Prague would continue to be what she immutably was, an utter Czech cow of a city.

He plodded slowly up the stone staircase. Bergmann's suite of offices was in the long wing on the south side of the castle. The outer office which housed his adjutant, *Scharführer* Peter Eckhardt, was the very one from which, they said, Hitler had first looked out upon the newly annexed capital. There was a framed print of the event on the wall showing Hitler in a peaked cap, hands on the sill, looking down. In the cobbled square below were photographers, a child waving, crowds held back by soldiers in steel helmets and greatcoats. Had they really cheered Hitler, these sullen-faced Czechs? They wouldn't cheer him now, Abendschon thought. He came up to the Hradschin once a week to turn in his report on Kramer. Not that there was much to report. Until now, he thought, with almost sensuous pleasure. He went into the outer office. The Hitler picture was in its usual place. He turned round to see Eckhardt holding up a coffee mug, eyebrows raised.

"Why not?" Abendschon said, slumping into a leather chair. "How are you, Peter?"

"Overworked and underpaid," Eckhardt said. "What brings you here—the usual?"

"The usual," Abendschon said, sipping the coffee. It was the real thing, not *ersatz*.

"Sign the book, will you?" Eckhardt said. "You'll probably have to wait. He's got the Chief with him."

Abendschon sipped the coffee and looked out of the window. It was a miserable, grey October day. The relentless drizzle was like a grey veil dropped over the city. The pleasant prospect disappeared into it, leaving only the rain-slick cobblestones, the dull, faceless office blocks, the hulking public buildings, the screech of trolley wheels on iron tracks, bowed heads, thin faces, the smell of sausages and damp wool. God, he thought, I wish I was back in Berlin. They said there had been more air raids.

At that moment the door of the inner office opened, and Bergmann's staff leaped to rigid attention. Abendschon lumbered to his feet as *Reichsprotector* Heydrich emerged from Bergmann's office, his thin, fox face relaxed in a not-un-pleasant smile. Abendschon had not been this close to the man before. He found himself looking at a tall, athletically-built, fit-looking man just too narrow-faced to be called handsome, too austere to exude warmth. Abendschon noticed Heydrich had what they called wishbone hips.

"Until tomorrow evening, then, Bergmann," he said in a thin, high-pitched voice. "Lina is looking forward to seeing you again."

"And we her, *Reichsprotector,*" Bergmann said, fawning. Heydrich nodded and crossed the room as though the men standing in it did not exist. His chauffeur, the giant Klein, was already holding the swing door open.

"Home, Klein!" Heydrich said.

The SS sergeant nodded and ran down the stairs ahead of Heydrich, the skirts of his leather coat flapping. Home, Abendschon thought. You never thought of men like Heydrich sitting by a fire, playing with their children. But even a Heydrich must have some time with his family. The *Reichsprotector* had moved into the former residence of Baron von Neurath at Panenske Brezany, a small village twenty kilometres north of Prague. The name of the village had been changed to Jungfern-Breschan, and a fortune spent on refurbishing the white manor house, once the home of a Jewish sugar-millionaire named Bloch-Bauer. Rumour had it that Heydrich was spending a fortune laying out a racing track and building stables: he fancied himself as a connoisseur of horseflesh. Every servant had a servant: very Austrian, Abendschon thought sourly.

"Walter," Bergmann said, interrupting his reverie. The staff had visibly relaxed in the wake of Heydrich's departure. "Right on time, as usual." He did not make it sound like a compliment.

"You sound cheerful," Abendschon said, following him into his office. Apart from the white and gold walls, and the huge windows, it was a duplicate of the one Bergmann had occupied in Berlin. Even the tattered Party flag had been brought to Prague. Abendschon had asked Eckhardt about it, and learned it was one of the banners carried in the 1923 *putsch* attempt in Munich.

"I am cheerful," Bergmann smiled. "*Reichsprotector* Heydrich has just done me the honour of inviting me to dine at his home. With *Reichsführer* Himmler."

"The *Reichsführer* is coming to Prague?"

"He arrives this evening."

And Frau Heydrich was giving him dinner. Cooked with her own fair hands, no doubt, Abendschon thought. Well, I don't envy you your social success, Colonel. He had met Lina Heydrich and she was not his type at all.

"You're old friends," he observed. "You and the *Reichsführer*."

"Well," Bergmann said, deprecatingly. "Not quite old friends. Although the *Reichsführer* did once honour my home by dining there. It was on the occasion of my founding the first Party branch. In Königsbrunn."

"You told me," Abendschon said. "What brings him to Prague?"

"*Reichsprotector* Heydrich wishes to show him some of our achievements here," Bergmann said.

Achievements, Abendschon thought, that's a new word for it. Bergmann's breed were adept at coining euphemisms. They called mass killings 'part of the process of Germanisation'. 'Unsuitable' Czechs were being deported to the far north, where they were to be 'resettled'. Like the Jews, he thought. He did not at all like what he was hearing about the Jews.

"The *Reichsführer* will also attend a gala performance of *Don Giovanni*," Bergmann was saying. "At the Tyl theatre. It's the hundred and fifty-fourth anniversary of its first performance, you know."

Abendschon did not think he was required to comment. Anyway, he was not a Mozart fan. What was it that critic had said? 'Too many notes.' That was it exactly. Opera, yes: but something with blood in its veins, like *Carmen* or *Trovatore*.

"Well, Walter?" Bergmann said, with a small sigh that might have been exasperation at the detective's lack of enthusiasm. "Your report?"

Abendschon let a moment or two pass before he spoke. Bergmann liked reports to be delivered sequentially: so and thus, then thus and so. He wanted to be sure he had everything in the right order in his mind.

"I've had Kramer under surveillance ever since I got here," he began. "As you know. His *Abwehr* performance seems to be completely satisfactory. He has been to Belgrade twice, Berlin once."

"Walter," Bergmann said, wearily. "I know all this."

"Bear with me, *Standartenführer*," Abendschon said. "Kramer is not a fool. He covers his tracks automatically, even though he has no idea we have him under surveillance. His liaison with your department, with the SD and the Gestapo is unexceptionable. He observes his routines meticulously. You can almost set your watch by him."

"Yes, yes," Bergmann said, testily. "Hurry it up, man!"

"He's broken his routine for the first time," Abendschon said.

"In what way?"

"He has never actually tried to shake off a tail before," Abendschon said. "Not in Prague. But last week he did just that. He took a trolley to the Brevnov terminus. I had a man right behind him, and he's certain Kramer didn't spot him. Just the same, he got to Brevnov just as the gates of that radiator factory opened and the workers came pouring out. My man had no chance in such a crowd, of course. Kramer disappeared for the evening. He turned up at his place in Smichov about midnight."

"And your conclusion?"

"That he has another place, somewhere in Brevnov. And that he was probably using it to rendezvous with someone."

"It could be part of his *Abwehr* work."

"It could," Abendschon said. "I'd have believed it was, if he hadn't gone to so much trouble to make sure he was not followed."

"Go on," Bergmann said. He was getting interested. You wait, Abendschon thought. You wait, my gleaming little *Standartenführer*.

"You remember the parachutist who was captured? The one who landed at Kledno? His name was—"

"Pavelka," Bergmann said, curtly. "For Heaven's sake, man, do you think I don't even read the Gestapo reports?" Satisfied that he had put Abendschon in his place, he nodded, continue.

"Pavelka was . . . interrogated. He revealed that he had been helped by a man named Vladimir Horacek. Leiche rounded up the man's family and took them down to the Petschek. Horacek's brother broke. He told Leiche that Vladimir had been given a telephone number, to be used only in the most serious emergency. The number was 77558. The *Forschungsamt* records showed that it was allocated to an apartment in Brevnov."

"And you conclude that Kramer was the occupant?"

"You tell me," Abendschon said, relishing the moment. "The apartment had been rented in the name of Bergmann. Dr Kurt Bergmann, formerly of Berlin." He leaned back, watching with sweet relish as the look of astonishment on Bergmann's face changed slowly to one of thunderous rage.

"What?" Bergmann choked. *"What?"*

"The apartment was rented in—"

"I heard, damn you!" Bergmann shouted. "Be quiet a moment while I think!"

Abendschon shrugged, stifling the need to grin. He was well aware of what was going through Bergmann's head. Because his name had appeared in an investigation of anti-Reich activities, the Gestapo report would have been placed directly before Heydrich. And, of course, before *Reichskriminaldirektor* Heinrich Müller, the head of the Gestapo in Berlin. That would be a nice, juicy little tidbit to drop on Himmler's desk just before his visit to Prague. Abendschon knew all about the damned Gestapo: they were prepared to believe anything about anybody. He could see the bullet-headed Müller now, suggesting to the vapid Himmler that while he was in Prague, perhaps it might be an idea to speak to *Reichsprotector* Heydrich about the matter of his counter-espionage chief's name appearing in this investigation? He had amused himself imagining the delicacy of the phrasing that would be used. *Although it is confidently expected. The possibility cannot altogether be excluded. Discreet but intensive examination.* Oh, yes, they'd have had a field day with that one. He looked up. Bergmann had control of himself again, the icy manner as usual. The panic still burned in the eyes, though, Abendschon thought.

"The apartment was thoroughly checked?" Bergmann said.

"Of course," Abendschon said. "It was anonymous. I don't think anyone had actually lived there for any length of time. It was a rendezvous. Or a drop. I examined the landlady, woman named Koch. She said that Ber—, the man had moved out a few days before the Gestapo arrived. No doubt one of the Horaceks tipped him off."

"Did the woman provide a description?"

"She did. Leiche was vastly disappointed. He thought the

place might belong to Vaslav Morávec. They still haven't caught him."

"They will," Bergmann said coldly.

Maybe, Abendschon thought. Morávec had been on the street since 1939. There couldn't be many tricks he didn't know by now. There was a story that in one of the places Leiche had raided, the Czech had left a pile of shit on the floor with a note that said 'For the *Winterhilfe*', the official Nazi charitable organisation. Gerhard Leiche was almost monomaniacal about Morávec. Catching the Czech had become a personal crusade with him.

"I didn't tell the Gestapo," Abendschon said. "But the description that Frau Koch gave me fits our man Kramer perfectly."

"Kramer!" Bergmann hissed. "Of course. Kramer."

"I have to say, *Standartenführer,* that I find it increasingly difficult to believe Kramer is acting in concert, as we originally thought, with other *Abwehr* officers. With the exception of that one trip to Berlin, he has not seen any of them. He keeps very much to himself. A loner."

If you don't count several visits to your wife, *Standartenführer.* Only if you don't count those.

"And that's it?"

"That's it," Abendschon said. "But there is something I'd like to ask."

"Go ahead," Bergmann said, looking at his watch.

"I want open access to the files of the Prague Gestapo," Abendschon said. "No restrictions."

"Why?"

"I was talking to Leiche. He was telling me about a case they've had open ever since 1939. Traitor X, it's called."

Bergmann frowned. "I don't think I've seen it."

"Probably not. It's a ragbag, Leiche said. But they've been picking up little items here and there for years pointing to the fact that the Czechs had a very well-placed source. He has used half a dozen code names. 'Franta', 'Eva,' 'Rene,' 'Steinberg', to name a few. They've never been able to pin him down. Like hunting a phantom, Leiche said."

"What has all this to do with Kramer?" Bergmann said, and then all at once it dawned on him. "By God, Abendschon!" he said. "Do you think—?"

"That's why I want clearance to go through the Gestapo files," Abendschon said. "Will you get it for me?"

"Kramer," Bergmann said again, but this time with a note of wonder in his voice, as though to say, what a fool I've been. "Kramer!" He banged his fist down on the desk. The inkpot jumped and a blob of ink plopped on to the smooth rosewood. It looked like blood.

"Yes," Bergmann said, as though Abendschon were not in the room at all. "You've had your little joke, my friend. And now I'll have mine." His smile made Abendschon's blood run cold.

Prague, November 1, 1941

"Well, Bergmann," Heydrich said. "What did you make of Uncle Heini's little surprise, eh?"

"You mean the Hess business, *Reichsprotector?*"

"What else?" Heydrich snapped, impatient, as always. When *Reichsführer* Himmler learned about Rudolf Hess's flight to England, he had launched *Aktion Hess,* a full-scale investigation of the whole affair. Warrants were issued for the arrest of Hess's adjutants, a number of his closest friends, even his chauffeur. On June 9, the Gestapo had gone to work all over Germany, arresting astrologers, faith healers, anthroposophists, clairvoyants and fortune tellers. Heydrich had watched the proceedings with undisguised amusement, powerless to prevent Himmler's misuse of the hundreds of man-hours necessary for his stupid, and, in the event, totally unproductive investigation. Goebbels's Propaganda Ministry had meanwhile informed the people that Hess's 'tragic hallucinations' had been the cause of his flight, and it had passed into that special limbo reserved, in Germany, for things it was better not to wonder out loud about. 'Onkel Heini'—the contemptuous nickname Heydrich and many others used behind Himmler's back—tapped his nose with a finger and regarded them owlishly. *Aktion Hess,* he told them, had been nothing but a 'cover' for a far more serious and far-reaching investigation which he had conducted personally and in the greatest secrecy. He had uncovered evidence, he claimed, that the *Abwehr* had worked with the British Secret Service in a plot to get Hess to Britain.

"I regret having to tell you this, Heydrich," he said. "I know you and Admiral Canaris are on friendly terms. But when it comes to the security of the Führer and the Reich, personal friendships must be put aside, and duty placed before everything!"

"You suspect Canaris personally, Herr *Reichsführer?*" Heydrich asked, silkily.

"I suspect the *Abwehr*," Himmler said, pompously. "The *Abwehr* is Canaris, Canaris is the *Abwehr!*"

Bergmann listened and watched. There might be an opening here. Perhaps he could use it. Find a way to manipulate Himmler? God alone knew how: the man was humourless, obsessive. He worked compulsively, from eight in the morning until sometimes as late as two a.m. They said he had a list of every person to whom he had ever given a gift. From their letters of thanks, he cut off the signatures, pasting them on the file cards with their names 'for graphological interpretation' should the necessity ever arise.

"He's got a lot in common with Brauchitsch," Heydrich sneered. "They both think of nothing but stars—Brauchitsch the ones on his shoulders, and Onkel Heini the ones in his horoscope!"

"Just the same, *Reichsprotector,*" Bergmann said. "If there's anything in it, it could be very useful to us." To me, he thought.

"We'll have to take it out of his hands, Bergmann," Heydrich said. "You'll have to do it. You know what will happen otherwise: he'll make a *Schiesse* out of it. And this time . . ." He let the sentence trail off, as he often did, expecting Bergmann to know the way his mind was working. He tolerated no one for long who could not do so.

"I'll start immediately," Bergmann said, thinking, yes, it might be an opening. It just might.

"If you can come up with something *hard,*" Heydrich

said, "perhaps we can nail down the lid on the coffin of those shady Barons at the Tirputzufer once and for all!"

It was no secret he wanted Canaris out of the way, indeed, the whole *Abwehr*. Heydrich wanted it all: total power. Bergmann knew that his boss had sized up the opposition long ago, and found it wanting. Heydrich felt certain he was intellectually, physically, and emotionally better fitted for leadership than any other man in the Reich. Look at them, he would say. Stupid or senile, all of them. Heydrich had only one passion, and that was ambition. He was aiming high: perhaps for the very top. They said Hitler thought highly of him, and that was always important. Nobody got to the top if Hitler didn't like him. As for himself, Bergmann had no liking at all for Heydrich. Well, who did? he asked himself. The man was hard to like. He excelled at everything: playing the violin, riding, skiing, a good enough fencer to take on Erwin Casmir. He was a fine pilot, and there was no doubt of his personal courage—hadn't he flown a fighter plane on the Russian front for six weeks during Barbarossa? Yet nobody liked him, and nobody trusted him. In any other world, Heydrich would have been a misfit, an outcast. In this one, he was as perfectly suited for what he did as a shark is.

They had discussed *Aktion Hess* at length with Himmler. Heydrich and he were the only ones in the Reich to whom he would entrust such information, he told them. He had not yet even shown his findings to the Führer, preferring to seek Heydrich's advice before doing so.

"You always manage to put your finger on the main point, Heydrich," he said. "Spot the fallacy."

"The Herr *Reichsführer* is too kind," Heydrich murmured, laying it on with a trowel. "Altogether too kind." Bergmann watched, amazed, not so much by the syrupy deference, but because Himmler—who had personally issued an order forbidding anyone in the SS to address him as anything but plain *Reichsführer*—was clearly swallowing it. A technique to remember, Bergmann thought. Heydrich was buttering Himmler up the way a very junior Prussian second lieutenant might have treated a very senior General. And Himmler was loving every minute of it.

"Heydrich, I want decisive steps taken," Himmler said. "I

want you to find out exactly how the *Abwehr* was involved in the Hess thing. I want you to handle it personally. Nothing is to take priority over it!"

"Of course, Herr *Reichsführer,*" Heydrich said. "If that is your wish."

"I wish it," Himmler said, nodding self-importantly. He clearly believed Heydrich's sycophantic flattery was genuine admiration. "There is something about this Hess thing that makes me uneasy. *Etwas verdächtig.*"

His looks had not improved much over the years, Bergmann thought, his mind wandering as Heydrich and Himmler beamed at each other. Himmler had a pudgy, unattractive face and a receding chin. His hands were small, his fingers short and fat. His mild blue eyes blinked constantly behind steel-rimmed glasses; he always kept his head slightly averted towards the right shoulder, so that the reflection of the glasses would hide his eyes. Nonetheless, he'd come a long way for a cheap ponce who'd very nearly hung for murder, a frightened-eyed revolutionary in Rohm's *Reichskriegflagge,* full of a bluster that was meant to accentuate his masculinity and only succeeded in underlining his lack of it. Well, we were all at the bottom of the pile in those days, Bergmann thought. I wonder what the ones who died on the march through Munich in 1923 would say if they could see us now, sitting in palaces, with all of Europe ready to jump if we snap our fingers?

"Before any action is taken, however," Himmler was droning on, "let me stress that I have already personally exonerated Frau Hess and Willi Messerschmitt. I am satisfied that neither of them is in any way implicated in the matter."

Heydrich looked at Kurt Bergmann, and his eyes said all the things he dared not say in front of Himmler. Bergmann knew what he was thinking. *Does this Dummkopf presume to instruct me?* Himmler infuriated Heydrich as much as Bormann, perhaps more. Although for totally different reasons.

"We shall have to tread warily, *Reichsprotector,*" Bergmann said. "Or the *Abwehr* will know what we are up to ten minutes after we begin."

"Bergmann is right," Himmler said primly. "This must

be handled just so, Heydrich. We don't want everyone in Berlin gossiping about it."

"Of course, Herr *Reichsführer*."

Himmler did not stay in Prague any longer than he had to. He never stayed anywhere long. Heydrich's anger simmered long after the *Reichsführer* returned to Berlin.

"That damned man will drive me insane one day," he said, mimicking Himmler's prim manner and voice. "'We don't want everyone in Berlin gossiping about it, Heydrich.' Does he seriously think we can investigate an *Abwehr* conspiracy without anyone in Berlin even knowing?"

"It may just be wishful thinking," Bergmann said.

"Ha!" Heydrich said, slapping his thigh. "That's the understatement of the year, Bergmann. Wishful thinking! The damned man does no other kind!"

Don't you be too sure of that, Bergmann thought. Himmler had taken him quietly to one side during a long evening at the opera.

"Bergmann, I want you to ensure that I see everything you uncover in this Hess matter, do you understand? Everything!"

"But of course, *Reichsführer*!" Bergmann had said.

"Be sure you know what I mean, Bergmann," Himmler said, the mild, blue eyes unblinking. "Do not misplace your loyalty."

Chilled by the menace implicit in the words, Bergmann could only nod. Needless to say, he had not mentioned it to Heydrich. If Himmler didn't trust the man, there was no reason why he should. Look after yourself was the first rule for survival in Heydrich's jungle.

". . . you've heard about his love-child, of course?" Heydrich was saying. Bergmann sharpened his attention. Wait, wait, he thought.

"It's true?"

"Yes, he's got that simpering little cow pregnant. What's her name, again?"

"Potthast," Kurt supplied. "Hedwig Potthast."

"God, even her name is unfortunate," Heydrich said. "Can you imagine going to bed with anybody called Hedwig Potthast?"

From a man they said would fuck a snake if someone would hold its head, Bergmann thought, that was pretty rich.

"He calls her *Häschen*," he said. "'Bunny'."

"Imagine the pair of them," Heydrich said. "Uncle Heini and his little Bunny, dressed up like a pair of Alpine yokels on the Obersalzberg! Having *tea* in their little love nest!"

According to rumour, Himmler was building a house for his mistress on the Obersalzberg, borrowing eighty thousand Reichsmarks at some enormous rate of interest from the Party funds. He had no salary to speak of; he professed no interest in wealth. You could not imagine Heydrich borrowing money off Bormann to build his mistress a house, Bergmann thought. Heydrich owed nobody anything, loved no one, trusted no one. Except perhaps his baby daughter, Silke. There was no question about it: he doted on her. Funny, that.

"It occurs to me that there may be a better way of bringing down Canaris and the *Abwehr, Reichsprotector*," he said.

"Really?" Heydrich said, eyes narrowing.

"Let me try it out on you," Bergmann said, feeling his way. You had to be damned careful with Heydrich. And this—Christ, one false step and it would be the end! Bergmann steeled himself: the prize was worth it. There was no point in being second at anything. As long as Heydrich was at the top, there would be no chance for anyone else.

"There really is no way we can mount a major investigation of the *Abwehr*'s part in the Hess flight—if they *were* involved, you may be sure they have covered their tracks carefully—without their knowledge. And the minute they find out, Canaris will run complaining to the Führer and that will be the end of that!"

"So?"

"If we went after one man," Bergmann said, thinking, careful, careful. "One man whose actions have been so injurious to the Reich that they would discredit the entire *Abwehr*—." He paused, watching Heydrich closely.

"You're telling me such a man exists?" Heydrich said.

"If the *Reichsprotector* will bear with me for a moment? On the night of October 2, the Gestapo raided a house in the suburb of Lieben. A transmitter and coded material were captured. I sent the material to the *Entzifferungsamt* immediately, taking the liberty of saying that it was the *Reichsprotector*'s desire that the material be immediately decoded."

"And what did the Decyphering Section say?"

"The documents confirm that top secret Reich material is being passed to the Czechs for transmission to London. By someone here in Prague."

"In Prague?" Heydrich said, sitting bolt upright. Anger mottled the pale face. "In *Prague*? What have you got on this, Bergmann? Anything? Any leads?"

"Well," Bergmann said. Heydrich's lynx eyes narrowed. He had no patience with anyone who held out on him, none at all. You could not keep him in the dark, you could not keep him waiting. He simply did not permit it. Yet Kurt Bergmann knew that in this business of Hess and the *Abwehr* traitor, it was he who must retain complete control and not Heydrich. It could be his passport to the top. How, he did not yet know, but he sensed there was something. Its outlines were hazy, unformed. But there was *something*, if he could find it and use it.

"A parallel investigation produced something which may be connected with the matter," he said. "Subsequent to the capture and interrogation of the British parachutist Pavelka, a number of corollary arrests were made. Under sharpened interrogation one of the arrested Czechs disclosed the fact that if the resistance circle of the Czech, Morávec, was infiltrated, that fact was to be communicated to a telephone number. Through the *Forschungsamt* we traced the number to an apartment in Brevnov which we thought might be Morávec's hiding place." This is the tricky part, he thought. He hesitated, and saw Heydrich note the hesitation. Damn the man, was there nothing he missed? "Our inquiries there revealed something . . . unusual. Unsettling," he corrected himself. "Before I continue, may I ask the *Reichsprotector* for his assurance of complete confidence in my loyalty and honour?"

Heydrich pursed his lips, a slight frown touching his forehead. "What the devil is this, Bergmann?" he said.

"May I take it, then, that—."

"Oh, damn it, man, of course!" Heydrich snapped. There was no way round it, Bergmann thought, and plunged.

"The name that the man who rented the apartment used was mine," he said.

Heydrich looked at him for a long moment, which felt to Bergmann like an eternity. Then he burst out laughing. It was so unexpected, and so unusual, that Bergmann was startled. He had never seen Heydrich laugh out loud before. Yet there he was, slapping his thigh, tears trickling down his cheeks.

"Jesus Maria!" he said, wiping his eyes. "That's funny, Bergmann. Don't you think it's funny?"

"The *Reichsprotector* will forgive me if I find it less amusing than he," Bergmann said.

"Ah, I see," Heydrich said, all trace of humour vanishing. "Keeping your arse protected, are you?" Bergmann knew the fact that the apartment had been rented in his name would have been in Geschke's report, and probably in the SD dossier, too. Heydrich knew he would know it.

"Something like that, *Reichsprotector*," Bergmann said, risking the hint of a smile. Careful, he thought, don't overdo it. Just let him know that there are no hard feelings.

"You aren't passing *Geheime Reichssache* to the Czechs, are you?" Heydrich said. There was the same small hint of a smile on his face now. Cat and mouse, Bergmann thought. It's the only game he knows.

"Of course not!" Bergmann snapped. Heydrich waved a hand: get on with it.

"Since 1939 Amt IVE here in Prague has been coming across indications that the resistance was receiving information from a high-level source. They maintained an open file on this unknown person. It is headed *Verräter* X."

"Unknown Traitor," Heydrich said, leaning forward again. "And?"

"We . . . I only just came across it. I immediately put it together with the matter I've just told you about. The material from the *Entzifferungsamt* could only have come from a high-level source. Nobody below the rank of ourselves, or Dr Geschke, would have had access to it. Except—"

"*Abwehr*," Heydrich murmured.

"It is my belief that *Verräter* X, the man for whom the Gestapo here has been searching for years, and the man who rented the apartment in Brevnov under my name, could be one and the same person," Bergmann said. "And I think I know who he is."

"What?" Heydrich shouted, leaping to his feet. He came around the table, his eyes burning like Lucifer's. For a moment, Bergmann thought Heydrich was going to grab hold of him and shake him as a terrier shakes a rat.

"The *Abwehr Hauptvertrauensmann* here in Prague," he said hastily. "*Oberst* Paul Kramer."

"Kramer?" Heydrich said, the anger turning suddenly to wariness. "Kramer? This could be dynamite, Bergmann. What evidence have you got?"

"That's just it, *Reichsprotector*," Bergmann said. "I haven't got anything on Kramer that would really *prove*, once and for all, that he is our man. He's too well-connected for me—for us to go after him with circumstantial evidence."

"We've got to be damned sure he's our man, Bergmann," Heydrich said. "It could become political."

"I know that, *Reichsprotector,*" Bergmann said. "The minute we arrest Kramer, all hell will break loose at the Tirpitzufer. I don't want there to be any mistakes."

"I'm glad to hear it," Heydrich murmured. Bergmann shrugged off the sarcasm: he was beginning to see what he could do with what he knew, and if he had to take a little sarcasm along the way, he could live with that. "Well, what do you propose to do?" Heydrich said, sitting down again.

"I intend to see to it that Kramer obtains highly classified information about a secret investigation undertaken by my department. At the same time, I will place all his contacts under concentrated surveillance. If one word of my investigation leaks, we have him. And the whole damned *Abwehr* with him!"

"What secret investigation?"

Bergmann smiled. "Why, the one the *Reichsführer* wishes us to carry out, *Reichsprotector*! An investigation of the *Abwehr*'s involvement in the flight to Britain of Rudolf Hess. I was thinking of calling it *Aktion Fuchse*. Does that appeal to you?"

He held his breath: this was where it could all go wrong. Heydrich smiled his hooded smile. 'Fox' was Canaris's nickname.

"Perfect," he murmured. "But Bergmann, there's a flaw in your plan."

Bergmann went cold. He waited, it seemed forever. "How do you mean, *Reichsprotector?*" he managed at last.

"How do you give Kramer the information so that only he knows it? He can simply claim to be one of many who were told."

"No, *Reichsprotector,*" Bergmann said, hoping his relief was not showing. It was all right: he was going to go for it. "I have a foolproof way of getting the information to him. It involves only one other person."

"And who is that?"

"My wife," Bergmann said.

Prague, November 7, 1941

As the snow which was to be Russia's salvation swirled around the rostrum above Lenin's emptied tomb, Josef Stalin exhorted the Red Army, on this twenty-third anniversary of the great Bolshevik revolution, to hurl back the Fascist invaders from the gates of Moscow. It was an impassioned, not to say desperate appeal to their national pride. He invoked the names of a pantheon of Russian heroes: Alexander Nevsky, Donskoi, Pozharsky, and Kutuznov, the famed General whose army conquered Napoleon. See our might arrayed here today, he told the soldiers, think of how much we have done. Think of how it was, only twenty-three years ago, when we brought down the mighty autocrat. Does any of you doubt that we shall beat the Fascists? The massed soldiers, their greatcoats frosted with snow, cheered their commander-in-chief to the echo, as patrol planes growled overhead, and the sound of German guns thudded dully in the west.

That same afternoon, in the forested enclave near Rastenburg in East Prussia which he had named *Wolfschanze,* Adolf Hitler decreed that the attack upon Russia must be
continued. The Bolsheviks had lost nearly two million men,
he told the officers at the *Lagebesitzung,* his daily conference.
Leningrad was being starved into submission. General
Guderian was to break through the Russian defences and
encircle Moscow. No German soldier, however, was to set
foot in the Russian capital. The Führer had already decided
that Moscow was to be wiped from the face of the earth.
Hitler was in an ebullient mood which lasted all through
the evening. He was in good form at dinner, telling jokes
and reminiscing about the old days, relaxed and happy. Arrangements had been made for him to leave *Wolfschanze* the
following morning and fly to Münich for the anniversary
celebrations of the 1923 *putsch.*

That evening, while Adolf Hitler and his aides relaxed in
the camouflaged encampment deep in the Görlitz forest,
Noël Mason-Morley, together with three graduates of
Camusdarach—Bartos, Valcik and Potucek—left Bellasis
House and, with Captain Sustr of Czech Intelligence driv-
ing the car, made their way to Tangmere aerodrome, near
Chichester.

'Percentage'—the code name for the flight which had
dropped Frantisek Pavelka into Czechoslovakia—had been
'out' for over a month. No word had been received by the
waiting monitors at Woldingham. It had to be assumed that
Pavelka had been captured. This time, three men would go
in. Their mission: to re-establish, at any cost, the broken
contact with Czech resistance, and most important of all
with the man called 'Karl'. The Avro Lancaster Type 683
carrying the three parachutists—code-name 'Silver'—took
off from Tangmere at 18.14 hours, crossing the Belgian
coast at 19.21 hours and reaching a point south of Prague at
22.10 hours. On arrival at the drop area, the pilot discovered
that a blizzard was blowing below. Visibility was zero. He
spent more than half an hour trying to fly around the storm
without success before turning his almost-new aircraft
around and heading back for England. The return flight
was completed without incident, and the Lancaster landed
again at Tangmere at 02.12 hours precisely. By two-thirty

both Mason-Morley and Captain Sustr had been informed that 'Silver' had aborted.

Less than eight hours later, Mason-Morley stood in the Storey's Gate office of Colonel the Honourable Oliver Stanley and told him the news. He did so rather warily. Stanley was a man of sudden, towering rages, which erupted without warning. They could be brought on by almost anything: the news that the German Embassy in Gøteborg was recruiting Swedish men for service in the German army, or simply because his coffee was cold.

"Sustr is over in Bayswater now, sir, telling Colonel Morávec," Mason-Morley said. "I rather fear we've missed the boat."

To his relief Stanley took the news with equanimity, running a hand through his hair and yawning. He looked wan and pasty, as if he needed a long holiday.

"Disappointed?" he asked Mason-Morley.

"It was always a pretty long shot, sir."

"True," Stanley said. He frowned, and got up from behind the table which he used as a desk, picking up the figurine of a dancing faun which stood in the centre of it and moving it a fraction, like a pernickety housewife.

"What about 'Jonathan'?"

"Ready and waiting."

"Any news from the other side?"

"Nothing."

"It's messy, Noël," Stanley said. "I'd like to terminate it. Is that possible?"

"He's their man, sir. Not ours."

"Can you get word to Germany?"

"It would be difficult. But we could do it. We could ask Donovan to send Gray to Berlin."

"Thought they'd thrown out all the Americans?"

"No, sir. Leland Morris, the chargé d'affaires, is still there."

"How much do they know?"

"About 'Jonathan'? Nothing, sir."

"You think you could tell our friends to close all the doors without our Americans finding out what we're up to?"

148

"I think so," Mason-Morley said.

"All right," Stanley said. He managed a smile, although he did not seem to be enjoying it. "Go ahead."

The same day 'Silver' aborted in the snow-filled skies above Prague, Paul Kramer arranged to meet Jan Novak in a restaurant called 'The Dutch Mill'. It was on the first floor of a building on Frauenstrasse, only a little way from Gestapo headquarters. Jan hugely enjoyed using the place as a rendezvous. "If those Nazi bastards knew what we were talking about, it would take the edge off their appetites, by God!" he would gloat.

"Jan, you shouldn't!" Maria would admonish him. "You know it's dangerous!"

"The best place to hide something is right out in the open," Jan quoted, sententiously.

"Try your proverbs on the Gestapo!" Maria retorted tartly, crossing herself hastily a moment later to banish the evil from the words.

Paul climbed up the stairs and gave his coat to the girl at the door. The restaurant smelled of sauerkraut and cigarette smoke. Reproductions of Dutch paintings hung on the walls: Vermeer, Rembrandt, van Dyck. The tables were separated by low partitions, in each of which was a radio which customers could switch on, thus ensuring that nobody heard what they were talking about. It was a favourite haunt of German officers: hence Jan's delight in meeting there. Paul looked around, but could not see the big man. Then he saw someone wave. It was Antonie. Her long hair hung unbraided around the pale oval of her face, and her smile was enchanting. Paul greeted her gravely.

"Tonie," he said. "This is unexpected."

"I wanted to see you."

"Where is Jan?"

"He was held up," she said. "He'll be here in half an hour."

"I'm glad you came," he told her. Before he had time to say anything else, the owner of the restaurant came across to their table. He was a big, burly man with a jolly face and a double chin. His name was Frantisek Pisek. "Goulasch is good," he said. "Or there's duck with sauerkraut and dumplings. That lot seem to like it, which is no recommendation." A jerk of the head at 'that lot' indicated his opinion of every German in the room. Paul grinned up at him.

"You ought to be more careful, Franta," he said. "I might be Gestapo."

"Never!" Franta scoffed. "*She* wouldn't sit with you if you were. Anyway, they've got their own trough at the Esplanade."

"Can you find us a bottle of white wine?" Paul said.

"If that lot haven't guzzled it all," Franta said. "They eat and drink as if somebody just announced a famine!"

He brought them a bottle of sparkling Valtice, chilled beads of moisture on the bottle. They clinked glasses.

"*Vitezstvi!*" Paul said.

"Victory!" she echoed. They were silent for a moment or two. Out of some forgotten corner of his memory he saw her as a slender girl, dark eyes unreadable, watching as he laughed and joked with her father.

"You're beautiful," he said. "Did I tell you that?"

She looked into his eyes and smiled. "I've been thinking about what you said, Paul," she said.

"And?"

"I want to be with you," she said. There was no artifice in her voice: no coyness, no arch flirtatiousness.

"You know what you're saying?"

"I thought about it a lot. About nobody being any good alone. You were right. You are right. And so I want to be with you. From now on, always."

He felt desire surge through him. It must have shown in his eyes. Tonie's smile became a mischievous grin.

"But not in front of all these people, *Oberst*," she whispered.

Paul threw back his head and laughed. It felt good. It was a long time since he had laughed out loud like that. One or two heads turned his way; he ignored the curious stares. He took Tonie's hand in his own and kissed it. She nodded, yes.

"A toast," Paul said. They picked up their glasses. "*Salud y pesetas y amor, y el tiempo para le gustar.*"

"It's Spanish."

"You're right. It means 'health and wealth and love—and enough time to enjoy them'."

"Enough time," she said, softly. "Do people like us ever have enough time, Paul?"

"I don't know," he said. "Perhaps we can make it."

At that moment, Jan Novak loomed over them. His cheeks were flushed from the wintry wind. There had been snowstorms all night; it was still snowing outside. They said it was a couple of metres deep out in the country.

"Well, well!" he said. "You two look like a couple of lovebirds!"

He sat down and waved at the waiter, unaware of the effect his words had had upon them. When he turned around they were grinning, delight bubbling up inside them like champagne. Franta came across and greeted Jan like a long-lost brother.

"Good to see you, man!" he said, slapping Jan on the shoulder. "You don't come here often enough!"

"At these prices, it's not surprising!" Jan said. "You must be making a fortune, you damned pirate!"

"Oh, yes," Franta said, sardonically. "A fortune. I suppose you imagine that lot pay their so-called 'accounts' punctually on the first of every month, eh? Bastards! They'd steal the straw from their mother's kennel!"

"Good job they don't speak Czech," Jan said. "If they heard you, you'd be sitting in the *kino* up the street, waiting for your interview."

"*Prasata!*" Franta spat. "Pigs!"

"That's the trouble with you Czechs," Paul said. "You don't know you've been Germanised."

"Germanised!" Franta snorted. "Hah!"

They ordered the goulasch and he went away smiling, a big man with a paunch. He would never become 'Germanised', no matter how many Heydrichs came and went. There was no way to force it upon them. They couldn't all be sent to the KZs.

"Well, Paul," Jan said. "What was so urgent?"

"I thought I'd better tell you, Jan," Paul said. "They're getting close to me." Jan looked thunderstruck. Paul tried

151

not to see the fear in Tonie's eyes. But she had to hear it too. He told Jan how the Gestapo had raided his apartment in Brevnov.

"I got out half an hour ahead of them," he said. "If it hadn't been for Morávec's call . . ."

Jan shook his head. Franta was coming back to the table with their food. He made a ceremony out of laying the plates in front of them, and stepped back with a flourish.

"I put in extra meat for you," he said, in a stage whisper. "Shame to waste it all on Fritz, isn't it? You want some more wine?"

"Bring us a bottle of Znojmo," Jan said. "And some sticking plaster for your mouth. Are you trying to get us all arrested?"

"They only arrest honest Czechs, Novak!" Franta grinned. "So we're in no danger!"

They were silent for a few minutes after he left, enjoying the food, and when he came back with the wine, they complimented him on it.

"Of course it's perfect!" he said. "Eat! Enjoy!"

"Well?" Jan said. "Tell us what happened."

"Your parachutist talked," Paul said.

The young Czech, Frantisek Pavelka, had landed near Kledno, miles from where he was supposed to come down. He made his way into Lidice, where he contacted a family named Horak. They handed him on to another family in Prague, the Horaceks. One of the Horacek boys, Vladimir, was a courier for Morávec. When Pavelka was arrested, the Gestapo, in their usual fashion, arrested everyone with whom he had been in contact and every member of those families. Vladimir was one of them. He had the phone number of the apartment, although he had no idea who lived there or where it was. All he knew was that if he called that number he would get instructions for a 'drop', pick up something, and take it somewhere else. Fortunately for Paul, Morávec was informed immediately of Vladimir's arrest. He telephoned Paul and told him. Paul quit the place at once.

"Next time we may not be so lucky," Paul said. "I can probably talk my way out of this, but Morávec. . . . How is he, by the way?"

"Like me," Jan said. "Angry. Nervous. Frustrated."

"Tell him to lie low for a while," Paul said. "It's too risky."

"He hasn't got much choice," Jan said, gloomily. "The resistance is paralysed. People are terrified. Nobody will help us any more."

Heydrich's relentless purge had been completely effective. In one month, October, his Gestapo and SD units made more than three thousand arrests. The ruthless execution of the Army Generals—Bily, Vjota, Pechlat, Wunsch, Groh and Fischer—and the out-of-hand shooting of anyone caught monitoring BBC broadcasts or committing minor acts of sabotage, had had a salutary effect. The Gestapo had picked up more than five hundred abandoned weapons on the streets of Prague during the last weeks. Nobody wanted to attract the vengeful lightning-strike of Heydrich's merciless hunters.

"The Gestapo and the SD have put capturing Morávec at the top of their priority list, Jan," Paul said. "Thirty or forty men have been assigned to his case. They do nothing else, day in and day out. If they take him, they take you, too. Perhaps all of us. So for God's sake tell him to be careful."

"Careful!" Jan said. "Like you, you mean?"

"I'm careful," Paul said, with what he hoped was a confident grin. "Tell me, what is Operation Wolf Trap?"

"I don't know," Jan said. "Should I?"

"I read the Gestapo report of Pavelka's interrogation," Paul said. "He told them he was a member of a team which had been trained in Scotland, at a big country house near Dorking in the south of England. He gave them all the names, even the instructors."

"It doesn't mean anything to me," Jan said. "They said they were going to drop in parachutists and that they would need help for a special mission. They didn't tell us what it was."

"From what he said, Pavelka seems to have been told things were considerably different here than they are. He said the British were confident the war would be over within a year.""

"Chance would be a fine thing," Jan grumbled. "Are they really that naïve, these kids?"

"You remember those leaflets they dropped, Papa?" Antonie said. "Do you think they told the parachutists the same thing?"

On Czech National Day, British planes had dropped tracts on the capital entitled *The Message of the British and Czech Airmen On The Occasion of 28 October*. The leaflets exhorted the resistance to keep fighting, and told them they were faced with not another three hundred years of slavery, but perhaps one at the very most. At a time when Heydrich's terror squads were carrying out executions and reprisals around the clock, and even the mildest and most meek Czech was keeping well out of trouble, the leaflets were like an insult. Can they truly be so stupid? people asked.

"If only we had a radio," Jan said. "If only we could find out what is happening."

"Don't get downhearted, Jan," Paul said.

"That's right, Papa," Tonie added. "They'll try again."

"In this?" Jan growled, jerking his chin towards the window. Snow was falling thickly; soft, heavy flakes settling fast on the streets. The sky was the colour of a bad snapshot. They asked for a pot of tea and Franta brought it to them. Paul looked at his watch. It was nearly three.

"There's something else," he said. Jan looked up, puzzled.

"I'm going with Paul, Papa," Antonie said.

"Yes?"

"Jan," Paul said, gently. His friend looked at him for a moment, and then, all at once, his washed-out blue eyes filled with tears. He seemed not to be able to speak. After a long moment, he got to his feet and put one arm around Antonie's shoulders and the other around Paul's.

"I'm a stupid old man," he said. "I should have expected it. I should have known."

"Nobody knew it would happen, Papa," Antonie said. "It just did."

"Well," Jan said. He took out a big, blue-checked handkerchief and noisily blew his nose. "Well."

"It feels strange," Paul said. "To ask your blessing."

"And stranger still to give it," Jan said. "But give it I do,

154

with all my heart. And your Mama, child? Does she know?"

"I told her, Papa," Antonie said. "And she said, 'I've been expecting it'."

Jan hugged his daughter close to him and kissed her roughly. Then he clapped Paul on the shoulder. "Go on!" he said. "Get out of here before I make a complete idiot of myself! And you, Franta—don't stand there gawking! Bring me a Becherovka! Better still, bring me two!"

Paul and Antonie went down the stairs and out into the street. The snow was already whitening the world, its sibilant half-sound damping down the city's noises. She put her arm through his and looked up at him. A snowflake melted on her long lashes. It looked like a tear. He kissed her.

"Where shall we go?" he asked her.

"It doesn't matter," she said.

Prague, November 22, 1941

Kurt Bergmann's dinner invitation took Paul completely by surprise. Having no real excuse ready, he accepted, even though the idea of spending what Bergmann referred to as 'a quiet evening, talking over old times', was somewhat less than enticing. He had no 'old times' to talk over with Bergmann, unless you counted those early years in Königsbrunn. Somehow, he couldn't bring himself to believe Bergmann wanted to talk about that.

He had never relished socialising with the Bergmanns as a couple. Erika had sometimes drunk that glass too many of wine, and made little effort to conceal from her husband that her relationship with Paul was something more than platonic. She had phoned him in October, soon after their arrival in Prague. She was bored, she said. Prague was such a *provincial* dump after Berlin, and she wanted some fun. Paul was to come and take her out, dinner, the theatre, a party, anything. It would be just like it had been in Berlin, she said, and the way she used the words was an invitation. Paul managed to avoid a commitment: a trip to Belgrade coming up, pressure of work: perhaps when he got back. He sensed her pique, but ignored it, and so avoided even calling at the lovely château on the crest of Petrin Hill which Curt von Gottberg's *Grundbesitzamt* had commandeered for the Bergmanns.

Kurt Bergmann was the picture of smiling affability as he greeted Paul, ushering him into the huge library and nodding in agreement as Paul admired the fine Aubusson carpets and the magnificent Tintoretto which dominated one wall. A maid discreetly brought them champagne in a silver bucket on a silver tray, then withdrew.

"Place belonged to some Jew or other," Bergmann said off-handedly as he poured the champagne. "The painting is from the National Gallery. On loan, as it were."

"Better not let the Fat Man know you've got it," Paul said.

"Göring?" Bergmann said, raising his eyebrows. "Ach, he's out of favour, according to Heydrich. The Führer will have nothing to do with him since the British started bombing Berlin. Here, my dear fellow, let me give you a refill."

It was a good wine: Krug '35. The maid reappeared noiselessly to say that dinner was ready. Surprised, Paul asked Bergmann a question.

"No, no, my dear Paul," Bergmann said, wreathed in smiles. "No one else is coming. We want you all to ourselves this evening. Erika has been dying to see you again." Was there a nuance in the words? Paul wondered. Or was it only his own guilty conscience trying to hear one?

They walked out into the hall just as Erika came down the wide staircase. She was wearing a black silk dress, cut very low, with straps that were little more than threads of black across her creamy shoulders. The long skirt caressed her hips. She extended her hands as she saw Paul, and ran down the last couple of steps, coming into his arms and speaking his name. She was beautiful, and she knew it.

"Darling Paul!" she said, kissing him on the lips. "Oh, it's so lovely to see you after all this time! You're really bad to have neglected us so shamefully, isn't he, Kurt? I don't even know why I'm being nice to you! Come, let's go in to dinner, and you can tell me what you've been doing with yourself since you left Berlin. I want you to myself all evening!"

She gave him no time to speak, and again, Paul found himself puzzled by the extravagance of her welcome: he had expected ice, not fire. Bergmann's beaming bonhomie was even more untypical. It was as if both of them were playing roles in a play whose ending they did not yet know. He could not begin to understand why, but he remained watchful and wary. Something, he thought, something.

They went into the dining room. Candles on the tables shone yellow-gold; silver flatware and crystal goblets sparkled. The table was laid with a beautifully-woven lace cloth, and the centrepiece was a gold and silver salver on which stood a beautiful spray of orchids. The walls of the room were panelled in white with golden beading. Above the ten-foot high doors was a gilded carving of a reclining Venus surrounded by cherubs. In one corner of the room stood a blue and white tiled stove which gave off a gentle warmth. It was a beautiful room, and he said so. They took their places, and the servants brought in the first course.

"A celebration," Bergmann said. "You like caviar?"

"When I can get it."

"Easy enough, if you know the right people," Bergmann said.

"You seem to," Paul said. "Getting a place like this to live in."

"That wasn't too difficult," Bergmann said.

"Did you keep the place in Berlin?"

"Of course, darling!" Erika said. "We won't be here for ever, will we, Kurt?"

"Six months at the most," Bergmann said. "Heydrich has other plans."

"Oh?" Paul said.

"Once he's tamed these damned Czechs, he'll be looking for a bigger job," Bergmann said. "He has his sights set high."

"So I've heard," Paul said.

The talk turned to the war, as it always did. The 'Autumn offensive' against Moscow had been scheduled to begin three days ago. According to the radio, Kleist's First Panzer Group had taken Rostov, Leningrad was ready to surrender, and the Third Panzers were within twenty miles of the Kremlin.

"And they'll take it by Christmas!" Bergmann said. "A fine present for the Führer, eh? By the way, what was this I heard about the British trying to assassinate your friend Rommel?"

"I don't know General Rommel all that well," Paul said. "The word from the *Fuchsbau* is that the British sent a Commando squad in by submarine. They travelled overland to a place called Beda Littoria, which they thought was his headquarters. In fact, it was a quartermaster's office. General Rommel had never been anywhere near the place."

"What happened to the Commandos?"

"They were shot to ribbons," Paul said. "It was a fiasco."

"Yet British Intelligence is supposed to be so good," Bergmann said, smoothly. "Or at least, that's what you *Abwehr* people are always telling us."

"We have the highest respect for them," Paul said. "But we never believed they were miracle men, and only a miracle man could know for sure where General Rommel is going to be at any given moment. The British call him 'the desert fox', you know. And not without reason."

"Did you know Ernst Udet, Paul?" Bergmann asked, too casually. He signalled the servants to take away the dishes, and they were silent for a moment.

"I met him a few times in Berlin," Paul said, in reply to the question. "But I wouldn't say I knew him."

"Funny business, that," Bergmann said. "You know it was suicide, of course?"

"I heard something," Paul said. "There are always rumours."

"No rumour, this time," Bergmann said. "Darling, give Paul some strawberries."

"Just coffee, thank you," Paul said. "I never eat dessert."

"That how you keep so thin?"

"No," Paul grinned. "I worry a lot."

"Do you?" Bergmann said. He got up and brought a port decanter across to the table. Erika murmured something about seeing to the coffee, and went out of the room, leaving them alone. Once again, Paul had the strange feeling that he was watching an under-rehearsed play. Their movements were stagey, badly synchronised.

"Yes, poor Udet," Bergmann said, pouring some port into his glass and sliding the decanter across to Paul. "Of course, the Führer ordered the whole thing hushed up."

"Of course," Paul murmured. Udet, a flying ace of the Great War who had turned barnstormer, had been given a job by his old friend Göring when he started to re-build the Luftwaffe. Udet had risen to the rank of *Generalluftzeugmeister,* Chief Air Inspector-General, in charge of all design, production and inspection of German aircraft. He had been found shot in his Berlin apartment. The official story was that he had been testing a new weapon which wounded him severely, and he died on his way to hospital.

"They say there was a message scrawled on his bedroom wall with red crayon," Bergmann was saying. "Something to the effect that the 'Iron Man' had ditched him. Then he shot himself." His eyes met Paul's. "You know who the 'Iron Man' is, of course."

"I'm not up on Air Ministry politics," Paul said. "I have enough trouble keeping up with what's going on at the Bendlerstrasse."

"A lot of strange deaths, all at once," Bergmann said, darkly. "Udet. General Wilberg. Werner Molders."

"Molders' death was an accident, surely?" The Luftwaffe ace's plane had collided with a power cable en route to Udet's State funeral the preceding day.

"So it seems," Bergmann said. "So it seems."

Paul shrugged. He could not escape the feeling that Bergmann was playing some sort of game, but why? Paul knew that Udet and Molders had been what the Oster group in Berlin called 'reliable', but nothing more.

Erika appeared in the doorway and told them coffee was waiting in the drawing room. They joined her in front of a crackling log fire, and she served black coffee in fragile Meissen china from a silver pot on a silver tray set on a low table before the huge hearth. The talk turned to *Abwehr* matters, Paul's duties.

"Most of it consists of reading," Paul smiled, fending off

any deeper probes. "News magazines, newspapers, statistical reports, government publications. The rest is arithmetic and a good memory."

"You don't do yourself justice, my dear fellow," Bergmann said, sipping his coffee and watching Paul over the brim of the cup. "I'm told they think very highly of you in the *Fuchsbau*." He paused, as if debating what to say next. "Do you know Canaris, at all?"

"Not really," Paul said. "He's not an easy man to know, and he's not at the Tirpitzufer any more than he has to be. If anyone knows him well, I'd say your boss does."

"They say he always leaves parties at ten o'clock sharp," Erika said. "Even the Führer's." There was just the faintest hint of a slur in her voice, and Paul saw Bergmann's eyes narrow as he noticed it. The light which lit his eyes was loathing, not affection. Then he put on a smile, the way another man might don a mask, and turned to Paul.

"Heydrich once told me that the old man once cooked a whole saddle of boar in a black bread crust for him and Lina. The whole thing, with his own hands."

"I'd heard he likes to cook," Paul said, wondering where all this was leading. A certain amount of 'shop' was inevitable at any dinner party, but there seemed little point to this topic.

"There's talk in Berlin that he's pro-British," Bergmann said. "What do you think, Paul? Is he against our war with Britain?"

"The only thing Canaris is against, as far as I am aware, is our war with Russia," Paul said. "He advised against it right from the start. And he may yet be proven right."

"Is that the general consensus among you *Abwehr* people?"

"Kurt, we '*Abwehr* people', as you call us, are concerned only with obtaining, interpreting and acting upon military intelligence. We leave consensuses to the politicians!"

"Well said, my dear fellow!" Bergmann smiled. "But I'd have been surprised if you said anything else. Could hardly expect you to tell me Canaris is disloyal, could I? Even if he is, I mean."

Paul frowned in annoyance, half-listening as Bergmann turned to Erika and regaled her with stories of how friendly

160

the Heydrich and the Canaris families had been in Berlin, riding together in the Tiergarten, tennis games, Heydrich's violin sessions with Frau Canaris. It was difficult to imagine Heydrich playing the violin and even more difficult to imagine him crying as he did so, as Bergmann was insisting he often did. Paul managed not to smile. It was like someone boasting that they had a rat which could sing.

"Don't you miss Berlin, Paul?" Erika said.

"Sometimes," he said. "But I like Prague. And I can still get to Berlin once in a while."

"Kurt is going next week," she said, mock-pouting. "But he won't take me with him. Could you persuade him, darling?" She looked right at him, and he saw the invitation in her eyes.

"I've told you a dozen times, I can't!" Bergmann said, impatiently. "We're flying in Heydrich's personal plane."

"A conference?" Paul guessed.

"Yes, and an important one," Bergmann said. "Heydrich, Frank and I will chair it. The Führer wants the Jewish problem solved once and for all. And not before time, if you ask me. The task of coordinating State and Party agencies has been given to the RSHA."

"To Heydrich, you mean."

"They are one and the same thing," Bergmann said, delivering the words almost like a reprimand.

"Where will it be held?"

"You know the villa on Grosser Wannsee?"

"The Interpol headquarters?"

"That's it. We meet on December the ninth."

"Which *referat* will be the executive agency?" Paul asked. The RSHA, the Reich Main Security Office, was a bewildering maze of sub-sections, 'desks', and *referaten*. They said that anyone who could understand how it worked automatically received a degree from Berlin University.

"Four-B-four," Bergmann said. Paul ran through the index in his mind of the various RSHA sections. One was personnel, two was administration, three and six were the *Sicherheitsdienst*. Four was the Gestapo. Four-B was the sub-section, commanded by Hartl, which dealt with churches, sects, Jews and gypsies. 4-B-4 was a 'desk' within that sub-section.

"Jewish Affairs," Bergmann said, impatiently, with the expression of a man having to explain something every fool ought to know.

"Oh, that big place on the Kurfürstenstrasse?"

"That's the one. I've put one of my assistants in there. Eichmann. Little Adolf, we used to call him. That was in the old days. You remember, Paul? When the SD was in that pokey little house near the Branitzerplatz?"

"Eichenallee," Paul said. "I remember it."

"What times we had there!" Bergmann enthused, his voice warming with the first genuine emotion Paul had heard all night. "You remember what a team we had, Paul? Not only Heydrich and Schellenberg, but Werner Best and Alfi Naujocks. And Helmut Wolff. Remember him?"

"He was sent to Russia, wasn't he?"

"Argued with the *Reichsführer*. Questioned an order. Damned fool!"

"This Eichmann. Why do you call him 'Little Adolf'?"

"So nobody would think we were making jokes about the Führer, of course! Little Adolf. He used to keep the card indexes up to date."

And now he's in charge of killing the Jews, Paul thought. What kind of insanity made a man pursue such obscene promotion? In the hall a telephone began ringing. After a few moments, a main knocked on the door and said there was a call for the Herr *Standartenführer*.

"Who is it, Marta?" Erika said.

"*Reichsprotector* Heydrich, madam," the maid said.

Bergmann bounded to his feet and hurried out of the room. Erika smiled at Paul as the maid soundlessly closed the double doors.

"You weren't coming to see me, were you?" she said, after what seemed like a long silence.

"I thought it better," he said. "Not to." It sounded lame and unconvincing. Erika said nothing for a moment. She leaned across to the silver box on the table and took a cigarette out of it. He held the lighter for her, her hand touching his.

"A little late for scruples, wouldn't you say, darling?" she purred.

162

"It's not that," he said.

"Ah," she said. "Then what can it be, I wonder?"

"I suppose I realised. That there was no . . . love in it."

"But darling," she said. "There never was. Why should that make any difference now?"

Well, if irony was to your taste he was getting his share tonight, Paul thought. He started to say something, but at that moment Kurt came back into the room. "That was Heydrich," he announced. "He wants me at the Hradschin, right away." Paul rose from his chair, but Bergmann waved him back. "No, no, my dear fellow, stay. Erika will take care of you." Did something pass between them? Paul thought he saw a signal in Bergmann's eyes, but it might have been imagination.

"Give Paul another drink, darling," Bergmann said to his wife. "Some of that Napoleon brandy, perhaps. Forgive me, my dear fellow. You know how it is." He shrugged, as if to say, we men, the things we have to do. "God knows what time I'll get back. So I'll say goodbye now. It was good to see you. We must do this more often."

"Yes," Paul said. "We must."

"Fine," Bergmann said. Paul wondered what he was so edgy about. Being around Heydrich would make anybody edgy, he decided.

"Here," Erika said, handing him a crystal goblet. "It really is Napoleon." They heard Bergmann's car purr away down the drive. Paul swirled the golden liquid in the glass, warming it with his hands to release its fine bouquet.

"Come," Erika said. "Let's sit by the fire."

She took his hand and led him back to the big sofa standing before the open hearth. The standard lamp and two table lights bathed the walls in a soft, rosy glow. Erika turned towards him, moulding her body against his. Her lips were hot, knowing.

"Make love to me, Paul," she whispered.

He took hold of her soft bare shoulders and pushed her gently back, shaking his head.

"No, Erika," he said. "It's over. Finished."

"Is it?" she said, her eyes narrowing. Her voice was no longer soft.

"It has to be," he said. "Prague isn't Berlin. My seeing you would be in a Gestapo report within a day of its happening."

"And so you want me to make it nice and easy for you, is that it?"

"That would be . . . generous."

"Generous!" she said. "He wants me to be generous! Well, I don't feel generous, *darling*. You were glad enough to share my bed a few months ago in Berlin. What's so different now?"

"I am, I suppose," Paul said. "Try to understand, Erika."

"Oh, lovely," she said. "Understand! You clump up my stairs and use my body, then piss off into the night like some Hemingway hero, thinking what a wonderful fellow you are. Then when you've had enough of it, you ask me to be *generous* and *understanding*! My God, you're like all the rest of them!"

"Ah," he said, softly. "There were . . . others?"

"Others?" she said, her voice rising. "Yes, darling, there were others. Others and others and others. You——." She shook her head angrily. "You don't know anything. Let me tell you about the others, darling. Let me tell you about the parties where they make daisy chains, a man and a woman and another man and then another woman, or the ones where they bring animals, a dog, a horse, a snake. Let me tell you about the lovely weekends at secluded chateaux in the country where we do things that would make hyenas vomit. Let me tell you——"

"Stop it!" he snapped, suddenly loathing her and loathing himself for being part of this. Erika glared at him, her eyes flooded with rage. He watched her as she stubbed out the cigarette and angrily lit another, as if to say, defiantly, I *will* be bad.

"You don't want to hear it, do you, my little soldier boy?" she said. "You don't want your nose rubbed in the dirty truth. Well, you're going to, whether you like it or not!"

"I think I'd rather leave," he said, getting up.

"I'm sure you would," she purred. She shook her head again, the long blonde hair swinging. "You still don't understand, do you?"

"Understand? Oh, I understand, all right."

"I'll put it into words of one syllable," she said. "Kurt uses me. As bait."

"What?"

"He tells me who to sleep with. And what to tell them."

"Oh, Jesus Christ, Erika." Paul said, softly. "And . . . you do it?"

"What choice do I have?" she said, seeing Kurt in her mind's eye, towering over her and the vile, epicene things he did, things which hurt her, disgusted yet simultaneously excited her, dirty, nasty, painful lovely things that could make her beg and whimper for release and never wanting it to stop all at the same time.

"I used to . . . regret not feeling more," Paul said. "And all the time you were betraying me."

"There are all kinds of betrayal, darling," she whispered. "We all do it, in the end." She turned her head away, and he thought he saw the glint of tears in her eyes. Then she spoke, her voice pitched so low that he could hardly hear her.

"Oh, Paul," she said. "We could have had such good times."

He managed a grin, although it was a poor one. "You know what we Hemingway heroes say to that line, Erika," he said. He stood up. "I'd better go."

"Yes, go!" she said. "You're finished, anyway. You and all your damned traitorous friends!"

"What does that mean?" he said, suddenly cold.

She shook her head, no. He bent down and gripped her shoulders, shaking her.

"What did you mean, I'm finished?"

She glared up at him. "You're mixed up in that Hess business. You helped him to escape to England!"

"You're crazy!" he said. "Nobody helped him!"

"Kurt says the *Abwehr* helped him. It was part of a plot to depose the *Führer*. Heydrich has begun a secret investigation. *Aktion Fuchse*. Kurt is in charge of it."

"Did he tell you to tell me this?"

"He says it will be the end of you," she hissed. "The end of the whole *Abwehr*. And you know what, my little soldier boy? *I don't give a damn*!"

Oster, he thought. Oster, and the mysterious Operation

Jonathan which he had picked up rumours of. Had they really connived to spirit Hess out of Germany? A plot to depose the Führer? His mind was racing. Was that the reason for Bergmann's thinly-veiled questions about Udet and Molders? Had they been involved? If it was true, then it was death for all of them. Himmler and Heydrich had been trying for years to find an excuse for purging the *Abwehr*. If their *Aktion Fuchse* established that there had been such a plot, Hitler would tell Himmler to let slip his dogs of death.

"Goodbye, Erika," he said.

"Don't think it hasn't been wonderful, darling," she sneered. "Because it hasn't. You weren't even good in bed!"

"Bitch!" he said, restraining the urge to slap her. She laughed, throwing back the golden head. If I had played along, made love to her, would this scene have been different? he wondered. He went out into the hall. The maid brought his overcoat. It was bitterly cold outside. He felt uneasy and off-balance. He had always kept at bay the ugly thought of what they would do if they ever caught him. It was like a nightmare from which you awakened yourself before it enmeshed you. You had to: it was not possible to think rationally about the long, slow agonies of the final days of your life in the hands of the Gestapo, your precious little bundle of dreams and achievements snuffed out like the flame of a candle.

He got into his car and drove back to his apartment deep in thought. Had he been able to see Erika Bergmann's face after he left, he would have been even more deeply uneasy than he was. After sitting in silence for long minutes after his departure, she lit a cigarette and picked up the telephone, dialling 31549. Bergmann answered at once, as if he had been waiting.

"Well?" he said.

"It worked," she said. "He believed me." He hated me, too, she thought, but she did not say that. That would not matter to Kurt at all.

"Good," Bergmann said. She could almost see him smiling. "You've done well. I'll tell Heydrich. He'll probably want to see you and thank you. Personally."

Erika put down the phone and crossed the room to where the decanter of cognac stood on the serving trolley. She gulped back the drink, coughing at its potent bite, then poured another. She lit a cigarette and sat down on the sofa, staring into the roaring fire. Its warmth, and the inner heat of the cognac, made no difference at all. She could not stop shivering.

Berlin, November 30, 1941

Sam Gray hurried across the Pariserplatz, shoulders hunched against a driving east wind with a thin edge of sleet in it. An official car hissed along the Unter den Linden towards the Brandenburg Gate, two narrow slits of light emerging from its masked headlamps. The cobblestones glistened in the lowering light. Heavy clouds with snow in them scudded above the darkened city. Berlin was much the same, but it was strange to be back. It seemed like only yesterday he had been kicking his heels in Washington, shuffling papers in the still haphazardly organised Office of the Coordinator of Information. Then the request to meet Mason-Morley in Lisbon, and the almost familiar boredom of the long hours in the trans-Atlantic clipper.

An Embassy car was waiting at the dock. The driver was a smiling man in a dark suit, short, sturdily built. He introduced himself as the Passport Control Officer, Edward Giles. SIS, Sam thought: he knew enough about British Intelligence now to know that all PCOs were in the Service.

"You know what this is all about, Edward?" he asked Giles.

"'fraid not, sir," Giles said disarmingly. "I'm not in on the hush-hush stuff." Sam smiled; not much, he thought. "And people usually call me Ted," the Englishman added.

He had been in Lisbon since the outbreak of the war, he told Sam as they drove through the city. Untypical Foreign Service background, he said: a scholarship, a commission, Oxford, and then the service. He pointed out one or two places of interest as they threaded through the narrow, hilly streets, the Basilica de Estrela opposite a spacious garden square, a street market in the Largo do Rato, but Sam wasn't really listening. He was asking himself the same questions he had asked Donovan when the request for a meet came through. What do they want? What was all this about? And getting the same lack of answers.

Ted Giles conducted him through the Embassy to a sun-filled library, where he found Noël Mason-Morley awaiting him. On an otherwise-empty table stood a silver tray with a matching coffee pot, milk jug and sugar basin. Bone china cups patterned with a light tracery of leaves and flowers stood to one side.

"Good to see you again, Sam," Mason-Morley said, after they had exchanged greetings. "Help yourself to coffee."

"No, thanks," Sam said. Bob Hope had a joke about the British coffee. If this is coffee, can I have tea? And if this is tea, can I have coffee? Hell, everyone had a joke about British coffee.

"General Donovan said we could ask you to do something for us," Mason-Morley said. "We wondered whether you would."

"Of course," Sam said. "What is it?"

"We want you to go to Berlin."

"And?"

"Get a message to someone."

"That's all?"

Noël Mason-Morley pursed his lips. "How much do you want to know, Sam?" he said.

"That's a hell of a question."

"All right," Mason-Morley said, as if coming to a decision. "I'll tell you. What do the words *Schwarze Kapelle* mean to you?"

"Nothing," Sam said. "Other than that they mean Black Orchestra."

"In German intelligence circles, an 'orchestra' is a network of agents," Mason-Morley explained. "In this case, it is a resistance circle inside the German High Command. We don't know much more about it than that. And the fact that it exists."

Sam said nothing, but his mind was busy. He nodded, go on.

"We have . . . we had some contact with them," Mason-Morley said. "I think you knew that. Through Geneva. They told us about a plot, within the German High Command, to depose Hitler."

"I remember," Sam said. "Late last year, wasn't it?"

"That's right," Mason-Morley said. "November, I think it was. We weren't sure how much faith to put in the story, but we thought it might be worth encouraging them."

"How?"

"We told them that we would try to put in a team to assassinate Hitler. They would then seize the SS barracks at Lichterfelde, the aerodrome, the broadcasting station at Königswusterhausen, railway stations, government offices, and all known SS and SD premises."

"And then?"

"If they were successful, they planned to offer us peace terms."

"Peace terms?" Sam frowned. "Would Churchill have accepted peace terms?"

"Of course not," Mason-Morley said firmly. "But we let them think we might."

"How?"

"We mounted Operation Wolf Trap. The idea was to provide a dramatic attempt on Hitler's life. If it succeeded, they could seize power without hindrance. If not, they could grab him and take him away somewhere. For his own protection, as it were."

Sam shook his head. Did no one in British Intelligence know what life was really like in Hitler's Germany? Nobody could plot a coup d'état without the Gestapo knowing about it.

"I'd be prepared to bet the Gestapo know all about your *Schwarze Kapelle*," he said. "And probably Wolf Trap, too, by now."

"We know that, too," Mason-Morley said. "It was an acceptable risk."

Acceptable to whom? Sam thought. The well-intentioned officers of the German High command who would die in Gestapo cellars? The idealistic Czech parachutists who would be exterminated on the streets of Munich?

"I know what you're thinking, Sam," Mason-Morley said.

"But we'd set out to defeat Germany and, right then, we weren't too particular about how we went about it. Frankly, we were grasping at any straw that came our way. And this seemed like a God-given chance to throw Jerry into utter confusion."

"Then Wolf Trap was more or less a suicide mission?"

"There are always casualties in a war, Sam," Mason-Morley said.

"Acceptable ones," Sam said. Mason-Morley went a shade pinker, but he did not reply. Sam shrugged. "So why do you want me to go to Berlin?"

"If it's possible to keep the link with the *Schwarze Kapelle* open, we want to do it," Mason-Morley said. "We have precious little information coming out of Germany as it is. There's no chance of us putting the Wolf Trap team in now until at least after Christmas. So we want to get word to them to go to ground. There may be another chance, there may not."

"How do I contact them?"

"Here's a Berlin telephone number," Mason-Morley said. He handed Sam a slip of paper. On it were written two telephone numbers: 21 81 91, and 4844. "The second number is the extension. The name of the man is Veick, Werner Veick. Make arrangements to meet him. We'll give you passwords and so on."

"And if I'm blown?"

"Try not to be," Mason-Morley said, unsmilingly. He must have pressed a bell somewhere, because at that moment, the young PCO, Ted Giles, came in.

"Yes, sir?"

"Mr Gray will be leaving us tomorrow, Ted," Mason-Morley said. "I think we ought to give him a decent meal before he goes, don't you?"

"How about a table at Aviz, sir?"

"Splendid," Mason-Morley said. "Fix it up, there's a good chap."

The rich green brocades and velvet upholstery of the restaurant in the Rua Serpa Pinto were like a memory from another life, Sam thought as he hurried towards the Friedrichstrasse station. It wasn't difficult to spot the tail.

The Gestapo rarely made any attempt to conceal themselves. Who was going to complain? Certainly not an American. The Germans were making absolutely no attempt to conceal their disaffection with Americans. Leland Morris, the chargé d'affaires at the Embassy, had told him that he spent most of his time these days cooling his heels in Foreign Minister von Ribbentrop's outer office, waiting to hear another tirade against President Roosevelt's 'warmongering'. Morris said the Gestapo listened to his phone calls and followed him everywhere as a matter of course.

"Maybe they won't be interested in me," Sam said.

"Don't bet on it," was the weary reply.

Sam went into the station and loitered near the newsstand, browsing through a copy of *Signal*. People with suitcases bustled past; groups of soldiers in *feldgrau* stood waiting for the departure of their trains. Uniforms, so many different uniforms: Sam smiled, remembering Morris's story about the shot-down RAF man who had walked down the Wilhelmstrasse in uniform and everyone saluted him. A station tractor towing a train of clanking baggage cars wove its way through the crowd, klaxon sounding. When it was almost level with him, Sam moved quickly away from where he was standing, putting the line of moving cars between him and the Gestapo agent. He went out of the station into Georgenstrasse and turned into the Central Hotel. He took an elevator to the third floor and then walked down the stairs to the lobby. There was no sign of the Gestapo agent. Sam shrugged and went out into the night. He walked past the Land Registry office in the Dorotheenstrasse; there was a school on the opposite side. He went into the Ministry of the Interior and walked down the great central hall to the information desk. The clerk told him that the office for the *Reichskommissar* for Price Control was not in this building, but on the Behrenstrasse. Sam already knew that: he was merely using the echoing, marble-floored hall to doublecheck that the Gestapo tail had not picked him up again.

He stopped one more time, on the far side of the Unter den Linden, watching the wide steps of the Ministry down which he had just come. Nobody came out. He shrugged again and set off down the Unter den Linden. The wind sang along its broad emptiness. There was a rime of frozen sleet on the statue of Frederick the Great. Scraps of paper whirled like birds, then flopped to the wet ground.

Baarz's beer hall was full, as usual. It was warm and noisy, and there was a rich fug of tobacco smoke, the smell of wet clothes and stale beer. The *Blasorchester* was pounding away, all but drowned by the roar of voices. Hefty-looking waitresses carried stone tankards, five to the fist, from bar to table. They smiled as they set them down; their customers smiled back. Things were going well. According to the radio and the newspapers, the fall of Moscow was imminent. There was a rumour that Stalin had put out peace feelers through King Boris of Bulgaria.

Sam went upstairs to the restaurant on the balcony. Round tables with white cloths on them, a tinned-steel condiments set plonked dead centre on each, were occupied by working men having a night out, couples having supper. A man in a corner raised a hand, and Sam smiled a greeting. It was Veick.

He was a tall, thin man with a long jaw and deeply-sunken eyes. His bony frame made him look under-nourished, but Sam knew that this was not the case. Berliners did quite well for food. There was plenty of bread, cabbages, potatoes. They received a pound of meat a week, a quarter of a pound of butter. The only thing in short supply was fresh fruit. That didn't bother the average German much, not with fourteen hundred different kinds of *wurst* to choose from.

"Werner," Sam said. "Let me get you something."

"Tea only," Veick said. He had a strange, seemingly arrogant way of speaking. It had taken Sam a little while to realise that it was just Werner's reaction to his own inner tension. Men like Veick lived on the edge of a volcano all the time. Why they did it, Sam was only just beginning to understand. How they did it, he would never know.

"Have you any cigarettes, Sam?" Veick asked. Sam took out a pack of Camels and slid it across the table. Werner tore the pack open and lit one.

"Ah!" he said, inhaling hungrily. "*Wunderbar!*"

He had a habit of wetting his lips with his tongue before he spoke. His thinning hair was combed across his scalp from a parting above the left ear, in a vain attempt to conceal his baldness. The waitress came across and Sam ordered tea for both of them.

"You want something to eat?" he said. "I've got coupons."

"Tea only," Werner said again. Sam shrugged and the waitress went away.

"Well, Werner, have you been able to find anything out?" he said.

"Yes," Veick said. "A little."

He looked up as the waitress brought their tea. She was a dumpy, vacuous-looking woman of about thirty-five. Her hair was done up in ringlets, and she had a sulky Cupid-bow mouth. Werner grimaced and waited until she was gone.

"I'm permitted to tell you this much," Werner said. "The British were in on the Haushofer plan."

"The Haushofer plan?"

"It was Haushofer's idea that Rudolf Hess fly to Britain."

"I see. And?"

"The British helped us."

"To get him to England?"

Werner hesitated for a moment. "Yes," he said. "To England."

"Then why do they act as if he's some kind of embarrassment?" Sam said. "They've got him locked away where nobody can talk to him."

"I don't know," Werner said. He looked strained, worried. Sam eased off: too much pressure and Veick would clam up completely.

"Anything else?"

"There's something big on," he said. "The lights are burning all night at the Prinz Albrechtstrasse, but nobody will say why."

"What do you think?"

"We thought Himmler. But we think now perhaps it's the organ-grinder, not the monkey."

"Heydrich?"

"Very probably," Werner said. "We got word there is to be a big investigation into the Hess business. Everyone was very worried. Those black-shirted bastards will hang people for a lot less than that. Yet, it's strange, nothing much has happened."

"What does that mean?"

"We don't know, Sam," Werner said, frowning. "We have the feeling it's a smoke-screen. They're not . . . intent. You know what I mean?"

"Not serious enough?"

"Exactly. As if they are really after something else. Or someone."

"Who?"

"I don't know," Veick said. "Someone in Prague, perhaps."

"Why do you say that?"

"It was from Prague we got our warning."

"One of your people?"

Werner shook his head. Sam frowned, chilled by a sudden thought.

"Do you know a man named Rauth?" he asked Werner. "Karl-André Rauth?"

Now it was Werner's turn to frown. "I don't think so," he said.

"He's an *Abwehr* officer. Counter-espionage."

"I know most of them," Werner said. "But no one of that name."

"He'd be quite highly-placed."

"Rauth, Rauth?" Werner said, with a grimace. "Here in Berlin?"

"No," Sam said. "He's in Prague."

"I know the *Hauptvertrauensmann* in Prague," Werner said. "His name is Kramer. Paul Kramer."

"Describe him."

"Thirty-five or so. Tall, blond, well built."

Sam nodded. "How difficult would it be for me to get to Prague?"

"Very difficult."

"But not impossible."

"For you, probably just possible," Werner said. "Perhaps a forty-eight hour permit. I doubt more."

"That would be enough," Sam said. "Can you help me arrange it?"

"Why do you wish to go to Prague?"

"A hunch," Sam said, not explaining. "What would I have to do?"

"You would have to go to the Office for Foreign Trade. You know where that is?"

"Isn't that the one down by the Elizabeth Hospital?"

"That's it. Why do you want to go to Prague?" Werner asked again.

"I told you, a hunch."

"To do with Kramer?"

"Yes."

"He's not one of us, Sam."

"I know that."

"Then I don't understand."

Sam shook his head. "Even if I thought you would understand, I wouldn't tell you, Werner," he said. "Do you know anybody in the Foreign Trade Office?"

"We . . . have someone there. His name is Christian Zittwitz. He is in charge of arranging travel permits for neutral aliens." He smiled his twisted smile. "I'd say you just about qualify."

"Could you speak to him?"

"Tomorrow," Werner said. "You know you'll have to tell the Gestapo why you're going? And you'll have to report to them when you reach Prague?"

"I know," Sam said.

"They'll ask you a lot of questions," Werner persisted.

"Then I'll have to think of some good answers," Sam replied.

"Yes, you will," Veick said, without the trace of a smile. "*So!*" He got up and went across to the coat rack, putting on his long black overcoat as he came back across the room.

"Heard the latest one about Adi, Sam?" he said.

"Werner—" Sam protested. Jokes about Hitler were punishable by imprisonment, even death.

"This one only carries a three-year sentence, Sam," Veick reassured him, with macabre glee. "You know why he stands like that?" He crossed his hands over his crotch to demonstrate.

"All right," Sam said. "Why?"

"Protecting the unemployed," Werner said. He looked over his shoulder nervously, a quick check for possible eavesdroppers. They called it *der Deutsche Blick,* the German twitch.

"Is there anything I can do for you, Werner?" Sam asked.

"Have you got any more cigarettes?"

"I'll get you some."

"Don't send them to the office," Werner grinned. He laid a hand on Sam's arm. "Take care of yourself, Yank. We're in a minefield."

"You, too, Werner."

"Wiederschau'n," Veick said, and went out into the night, a tall, thin nondescript man. I wonder how many thousands like him there are? Sam thought. He ordered another pot of tea and sat in the beer hall for another half hour, deep in his own thoughts. Something big was on, Veick had said. An investigation without teeth; perhaps a smoke-screen. Not the monkey, but the organ-grinder. An investigation originating in Prague. Heydrich was in Prague. So was the man who called himself Karl-André Rauth. Or Paul Kramer? Was there a connection? Between Hess and Wolf Trap and *Hauptvertrauensmann* Kramer? There was something there: but what? Wolf Trap, Hess, Prague, Karl, Heydrich. Had the 'something big' which had them working round the clock at *'Nummer Acht'* anything to do with all this?

He paid his bill and went out into the street. It was snowing in earnest now, blanketing the sidewalks. He turned up the collar of his trench coat and hurried across to the U-Bahn station. He went down the steps, still frowning with concentration. Whatever the answer was, the key to it was in Prague. The train roared into the station and he got on. At the next station he waited until the doors were closing, then jumped off. Nobody else got off. There were only three other people on the platform: an old woman, a young soldier, and a middle-aged man in a soaked raincoat. Sam nodded: he had not been followed from the restaurant. He got on the next train and headed home. Without knowing how or why, he could not shake off the feeling that Karl-André Rauth was in deadly danger.

Berlin, December 4, 1941

Walter Abendschon walked along the corridor of Gestapo headquarters behind the woman clerk who had been assigned to help him. His interview with *Kriminalrat* Matzke, head of RSHA Amt 4C/1, had been brief to the point of perfunctoriness. He had given his name, and presented the letter from Heydrich authorising his use of the records of the *Hauptstelle*. It had the desired effect: Matzke fell over himself to be helpful when he saw the jagged, imperious signature.

The woman clerk was an attractive blonde in a crisp white blouse and a black skirt. Her hair was tied back at the nape of her neck. She looked efficient, clean and cool. Her heels clicked rhythmically on the marble floor. Her blue eyes caught and reflected the flat November light.

'*Nummer Acht*', as every police officer in Berlin called Gestapo headquarters, was the one-time Schools of Arts and Crafts, designed by the famous architect of the Neue Wache and the Werderschekirche, Karl Friedrich von Schinkel. Fronting the Prinz Albrechtstrasse opposite the Air Ministry, it was an undistinguished building in the shape of an H, with high, vaulted ceilings, thick walls, and windows that rose from the floor to twice the height of a tall man. It had been closed down by the police after the Reichstag fire, then commandeered by Göring when he set up the new secret police later in 1933.

Abendschon remembered how the place had looked the first time he ever saw it, that same year. Empty, then, abandoned, its corridors littered with debris, dust, broken glass. Doors hung askew on their hinges. The walls were defaced by illiterate graffiti. He remembered wondering how they would ever get the place cleaned up and turned into a functioning office. He remembered Rudi Diels striding about, shouting orders.

Well, Rudi didn't last long as head of the Gestapo, Abendschon thought, Heydrich saw to that. He and Himmler wanted the secret police for themselves, and they got it. It was they who had changed its name to the one that every German feared: Gestapo. And beer-drinking, glass-chewing Rudi Diels, who had been Abendschon's first boss, had been kicked upstairs into an executive job with the RHG. One of the advantages of being married to Göring's cousin, Abendschon thought. He marched along a corridor that reminded him of the colonnade alongside a cloister. Beyond the windows lay a bloomless lawn. On its far side stood the squat bulk of the Ministry of Labour. People bustled past, men in uniform, women in the same white blouses and dark skirts as his escort. None of them smiled or said hello. Well, Abendschon thought, there wasn't much to smile about at *Nummer Acht*.

"*Bitte,*" the woman said, opening a door. He followed her into a huge room crammed with metal filing cabinets. My God, he thought, look at them. They stretched in rigidly-aligned rows from the door to the farthest end of the room. And it was a big room.

"There must be thousands of them," he said.

"This is just Army records," she said. "Civilian records are further along. Three rooms for German citizens. Then beyond that there are the rooms for the records of the Greater Reich."

"How many people work here?" he asked. "In Records, I mean."

"Oh, I don't know," she shrugged. "Hundreds. Hundreds."

He told her he knew how the card index worked: he had used it before. The section he was going to start on was A-1, 'enemies of the State.' A-1 was divided into sub-sections: A-1/1 was Communists, A-1/2 Marxists, and so on. Jews, priests with unacceptable political views, reactionaries, political malcontents, industrial saboteurs—each section had its own code number, whether for habitual criminals or opportunists, black marketeers or abortionists, homosexuals or unreliable journalists. Each card was colour-coded in two ways. A red tab on the left-hand side of the card indicated Communist affiliations, blue, suspected criminal activities, green, dangerous tendencies. A secondary colour code for the right-hand side further cross-referenced the subject: brown for a known assassin, brick red an escaped prisoner, alternate red and white stripes a deportee. Thus, an index-card from A-1/6 with a red tab on the left and a brick red on the right indicated that the subject was a political malcontent with Communist affiliations who had escaped from custody. A reference number in the top right-hand corner of the index card, which carried a passport-size photograph of the subject, referred to the full Gestapo dossier. Other numbers cross-referred to the dossiers of other subjects known to or affiliated with the subject, and still others to SD, Sipo, Kripo or *Ordnungspolizei* files in which his name appeared. All cards were checked twice annually, on April first and October first. It was vast, mindless, and utterly comprehensive. Practically every citizen of the Third Reich, not to mention the inhabitants of all the conquered countries, were listed in Gestapo files for one reason or another. In addition, of course, there were files on foreign nationals of interest to Gestapo investigators, and the counter-espionage files of Amt 4/E. God alone knew how much it all cost to maintain. The last time he had looked, in 1937, the Gestapo was spending more than forty million Reichsmarks a year. Probably double that, now, he thought.

He signed the logbook and then stood looking at the featureless grey cabinets in their impeccably aligned rows. Kramer's index card was easy to find. He gave it to the woman. She picked up a telephone and spoke into it, giving someone the number on the card.

"We'll have to wait a few minutes," she said. "For the messenger."

"All right," he said, looking around. He tried to imagine someone holding a class in arts and crafts in this room, and failed.

"Would you prefer to wait in the reading room?" the woman said. "It's just through here."

She led him to a heavy, iron-studded door with a metal ring for a handle, and opened it. The reading room seemed almost monastically austere: grey walls, stone floor, small windows set high, a simple polished table with goose-neck reading lamps, high-backed wooden chairs with brass-studded leather seats. On one wall hung a framed portrait of Hitler. Opposite it hung a painting of Frederick the Great. The door opened and a young man wearing the dark blue uniform of a messenger came in. His complexion was pasty and he wore thick-lensed glasses. He was carrying a bulky dossier.

179

"You the one for Kramer?" he said.

"That's me," Abendschon said.

"Sign here, please."

Abendschon scribbled his signature and the messenger went out, closing the door. I wouldn't mind betting he gets down on his knees every morning to thank God for those weak eyes and that spindly body, Abendschon thought. No chance of being sent to the Eastern front, to die in the merciless cold like the poor bastards whose death announcements filled pages every day in the *Volkischer Beobachter*. The saddest thing of all was their age: twenty-four, twenty-six. Fallen for Germany. *Führer, Volk und Vaterland*. Empty, empty words: it made the heart weep to read them.

"Do you want me to stay?" the woman said.

"Oh, yes," Abendschon said. "This is going to be quite a job."

"Would you like some coffee first?"

He smiled. "You've really got some?"

"I have a cousin who was in Holland," she said. "She bought some on the black market."

"I'd walk through fire for a cup of real coffee," he said.

"Oh, I won't make you do that," she said, smiling. It seemed to Abendschon there was more to the words than just the words, but he told himself not to be stupid.

"Then, yes, please," he said.

"With or without?"

"Without."

"Don't go away," she said. "I'll be right back."

He opened the dossier. He had no preconceptions: he did not know what he was looking for except that he needed a handle, a clue, a lead, a hint. Bergmann's so-called *Aktion Fuchse* might or might not flush their quarry. But Abendschon felt sure there must be something, somewhere, that would confirm, once and for all, that Paul Kramer was the mysteriously elusive 'Traitor Unknown' who had been working against the Reich since the beginning of the war. He laid the file he had brought with him from Prague alongside the bulkier one of Paul Kramer. Common denominators, he thought. That's going to be the way. The same name recurring. The same places. You always looked for the same thing when you were investigating: motive, opportunity. Murder or treason, it made no difference. If Kramer was a traitor, there was a reason for it. That might emerge from the Gestapo files, although Abendschon doubted it: the 'blacks' didn't score too highly on subtlety. Opportunity, however, was another matter.

He looked at Kramer's photograph in the dossier: a confident, assured smile. He skimmed the details of the man's life, most of which he knew already. Parents Walter Kramer, a music teacher and critic, and Libena Kramer-Fafek, born in Pilsen. That's why he speaks Czech so well, Abendschon thought. A sister, two years younger, named Hannelore, and a brother, Peter, four years younger. Reference numbers for their personal dossiers were entered alongside their names: Abendschon made a note of them. Kramer's school reports showed he had been a good student, punctual and industrious. He was in the third grade in 1917, Abendschon thought with a grimace, while I was being shot down *and the wind howling in the struts as the Pfalz spun down and down and he thought Jesus Christ don't let me die.* It made him feel very old to remember that. All the usual stuff: *Dienstlaufbahn* with Kramer's Army commission, and the various *Beauftragen* informing him of his promotions: *Leutnant, Hauptmann, Major, Oberstleutnant,* and most recently, *Oberst.* Height, weight, medals, religion. *Fragebogen.* Personally-written biographical details: a neat admirable script. Marriage papers. A photograph of Brigit Schafer. Pretty thing, Abendschon mused. Just at that moment, the woman clerk came back into the reading room with two mugs of coffee. She put them on the table.

"What do I call you?" Abendschon asked.

"My name is Elchens," she said. "Angela. Call me Geli."

"Geli," he said, saluting her with the coffee mug.

"Your name is Walter," she said. "I saw it on the letter. Do they call you Walti?"

"Not if I'm in the room," he said.

"Walter, then." She sat down in the chair next to his and sipped her coffee. "My God, there's enough of it," she said, grimacing at the files. "How do you want to do it?"

"I want to excerpt the names of everyone he knows. I want a list of all the places he has been. Then I want to pull the dossiers on those people, and so on and so on. I want to put together, as nearly as I can, a complete breakdown of *Oberst* Kramer's movements for the last two years at least."

"That's a big job," she said.

"Then we'd better get started," Abendschon said. "That was good coffee."

"Glad you liked it."

"We'll split the dossier," he said. "You work from the back forward, and I'll work from the beginning to the middle."

"All right," she said. She hesitated slightly. "Do you mind if I ask you a personal question?"

"No."

"Where did you hurt your leg?"

"In the Great War," he said, gruffly. "Before you were born."

"I was twelve when the war ended," she said. "I'm thirty-five."

"You don't look it."

"Thank you," she said. She had a nice smile. She hitched her chair forward and crossed her legs. She had good legs. She caught his glance and held it. He looked away. Come on, Walter, he told himself. Don't let your imagination run away with you. He bent over the dossier, frowning. Kramer's photograph smiled up at him. Is that a traitor's smile? he wondered. Probably. It did not make him angry. Nothing people did made him angry or surprised him any more. He always thought policemen had a lot in common with doctors. Both professions got to know very quickly that there was never going to be any end to it. There was a never-ending supply of sick people waiting for you to come and cure them. And there was an equally inexhaustible supply of thieves, and thugs, and killers. That was why there were doctors, and that was why there were policemen.

The silence was companionable, broken only by the rustle of turned pages. Abendschon tried to shut out the insistent awareness of the young woman at his side, but he could not do it. He could smell the light perfumes of face powder, clean hair, starch.

"Where are you staying?" she asked, breaking the silence.

"I've got an apartment," he said. "You forget, I live here. I'm just on secondment to Prague."

"I forgot," she said.

They worked steadily on. The lights came on automatically at three-thirty. The winter night was setting in. At five, bells rang to announce the end of the day roster's eight-hour shift. Geli Elchens got up and stretched her arms above her head. Her breasts lifted beneath the white blouse. She smiled.

"I'll see you tomorrow, then," she said.

She left the room, but he didn't feel as if she was gone. He could still smell the light perfume. He wondered whether she had noticed him looking at her breasts when she stretched, and decided that she had, and that it hadn't exactly ruined her day. He shook his head, annoyed at himself for allowing thoughts of her to distract him. No fool like an old fool, he told himself, irritably. Frowning, he concentrated on the work at hand. It was going to be a long grind. It would have been a damned sight easier to go to the Tirpitzufer and demand to see Kramer's *Abwehr* file, but he knew that within ten minutes of his asking for it, someone would be telephoning Kramer on the *Abwehr*'s scrambler phones, telling him that someone from the Gestapo was poking around. Bergmann wouldn't be thrilled if he started the hare too soon.

He worked on until nine-thirty, then gathered up his papers. A messenger came and took the files away. Abendschon walked slowly back to the Magdeburgerplatz. The apartment was cold and unwelcoming. He had no affection for it. It was just a place to sleep. He didn't care where he lived any more. It was well over a year since the raid in which Eva and the boys had been killed, the little house sliced out of its row as neatly as a piece of pie. It had been a nuisance raid, the VB said the next day: only twenty-two civilians killed, no real damage done. Some factories north of the city hit, a gas works, the railroad yards outside Lehrter station. Eva, Friedrich and Georg Abendschon gone, without trace. No real damage. He tried not to think about it any more than necessary, but once in a while it flooded into his mind and he wept without weeping.

He thought about switching on the radio, then decided against it. He didn't want to hear the news: it was always the same, anyway. He looked out of the window at the dark hulk of the market across the square. I must buy some food, he thought. I haven't eaten all day. He got a bottle of Rudesheimer out of the cold cupboard and opened it. It tasted of sunshine. He remembered crossing the Rhine on the ferry to Rudesheim. Eva and the boys were excited, they were going to climb up the path to the Lorelei. Later that day, they tasted wine in a stone cellar in the Oberstrasse, and ate dinner in the terrace of a café looking out across the river. He emptied the glass and poured another. He was asleep in the chair before he finished it.

On the third day at Gestapo headquarters, they made the first breakthrough. Working on the as-yet unproven assumption that Kramer really was a traitor, Abendschon pulled the files on all the senior officers of the Czech Intelligence Service. It was not unlikely that if Kramer was passing information to the Czechs in Prague now, as the captured material from the house in Liben indicated, he had done so before. One by one, he and Geli Elchens worked through the dossiers. Lieutenant-Colonel Oldrich Tichy, Major Emil Strankmueller, Major Josef Bartik, Captain Jaroslav Tauer, Captain Josef Fort, Major Alois Frank, Captain Vaclav Slama, Captain Bohumil Dite, Captain Ladislav Cigna, Captain Karel Palecek, Captain Frantisek Fryc, and, of course, the head of the Service, Colonel Frantisek Morávec. Each of the files was voluminous. Each took hours to read, but they ploughed on, jotting down details of the meetings these Czech officers had effected with agents, spies, informers, or 'unidentifiable suspicious persons', to use the Gestapo jargon. In the file of Fryc, one of Morávec's case officers, and a 'German expert', was a notation that in February, 1939, he had met an "unidentifiable suspicious person", thought to be an officer of the German army, at Turnau.

"Well, well," Abendschon said, leaning back in his chair. "In February, 1939 our *Abwehr* friend requested permits to travel from Prague to Vienna and Graz."

"What does that prove?" Geli asked, pushing back a strand of hair that had come adrift.

"Maybe nothing," Abendschon said. "But Turnau is only a few kilometres off the Vienna-Graz highway. And the timing is right."

"That's hardly proof," she pointed out.

"No," he agreed. "But it's encouragement. Let's keep going."

It could be coincidence, he thought, stilling the pulse of excitement rising inside him. But he *knew* it wasn't. And he was right. He found what he was looking for in the dossier of Major Alois Frank, another of Morávec's 'German experts'. In April, 1930, Frank had made a 'treff' in the Hague with two British Intelligence agents and an unidentified German in civilian clothes. Papers had changed hands: the German had brought them. He had been followed, but eluded the pursuit. There was a description of sorts, but Abendschon ignored it. A glance at Kramer's dossier showed that in that month he had travelled to Holland: unspecified *Abwehr* duties. Opportunity again, but this time something else. The two British agents were SIS officers, Richard Stevens and Payton Best. They had been the heads of the British secret service in Holland, and the victims of a baroque plot concocted by the *Abwehr* and carried out by Heydrich's infamous '*Elite-truppe*' which ended in their being kidnapped at the Dutch border town of Venlo. They were now imprisoned in the concentration camp Oranienburg. And would, Abendschon thought, laying the dossier down, more than likely be able to identify that 'unidentified German in civilian clothes' if shown a photograph. He had no doubt it would be Kramer. He felt no triumph, just satisfaction. The old plodding police methods again, he thought. They hardly ever fail.

"You look pleased," Geli Elchens said.

"I am."

"How about celebrating together?"

Abendschon just looked at her.

"We could go back to my place and have a drink," she said. "I'll put on a pretty dress and you can take me to Horcher's for dinner."

"Horcher's," he said. "You don't want much." It was the most expensive restaurant in Berlin.

"I'm joking!" she said. "Can't you take a joke? Listen, there's a nice little place near where I live. It's called the *Kerzenstüberl*. Very Viennese. Good food. Candles on the table. It's very romantic. I could do with a little romance in my life."

"Isn't that a wedding ring you're wearing?"

"Yes," she said, pouting a little. "But Franz is in Russia and I'm here. Are you married, Walter?"

"My wife died," he said. "In an air raid."

"I'm sorry."

"It's all right."

"What about it, then?"

"I don't think—"

"Let me go home and put on my nice red dress," she said. "We'll have an early dinner. After that . . ." She raised her eyebrows and shrugged.

"Geli," he said. "I can't."

"All right," she said, getting up.

"Geli—"

"No, really, it's all right."

"I'm sorry."

"No need," she said, too brightly. "No need at all."

She went out and left him alone in the reading room. He could smell the faint perfume of her. Now, why the hell do I do that? he asked himself, angrily. He slapped the dossiers shut and rang for the messenger. For some reason the image of Karin Graumann came into his mind, a pert, high-cheek-boned face, green eyes with the faint hint of an Oriental slant. He remembered putting his arm around her shoulders when she cried. She was slender but not frail. With a strange feeling of anticipation that he did not understand, Walter Abendschon decided to go and see her.

Prague, December 6, 1941

Sam Gray sat by the window of his room in the Esplanade Hotel and scowled at the snow-covered little park below and the twin towers of the old Wilson Station beyond it. A whole day gone, he thought, and still no word. His help-lessness was frustrating, but it had to be endured. As did the maddening, inescapably omnipresent Herr Ludwig Winkel from the Office for Foreign Trade. Sam looked at the telephone. Ring, damn you, he willed it.

At least he had this morning free of Herr Winkel. The little man from the RFA was not due back until three, to assist Sam through difficulties which did not exist in his dealings with the Czech museum authorities and music publishers. Sam was rather pleased with the cover he had invented for himself: that of a mildly-venal American Embassy official who was lining his pockets by acting as the middleman for a Lichtenstein corporation interested in publishing facsimile editions of the manuscripts of Antonin Dvorak and Bedrich Smetana. The printing would be done in Czechoslovakia, the finished unbound pages shipped to Vaduz, and the account paid in American dollars. They knew all about Lichtenstein corporations at Foreign Trade, and middlemen from neutral countries. All they were interested in was the dollars: Sam Gray was not their problem. The Gestapo would take care of that.

Herr Winkel did not look as if he belonged to the Gestapo, but if he didn't, Sam thought, he sure as hell worked for them. He met Sam's train at the station, and he had stayed as close to Sam since as a flea to a dog. With him Herr Winkel carried notebooks, a briefcase, a greasy-collared raincoat, and the air of a man perpetually forced to gladly suffer fools. I know my worth will never be recognised, his manner said. He never stopped being helpful. He insisted, after their initial meeting with the Director of the National Museum, on giving Sam a conducted tour of Prague.

"There is time enough," he said. "Leave to me. I will show you everything worthy."

It was hardly the weather for sightseeing, but that didn't deter Ludwig Winkel. Hradschin, the Old Town and the Middle Town, Winkel directed the chauffeured Mercedes from Faust's house to Kafka's, from the Belvedere to the Bethlehem Chapel, sprouting a nonstop torrent of guidebook clichés so awful that Sam could not even find them funny. Herr Winkel's verbosity was not dampened in the slightest by Sam's monosyllabic response to it. Nor did it slacken that afternoon, in the offices of the Director of the

Academy of Musical Arts at the Palace of the Counts Lazansky, or during the extended dinner Winkel arranged with the Czech music publisher, Josef Nemkova. Any other time, Sam would have found him funny, perhaps even a little sad. Fuming with impatience to hear from Karl as Sam was, Winkel was insufferable. At times it was all Sam could do not to tell the little man to shut his damned face.

Finally, they bid Nemkova and his fellow directors good night. The Czechs had lingered over their early dinner: it was rarely that they got the chance to eat as well, and Sam's allowances as a diplomat enabled him to be generous. He just hoped they wouldn't be too let down when the 'deal' fell through.

"So," Winkel said, as they stood on the steps of the hotel. "You will go now to your room?"

Like a good boy, Sam thought. "Not yet," he told the little man. "I always like to take a long walk after dinner. For the digestion."

"Oh?" Winkel said, dismay showing. "You will go where?"

Sam shrugged. "Down to the Old Town, maybe. Not far."

"Perhaps it would be better if I were to accompany you," Winkel said, dubiously. "The curfew—"

"I really need a breath of air," Sam said.

"You are strange here," Winkel said. "Better I come." He looked up at Sam, spaniel eyes wide. Strange is right, kid, Sam thought: if only you knew. What Winkel was saying was: you're not going anywhere unaccompanied.

"Half an hour," he said to Winkel. "Then I'll buy you a nightcap."

"I do not wear one," Winkel said. "And thank you, I am not permitted the accepting of gifts."

There were times when Herr Winkel's English just didn't stretch to it, Sam thought. He explained to Winkel that he was talking about a drink, *Natchttrünk,* not a hat to wear in bed, *Nachtmütze.* Winkel looked annoyed, as though Sam had tricked him.

The hell with Herr Winkel anyway, Sam thought, walking impatiently across to the window again. He looked at his watch. Eleven forty-five. Come on, damn you! he told the telephone, and then jumped as it rang as if in response to his unspoken command.

"Yes?" he said.

"*Grüss Gott!*" a voice said. "*Karl hier.*"

"You must have the wrong number," Sam said.

"I beg your pardon," the voice said. "I wanted Mr Charles Travers."

"There's nobody of that name here," Sam said.

"Is that Room 101?"

"No."

"I'm sorry," the voice said, and rang off. Sam put down the telephone and wiped his hands on the towel. He felt very exposed, much more than he had expected to. It was up to him now. The code was simple. Charles Travers. Traverse equals bridge. Time, 1.01. He hoped the Gestapo were no good at word games. He didn't want Leiche waiting for him when he kept the appointment on the Charles Bridge. In fact, the less he had to do with that ugly bastard the better, he thought, remembering the huge, monumentally-ugly Gestapo Superintendent who had visited his hotel room while he was still unpacking. He had examined Sam's papers minutely, as if hoping somehow he would find something wrong with them. Then, tossing them on the bed, he had said loudly that aliens ought not to be permitted *laisser-passez* in time of war.

"The United States is not at war with Germany," Sam remonstrated. "I am here on legitimate business. The *Reichstelle fur Aussenhandel*—"

"I know all about that!" the big man said. "We are well aware who you are, Herr Gray." He said the name as if it rhymed with 'rye'. Sam looked at Winkel. The little man from the RFA looked as if he wished he could make himself invisible. Sam shrugged. The Gestapo man's words could mean anything or nothing. That was the way they worked. He had no intention of volunteering one word he did not need to speak. After a long pause, the Gestapo Superintendent spoke again.

"I will require a list of all your appointments," he said. "And the name of every person you propose to visit in Prague." He looked at Winkel as he said it. "All your movements must be accounted for."

"No problem, Superintendent Leiche," Sam said. He was determined not to let this rough-tongued strong-arm man get under his skin. That was just what Leiche was trying to do.

"You have handed your passport to the proper authority?"

"Of course," Sam said. And they're probably copying it even as we talk about it. Karl had once told him how the system worked. All foreign passports were retained 'for inspection' for twenty-four hours. They were taken from the Foreign Office to the *Sicherheitsdienst,* who had a printing plant in a side street not far from Tempelhof aerodrome. All foreign documents, letters, passports and visa stamps were copied and filed. An SS Major named Alfred Naujocks was in charge of the operation.

"So," Leiche said, nodding to the other man who had come in with him. This one wore rimless glasses, an ankle-length leather overcoat and jackboots. He had not spoken at any time, nor did he ever take his right hand out of the coat pocket. "Everything seems to be in order. Go about your business and all will be well. Winkel here will arrange everything."

Leiche left the room scowling, as though he was annoyed he had been unable to find anything wrong. He left behind him the smell of cheap soap and perspiration. Well, they didn't employ beauty queens in the Gestapo. Sam recalled the scowling face as he left the hotel and turned right past Gestapo headquarters and right again into Wenceslas Square. In fact it wasn't a square at all, but a boulevard, dominated at this end by the imposing façade of the National Museum. Thanks to the unquenchable Herr Winkel, Sam knew that the statue in the centre of the street, looking down the hill towards the Old Town, was that of the patron saint of Czechoslovakia for whom the square had been named, and that Wenceslas had not been a king but a duke, ruler of Bohemia a thousand years earlier. He was assassinated by his brother at the age of twenty-nine. His Czech name was Svaty Vaslav, and the faithful servant who had followed his footsteps in the snow was called Podiven. Podiven, Winkel said, had been hanged when he tried to avenge the murder of his master. He said it with some satisfaction, as though it had served Podiven right. Well, the snow isn't deep and crisp and even this year, Vaslav, Sam thought.

He set off down the hill, wary of the icy skim on the mosaic-stone sidewalks. Snow cleared from them was banked high in the gutters. Passing vehicles spattered slush on top of it; it looked like bad stewed apple, frozen stiff. The street would be wide and pleasant in fine weather, Sam thought, with pavement cafés shaded by handsome trees. The shops had very little in them: a dress store with two drab print frocks, the price and number of clothing coupons scrawled on a piece of card. A completely empty dairy shop, a grocery store whose window was filled with a pyramid of tinned carrots. A small queue of women waited patiently to buy, their food cards ready. A German policeman watched them impassively.

Sam dawdled purposefully. In a bookshop on the corner of Stefanstrasse there was a big display of *Mein Kampf* with its distinctive diagonal stripe. Most of the other books on sale looked like propaganda: *Der Sieg in Polen, Jahre Soldat Adolf Hitlers,* a book about the Hitler Youth, picture magazines.

Sam stopped at the bottom end of the boulevard to let a number three trolley clang past, using the pause, as he had used the earlier ones, to check the whereabouts of his shadow. It was the thin-faced man with the rimless glasses who had been with Leiche the preceding day. His leather overcoat flapped in a sudden gust of wind, and Sam smiled. *Bye, bye, blackbird,* he thought and crossed the street, hurrying into the winding alleyways of the Old Town.

He threaded his way through towards the Old Town square and skirted the church of Our Lady of Tyn. In back of it there was a narrow alley called Teyngasse. It ran beneath an arch and broke sharply to the right. On the right a carved and metal-studded wooden doorway was set into a stone arch. The door was ajar: it led into an alley beyond which were some of the old town tenements the Czechs called *pavlace.* An Opel van was parked against the wall. Sam stepped quickly into the dark hallway and pushed the door closed. He leaned against it, his heart bumping. He heard Blackbird's feet on the gritty cobblestones outside.

They hesitated, and then Sam heard them hurry away. He grinned and eased the door open. Blackbird would come out somewhere near the Hotel Paris. Which was in the opposite direction to Sam's destination, the Charles Bridge. He crossed the Old Town Square again, passing the gilded astronomical clock outside the Town Hall. Photographers were taking pictures of a young couple beneath the elaborately-carved entrance to the building. The girl was wearing a white bridal gown; the young man the uniform of a sergeant in the Waffen-SS. Ahead, a galleried street curved right, widening at the far end and leading him directly to the Clementinium, beyond which lay the Charles Bridge. Sam checked his watch: twelve forty-five. A damned close-run thing, he thought, looking back the way he had come. There was no sign of Blackbird. Nobody else showed any interest in him at all. Even so, Sam walked all the way down to the Smetana Museum to make sure. The river gave off a sullen roar as it cascaded over its weir. Gulls shrieked and wheeled above the water. The cathedral of St Vitus was limned against the pale blue winter sky.

He walked purposefully back along the river to the Charles Bridge. There were plenty of people about. Two *Wehrmacht* corporals were taking photographs of a pair of giggling Czech girls beneath the arch leading on to the bridge. An old lady smiled at him, and Sam touched the brim of his hat and said "*Dobry den*". The bridge was quite wide, with a solid stone balustrade on both sides. At regular intervals stood expressive Baroque sculptures, saints, a gilded Calvary, John the Baptist. Sam wondered who Saint Cyril and Saint Methodius were: a statue of them stood on the right hand side, about half way across. He saw a young couple coming towards him, arm in arm, and realised with a shock that it was Karl. He looked tired, Sam thought, older, more drawn. Maybe the strain is beginning to tell, Sam thought. It was a deadly game, and Karl had been playing it for a long time.

"*Grüss Gott!*" he said. The Austrian greeting had always been their recognition code. Rauth smiled, and the tiredness fell away from his expression as he did.

"Well, well," he said. "It's good to see you, Sam."

"I thought you'd be alone," Sam said.

"This is Antonie," Karl said. Sam gravely shook hands with the girl. She was shy-looking, not tall, with the face of a madonna framed by long black hair. Something about her drew his attention: the way she looked at Karl, her eyes at once loving, protective, yet fearful. She loves him, Sam thought. He wished there was a woman in his life who would look at him like that.

"Let's walk up to the Malostranskeplatz," Karl said. "There's a little café near the church. We can go there."

It was warm and cheerful in the café, which was called *U Zeleny Zaby,* the Green Frog. Above its entrance was a stone carving of a frog, painted bright green, with golden eyes. There was fresh sweet bread on sale to go with the tea. Bakers worked all night in Prague; the best time to eat bread was early in the day.

"How did you find me?" Sam asked.

There was a daily report, Karl said, a routine police listing of all visitors staying in the city at hotels, guest houses, or in private homes. It was circulated to all security agencies.

"The purpose of your visit is listed as 'international trade'," the German went on. "I thought that was rather good, in the circumstances."

"I quite liked the idea of the Gestapo reading it," Sam said.

"You've already had your visit, I imagine?"

"Indeed I have," Sam said. "Guy by the name of Leiche. He doesn't go out of his way to be charming, does he?"

"He had you followed."

"I know," Sam said. "A thin-faced character in a black leather coat. Rimless glasses. Not tall."

"Herschelmann," Karl said. "You lost him?"

"More than somewhat," Sam said.

"Leiche won't be delighted about that."

"Well," Sam grinned. "He'll just have to do the best he can to bear up." He looked at the girl. He didn't say anything. Then he looked at Karl.

"Sam," Antonie said. "Can I call you Sam?"

"You smile like that, and you most certainly can."

"Sam," she said, again. "I like that name. It sounds . . . reliable, somehow. Sam, don't worry. I know what you are thinking. I will go for a walk while you two . . . do your business. I'll meet you later. Don't get up."

She rose and put on her coat. Two soldiers in *feldgrau* looked up as she went past their table. One of them pursed his lips ruefully, and Sam felt a touch of sympathy for the lad.

"Karl," he said. "Or Paul. Which is it to be?"

"You know my name?"

"Worked it out."

"Paul, then."

"Tell me about the *Schwarze Kapelle*."

"I'm not a part of that."

"I know that, too," Sam said.

"You seem to have worked out a great deal, Sam," Paul said, with a smile. "All right, what do you want to know?"

"Did you warn them? About an investigation called *Aktion Fuchse*?"

"Yes, I did," Paul said. "Many of them are my friends. Colleagues."

"Is it true about Hess?"

"That they helped him? Yes, I believe so."

"Why?"

"I don't know. Some plan they had cooked up with the British, a coup d'état to depose Hitler. It was insanity. It never could have worked. Even if they had brought Hess back with a peace offer signed by Churchill, nobody would have listened to him. But they went ahead with it. They put everyone at risk for a damned crazy thing like that!"

"You know Werner Veick?"

"Casually, why?"

"He says that *Aktion Fuchse* is just a smoke-screen. He thinks that they're after someone here in Prague. And I think that someone is you."

"They've been after me for years, Sam," Paul said.

"Think!" Sam said. "Has anything happened recently? Anything that could have given them a line on you?"

"Yes," Paul said. "A few things." He told Sam about the arrest of the radio operators in Nusle, Pavelka's confession, the raid on the apartment in Brevnov.

"Then *Aktion Fuchse*—?"

"I see it now," Paul said. "She said it would be the end of the *Abwehr*. I see it now."

"She?"

"Someone I know," Paul said. "And now I know why she told me."

"I'm sorry," Sam said. "I don't understand."

"Veick was right," Paul said, flatly. "*Aktion Fuchse* was invented for my benefit." He frowned. "But they know I can't use it. They know the resistance has no radio contact with London."

"Pavelka would have told them that more radios are to be dropped when Wolf Trap gets in," Sam said.

"Ah," Paul said. "Wolf Trap. Yes. I want to know about that."

"You think you should?"

"I appreciate your caution, Sam. But yes, I think I need to know."

Sam told him the story: everything, from the moment that he had been instructed to obtain information on Hitler's security through the postponement of the undertaking, when bad weather prevented the team from parachuting into Czechoslovakia.

"They told me to get word to the *Schwarze Kapelle* in Berlin. When I talked to Veick it sounded . . . unright, do you know what I mean?"

"I know exactly what you mean," Paul said.

"I decided to come to Prague. I asked Veick to get word to you. How do you keep in touch with each other?"

"We use the mails, Sam."

"But the censor—?"

"Only reads letters. Our messages are sent as invoices or estimates. The censors don't open bills, you see. Our Gestapo geniuses haven't caught on to that one, yet."

"Let's hope they never do," Sam said.

"Amen to that," Paul said. "Why did you come?"

"Like I said. There was something unright about it all. I got the feeling there was some connection between the Hess thing and Wolf Trap that I don't know and you don't know, and that it puts you at risk. But I can't get a handle on it."

Paul shook his head and lit a cigarette. "I could try to find out," he said.

"Too dangerous," Sam said. "Stay the hell away from it, Paul."

"I think it's probably a little late in the day for me to worry about danger, Sam," Paul said. "I fear those black-shirted bastards are on to me, one way or another. It doesn't make much difference how they did it."

"Is there anything I can do?"

"No, there's nothing you can do," Paul said, with a try at a smile. He mashed out the cigarette. "I'll just have to give them a good run for their money."

"Why?" Sam asked. "Why do you do it?"

"A good reason, Sam," Paul said, softly. "A good enough reason." His eyes veiled, as though his thoughts were far away. For a moment, Sam thought Paul might tell him, but the moment passed. The German took a small book out of his pocket and slid it across the table. It was a battered copy of a Baedeker guide to the Rhine and the Black Forest, dated 1911. Sam raised his eyebrows.

"I'm going to give you some papers," Paul said. "They're coded. Each sheet has a number in the top right hand corner. It refers to the appropriate page and line in this Baedeker. So take good care of it."

"I will," Sam promised. He knew the documents would be meaningless without the book. "What are the papers?"

Paul took an envelope out of his pocket. It was plain, used, creased. He slid it across the table, and grinned.

"What's funny?" Sam said.

"Nothing," Paul said, thinking of Bergmann's elaborate, useless trap. This shambling, likeable American had saved his life. Had the British got the Wolf Trap team in with radios, he would have warned them about *Aktion Fuchse*. And delivered himself into Bergmann's hands.

"I've given you a report on a new type of plane, the Messerschmitt 162," he said. "Another about a glider bomber to be carried beneath a bigger plane. And the agenda for a conference which will be held in Berlin next week. The chairman will be Heydrich. All State Secretaries, together with representatives from the Ministries, the Foreign Office, and the Gestapo will be there."

"Sounds important."

"It is," Paul said, grimly. "Some time last summer, Hitler let it be known that he wanted the SS to devise what he called a final solution to the Jewish problem. Heydrich has been put in charge of carrying it out."

"Heydrich again," Sam said.

"Mr Suspicion himself," Paul said. "You know him?"

"We've met."

"He's a busy fellow," Paul said. "Apparently, our beloved Führer feels that the treatment of the Jews is still too benign." He gave a short, bitter laugh. "Benign! There is to be a drastic change in policy. All Jews are to be evacuated to the East."

"All Jews?" Sam said. "But that's not possible! There are millions of them! Where could they all be sent to?"

"The phrase in vogue at the moment is *in Nacht und Nebel*," Paul said, drily. "Into night and fog."

Sam frowned, thinking of the colossal logistical problems such a movement of people would entail. Supervision, transportation, relocation, food: it would be like moving the biggest army the world had ever seen.

"What will they do with them?" he said. "Use them as slave labour?"

"No," Paul said, quietly. "They are planning to exterminate them."

Sam shook his head, no, impossible.

"Yes, Sam," Paul said, inexorably. "I told you about Poland, Latvia, Lithuania. They're doing it there and now they're going to do it here. They've already started. Seventy-five thousand Jews have been removed from Bohemia and Moravia to Theresienstadt. And from there to God knows where."

Sam knew, as did anyone who lived in Germany longer than a week, that anti-Semitism was a cornerstone of the Nazi credo, and that Jews had been systematically reduced to the status of caged animals. Since he had last been in Germany it had become mandatory for every Jew over the age of six to wear a yellow Star of David sewn to his clothing. Millions of decent Germans countenanced the cruelty, bludgeoned into acceptance of it by Goebbels's vicious propaganda. But to exterminate an entire race? The mind refused to encompass such a proposition. How many Jews were there in Europe? Eight, ten million? The machinery did not exist by means of which it could be done, and Sam said so again to Paul Kramer.

"If it does not exist, they will manufacture it," Paul said. "Take my word for it, Sam. They are building death factories, in places no one has ever heard of. They are going to systematically destroy the Jewish race. They are already shipping treasures looted from synagogues to the ghetto here in Prague. When the Jews have been done away with, there will be a museum where Germans can go and see the strange relics of the vanished race."

"Can you find out more?"

"After the conference, perhaps," Paul said. "If your people get a radio in."

"They're still trying," Sam said. "I heard just before I left Berlin that they tried last Sunday night. The weather was too bad."

"Do they care, Sam?" Paul asked. "Does anybody care about what is happening to the Jews?"

"Yes," Sam said. "You do. I do. There are others. But not enough. Nothing like enough, yet."

He told Paul about the memorandum he had written for General Donovan. Officially, he said, there had been no reaction other than an acknowledgment that the US Department of State and the Foreign Office in London were 'aware of the problem'.

"So are the Jews," Paul said, grimly. "Make them understand, Sam!"

"I'll do my best."

"That's all any of us can do," Paul said. "Tell me, Sam, do you ski?"

Sam shook his head, surprised by this turn in the conversation, and Paul grinned. "What a pity," he said. "You could have come with us to the Tatras."

"Us?"

"Tonie and I," Paul said. "We're spending Christmas in the mountains. Come, we'll go and meet her." He shrugged into his overcoat, and Sam put on the Burberry trench coat he always wore. Paul paid the bill at the cash register near the door and they went out into the square. It was sharp and clear and cold.

Antonie was waiting in an arcade across the street. She waved and came towards them. She wore a dark blue serge coat like a pea-jacket, and a bright red woollen scarf and hat. She was, Sam thought, one hell of a pretty girl.

"Well," he said. "I guess this is where we say goodbye."

"You can get a trolley here," Paul said. "Number twenty-two. It will take you right back to Wenzelplatz. Wenceslas Square."

They stood for a moment, not speaking. Then Paul put out his hand, and Sam shook it. "Enjoy yourselves," Sam said. "In the Tatras."

Antonie laughed. "Oh, we will," she said. "I promise you that we will."

"Sam," Paul said. "Thank you."

"Sure," Sam said. A number twelve trolley grated into the square and Paul and Antonie got on it. Leaning against the lamp-standard, Sam watched the trolleycar pull away. He wondered whether he would ever see either of them again. After a while, his trolley came along and he headed back to the Esplanade. It was a little before two-fifteen when he pushed into the long lobby. The Gestapo agent, Herschelmann, was sitting in a chair by the entrance to the lounge. He jumped to his feet when he saw Sam, and rushed towards him.

"Do not move, Herr Gray!" he shouted, producing a gun. Everyone in the lobby froze stiff. Sam saw the peculiar blank look that he had seen so often in Germany come over the features of the spectators in the lobby and the adjoining lounge. I do not see, it said, I do not hear; I am not even here. What was happening to Sam, their faces said, was nothing whatsoever to do with them. They did not know him and they did not want any part of his troubles.

"You will come with me at once, Herr Gray!" Herschelmann shouted, grabbing Sam's arm.

"The hell I will!" Sam snapped, pulling his arm out of the man's grip.

"You will come at once!" Herschelmann repeated, loudly.

"What do you want?" Sam said.

"There are many question—" Herschelmann snapped, but Sam didn't let him go any further.

"You got any questions, you ask them right here," he said, putting some anger into his own voice. "Or I make some calls to Berlin. Which is it to be?" Herschelmann looked at him, indecision battling for supremacy with anger on his face. He's just not sure enough, Sam thought, putting his money on indecision. He won.

"You will wait there!" Herschelmann said, and gestured peremptorily for a telephone. The desk clerk hastily gave him one, eyes shuttling from the Gestapo man to Sam and back again. Herschelmann made a call, spoke briefly, shook his head, spoke again, telling whoever he was talking to that the swine of an American would not do what he was told. Leiche, I'll bet, Sam thought, as Herschelmann put down the telephone, and came across the lobby.

"You will to kindly wait, please," he said. Well, Sam thought, at least he said please. They did not have long to wait. The velvet curtain inside the street doors was thrust aside, and the unmistakeable figure of Superintendent Gerhard Leiche barged into the lobby. People fell back from his path as if he were red hot. He came across to Sam, the anger vivid in his eyes. Herschelmann looked almost as frightened as the silent spectators in the lobby. Leiche waved his assistant contemptuously to one side.

"You will explain instantly where you have been, and whom you have met, Herr Gray!" Leiche rasped. His voice was loud enough to carry, and Sam saw the people in the lobby cringe. Now they were part of it: the Gestapo might very well arrest everyone in sight for no other reason than the fact that they were present.

"Superintendent Leiche," Sam said, quietly, "this is the second time you've tried to bully me. May I again remind you that I am an American diplomat, and that—"

"Silence!" Leiche thundered. *"Silence!"*

Sam shrugged, making it the expression of a man dealing with someone who will not listen to reason. He saw the anger brighten in Leiche's eyes, and then watched as the man put the anger under iron control. When Leiche spoke, his voice, if harsh, was almost normal. It was an impressive performance.

"Herr Gray, it is mandatory that you cooperate with the police at all times," he said. "There is no choice in the matter."

"I am more than willing to cooperate with you," Sam said. "I just don't like being yelled at."

"That was . . . unfortunate," Leiche said, stiffly. It was about as near to an apology as he was likely to get, Sam decided, and nodded to accept it as such.

"You say you want to ask me some questions?" he said. "Does it have to be here, in public?"

"Have you anything to hide, Herr Gray?"

"Of course not."

"Then you would not object to being searched?"

"I wouldn't object," Sam said, slowly. "As long as you wouldn't object to an international incident, Superintendent."

He let Leiche digest that one. He was well aware that the massive Gestapo man could slap him into a cell in the Petschek Palace and spend all night kicking him in the balls, and he could see in Leiche's hooded eyes that that was just what Leiche would love to do. Weighed against the repercussions, however . . . Leiche nodded, coming to a decision.

"Where have you gone this morning, Herr Gray?" Leiche rasped. "Exactly, please!"

"I walked down to the Old Town Square. Over that bridge with all the statues on it, and up to the Hradschin. I stopped and had some tea in a café."

"The name?"

"I can't remember. It was by the river, below the bridge."

"*Zum Goldener Adler*?" Leiche asked.

"I don't think so," Sam said. Leiche was clumsy. It was one of the oldest tricks in the book to give a suspect the name of a place which, not having been there, he agrees he visited so as to conceal the location of the actual place he went to. The interrogator, knowing there is no such place as the one he named, now knows that the suspect is lying.

"You spoke with no one?"

"Not unless you count the waitress."

"You met no one?"

"I don't know anybody in Prague, Superintendent," Sam said. "I have never been here before."

"Then who is Karl?" Leiche shot at him.

Sam looked blank. "I don't think I understand you."

"You received a telephone call. This morning. From someone who said his name was Karl."

"Oh, that," Sam said. "That was a wrong number. He wanted someone else. Do you tap everyone's telephones, Superintendent?"

"You know nobody named Karl in Prague?" Leiche persisted, ignoring Sam's question. "Nobody named Charles Travers?"

"I told you before, Superintendent, I know nobody in Prague except the people on the list I gave you. Herr Winkel, your man there, and you. I must say, I seem to be seeing a lot of you."

"And you may be sure, Herr Gray, that if you attempt to disappear on the streets of Prague again, you will see a lot more of us!" Leiche said, heavily.

"Look, all I did was go for a walk. There's no law says I can't go for a walk, is there?"

"In Prague, Herr Gray, the law is precisely what we decide it is to be," Leiche said. "You will do very well to keep that in mind at all times. And do not, I warn you, leave this hotel alone again!" He stared at Sam for another long moment, as though wanting to say more. Then he turned abruptly and marched away, shouldering through an incoming group of guests, sending one man reeling. No one murmured a word of protest, but as the curtains closed behind Leiche, Sam heard a just-audible sigh of relief from the men and women sitting nearest to him.

He went over to the desk and got his key. The clerk looked at him warily, as though his trouble with Leiche might be contagious. Sam walked up the three steps to the elevator on the right. As he did, the Gestapo agent, Herschelmann, stubbed his cigarette in the sand tray and followed Sam into the elevator. He got off at Sam's floor, no word having passed between them. At the end of the hall was a chair where he could sit, commanding a view both of the emergency doors and the elevator.

"*Wer warten kann, hat viel getan,*" Sam said, grinning. He closed his door before Herschelmann could reply. Telling the man he deserved a rest after so much work, wouldn't make his vigil out there any more enjoyable. Especially after the roasting Leiche had no doubt given him for losing Sam in the first place. Still smiling, Sam looked at the calendar on the wall. He could finish his 'business' with the afternoon meeting. Tomorrow was Sunday. If he got an early train he could be in Berlin for dinner. He took the Baedeker guide and the papers Kramer had given him out of his inside pocket. So damned little to risk so many lives for: if Leiche had searched him . . . He shrugged. No use thinking about that. He remembered Paul Kramer's words. A good reason, Sam. A good enough reason. *I wonder if he'll make it?* he thought. *I hope to God he does.*

Prague, December 18, 1941

Walter Abendschon was depressed.

How much of the depression was due to being back in Prague, and how much to frustration, he did not know. He wished he was back in Berlin. He wanted to see Karin Graumann again, very much indeed. He had spent one of the nicest weekends he could remember having for a long time, taking her to the cinema to see Franziska Kinz and Otto Wernicke in *Die Kellnerin Anna*. Afterwards they had dinner in a restaurant called *Jagdhütte* on Eisenzahnstrasse. He had plenty of coupons: he hardly ever used them. They drank a bottle of Rudesheimer: she said it was one of her favourites, too. Afterwards, he took her back to the little house in Schmargendorf.

"I enjoyed myself," he said. "I hope you did."

"Very much," she said. She took out her key and put it in the lock. He hesitated, and she sensed his hesitation, turning to face him.

"I'd like to see you again," he said.

"I'd like that, too," Karin said.

"You don't mind—an old man, taking you out?"

"You're not an old man," she said. Her nose wrinkled when she smiled. "And you're nice."

"I'm no Lothario," he said, ruefully.

"You don't have to be," she said. She kissed him lightly on the lips. "Come back whenever you like."

He smiled and nodded, feeling foolish, yet happy. She waved to him as he turned the corner.

On the Sunday he took her with him to Oranienburg. She waited at the Hotel Sonne while he drove across to Sachsenhausen and saw the two English prisoners. The camp was on the far side of a canal, a dour and depressing place that stank of despair. Prisoners in striped overcoats were clearing the snow in front of the *Schutzhaftlagergebäude*, the squat administration building with a slogan on its gate announcing 'Freedom Through Work'. The SS guards led him to the hut set aside for the special prisoners, the *Prominenten*. On each of the barrack huts a word was painted. He asked one of the guards what they were.

"Camp motto," the guard said laconically. Abendschon read them, one after the other. *There is one road to freedom. Its milestones are: obedience, assiduity, honesty, order, cleanliness, sobriety, truthfulness, self-sacrifice, and love of the Fatherland!* Barbed wire-topped walls, electrified fences, guard dogs: Abendschon suppressed a shudder, and tried not to see the slouching, defeated men all around him.

He had asked to see only the junior of the two Secret Service men. Ex-Captain Payton Best was a very English Englishman. He wore a monocle. He spoke perfect German, and Abendschon interrogated him carefully for more than two hours about his connections with the Czech Intelligence officers, Bartik and Frank. Best was anxious to please: the fact had been noted in his dossier, which was why Abendschon had chosen to talk to him and not his superior, ex-Major Richard Stevens. Stevens, his dossier said, was unreliable, and given to 'romancing'.

Abendschon's patient questioning put Best at his ease, and he talked freely. He said Stevens had been contacted through NV *Handelsdienst Veer Het Continent,* the genuine transport firm which was British Intelligence's cover operation in Holland, by some Czechs who said they worked for the German *Sicherheitsdienst*. Stevens thought he might be able to 'turn' them. He asked Bartik of Czech Intelligence to come and look the men over. Bartik was mistrustful; perhaps he sensed a trap.

"Stevens wouldn't listen to him," Best told Abendschon. "He thought we had a fine chance of penetrating German Intelligence. Insisted we press on with the operation."

They fixed another meeting with the Czechs, who brought them more information. They said there were others who might work with them, and who might be amenable to a *treff*. It seemed too good to be true. Stevens was very excited. This time they asked Colonel Frank, who divided his time between Holland and England, for his advice.

"He said there was someone who could tell us if what the Czechs were telling us was true," Best said. "He told us he had a very highly placed source inside the German *Abwehr*, a man of complete reliability."

"You met this man?"

"Yes, he came to our offices on Nieuw Uitleg."

"His name?"

"As I remember it, he called himself Rauth. Captain Rauth. He was in Army uniform."

Abendschon took out his photograph of Kramer. "Is this him?"

"Yes," Best said. "That's the man."

As easy as that, Abendschon thought. "What did he tell you?"

"He told us we were being tricked. He said the Czechs were agents of Heydrich's *Sicherheitsdienst*."

"Were they?"

"We fixed another meeting, faced them with it. They acted as if *we* had betrayed *them*. They promised to prove that they were genuine. They would bring a senior officer to meet us. A Captain Schemmel, who was one of the most important officers in *Abwehr* III. We agreed to another *treff*, this time in a café on the border. It was a trick, of course. They grabbed us and made us prisoner. They took us to Berlin and after that they brought us here. We should have listened to Rauth."

Simple, Abendschon thought. Even sad, in a way. Using

Kramer to help the British, Frank had unwittingly betrayed him. And pointlessly: Heydrich's men had kidnapped the Englishmen anyway. There was no longer any question about it: Kramer was the traitor for whom the Prague Gestapo had been searching all these years. Strangely enough, the knowledge did not make him happy. Poor bastard, he thought. He drove across to the Hotel Sonne at Oranienburg. It was a pretty little town, surrounded by wooded heathland. It was hard to believe Berlin lay on the other side of the rolling hills, thirty kilometres away. Harder still to believe that beyond the stand of pines that crowned the bluff which Abendschon could see through the hotel window, lay the monstrosity that was Oranienburg concentration camp. He picked at the meal of stew which was all that was on offer.

"Aren't you hungry?" Karin asked.

"Not very," he said. "That damned place——."

"Is it—are they as awful as people say?"

"Worse," Abendschon said, angrily. He wanted to say more, but one or two of the other guests in the dining room were looking at him. There were plenty around who would report you to the Gestapo for a good deal less than talking about the KZs.

"Did you find out what you wanted to find out?" she asked. She was wearing a lemon-yellow woollen sweater and a brown corduroy skirt. Her hair shone in the bright, hard winter sunlight, a warm gold colour. She had a good figure too. Not the kind that stopped traffic; just well-made, everything in the right amounts and in the right places. He thought: if I wasn't sure she would call me an old fool, I'd tell her I was falling in love with her.

"I have to tell you something," he said. "I'll have to go back to Prague."

"Right away?"

"Tomorrow. As soon as I can. Karin—I know who killed your husband."

"Oh," she said, softly. "Can you tell me?"

"Not yet," he said. "But I will."

"What will you do?"

"Hand him over to the Gestapo, I suppose."

She shivered. "Alben always used to say that was the part of his job he hated most. Bringing in prisoners. For the executioners, he used to say."

"They're that, all right," Abendschon said.

"Could we go now?" Karin said.

Neither of them wanted to go back to Berlin. To hell with them, he thought. Being with her made him feel like that. They went for a drive. It had been a very cold night, and frost had woven delicate lacings of ice on the bare branches of the trees. They saw children skating on frozen ponds, and snowmen with eyes made of pebbles.

He told her about Eva and the boys; she talked about her husband.

"I was working in a bookstore," she told him. "It went bankrupt in 1932. I couldn't get another job. My father was at home, he had a stroke. I left home every morning as if I was going to work. Then came 1933 and there was work again. My father read *Mein Kampf* and he wouldn't have anything to do with the Nazis, Mütti either. But what good was that? They couldn't give me work, the Nazis could. Then I met Alben."

"Was this in Berlin?"

"No, in Nürnberg. We were both from there. He warned me that if I wanted to keep my job, I'd better join the Party. I joined to please him as much as anything. It wasn't till I'd joined he told me what his job was. I didn't know what it meant. I thought he was some kind of detective."

"When did you move to Berlin?"

"1938," she said. "Alben was doing well. He had reached the rank of *Kriminalobersekretar*."

The sky was turning the colour of slate. Flecks of snow touched the windshield, and Abendschon turned on the wipers. They made hardly any difference.

"I miss him, you know," she said. "I still half-expect him to come in through the door, asking me what's for supper."

"I know," Abendschon said. "I know."

He drove to the little house in Schmargendorf. They had spoken little during the ride through the city. It had started to snow again; feathery flakes mantled her coat. He patted her shoulder clumsily.

"Take care of yourself," he said.

Karen Graumann smiled. "Do you really want to go, Walter?"

"Yes," he said. "No. No, I don't. I want to stay with you."

"Well, then, you fool," she said. "Come in out of the snow."

The following morning, Sunday, December 7, the Japanese launched a surprise attack on the American naval base at Pearl Harbour in Hawaii, virtually destroying the entire American navy. Next day, Roosevelt declared war on Japan, and the British immediately followed suit. There was pandemonium at the Wilhelmstrasse and in the Bendlerblock. Walter Abendschon tried a dozen times to reach Bergmann in Prague, only to be told that every line was busy. When he finally got through on the Wednesday afternoon, he was told that Heydrich, Frank and Bergmann were already in Berlin. They had flown in to meet the Führer on his return from the Eastern front the preceding day.

"All hell has broken loose down here, Walter!" Bergmann's aide, Peter Eckhardt told him. "We're on the telephone twenty-four hours a day, trying to let everyone who was invited to that damned conference at Grossen Wannsee know that it's been cancelled."

"What am I supposed to do, then?"

"Try and contact Bergmann at RHSA headquarters," Eckhardt suggested. "And Walter—?"

"What?"

"Buy yourself a steel helmet," Eckhardt said. Abendschon could almost see his boyish grin. He tried to reach Bergmann at Wilhelmstrasse 102 a dozen times; each time he was told the *Standartenführer* was not available. Well, Abendschon thought. He's your damned traitor, Bergmann, not mine.

On the evening of Thursday, December 11, speaking to the Reichstag in the Kroll Opera House, Hitler declared war on America.

"Is he insane?" Abendschon said, hardly believing what he was hearing. "Has he finally gone absolutely insane?"

"Walter, listen!" Karin said. She was sitting in the armchair opposite him, on the other side of the little fireplace.

They liked listening to the radio in the evening. Karen was fond of operetta music; Lehár, Strauss.

"We will always strike first!" Hitler was shouting in that rough, compelling, unique voice. "We will always deal the first blow!"

"It's true!" Abendschon said. "He's gone crazy!"

Roosevelt, Hitler was saying, was as mad as Woodrow Wilson, first inciting war, then falsifying the causes, slowly but surely leading mankind to war. International Jewry, Bolshevik Russia, Roosevelt's régime were equated. "I have therefore arranged for passports to be handed to the American chargé d'affaires today and—" The rest was drowned by cheers.

"America!" Abendschon said. "Can you believe it? He's not content to fight Russia in the East and Britain in the West. He's got to take on America was well!"

"Will it be bad, Walter?" Karin asked.

"Worse than bad," he told her, darkly.

He managed to contact Bergmann the next day, and, as he had both feared and expected, Bergmann told him to return to Prague.

"What about Kramer?" Abendschon said. "Do you want me to arrest him?"

"Do nothing!" Bergmann shouted at him down the telephone. "This matter is too sensitive to be handled by anyone except the *Reichsprotector*!"

Sensitive, Abendschon thought. As I'll bet your arse is, from being kicked by Heydrich for the complete and utter lack of results achieved by your stupid *Aktion Fuchse*.

"And what shall I do when I return to Prague, *Standartenführer*?"

"Prepare your report. Have it ready for my return!"

"And when will that be?"

"You will be advised," Bergmann said, coldly, and hung up. *Zu befehl, Standartenführer,* Abendschon thought sourly. That was what Bergmann's kind always wanted, the mindless robot obedience they taught them in the SS. Loyalty is my honour. Yes, and stupidity is my reason, he added.

Well, he was back in Prague. He still hadn't done the report. He hated paperwork like the plague at the best of times, which this most certainly was not. He was down in the dumps; *schwermütige Stimmung,* they called it. He missed being with Karin. No fool like an old fool, he thought, skirting the baroque bronze fountain in the Second Courtyard of the Hradschin. Prague was cold and cheerless, a damp and unpleasant cold that penetrated even the heaviest overcoat. Most days it snowed; the gangs of forced labourers usually had it cleared off the streets by midday, but Peter Eckhardt, who had been out to Jungfern-Breschan, said it was still quite deep out in the country. The weather did nothing to lift Abendschon's depression, and neither did his enforced inactivity. Heydrich and Bergmann were still in Berlin. Our little yellow friends certainly spoiled things for everyone at the Wilhelmstrasse, he thought, not without satisfaction. The way things were looking, they'd all be working overtime right through Christmas.

He had checked on Kramer, in spite of Bergmann's embargo. To his surprise, he learned that Kramer had gone skiing with the Novak girl in the High Tatras. Bit young for him, he thought, and then grinned. Look who's talking.

He went up the stairs to Bergmann's office. Peter Eckhardt lifted a hand in greeting. Phones were shrilling; the air of suppressed excitement was almost tangible.

"What's going on, Peter?" Abendschon called across the room. Peter Eckhardt made a 'wait a moment' signal. He was standing next to the big teleprinter. It was chattering busily, pumping up the twin sheets of paper with the carbon between them. It stopped. Eckhardt tapped out the acknowledgment and tore off the message.

Eckhardt came across the room. "By God, Walter, it's all happening in Berlin!" He waved the teleprinter message. "The Führer's sacked old Brauchitsch! He has personally taken command of the armed forces!"

"The Führer?" Abendschon said. "Commander in chief?"

"He's kicking generals downstairs by the dozen!" Eckhardt said. "Strauss has lost Ninth Army, Leeb has lost Army Group North. Kluge is to go, von Bock! And . . . *Himmelswille!* Even Guderian!"

He once boasted he had created more Field Marshals in a single day than even Napoleon, Abendschon thought. He remembered listening to the harsh voice on Karin's radio,

210

and thinking how full of hate it was. Did the man know no other emotion?

"If he goes on like this," Eckhardt said, "we may all get four stars yet!"

"What it is to have such a leader!" Abendschon said. Eckhardt looked at him uncertainly for a moment, then decided that he not heard the sour note in Abendschon's voice.

"Can I do anything for you, Walter?" he said.

"Yes," Abendschon said. "Give me a rough idea when your boss will be back."

"Not until at least January twenty-first," Eckhardt said, confidently.

"How do you know that?"

"Because the Wannsee conference has been scheduled for Tuesday, the twentieth," Eckhardt said. "There'd be no point in his coming back here before then. Anyway, nothing's happening in Prague."

"You're right," Abendschon said, thinking, at least I don't have to do the damned report yet. "Listen, Peter, I have some leave due."

"Don't we all, dear heart."

"The difference is, I'm taking mine. I'm going back to Berlin."

"You can't," Eckhardt said. "Every seat on every train and plane is full."

Abendschon produced Heydrich's letter and laid it flat on Eckhardt's desk. "Read that and weep," he said.

"Oh, Christ, Walter, I don't need any more problems!" Eckhardt said.

"Maybe," Abendschon said. "But you've got them."

"All right," Eckhardt groaned. "I'll try to get you out on Monday."

"Tomorrow," Abendschon said, and left Eckhardt to it. He walked down the stone staircase and out into the courtyard. The clouds parted; a weak sun laid a soft yellow light on the snow-limned lines of the fountain. *Stille Nacht, Heilige Nacht,* Abendschon hummed to himself as he walked through the archway to the main entrance. It looked as if it might be a halfway decent Christmas.

Stary Smokovec, December 22, 1941

The train pulled into the station, and as they got out the driver let off steam with a roaring hiss. Someone down at the far end of the platform shouted the name of the town. They crossed the tracks and walked behind the railway station and there was the *post-auto,* a yellow, single-decker bus with a basketwire rack fixed on the rear for skis. Paul put the skis in while Antonie got them a seat. Everyone was smiling. The driver came and clipped their tickets and then got into his seat. He put the bus in gear and they moved off through the narrow streets of Poprad, past shops whose lights glowed yellow against the grey of morning. The main street rose sharply, turning right and right again, then left. There were little shops on the corners, a butcher, a bakery, an *apotheke.* The bus stopped for a few minutes to pick up the post outside the main post office. The driver and a fat man in a blue smock exchanged a few words in Czech.

"*Kam pojedes na dovolenou?*" the postman asked.

"*Rad bych jel na Praha,*" the driver replied. "*Kam jdes, Tomass?*"

They were talking about going on holiday. The driver was going to Prague. Everyone in the bus had a cheerful face. There was a festive feeling in the air: Christmas was coming. The driver shouted goodbye to his friend, and the bus lurched into motion again up the narrow, snow-covered street. People walking ahead of them moved out of the way. Some of them waved at the driver. Then they were out of the town and going up a long slope. Through the window they could see the old town below. The railway station looked like a child's toy. The lines gleamed in the pale sunshine, factories and breweries beyond them.

Now they could see the towering peaks of the Tatras, rolling from one end of the horizon to the other, grey-black rising to meet pure whiteness, sloping lines of snow laid across the flanks of the mountains like foam on a galloped horse. Tendrils of mist clung to the lower slopes and threaded between the thick stands of trees.

"Oh, it's so beautiful!" Tonie whispered. "I wish I knew the names of all the trees: larch, pine, birch . . ." She slid her arm through his and they held hands, like schoolkids.

Up and still further up the bus climbed, at ten and sometimes fifteen miles an hour, the wheels slipping once in a while until the chains bit into the compressed snow. The valley below looked like a map now; they were above the thousand metre line. The snow was banked deep beside the looping road. Once or twice they saw people on skis, standing by the side of the road to watch the bus go by.

"When I was a little girl I used to love it when it snowed," Tonie said. "I was always impatient to go outside. I used to hop from one foot to the other while Mama buttoned my coat, thinking, hurry, hurry, or it will all be gone. And I would rush outside, and there would be nobody else there at all, and it was as if the whole world belonged to me. I always thought that was the best time of all, when the snow was still falling and nobody was there."

It was good to see her smiling, Paul thought. She was so young, and she had seen death and pain and she had done things no young woman should ever have to do. He wanted to make her forget that, just for a while. He had told Jan that, and Jan had nodded, clapping him on the shoulder.

"Go and be together," he said. "Be together. Take everything life offers you!"

The bus turned a corner and they saw the village, snow a foot deep on the wooden roofs. Up ahead, on a rise, they saw a big Alpine-style hotel with a spa-yellow exterior, all cupolas and balconies and dormers.

"Grand Hotel!" the driver announced, pulling the bus to a halt with a hiss of brakes. He worked the lever to open the door and got out, offering his helping hand to the ladies. As he handed Tonie down, he said something to her which Paul did not catch. He saw her smiling as he got the skis out of the basket at the rear of the bus. A porter with a green uniform saluted and put their bags and the skis on to a sled. They walked up the drive to the hotel.

"What did the driver say?" Paul asked Tonie.

"He said I look good in ski pants."

"He was right."

She was wearing a blue ski jacket and navy trousers with a white, roll-neck sweater. The pants were snug over waist and hip. Paul grinned as she went up the steps ahead of him. God had one of his better days when he designed the lines of a woman's thighs, he decided. A big, sandy-haired man bumped into him.

"*Prominte, prosim,*" he said.

"*Nic se nestalo,*" Paul said, automatically. The man reminded him a little of Sam Gray. He wondered what happened to the big American. Probably back in America now, he thought—an America at war with Germany.

He still found it hard to believe. He had listened to Hitler's speech on the radio, heard the bedlam of cheers which all but drowned the words, with mounting dismay. It had had to come, of course, but with Hitler's declaration of war Paul's last direct links with the Allies were severed. The only way to get information to them now would be by radio. The feeling of oppression and impending disaster swamped him.

I am not going to think about the war while we are here, he told himself, as they went through the formalities of registering. I am going to think of nothing but Tonie. Just for these few days: surely we deserve that much time together?

They went into the restaurant, empty at this time of day except for a blonde girl in a black dress with a white apron. They asked her for some tea. She shrugged to show that she was used to the unreasonable foibles of guests and stopped the lackadaisical straightening of tablecloths she has been engaged in. While they were waiting, they walked over to the window, and looked out at the view.

Paths cut deep in the snow led from chalet to wooden chalet. All the buildings were weathered a warm golden brown. The sky was intensely blue, and the pines and spruces looked black against the stark whiteness of the snow. Beyond the tree line, hulking huge against the sky, black and white and touched with golden sunlight and dark blue shadows, stood the mountains.

"What's the name of that big peak?" Tonie said, pointing. She squinted her eyes against the bright sun. Her nose wrinkled up. She was as excited as a little girl, he thought.

"Mount Gerlach," he told her.

"There's a little railway station at the other end of the street," she said. "Is there a train?"

"It's a funicular," he said. "It goes up to Hrebienok. There's a little café at the top. If it was summertime we could walk up there. The ground would be covered with gentians. We could pick raspberries, and whortleberries as big as cherries."

"Oh, it's all so beautiful!" she said again. Her face was flushed by the chill edge of the wind, and she looked very desirable in her blue ski jacket. She caught him looking at her, and saw what was in his eyes. She smiled the smile of a woman who knows secrets.

"I'm glad you brought me up here, *Oberst,*" she said. It had become an endearment. He remembered the first time she had used it, differently then.

"So am I," he said.

"It's not wrong of us, is it, Paul? To have a few days of happiness when there are so many unhappy people in the world?"

"I don't think so."

"We live so much of our lives on the edge of an abyss," she whispered. "I want to forget all that. Just for a while."

"All right," he said. "We'll try."

"And—no promises, darling Paul?"

"No promises that can't be broken," he said.

After they had their tea, they went outside to put on their ski boots. There were benches along the front of the hotel. The sun was warm on their faces. First, they laced up the inner lining, and then pulled the criss-cross rubber strapping into the hooked eyelets that closed the boots snug and tight against their ankles. Paul swung their skis up on his shoulder, grunting with the effort.

"You're puffing and panting already," Tonie laughed.

"I'm an old man," he said. "Show a little respect."

They took the cable car up to Hrebienok and walked across to the ski lift. It was a simple T-bar which would take them up a couple of hundred metres to the *Horna Luka,* the Upper Meadow. They stopped to put on the wooden skis, hooking the rear wires over the notches in the boot heels, and then pushing the binding lever forward.

"I'm not very good, you know," Tonie said. "You'll have to give me lessons."

"Just put yourself entirely in my hands, *Liebchen,*" he said, with a theatrical leer.

"With pleasure," she simpered. Then she looked at him

in the direct way he had come to recognise as typical. He kissed her on the lips. Her nose was cold.

"Race you to the lift," he said, and slid down to the cabin. The slope was not very steep. Paul put his arm around Tonie's shoulder as they went up. She sang a song about a red scarf, her voice light and happy.

Cerveny satecaku, kolem se toc, kolem se toc, kolem se toc,
Muj mily se hneva, ja nevim proc, ja nevim proc, ja nevim
proc . . .

At the top of the lift, a boy wearing an Afrika Korps hat with earmuffs deftly caught the towbar. He looked like the picture that Van Gogh painted of himself after he cut off his ear. Tonie stood on the crest of the slope, looking down.

"It looks steep," she said, dubiously.

"Just go easily to begin with," Paul said. "Sideslip a little. Don't be af—"

She was gone in a peal of laughter, soaring down the slope like a bird. Paul laughed out loud. Vixen, he thought, and pushed off after her, feeling the strain on muscles he had not used for a year. The wind was keen and cold on his face, making his eyes water a little. He did not like wearing goggles: they cut out the peripheral vision. He kept his knees bent to absorb the bumps, swaying into the turns, left and then right and then left again, up over the first crest and then swooping down the sharper incline between the trees. Flying, he thought, it was the nearest thing to flying you could do with your feet still on the ground.

He stopped at the bottom and looked back. Tonie had reached the first crest ahead of him, but stayed there, looking at the far mountains. He wished he could photograph her there like that, standing against an empty, cobalt sky, with the crisp edge of the white snow falling away in front of her. He watched her, loving every line of her body, as she zigzagged down the hill, graceful and sure. Then she was running across the level stretch towards him, the strong legs moving the wooden skis. She stopped in a swoosh of snow, a rime of frost on her hair, cheeks glowing, eyes dancing.

"Oh," she said. "That was wonderful!"

216

"Tomorrow we'll go on the sledge track," he said. "Maybe we'll see some chamois."

They went up to the top of the little lift again. This time the boy with the Afrika Korps hat smiled at them. Then down they swooped, luxuriating in the sheer physical pleasure of skill and speed, conscious only of white snow, yellow sunlight, blue shadow. At midday they had soup and bread in the Bilikova mountain lodge, and went back to the slopes while the afternoon sun was warm and strong. And slowly, Paul felt his nagging fears ebbing. It was no use worrying, anyway. The time for worrying would come soon enough.

When the sun began to sink behind the top of the mountains, it grew very cold. They took the funicular down to the village. As they came down they could see children outside the post office, helping to load parcels on to a sledge. Some of them were throwing snowballs at each other. Paul and Tonie slid-walked over to the shed in back of the hotel and took off their skis, stacking them in the pegged racks. They brushed the snow off their boots with a cane broom at the doorway and clumped into the hotel, up the stairs and along the corridor. The wood-block flooring squeaked and squealed beneath the coconut matting. Outside each room there was a big felt mat. They took off their boots and put them on the mat and went into the room. It was very warm. When he looked in the mirror, Paul saw that his hair was spiky with snow. I'll have to get a hat, he thought. They put their gloves on the radiator to dry, and took off their heavy sweaters. Then they just fell on the bed, happily tired. After a little while, Tonie kissed him, and then she said "Love me, Paul. Love me. Now!"

She turned on her side, the soft, strong sinuosities of her body hard against his own. Her lips were hot. He kissed her forehead, her throat. He could feel the soft, strong, slow throb of life beneath the skin. She held his head against her body and then sighed.

"Wait, my darling," she whispered. "Wait."

She got off the bed and undressed, standing before him almost defiantly unashamed. Her breasts were high and firm, the nipples the colour of coral. She watched with frank interest as Paul took off his clothes.

217

"You have a good body," she said. "Strong."

"Come here," he said. "Talk later."

She came to him. She made love the way she did everything else, with no coynesses or pretended modesty. Her mouth was hot. She bit his lips gently, caressed him. Her hands pulled him hard against her.

"I love the smell of you," she said. "The man smell."

She burrowed down between his legs, grasping him with both her hands, sucking him, nibbling. It was like an electrical current. He thrust his tongue into her dark, moist cleft. She moaned.

"Now, now, now," she said, writhing. "Put it in me now!"

She turned like an otter and sat astride him, looking down at him with blind eyes. He felt himself go up and into her like an oiled piston. He exploded, the long, hot, aching upwardness that took both of them out and away, in oneness, then, and then it was a long, quickening rushing, like a ski-jump, soaring into nothingness, the falling of a leaf on a still, summer day, down, down, returning to each other, united, spent.

And she was crying. She was thinking of Josef. It had been like a door, closed between them. Until this long, sweet moment of love brought it all back to her, and she remembered him, and wept.

"I'm sorry," she said.

"Don't be."

They were silent for a long time, apart together. He thought his thoughts; she thought hers. After a while, she stirred.

"You didn't mind," she said. It was not a question.

"No," he said.

"I don't want there to be any ghosts," she said. "I want to be with you, Paul. Always."

Always is a long time, he thought. He laid a gentle finger on her lips. "Hush," he said. "We have tomorrow and tomorrow. We have time." Snow began to fall. Somewhere in the village, the children were singing carols.

"Yes," Tonie whispered. "All the time in the world."

Washington, December 22, 1941

At precisely 6.58 p.m. the Lockheed airplane which had brought Winston Churchill from Hampton Roads, Virginia, touched down at National Airport. Followed by Averell Harriman, Lord Beaverbrook, Admiral Sir Dudley Pound, Air Chief Marshal Sir Charles Portal and General Sir John Dill, the British Premier came down the ramp from the plane and hurried to meet President Roosevelt, propped up against a black bulletproof limousine that had once been the property of Al Capone. They clasped hands with evident pleasure.

"Where are the rest of your people?" Roosevelt asked.

"Coming up by train," Churchill said gruffly. "I couldn't wait." The great 'Arcadia' conference between the British and American war councils had begun. Winston Churchill and his Chiefs of Staff had crossed the Atlantic in the *Duke of York,* bringing with them Britain's design for winning the war, the 'Germany First' strategy which Churchill wanted the Grand Alliance to adopt. Well, there'd be a lot of heated discussion about that, and many other things, Sam thought, on a day which had begun with the announcement of the Selective Service Act, conscripting all able-bodied males between the ages of twenty and forty-four, and ended with the news that Japan's Fourteenth Army, led by General Masaharu Homma, had landed at Lingayen Gulf in the Philippines. It was going to be a long war, Sam thought, as he lay on his bed in the Hay-Adams Hotel. He got up and poured some of the wine he had ordered, thinking back over the events of the past few weeks. Saying it had been hectic would be like calling hurricane weather 'windy'.

By the time Foreign Minister Joachim von Ribbentrop, wearing his most resplendent uniform and his most frigid expression, began to read aloud to Leland Morris, the American chargé d'affaires in Berlin, the official German declaration of war, Sam's plane had already touched down in Lisbon. He was glad to be out of Berlin: the chill correctness of the Germans had turned to ugly hostility, and for the first time in his life, Sam had been afraid to walk the streets of the capital. Lisbon was cold and unwelcoming, cheerless and windswept, with rain coming in off the Atlantic. He went to the British Embassy and filed a preliminary report, to be cabled to Donovan in Washington, and LCS in London. What strings were pulled to get him the priority seat on the Clipper which Pat Kelly, Pan Am's genial, smiling manager, told him he had, Sam neither knew nor asked. He went out to Horta and got on the plane as if he was in a dream; or a nightmare, he was not sure which. The whole journey had had a nightmarish quality.

He reached Washington on December 12, a blustery Friday afternoon with bright clear skies and a wind that took his breath away. He had only time to shower, shave, and hastily change his clothes before the car came to pick him up. The driver was morose.

"Them dirty Japs pick a goddamned fahn time to go startin' a war!" he complained. "Some Christmas present, man. *Some* Christmas present!"

He told Sam that when the news about Pearl Harbour had come in one 'patriot' had chopped down four of the Japanese cherry trees in the Tidal Basin.

"Dey even painted de windows of de White House black," he said. "*Some* Christmas present, man!"

Sam reported to Donovan, who listened intently to everything Sam told him. He did not speak, and his eyes never left Sam's face. Sam left nothing out.

"You took a lot of chances, Sam," Donovan said, when he finished.

"They needed taking, General."

"Your conclusion is that there was something about Wolf Trap that wasn't kosher?"

"This is what I've got, General," Sam said. "The British helped the German secret service to get Hess out. There is a connection between that and a plot to overthrow Hitler. The British mount Wolf Trap. Purpose, to kill Hitler, which in turn provides opportunity or spur to the same German secret service to stage a coup d'état. There is no mention of Hess. There can't be two simultaneous plots to depose Hitler going on in the German secret service. Therefore—"

"The British aren't telling us the whole story."

"I don't know, General," Sam said. "I just don't know."

"Well, you'll get your chance to find out," Donovan said. "The Brits want to reactivate Wolf Trap."

"What?" Sam said, incredulously.

"That's why you got priority transportation, son," Donovan said. "The minute they got your report from Lisbon, they cabled us asking for a meeting, A-1 priority. I needed you here to brief me."

"But there's no way they could get to Hitler now!" Sam said. "It's lunacy."

"I gather they're thinking of another target."

"Jesus Christ!" Sam said, impatiently. "This is beginning to sound like Alice in Wonderland! Don't they have any goddamned idea what it's like in Occupied Europe?"

"Sam, Sam, take it easy," Donovan said. "They've asked for a meeting. So we'll have a meeting. Maybe we can find out what the hell the connection is between Hess and the Wolf Trap thing."

"Maybe," Sam said, sourly.

"I'll give you the wisdom of the ages in three words, son," Donovan said. "Wait and see." He was silent for a moment. "You know that the Russians have counter-attacked?"

"I saw the papers." The Washington *Post* had run a headline story about the Red Army pushing the Germans back from Moscow. The Russian winter was doing to Hitler's Panzers what it had done to Napoleon's *Grande Armée*.

"Would that change things in Germany?" Donovan asked. "If Hitler started losing?"

"Maybe," Sam said again. "But I suspect the German secret service is going to have too much on its plate to play footsie with the British, or anyone else."

"I think we'll let it wait, then," Donovan said. "Let's hear what they have to say. They'll be here in ten days. Meanwhile . . . give it to me in writing, together with your . . . I won't call them suspicions. Your guesses, maybe. Will you do that?"

"Yes, sir, of course," Sam said. He hesitated for a moment, making the silence work for him. Donovan looked up, frowning.

"Something else?"

"This other thing Kramer told me about," Sam said. "Hitler's plans for the Jews. The final solution."

"I don't know what the hell we can do, Sam," Donovan said, running a hand through his hair. "It's not something this office is equipped to handle."

Do they care, Sam? he heard Kramer asking. *Does anyone care?*

"I put in a long report about this back in April, General," Sam said. "When the SS sent its *Einsatzgrüppen* into Russia and Poland. Now this. I'm beginning to wonder. Does anyone care?" Donovan's head came up and Sam saw the anger in the normally mild blue eyes.

"You've done a fine job, Sam," he said. "But it doesn't give you the right to ask me a question like that!"

"I'm sorry, General," Sam said, and he was.

"It's all right," Donovan said. "You're tired. I'm tired. We're all tired. I'll talk to State again. I don't know how much good it will do, but I'll talk to them."

"Yes, sir," Sam said. "Thank you."

"Tell me something, Sam," Donovan said. "How long have you been in the field?"

Sam did some sums in his head. He was surprised at the answer. With the exception of a fortnight's 'vacation'—which he used to go to Berchtesgaden to find out what he could about the layout of Hitler's Alpine retreat on the Obersalzberg—he had been 'out' for almost three years.

"I went to Berlin in May, '38," he said.

"A long time," Donovan said. "You need a break, son."

"I'm fine, General."

"Do it," Donovan said. "That's an order."

"Well," Sam said, thinking *why not?* Writing his report would take only three or four days. After that, he would have little or nothing to do until 'Arcadia' was convened. "I always wanted to go south, to look at some of the Civil War Battlefields. But I never got around to it. Maybe this would be as good a time as any."

"Draw a car from the motor pool," Donovan said. "I'll give you a warrant for gas."

"A warrant?"

"Scuttlebutt is that gas is going to be rationed," Donovan

told him. "There's already a 'gas-curfew' from seven at night till seven a.m."

"Thanks, General."

"You earned it," Donovan said.

So Sam borrowed a blue Dodge sedan from the motor pool and headed south on Highway 95, with no particular destination in mind. It gave him the strangest feeling to be back in America again. It was all so raw, so new. There were no old buildings, no great palaces and museums stained and darkened with the patina of centuries. And no sign at all of war: no martial displays, no massed banners and serried ranks of soldiers such as one always saw in Germany. In his memory he heard the brass bands thumping out the '*Badenweiler*', the march of Hitler's regiment in the Great War.

Here in America, the same roadside diners served the same truckers they had been serving for years. Huge billboards, extravagantly coloured, exhorted the public to visit amusement parks, motor hotels, vacation spots. While Sam had been keeping his rendezvous with Werner Veick in Berlin, the Navy had beaten the Army 14–6 in their annual football game at Municipal Stadium in Philadelphia. Again the thought came to Sam that his countrymen had no real conception yet of what war was. Once, a long time ago, they had known; but that time was forgotten.

He saw a sign for Fredericksburg. There had been a battle there, he knew. He turned off the highway and drove into the town. It was a pretty, sleepy sort of place. There was a National Parks Center on the corner of Lafayette Boulevard, where he picked up leaflets which directed him to the scenes of the fighting. He walked along a lane with a fieldstone wall on his right which looked down a gentle slope towards suburban houses. In 1862, it had been open ground, perhaps a mile to the town. On a bluff overlooking this ground was a house built by a French Huguenot family named Marye. The house was called 'Brompton', the bluff on which it stood Marye's Heights. He tried to imagine it crowned with row upon row of Confederate artillery. General Robert E. Lee had placed General Longstreet there to his left, with 'Stonewall' Jackson on the right flank, to await the Army of the Potomac, commanded by the newly-appointed Ambrose E. Burnside, he who had given his name to the mutton-chop side-whiskers, a stubborn ditherer who could not admit error.

As the fog lifted on the morning of December 13, with the earth like iron and snow hard on the nearby hills, Burnside committed his Army to action. In parade-ground order, his Federals advanced upon the astonished Lee's fortified positions.

Sam stood by the stone wall and tried to imagine the Georgia boys standing ready in the sunken road behind it, and blue-clad Federals advancing up the slope towards them, bugles blaring, bayonets glinting in the thin winter sun. Lee's artillery mowed them down like standing corn. They regrouped, came on again, only to walk into the withering hail of musket fire poured into their ranks at point-blank range by the Rebels behind that terrible stone wall.

The Federals died in battle-lines, felled in windrows. Hundreds of them, thousands. Yet still Burnside insisted that the wall be taken, the Heights invested. Brigade after brigade was hurled forward and slaughtered. Hopeless, condemned, line after line of fresh-faced lads in Federal blue walked knowingly into the jaws of death. Two days later, Burnside retreated. Twelve and a half thousand of his men were dead, wounded or missing. And all for nothing.

Sam got into his car and sat quietly smoking a cigarette, thinking about the battle, about men marching bravely towards certain death. Why do they do it? he wondered. What drives them on? Death sits grinning on a stone marked with your name, beckoning. Every sense, every nerve, every ounce of reason screams no, no, no! The body does not gladly offer itself to be torn apart by red-hot lead or whirring canister. Yet the man goes bravely forward to the slaughter, head high, singing to keep up his courage. Why?

He thought of Paul Kramer, of the young Czech soldiers who made up the Wolf Trap team. Why do they do it? Because it is their duty? Out of the nowhere mists of memory came a picture of his father reading Goethe. *'What then is your duty? What the day demands.'* He drove back to Washington on the Sunday night and checked into the Hay-

Adams: more string-pulling, he thought; hotel accommodation was harder to find than hen's teeth.

He went across to the window and looked out across Lafayette Square. Glimmers of light escaped through the makeshift blackout of the White House. Under the portico of the driveway leading from the Pennsylvania Avenue entrance, the great white light that had burned there for as long as Sam could remember no longer shone. He drew the curtains and put on the light. The wine bottle stirred in the melting ice. He poured himself another glass of wine and raised it to his reflection in the mirror.

"What the day demands," he said, thinking of the morrow.

The meeting to reactivate Wolf Trap was held in an anonymous room in the Treasury building. Its tall windows looked down on the equally anonymous 15th Street. The location had been selected partly for security reasons and partly because, as tired old Washington hands never failed to tell you, it would be another ten goddamned years before they finished building the new Army complex known as the Pentagon. It was not a large gathering: Stanley and Mason-Morley had come over on the *Duke of York*. General Donovan, Walter Landis from State, and Sam Gray represented the United States. The sixth member of the committee was a man whom Sam had previously only known by name and reputation. His name was Jan Masaryk, and he was Minister of Foreign Affairs in the Czech government-in-exile as well as its deputy Prime Minister. He was a balding man in his middle fifties with a corrugated forehead, and a chubby face with a heavy growth of beard that looked as if he might have to shave it twice a day. He acknowledged the introductions gravely and took his place at the table, watching Mason-Morley. There were no secretaries. This meeting was, at Stanley's request, to be strictly off the record.

"Gentlemen?" Donovan said. "Shall we begin?"

"By all means," Stanley said, urbanely.

"Good," Donovan said, in his no-nonsense voice. He looked at the Britishers with those mild blue eyes. "You've had a chance to study Sam Gray's paper?"

Mason-Morley nodded curtly. "We have."

"Then you'll know we have some questions," Donovan said.

Mason-Morley's eyes narrowed slightly. "Yes," he said. "Quite." He took a buff dossier out of his briefcase. It carried a red diagonal tab on its top right-hand corner, indicating that the material in it was classified Most Secret. He made no move to open it, placing his hands flat on the dossier and looking at Sam. There was hostility in his eyes. He doesn't like being questioned, Sam thought.

"Your questions, General?"

"We've got a number of them," Donovan said. "But they boil down to one. What was the connection between the Hess flight and Operation Wolf Trap?"

"It's a long story," Stanley said.

"We have time," Walter Landis said. There was no mistaking the edge on his voice. Mason-Morley flushed slightly and moved uncomfortably in his chair.

"You will remember at ABC-1, when Wolf Trap was first mooted," he began, "we told you that we had been contacted through Geneva by a man named Albrecht Haushofer?"

"Yes."

"Haushofer was a close friend of Hess. He had learned from him that Hess was taking intensive training lessons, with a view to flying to Britain to offer a plan for a separate peace to the King. He encouraged Hess, who thought very highly of him. What Hess did not know was that Haushofer was an active member of the resistance movement known as the *Schwarze Kapelle*. They were putting together a plan to overthrow Hitler—who had just announced his intention of going to war with Russia—but they were dithering. Nobody wanted to dirty his hands by killing the Führer."

"But you didn't mind," Landis observed. Again Mason-Morley flushed slightly.

"Haushofer came up with the idea of getting us to take on the job of killing Hitler in exchange for getting Rudolf Hess," he went on.

"And you agreed?" Landis said.

"Of course we did. We'd have made an accommodation with Beelzebub at that stage of the war, let alone the German *Abwehr*. However, we did make one condition. They were to provide us with a complete blueprint of their plan, timetables, everything."

"And they agreed?"

"They agreed. That was when we came to ABC-1, and why we mooted Wolf Trap. The trouble was, Hess took much longer than we all expected to make up his mind. It was not until he landed on May 10 that we could actively sanction the operation."

"You're saying Hess knowingly participated in a plot to kill Hitler?" Sam said. "I don't believe it. He worships the man."

"He knew nothing about the plan," Stanley said. "He was incidental to it. It was the plane we wanted. The documents were hidden in it."

"As soon as we had our hands on the documents, we set things in motion. The Ministry of Defence authorisation went through on May 19, nine days after we got them," Mason-Morley added.

"Then you didn't want Hess at all?" Donovan said, slowly.

"We did not," Stanley said, flatly. "The man was a damned embarrassment. The only thing we could think to do with him was lock him away where he would do the least harm."

"What did the documents contain?" Sam asked. "You never showed them to us."

Mason-Morley shook his head, not embarrassed by the animosity in Sam's voice. "They wouldn't have been any use to your people, although they were intelligence of the highest order. Not only did the plan list all SS, SD, and *Abwehr* safe houses, the names and private addresses of the commanders of every department of the Security Services and police organisation, but also the locations of arsenals, barracks, secret airfields throughout Germany. And, of course, the names of every member of the *Schwarze Kapelle*. The name of every man in Germany ready to turn traitor. Every one a potential double agent. It was worth putting on an assassination attempt for that alone—even if we knew it didn't have more than one chance in twenty."

"You'd have gone ahead with it?" Landis said.

"Of course, sir," Mason-Morley said. "We couldn't lose. If

we put Wolf Trap in and they made the hit, the *Schwarze Kapelle* would mount its coup d'état, and throw Germany into a state of anarchy. If—as turned out to be the case—we could not, we were still ahead of the game by virtue of having Hess in custody and the information they had sent us."

"Since this meeting is off the record, Major," Landis said, speaking slowly and distinctly, "let me say something. If Wolf Trap had gone ahead, a lot of people would have been killed, perhaps needlessly, for no damned good reason that I can discern. That strikes me as being a particularly treacherous way to repay your *Schwarze Kapelle* for its efforts!"

Sam saw two spots of colour appear high on Mason-Morley's cheeks. He felt a strong sense of *déjà-vu*; he ransacked his memory but could not recall the other time he had seen that same, guilty unease on the Englishman's face. Mason-Morley looked at Stanley. Help, his eyes said.

"You'll have to forgive me if I differ, Walter," Stanley said in that cold, precise way he had. "We make no apologies for what we had to do then. Our backs were to the wall. We had to fight with any weapon we could lay our hands on: lies, betrayals and double-crosses included. It's not cricket, of course. But war isn't cricket, as you people are beginning to learn."

His words struck home. Only the preceding day, after an heroic stand by its four hundred Marines, Wake Island in the Pacific had fallen to the Japanese. And it looked as if the Philippines would be next.

"Well," Donovan said, into the silence. "Doesn't that leave you with a problem, Colonel Stanley?"

"You mean Hess?"

"I do."

"Hess is a sick man. Very sick. He has been undergoing intensive electrotherapy," Stanley said. "For his nerves."

There was no emotion in the words, nothing. Yet somehow they made a chill run up Sam's spine. He wanted to ask questions whose answers he knew he would not wish to hear. He looked at Donovan, whose face was unreadable.

"He's your man, Colonel," he said.

"Quite," Stanley acknowledged.

"Well," Mason-Morley said, opening the buff dossier.

228

"Shall we proceed with the business at hand? Unless, of course, you gentlemen have any more . . . questions?" He looked at Sam as he spoke, as much as to say, that takes care of you.

"Just one more question," Sam said, gently. "Who, or what, is 'Jonathan'?" He watched Mason-Morley closely as he said the words, and for a moment he saw that same unease in the Englishman's eyes again. Mason-Morley looked at Stanley.

"'Jonathan' was our code-name for Hess," Stanley said, imperturbably. "Anything else?"

"No," Sam said, reluctantly. "Nothing else." He felt as though he had missed something important, but he had no idea what it was. He saw that Landis was watching him, waiting. He shrugged.

"All right, let's get on," Landis said. "You say you want to reactivate Wolf Trap, Oliver, but with a different target?"

"That's right."

"Who this time?"

"Reinhard Heydrich," Masaryk said, speaking for the first time. He had a striking, mellifluous voice. "The Butcher of Prague."

Sam felt astonishment, shock. He could not believe his ears. Of all the men in the world whom the British might have assassinated, they had chosen Heydrich! He stared at the table, hoping his reactions had not been observed.

"Why Heydrich?" Donovan asked. "What good would killing him do?"

"Sam knows the answer to that, General. Tell him, Sam."

"Kramer," Sam said. His throat was tight. He felt as if he was croaking. "Heydrich is probably the only man who could arrest Kramer and make it stick."

"And Kramer is the most valuable agent we have or are ever likely to have in Germany," Mason-Morley said. "When Sam told us that Kramer said they were closing in on him, we knew we had to act, and fast. There are other reasons, of course. Killing Heydrich will give the *Schwarze Kapelle* breathing space, which they desperately need. Heydrich and his minions are breathing down their necks. We want to keep the network alive if we can: any resistance to Hitler, no matter how weak, is valuable to us. All internal dissension must be encouraged. If Heydrich threatens that, then we must have him out of the way."

"Our first priority is to protect Kramer," Stanley said. "Then the *Schwarze Kapelle*. But even were that not the case, there would still be powerful political and economic arguments in favour of his assassination."

"Dr Masaryk," Mason-Morley said, by way of introduction.

"I have been here, as you know, gentlemen, since the middle of September," Masaryk said, "when the butcher Heydrich became the so-called *Protector* of my homeland. The weekly intelligence summary which is sent to me from London is one long saga of murder and terror. He has ruthlessly exterminated all resistance. My people are a cowed and subjugated people. Now Heydrich has set out to seduce them."

"Seduce them?" Donovan said. "How?"

"He is using a technique he calls *mit Peitsch und Zucker,*" Masaryk said. "The stick and the carrot, if you like. His larger plan, to turn Czechoslovakia into a war factory supplying the Reich, has become clear. 'You may imagine how many tanks the Czechs will make for us, if they do not benefit from doing so,' he says. So he now promulgates a system of increased rations for good workers, installs works canteens in factories, distributes 200,000 pairs of free shoes. He concerns himself with wage levels. He tours the big firms, winning the confidence of the workers. There is even talk he may release the students arrested in the October disturbances last year. The result of all this is that my Czechs—my people!—call this genocidical monster their 'friend', their 'benefactor'! They exchange their birthright for free vacations in Luhacovice!"

"From what we've been able to learn," Stanley said, coolly interrupting Masaryk's impassioned speech, "arms production, heavy industry, even agricultural figures are improving steadily. Czechoslovakia is turning into a combined quartermaster depot and a munitions factory for Hitler's Germany. We'd like to put a stop to that."

"You'll appreciate, of course, that killing Heydrich is one

230

small barb in Hitler's flank among many we're planning for '42," Mason-Morley said. "Commando raids on the French coast, perhaps even larger operations. The Prime Minister has brought with him a plan for the invasion of North Africa, codenamed Gymnast. We plan to attack Hitler wherever he is stretched, where we can be sure of victories. We want the people of Occupied Europe to know there is hope, if they'll resist."

"Our War Plans people see a full-scale invasion of Europe as the only way to end this war quickly," Donovan said.

"Won't work," Stanley said.

Donovan shrugged. Stanley's arbitrariness was well known—after all, hadn't he blackballed the Aga Khan from the Turf?—and there was no percentage in tackling him head-on. The Joint Chiefs could do that better than he.

"Getting back to Wolf Trap," Mason-Morley said into the slightly cooled silence, "we think that by assassinating Heydrich we'll be able to give Kramer a chance to cover his tracks. We protect the *Schwarze Kapelle* at the same time. And we show every one of that Nazi gang that they are not safe, that we can reach out and strike them down at any time."

"All right, Major," Donovan said. "Let's hear the proposition."

"Wolf Trap will go in as soon as we can get a plane over." Mason-Morley said. "Three teams. Seven to ten men. The first team will try to locate Vaslav Morávec, the head of the Czech underground in Prague. The second team will set up radio contact with London. The third team will go into hiding in Prague and, having found a suitable place to do so, will assassinate Heydrich."

"Sam?" Donovan said.

"They won't last ten days in Prague," Sam said, flatly. "The Gestapo already know everything. They got it all out of the first kid you sent across there, Pavelka."

"Pavelka only knew about the Hitler plan, Sam," Mason-Morley said. "They won't be expecting us to put men into Prague to kill Heydrich."

"All right!" Sam said. "Suppose they get in. Suppose they

231

can get close enough to Heydrich to kill him. Even suppose they do it, which is a hell of a lot of supposing—what about the reprisals?"

Landis looked at Dr Masaryk. He nodded gravely. "Yes," he said. "There would be terrible reprisals. There is no doubt of it."

"And?" Landis persisted.

"President Beneš believes, and I concur, that they would be within acceptable limits," Masaryk said.

Acceptable, Sam thought. He must have learned that word from Mason-Morley. It was one the Englishman seemed to like. Sam thought of the lovely girl with the madonna face he had met that December day in Prague. Antonie: she had been wearing a dark blue jacket and a red woollen hat and scarf. She, and hundreds like her, would willingly put their lives at risk to help Wolf Trap to succeed, and for no other reason than they knew someone must do it. Like those fresh-faced lads coming up the hill towards the stone wall at Fredericksburg, he thought.

"What the day demands," he murmured.

"Exactly," Noël Mason-Morley said, with surprise in his voice. He thinks I agree with him, Sam thought.

"We're buying time, Walter," Stanley said. "We need it."

"All right," Landis said. "Bill?"

"Fine," Donovan said, his voice low and tired. "Except for one thing. I'd like Major Mason-Morley's assurance that he has no more, ah, surprises in store for us?"

Mason-Morley managed to look wounded. "Of course not, General," he said, stiffly. Landis stood up. They all shook hands. Landis and General Donovan went out of the room. Sam went across to Noël Mason-Morley and Colonel Stanley, who were standing close together, as if for mutual protection.

"Am I in on this?" he asked them. "Wolf Trap?"

"If you want to be, Sam," Mason-Morley said.

"I want to be."

"Fine," Stanley said, with a strange look at Mason-Morley. For some reason that Sam could not understand, it seemed to him he saw a gleam of triumph in Stanley's eyes. What did the English think they had won?

Tangmere, December 28, 1941

Mason-Morley's signal to London was logged at 20.50 hours, Eastern Standard Time, December 27. It was brief and to the point: REACTIVATE WOLF TRAP IMMEDIATELY was all it said. Within ten minutes of its arrival at the Ministry of Defence, word was passed to Staff-Colonel Frantisek Morávec of Czech Intelligence in Bayswater, and, within an hour, a dispatch rider was roaring through Leatherhead on his way to Bellasis House. The operation was to be launched the following day. The weather forecast was good, the plane was ready, the plans drawn up.

Three teams were assembled at Bellasis. The first consisted of two non-commissioned officers, Sergeants Josef Gabcik and Jan Kubis. Their task was to kill Heydrich. The second team, under the command of First Lieutenant Alfred Bartos, consisted of Sergeant Josef Valcik and Corporal Jiri Potucek. Their job was to locate Vaslav Morávec. The third team, Skacha and Zemek, would set up radio contact from Czechoslovakia as soon as they could find a suitable, protected location.

The men were driven, that fine December afternoon, to the aerodrome at Tangmere. It was located on a small side road off the main A-29 to Chichester. Their final briefing took place at Tangmere Cottage, just opposite the main gates to the aerodrome. Extended on the skeleton of a tiny seventeenth-century cottage, the house was partly hidden from the road by tall hedges. Cars parked in the rear were concealed by lath screen fences. Entry was via the kitchen door, which led through the kitchen to two rooms: on the left the dining room, with its simple trestle tables, and on the right, the operations room. In an alcove by the window stood a plain pine office desk with a black telephone and a filing tray. On the wall above it was a map of France with the flak zones marked in red. A coal fire burned in a simple, brick-surround fireplace. Above the mantleshelf was a green felt notice board. The black-beamed ceiling was low, the walls thick, the windows small. An assortment of chairs was ranged around the fire.

The parachutists were joined here by the Canadian Air

Force pilot, Flight Lieutenant Hockey, and his crew of seven. Assembled in the Ops Room were the Navigation Officer, the Armament Officer, the Met Officer, and Squadron-Leader 'Dusty' Miller, the Senior Flying Controller. Each of them gave Hockey and his crew their relevant information. Then, the drop zones were selected. Gabcik and Kubis would be dropped near Ejpovice, three kilometres northwest of Pilsen. Bartos and his group would be dropped a little further south, and still a little further, Skacha and Zemek. While Hockey and his crew made their pre-flight checks of oxygen, weaponry and radio equipment and the navigator made sure the 'Gee', the radar grid-reference system, was functioning, the Czechs read and signed an undertaking that they would do everything in their power to carry out the mission for which they had volunteered. Then, while the plane was being fuelled, the two RAF Service Policemen who ran The Cottage, the tall, fair-haired Flight Sergeant Blaber, and his friend and amanuensis Sergeant Booker, a short, tubby, strongly built man, served the Czechs what they called an 'operational supper' of sausages, bacon, eggs, fried potatoes and kidneys.

Then they were driven in an Army lorry to the Halifax II standing on the apron, almost directly opposite the fire station facing the runway. At 22.00 hours, Flight Lieutenant Hockey was cleared for takeoff, waved the chocks away, and taxied the Halifax on to the northwest-southwest axis of the runway. The four giant Rolls Royce Merlin XX engines roared into screaming life, and the plane lurched and trembled like some impatient monster as Hockey built up to full power. Then, with a roar, she was on the move, four thousand, eight hundred and forty horses lifting her like a bird into the starlit sky above Selsey Bill.

Three quarters of an hour later the Halifax crossed the enemy coast. Flying on a line slightly south of east, she was over the Darmstadt area by 04.00. The parachutists, huddled inside their blankets on the makeshift metal and canvas seats rigged against the freezing metal struts of the aircraft, heard the crackle of the crew's radios, felt the plane swinging and banking. Hockey was taking evasive action: German night fighters had soared up to meet them. He eluded the pursuit by slipping into cloud, then altering his course several times while concealed within it. They passed over Bayreuth just after one–thirty in the morning. A grinning Sergeant/Observer brought the half-frozen, deafened soldiers scalding hot tea in tin mugs.

"Ah've purra lorra sugar innit," he told them, grinning as if to show them how few teeth he had. "Keeps ya warm."

The plane roared on, crossing the Czech border south of Cheb. They looked at their watches; it would soon be time. Their eyes moved over the length of the fuselage, along the metal-ribbed walls, the naked spars dripping with freezing condensation, to fix on the taut metal wire running the length of the plane. They automatically checked the release boxes and static lines of their harnesses.

As they approached Pilsen the flak batteries on the ground opened up. The parachutists could hear the exploding shells clearly: a sound like a man hitting an empty tin box with his fist. Once or twice the plane lifted as a blast of displaced air from one of the bursts reached it. The pilot turned to the navigator, his face lit green by the lights on his instrument panel. The navigator gave a thumbs-up sign and then pointed down at the ground. The pilot nodded and tapped Captain Sustr on the shoulder, one hand spread open. Five minutes.

"We're approaching the drop zone!" Sustr shouted. "Hook up! Warning light on!"

They shook hands, wished each other luck. They were the first Czech soldiers to return to the homeland since 1939. They had rehearsed all this so many times, yet now the real thing seemed almost not to be real. Sustr and the Sergeant/Observer got to their positions as the bomb doors opened. The Halifax slowed to a hundred and twenty miles an hour and dropped, bucketing, through thick cloud. Five, four, three, two and then one thousand feet. They could see the ground below rushing by: snow-covered, grey, hostile. Snow lashed at Sustr, braced near the open hatch. He did not look at Gabcik or Kubis, the first two men in line. His face was bathed in the rosy glow of the red 'stand-by' light. It changed all at once to a phosphorescent green.

"Go!" he shouted, clapping Gabcik on the back. The little man fell forward and out, closely followed by Kubis, soundless, ghostlike, gone. Sustr could not see their chutes open.

He turned to look at the light, which had changed back to red. He counted to one hundred and eighty. It turned green. Bartos and his two men jumped into the void. At 02.56 precisely, the green light came on for the third and last time, and Sustr watched the last two parachutists fall through the gaping aperture into the roaring darkness. The buckles on the lines danced and jangled in the screaming wind as the bomb doors slowly groaned closed. The comparative quiet was shocking: the navigator's voice seemed almost loud.

"All away?"

Sustr gave him a thumbs-up sign.

"All away, Skip!" the navigator shouted, banging Hockey on the back. "Let's go home!"

Prague, January 14, 1942

At a little after ten in the morning, the detective whom Walter Abendschon had assigned to watch Antonie Novak telephoned, to inform him that she had left the Lufthansa offices on the Wenzelplatz, and gone to the school where her father was a teacher. She was now standing at a tram stop on the Keplerstrasse, the detective said. She was obviously not waiting for a tram, since three or four had gone by and she had ignored them. Abendschon was out of his office in five minutes and sitting in his car opposite the tram stop in five more.

It was a bitterly cold day, with the wind coming from the east with sleet that occasionally turned to driving pellets of snow in its teeth. It battered the few pedestrians on the street back as if it were a sentient thing. The girl was standing with her back turned to the wind, coat collar up, woollen hat pulled low over her face. After perhaps another five minutes, Abendschon's face broke into a rewarded smile. Paul Kramer appeared, spoke to the girl, put his hands on her shoulders, kissed her. It was clear she was telling him something important. Her gestures were staccato, urgent. Kramer was frowning. He shook his head, no. The girl said something else, and he nodded, all right. Whether anything changed hands, an envelope, papers, Abendschon could not see. Kramer waited with the girl until a tram came along. A number twenty-two, Abendschon noted. It would take the girl back to the Wenzelplatz. Kramer watched as the tram grated away towards town, then thrust his hands into his pockets and began walking towards Dejvice.

Abendschon put the Opel into gear and eased along, passing Kramer on the opposite side of the street and parking some distance ahead. He saw Kramer turn into a side street a block back. Quickly reversing the car, Abendschon turned to follow his quarry. By the time he reached the corner, Kramer was at the door of an apartment building a little way down the street. Abendschon watched him go in, then got out of the car and hurried down the street, noting the name, Kupfergasse. He hurried to the rear of the building into which Kramer had disappeared. Behind it was a high brick wall at the end of a basketball court set up for local children. No way out there. With a nod of satisfaction, Abendschon limped back to his car and slid behind the wheel. He wondered whether he ought to have picked up his detective. He decided that if Kramer came out of the house alone, he would let him go, and devote his efforts to finding out whom Kramer had visited in the apartment house.

He was excited. This was the first move Kramer had made since his return from the High Tatras. The Gestapo had received reports of a low-flying British plane south of Prague on the night of December 28, and was intensively investigating the possibility that parachutists might have been dropped. If they had, it might explain today's activity. The girl's father had received word; he had called his daughter, told her to enlist Kramer's help. Kramer could warn them if the Gestapo was getting too close, perhaps even provide them with false papers: the *Abwehr* had its own forgery section.

He was an old enough hand to know Kramer would be on to all the standard shadowing tricks, so he had invented a few of his own. He bought a couple of old coats from a stall in a street market, a golf cap, a greasy old Homburg that looked as if it had been worn by a down-and-out. He bought a pair of spectacle frames with no lenses in them, and a heavy false moustache and some spirit gum from a theatrical costumier near the Tyl Theatre. All of these would help to change his appearance, although there was nothing he could do about his bulk and his limp.

He put the spectacle frames on and dabbed some spirit gum on his upper lip. The moustache was heavy and thick: I look like a grandfather, he thought. I wonder what Karin would say if she saw me now. Laugh, probably. She had a lovely laugh, infectious. He wished he had brought galoshes with him; the snow was beginning to settle. The windows were steamed up: he cleaned them with his sleeve.

About half an hour later Kramer emerged from the apartment block. He was accompanied by another man, short and swarthy, wearing a peaked cap and a dark blue overcoat. He was carrying a battered briefcase. The two men walked up the street away from Abendschon towards a small square, bleak and empty, the branches of its spindly trees winter-bare. At the junction of the two streets, Kramer shook hands with the swarthy man and went down the street to the left. The dark-haired man went the other way, and Abendschon let him go for a minute or two before he got out of the car and started in pursuit. There was something familiar about the man's appearance, but he couldn't put a finger on it. And what was this clandestine meeting about? What could have brought Kramer—he stopped in mid thought.

"Morávec!" he hissed.

The man he was following was Vaslav Morávec, the most wanted man in Prague! His heart bumped. Absolute proof positive of Kramer's collusion with he Czechs. Proof, perhaps, that there *had* been a drop, and that the parachutists had brought in a radio. Could Morávec be leading him to it, right now?

At the end of the street, Morávec turned sharply right into still narrower and more crooked byways. This was one of the drabbest parts of all of Prague's drab suburbs, Abendschon thought. He was cold; the grey clouds piled dark and heavy in the sky, and the light was flat and leaden.

He was torn by indecision. Continue tailing Morávec, which could be dangerous, or go back to the car and call in on the radio, perhaps losing the quarry in the process? He pulled the greasy Homburg down firmer on his head, and plodded on. He didn't look too much like a Czech workman, he supposed, but he certainly didn't look like a *Kripo* detective, either.

Morávec turned again, this time sharp left. Abendschon halted, approaching the corner cautiously. The man had given no sign that he knew he was being followed, but that didn't mean he didn't know. He eased up to the corner on the balls of his feet and risked a quick look around it. He found himself looking into a courtyard fronting a three-storey row of *pavlace*. Two cars were parked on the right-hand side, battered old Opels which didn't look as if they had been driven since the beginning of the war. A line of washing hung on the second floor balcony. The figure of a sad-looking saint reposed in a niche below it. Pigeons croo-croo'd in the eaves. There was no sign of Morávec. Abendschon heard music: a radio or gramophone. It sounded like Lale Anderson. A woman came out on the balcony and looked down.

"*Koho hledate?*" she demanded. "Who are you looking for?"

"*Hledem Pána Kovecs,*" he called back, cursing his poor Czech and worse luck.

"Nobody here named Kovecs!" the woman said, sharply. She turned abruptly and went into the tenement. *Verdammt und doppelverdammt!* Abendschon thought. He could not stay here any longer. Better get to a phone, call in some help.

He felt, rather than saw the movement behind him, and half-turned as a big man came around the corner, pistol in hand. Abendschon opened his mouth to speak, and the man pulled the trigger. The flat slam of the gun and the thud of Abendschon's body against the fender of the nearer of the two Opels were almost one sound. He went backwards over the hood of the car, legs kicking high, and fell in a befuddled sprawl on the other side. He could not see properly. He tried to get the gun out of his shoulder holster but he could not get his arm to move. He saw the big man loom dark against the light. He heard the gun go off and felt the solid smash of the bullet in the same moment. He rolled over against the wheel of the other Opel and lay still. I'm dying, he thought.

Pain roared through his body like a train through a tunnel. He opened his eyes wide. He saw Morávec come out of the tenement. The big man who had shot Abendschon went across to him. A curtain of black came down and rose again. Now there was only the big man. He turned and started back towards the detective. As he did Abendschon lifted his automatic and shot the big man through the body. The man grunted in surprise and tried to raise his own pistol. Abendschon's vision blurred. He pulled the trigger of his automatic and kept it pulled. He heard the stutter of the shots, saw the indistinct figure falter and then fold downwards. His vision cleared and he saw that the Czech was lying on the ground, the front of his body a tattered mess of blood and bone. He was trying to get up. The man must have the strength of a giant, Abendschon thought, terror drowning his pain. He watched in horror as the man struggled to one knee, his eyes staring and filled with hate. He lifted his gun and pointed it at Abendschon and then fell forward dead on his face.

Berlin, January 24, 1942

"Sit down, Bergmann," Himmler said.

Kurt Bergmann took the indicated seat uneasily. There was a silence. Through the windows of Himmler's office he could see sparrows foraging on the frozen lawns below. The room was like the man himself, cold and impersonal. A portrait of the Führer dominated the wall behind Himmler's antique desk. Beneath it hung a flag, the Imperial banner Himmler had carried that long-ago day in 1923 when Röhm's men had stormed General von Lossow's Schonfeldstrasse headquarters in Munich during the *putsch*.

Himmler was very proud of having been there that day. He liked to think of himself as a tough, no-nonsense soldier. Everyone in the SS knew he had the guts of a butterfly.

"Now," Himmler said in his schoolteacherish way. "You wish to see me privately, Bergmann? You see you have your wish. Every member of the SS has direct access to me."

"*Reichsführer*," Bergmann said, sombrely. "I come to Berlin on a very grave errand."

"So?" Himmler said. His eyes were expressionless. The very ordinariness of his face was chilling. Careful, Bergmann told himself. A wrong word with this man is peril. A wrong sentence could be ruin.

"*Reichsführer,* you and I are *alte kämpfer*," Bergmann said. "You honoured my home by visiting it in 1929, when I founded the first *Parteistelle* in Königsbrunn." Do no harm to remind him, he thought, watching Himmler carefully.

"Yes, yes," Himmler said, waving a hand. "Come to the point, man!"

"I must ask the *Reichsführer* a delicate question. That was why, before asking him, I took the liberty of reminding him how long is our association."

"And what is this delicate question?"

"Do you trust Heydrich?" Bergmann said, plunging.

Himmler's eyes narrowed. He ducked his head to the right so that the light hit his glasses obliquely. "Let us say that I do not . . . altogether trust him," he said. "Why do you ask?"

"Because, *Reichsführer*, if word were to reach him of what I am about to tell you, my life would be in the utmost danger!"

"I see," Himmler said, leaning forward, forearms on the desk. "Then let me assure you, my dear Bergmann, you may rely on me. I will honour your trust."

"Thank you, *Reichsführer*," Bergmann said. "I knew I was right to place my life in your hands." It worked well: Himmler beamed. He waved a hand again, a lordly signal to continue.

"You remember your visit to Prague, *Reichsführer*? You proposed a searching investigation of the *Abwehr*'s role in the flight of the *Stellvertretenderführer* to Britain?"

"Of course," Himmler said. "It was my own idea."

"Heydrich ordered me not to pursue the matter, *Reichsführer,*" Bergmann lied. "He said it was a stupid idea, and that all it would do was waste time and money."

"He said that?"

"Yes, *Reichsführer.* He told me he had an investigation of much greater importance, and that I was to devote all my energy and time to it and it alone."

"Go on."

"There was an investigation of long standing in Prague," Bergmann said. "The Gestapo there had suspected for some years that a highly-placed source was leaking state secrets to the Czech resistance, who were in turn passing them to the British. My department tentatively identified this man as Wehrmacht *Oberst* Paul Kramer, presently controlling all *Abwehr* activities in the Protectorate. Heydrich felt that if we could prove beyond a shadow of a doubt that Kramer was indeed the traitor for whom we have been searching all these years, it would enable him to topple Admiral Canaris. He said nothing else was as important."

"And when you got your evidence?" Himmler asked. "Just how did he propose to use it?"

"It was the *Reichsprotector*'s intention to take the information directly to the Führer, and to ask immediately for control of all the intelligence organisations, grouped under one commander."

"Heydrich, of course."

"Exactly, *Reichsführer.* I thought at first he was doing all this with your knowledge and authority. Later, I discovered that the very opposite was the case."

"And so you came to me?"

"I felt it was my duty, *Reichsführer.* I could do no less!"

"You think he is plotting to overthrow me?"

"I don't know what to think, *Reichsführer,*" Bergmann said. Puzzled, but sincere, he thought, watching Himmler's face. That's the way to play it.

"Well, Bergmann, I'm going to tell you something," Himmler said. "I was watching you, waiting. I'm glad you came to me. If you hadn't, I'd have assumed you were in it with Heydrich. Your coming here assures me that you are not."

"My loyalty is always first to my Führer, and then to my *Reichsführer!*" Bergmann said, putting all the sincerity he could muster into his voice. "Did I not swear that in front of the Feldernnhalle all those years ago?"

Himmler nodded. That was the kind of thing he liked to hear.

"He was using you, Bergmann," he said. "Using you, as he uses everyone. I trusted him, too, you know. Like a son. I put him where he is now. Gave him everything he asked for. And how does he repay me? With treachery, Bergmann! Treachery!"

"That can't be true, *Reichsführer!*" he said. Horror-stricken, awed. Yes, that was it. He could see again from Himmler's expression he was saying the right things. The pudgy face had a self-satisfied look which said, see how clever I am. he watched as Himmler took a key ring from his pocket and opened a drawer in the desk. From it he took out a red folder, the kind used for the most important state secrets. He unfastened the tapes and opened it.

"This is my personal dossier on the Hess flight," he said. "No one but myself—not even the Führer—has seen it."

Bergmann said nothing. He remembered the evening he and Heydrich had discussed Himmler's investigational abilities. Heydrich had laughed. Would he laugh if he was here now? What has Himmler got? How does it affect me? How much shock do I pretend? He doubted there would be much in the Hess dossier he did not know. He had done a great deal of work on that matter without informing Heydrich—or anyone else.

"What Heydrich doesn't know," Himmler was saying. "What nobody knows is this—that Rudolf Hess *never left the Reich!*"

"*What?*" Bergmann said. It was so unexpected that he started to his feet. Himmler regarded him impassively, and Bergmann sat down again, thoughts spinning. He had thought he knew exactly what the *Schwarze Kapelle* was up to—but *this!* Could it be true?

Was Himmler serious?

Himmler was always serious.

"I have established that when Hess took off from

Augsburg on May 10, he did not fly directly to England. There was no way he could have done so. The plane he was flying did not have the necessary range."

"Then where—"

Himmler held up an imperious hand: don't interrupt me. "Hess landed at Aalborg," he said. "In Denmark, at a Luftwaffe marshalling field for *Zerstörers* such as the one he was flying. He had been led to believe he would be able to refuel there and continue his flight. In fact, he was taken prisoner and smuggled by boat to Gøteborg, in Sweden. There he was handed over to the British Secret Service."

"By the *Abwehr?*"

"By a group which calls itself the *Schwarze Kapelle.*" So he knows that much, Bergmann thought. How much more?

"Some of them are *Abwehr, Reichsführer,*" he said.

"I know," Himmler said. "I have infiltrated the group. Personally."

"I can only say I'm awed," Bergmann fawned. Don't lay it on too heavy, he told himself. "But, tell me, *Reichsführer*—if Hess was taken to Sweden, who was the man who landed in England?"

"A double," Himmler said, his expression fatuously smug.

"A double?" Bergmann breathed. "A *double?*"

"Indisputably," Himmler said, prim as a nurse.

"But why?""

"Come, Bergmann!" Himmler said, his voice altering. "I know that Heydrich thinks I am a fool. You would be well advised not to make the same mistake!"

Bergmann went cold. Himmler's eyes were invisible, light glancing off the front of the steel-rimmed glasses tilted purposely to catch it. His childlike face with its twisted petulance held more menace than a thousand threats. Bergmann thought of all the things this man must know about him. Everything, every step of the way, since the beginning.

"Operation Wolf Trap?" he said, seeing it all at once. Himmler's pleased smile told him he was right. Why had he been so stupid? "They were going to use the double to kill the Führer!"

"Precisely so," Himmler said. "And then?"

"It might have worked," Bergmann said, softly. "It might just have worked."

"You're an expert in these matters, Bergmann," Himmler said. "How do you think they would have gone about it?"

Bergmann was still thinking. Parachutists, high-powered rifles, tracer bullets: the parachutist Pavelka had told him all that. It had sounded like utmost naïvety, but now, with the added dimension of the Hess double, he began to see the true parameters of the thing.

"The parachutists would merely create a diversion," he said, slowly. "Enough for the double to push through the cordon, shouting. Imagine it, *Reichsführer*! Right in front of the Feldherrnhalle! Hess appears out of the crowd, calling the Führer by name! The bodyguards hesitate. And in that moment, he would kill."

"Yes," Himmler said. His eyes were empty. What was he thinking? What was going on in that strange, tortuous mind? "And?"

"God in Heaven!" Bergmann said, putting everything he had into it. "You don't mean Heydrich knew all this?"

"He knew the *Schwarze Kapelle* plan," Himmler said. "He knew they planned to mount a coup d'état the moment the Führer was assassinated. But he had no intention of letting them do so. He knew every one of them by name. The moment the thing began, his murder squads would go to work. Who better to put down incipient revolution than Heydrich? Who better to step directly into the Führer's shoes?"

"What about yourself, *Reichsführer*?"

"Oh, he planned to kill me the moment the Führer was dead," Himmler said, almost jovially. "And he would have done it, too. But for one thing: the British could not land their parachutists."

"And Hess?"

"Dead," Himmler said, flatly. "The British killed him."

"Why?"

"What else could they do? There could not be two Hesses. I'm willing to wager the British Secret Service was acting without government sanction. They could never take the real Hess back to Britain."

He steepled pudgy fingers and looked over his pince-néz at Bergmann.

"I don't suppose you even know why you got nowhere, do you?" he said.

"I had a very good man working full time on the Kramer matter," Bergmann said stiffly. "Unfortunately, he was severely wounded in Prague while in pursuit of information. He is still unconscious. Until he comes round, there is nothing I can—"

"Tsk, tsk, Bergmann," Himmler said, impatiently. "Kramer passed word about your investigation to an American diplomat named Samuel Gray, who carried it back to London. As soon as the British secret service heard we were investigating the connection between the *Abwehr* and Hess, Hess was disposed of."

"May I ask the *Reichsführer* how he knows all this?"

"As I told you, Bergmann," Himmler said. "Heydrich doesn't know everything. I have access to sources not even he knows about. For instance—"

He produced a piece of paper from the dossier, adjusting his glasses. It bore the heading of *Forschungsamt* A, in Berlin's Schillerstrasse.

"The Research Institute of the Post Office has been working for some time from a secret location on the Dutch coast, trying to break into the British transatlantic telephone traffic. A few weeks ago they succeeded." He pushed the piece of paper across the desk. Bergmann picked it up.

TRANSCRIPT OF CALL MADE 19.00 HRS GMT
LONDON/WASHINGTON 15.1.42
Sam Gray here, General.
Hello, Sam.
I thought you'd like to know that Wolf Trap is in.
Good. Has there been any radio contact?
Yes. They say the target is not in Prague right now.
Where is he?
In Berlin. Until the middle of February.
That ought to give them enough time to get things set up.
I imagine so. One other thing.
What?
Morávec reports he and Kramer were followed by a man. Not Gestapo, not SD. Some special squad

whose job it is to get Kramer. He didn't know the
man. There was a shooting. The man was severely
injured but he got away. Morávec is afraid Kramer
is going to be arrested.
Anything we can do?
I don't think so. Just hope Kramer remains at liberty
long enough to get the information on Heydrich.
The Wolf Trap team will do the rest.
Okay. Keep me informed.
I will.
Goodbye, Sam.
Goodnight, General.

"Well?" Himmler said, as Bergmann almost reverently
laid down the document. He looked at Bergmann with unblinking, basilisk eyes. Sweet Jesus Maria, Bergmann
thought. If I say the wrong thing now, I'm a dead man. It
was as if a bell was ringing inside his head. They're going to
kill Heydrich, they're going to kill Heydrich.

"I will take the necessary steps immediately,
Reichsführer!" he said. "Special security for the
Reichsprotector. A round-the-clock guard, extra men at
Jungfern-Breschan—"

"No," Himmler said, tonelessly.

"Reichsführer?"

"You will do . . . nothing," Himmler said. His stare was
empty, unnerving. Jesus, Bergmann thought. How in the
name of God did I ever get into the middle of this? His
hands were wet with perspiration.

"Bergmann," Himmler said. "Can I trust you?"

"But of course, *Reichsführer,*" Bergmann said, hoping it
didn't sound *too* eager. This could still be some kind of
insane loyalty test. You just never knew with Himmler. One
minute he was the reincarnation of Henry the Fowler, and
the next he was signing death warrants for half a million
men, and never a blink between the two.

"I'm glad to hear it," Himmler was saying. "I'm going to
confide in you."

"I am honoured, *Reichsführer,*" Bergmann murmured,
thinking, don't expect the same in return, though.

"When he realised that the British plot to assassinate the

247

Führer was not going to be successful, Heydrich immediately changed his plans." Himmler said. "That was why he put you to work on the matter of the traitor Kramer. He intends, as you said, to use him to bring down Canaris and the *Abwehr*. But not so that he can become *Reichsführer*, Bergmann! Nothing as *ordinary* as that! Heydrich proposes to become Minister of the Interior!"

Leapfrogging Himmler, bypassing Bormann, rendering Göring powerless in one fell swoop, retaining all his former powers—Heydrich would be the most powerful man in Germany, next to the Führer, Bergmann thought. His determination wavered: what if he did it? By God, this was going to be a fine-honed game!

"Now you realise why I have confided in you, Bergmann," Himmler said. "I will need the help of a man I can trust. Someone who is close to Heydrich."

"Yes, *Reichsführer*," Bergmann said. He had to play along. If he refused, he was finished now. If he did as he was told and Heydrich came out on top anyway, he was still finished.

"If my judgment is correct," Himmler said. "If you handle this matter . . . judiciously . . . Heydrich will be out of the picture for good, and everybody's skirts clean. You realise what that would mean, Bergmann?"

"You would need someone to replace him, *Reichsführer*," Bergmann said. "Someone . . . whose loyalty has never been in doubt." It was a *sine qua non* of the Nazi hierarchy that the denouncer usually received as his reward the post of the man he had delivered to the executioner. Well, why not? He was as good as any man in the SS, as good in his own way as Heydrich. Why not?

"Precisely so," Himmler said, primly.

"I think you could rely upon me, *Reichsführer*," Bergmann said. Well, this was what he had wanted, wasn't it? This was why he had come to Berlin, wasn't it? It hadn't quite gone the way he originally planned it, but it came out as well this way as any other.

"I'm glad to hear you say that, Bergmann," Himmler said, seriously. He got up out of his chair. "It's good to know there are men one can always rely on. That is the thing we need right now. We *alte kämpfer* must stick together. So: go back to Prague. Keep me informed. I will give you a number where I can always be reached, day or night." He wrote the number 12.64.21 on a slip of paper and handed it to Bergmann. Bergmann took it as if it were a death warrant. Which in some ways, he thought, it well could be. If Heydrich even suspected that Kramer knew of an assassination plan but had not told him, then Kurt Bergmann would die a particularly painful death. Heydrich was a vengeful bastard.

Bergmann saluted Himmler and shook his clammy hand.

"I'm lunching with the Führer tomorrow," Himmler said, with as much warmth in his voice as Bergmann had ever heard there. "If the opportunity presents itself, you may be sure I shall bring the matter of your unswerving devotion to duty to his attention."

"Thank you, *Reichsführer,*" Bergmann said. "Heil Hitler!"

"Heil Hitler," Himmler said laconically. He stood watching as Bergmann went out. A faint smile touched his pudgy face.

Prague, February 4, 1942

LIBUSE TO SVOBODA + LIBUSE TO SVOBODA + DUE
TO OUR POSITION CAUSED BY INACCURATE DROP
WE HAVE BEEN UNABLE TO CONTACT "LEON" IN
PRAGUE + WE HAVE NOW RECRUITED COURIERS
AND WILL ATTEMPT TO DO SO IF YOU WILL SUPPLY
US WITH INSTRUCTIONS ON HOW WE ARE TO
LOCATE HIM + PLEASE TREAT THIS REQUEST WITH
THE UTMOST URGENCY + INTELLIGENCE
GATHERED IN THE PRECEDING TWENTY-FOUR
HOURS FOLLOWS . . .

SVOBODA TO LIBUSE + SVOBODA TO LIBUSE + YOU
WILL BE ABLE TO CONTACT "LEON" AND "VLK"
THROUGH B. *[First Supplement]* + "LEON" LIVES

WITH HER AT *[Second Supplement]* + ESSENTIAL
THAT YOU MAKE THIS CONTACT URGENTLY +
SUPPLEMENT FOLLOWS IN NEXT TRANSMISSION +

SVOBODA TO LIBUSE + SVOBODA TO LIBUSE +
FIRST SUPPLEMENT BOCKOVA + SECOND
SUPPLEMENT BISKUPCOVA 28 PRAGUE-ZIZKOV +
YOU MUST ENDEAVOUR TO MAKE CONTACT AT THE
EARLIEST OPPORTUNITY + "LEON" WILL HAVE
INTELLIGENCE INFORMATION OF THE MOST
IMPORTANT NATURE +

Tonie walked all the way to Zizkov. It was safer that way.
You could see if anyone was following you. It was a long
way from the centre of town. Under the railway arches
beyond the Wilson Station, and along the wide, empty Hus-
strasse towards Vitkov Park. The street itself was the foot of
a valley; the ground rose steeply on either side. On the left it
went up to the top of the park. On the right, steep streets
led to the top of Zizkov Hill. Biskupcova ran parallel to the
Hus-strasse. The apartment she was looking for was on the
corner of a little square, where trolleycars turned around.
She looked at the names on the mailboxes. Hladena, Kostal,
Janacek. . . . Ah, there it was: Bocek. Apartment fourteen.
She ran up the stairs and knocked on the door—three short
knocks, one long. The door was opened by a tall, thin, full-
breasted woman with dark hair, wearing a dark blue velvet
dress that looked expensive. Tonie could smell cigarette
smoke. The woman had a glass of wine in her hand.

"Yes?" she said, warily.

"My name is Antonie Novakova," Tonie said. "I am trying to find Captain Morávec. It is a matter of life and
death."

"Morávec?" the woman said, wrinkling her brow. "I
know no one of that name. You must have the wrong address."

"*Pani* Bockova, I beg you, listen to me!" Tonie said. "Let
me come in for a moment, please!"

"I'm afraid that will not be possible," the woman said,
frigidly. "I am entertaining."

"Is he here?" Tonie said, craning to see over the woman's
shoulder into the apartment. She cold see only some fur-

niture, an armchair. It all looked neat and depersonalised.

"See here!" the woman said. She made as if to close the door in Tonie's face. There was suspicion and fear in the dark eyes.

"We were told you would help us!" Tonie said. "We were told you could put us in touch with Captain Morávec."

"We?"

"Some . . . friends of mine," Tonie said. "They are . . . from abroad." The woman's face changed. Once again she made as if to close the door, and once again Tonie spoke hastily to stop her. "Look!" she said, pulling out her identity cards. "I'm not lying to you. Please, won't you help me?"

"I am afraid I cannot help you," the woman said.

"You must!" Tonie said. "You must! Where is he? Where is Leon?"

Madame Bockova's eyes narrowed. "How do you know that name?" she whispered.

"If I told you—someone sent it? By radio? Would you believe me?"

"You'd better come in," the woman said.

"I thought you said—" Tonie said, as she closed the door.

"There's no one here," Madame Bockova said. "I live alone. The *Blockleiter* comes around all the time. That's how I keep him out."

'Block leaders' were the building-bricks of the Party— and, by definition the Gestapo—spying system. Each province, or *Gau,* had a governor, a *Gauleiter.* His province was divided into 'circles' or *Kreise,* each of which in turn had a *Kreisleiter.* Every one of these areas had a group leader for a locality, a town, a village. And in each of these places, the *Ortsgruppenleiter* appointed 'cell leaders', who in turn collated and supervised the reports of the *Blockleiter,* responsible for perhaps thirty or forty families. The *Blockleiter*'s business was to know everything there was to know about 'his' families: quarrels, love-affairs, politics, professional activities, weaknesses, passions, salary, hours of work—everything. It all went into Gestapo records. There was no escaping the all-permeating spies of Hitler's Reich.

Tonie went into the sitting room. Madame Bockova gestured towards one of the armchairs. It was warm and cosy in the apartment. A cat lay on the sofa, fast asleep. In one corner, a rubber-tree plant stood in an earthenware pot, its top tied to a hook in the ceiling. Along the window ledge were potted plants: African violets, little cacti. Madame Bockova lit another cigarette.

"How could you have been given my name by radio?" she said, coughing a little as she inhaled the smoke. "Do you want a drink?"

"No, thank you," Tonie said. "I told you—some friends. From abroad."

"I don't understand."

I'll have to trust her, Tonie thought. "Parachutists," she said. "From England."

"Here?" Madame Bockova said. "In Prague?"

"I can't tell you where. But they are here. Please, will you help us?"

Madame Bockova was biting her lip. It was always the same, Tonie thought. Everyone was afraid. What she was saying might be genuine. On the other hand, she might as easily be an *agent provocateur,* trying to trap Madame Bockova into admitting complicity with Morávec, ready to whistle up the Gestapo *Abholwagen* and drag her off to the Petschek.

"Your husband, Colonel Bocek. He is in England, isn't he?"

"I don't. . . . My husband left Czechoslovakia in 1939," Madame Bockova said, as if she had been asked the question many times, and always answered it the same way.

"If we could get him to broadcast to you, would you believe us then?"

"You could . . . do that?"

There was doubt in the dark eyes. She wants to believe, Tonie thought.

"*Pani* Bockova, I beg of you, help me. It is vital that I contact Captain Morávec."

"I do not know anyone of that name," the woman said. "However . . . if you could do . . . what you said?"

"Yes, yes!" Tonie said. "I will!"

"We had a silly name we used. Chodsky. If he were to broadcast as Chodsky . . . and say something . . ."

"Yes, all right!" Tonie said. "What?"

"He would know," the woman said. She got up. "Nobody else would. If what you say is true, I will try to help you."

"Chodsky," Tonie said. "It will take a little while."

"Tell them March the fifth," the woman said. "He'll know why."

LIBUSE TO SVOBODA + LIBUSE TO SVOBODA + WE
HAVE MADE CONTACT WITH B. BUT SHE CLAIMS TO
KNOW NEITHER "LEON" NOR "VLK" + ASKS FOR A
MESSAGE FROM HER HUSBAND TO BE BROADCAST
[First Supplement] + SHE HAS GIVEN US ONLY THE
WORD [Second Supplement] AND SAYS HE WILL
KNOW WHAT TO SAY + END ITEM + CONDITIONS
HERE ARE NOTHING LIKE WE EXPECTED + BOTH
THE MILITARY AND POLITICAL ORGANISATION OF
THE RESISTANCE HERE ARE IN A STATE OF TOTAL
CONFUSION . . .

LIBUSE TO SVOBODA + LIBUSE TO SVOBODA +
FIRST SUPPLEMENT MARCH 5 + SECOND
SUPPLEMENT "CHODSKY" +

". . . and that is the end of the news. And now a message for our brave countrymen in Nazi-occupied Czechoslovakia. Here is our comrade, Colonel Chodsky" . . . "Good evening, I am Colonel Chodsky. Tonight I wish you, dearest Tatana, a happy birthday. The hour of liberation is near. We shall be together soon. Good-night and God be with you . . ."

SVOBODA TO LIBUSE + SVOBODA TO LIBUSE + IT
HAS BEEN A WEEK SINCE "CHODSKY" BROADCAST
+ WHAT IS YOUR SITUATION? + ADVISE
IMMEDIATELY WHETHER YOU HAVE YET MADE
CONTACT WITH "LEON" OR "VLK"" + THIS IS A
MATTER OF THE MOST EXTREME URGENCY + END
ITEM + IF YOUR VIEW OF THE ORGANISATION OF
THE HOME RESISTANCE IS CORRECT IT IS VITALLY
NECESSARY TO STIMULATE IT FROM ABROAD BY ALL
VALID MEANS + IT WAS WITH THIS INTENTION
THAT WE . . .

LIBUSE TO SVOBODA + LIBUSE TO SVOBODA + AS A
CONSEQUENCE OF MY INFORMATION OF SATURDAY

AND WITH THE HELP OF B. PERSONAL CONTACT
WITH "LEON" HAS BEEN ESTABLISHED +
COOPERATION WITH HIM WILL COMMENCE
IMMEDIATELY + HE HAS SUPPLIED US WITH A
CONSIDERABLE AMOUNT OF INTELLIGENCE + WE
BEGIN TRANSMITTING NOW + END ITEM + TROOP
MOVEMENTS IN EASTERN CZECHOSLOVAKIA
OBSERVED IN THE LAST THREE WEEKS INCLUDE . . .

SVOBODA TO LIBUSE + SVOBODA TO LIBUSE + BY
ACHIEVING CONTACT WITH "LEON" YOU HAVE
CARRIED OUT ONE OF YOUR MAIN TASKS + THAT
IS TO SAY THE RENEWAL OF LIAISON WITH THE
HOME ORGANISATION AND THE BEGINNING OF
YOUR COOPERATION WITH IT + YOUR CONDUCT
HAS BEEN BRAVE INTELLIGENT AND WELL
CONCEIVED + I THANK YOU FOR IT AND EXPRESS
MY GRATITUDE + END ITEM + WE ARE
PARTICULARLY ANXIOUS TO OBTAIN PRODUCTION
FIGURES OF LIGHT MACHINE GUNS . . .

They met in a restaurant called *U Medviku*, not far from the St Martinskirche. It was a place which specialised in Bohemian food; they had used it once or twice before.

"You said it was urgent," Paul said.

"Damned urgent," Morávec told him. "The parachutists are in contact with London. We're in business again."

He was a slight, balding, swarthy man with a mischievous smile. He looked perfectly at ease, as though he had more right to be where he was than most. His suit was neat, his shoes polished. There was nothing of the hunted man about him, yet Paul knew the Gestapo had put a price of fifty thousand *Korunas* on Morávec's head. It was the first time they had met since Novak's death in Dejvice.

"Where are they?"

"The ones with the radio are hiding in a quarry near Hlinsko. They're using the call-sign 'Libuse'." Hlinsko was a village near the town of Pardubice, east of Prague. "They dropped them all over the place. Miles from where they expected to land. So the contact addresses they gave them were useless."

254

"Are they all at Hlinsko?"

"No, a couple of them are in Prague. Uncle Hajsky is moving them around." 'Uncle Hajsky' was a schoolteacher named Zelenka, who acted as Morávec's 'housing agent'.

"I'll have to go very carefully, Vaslav," Paul said.

"You being watched?"

"Not as far as I know. But—" Paul shrugged.

"The one we shot—have you found out who he is?"

"A detective from the Berlin *Kriminalpolizei*. His name is Walter Abendschon."

"From Berlin, you say? What was he doing following you?"

"I don't know," Paul said. "That's what's worrying me. There's nothing on the record at the Petschek. Somebody's going to a lot of trouble to keep it covered up."

"Heydrich? Bergmann?"

"Maybe. I won't know till they get back from Berlin."

"When will that be?"

"Any day now."

"There was nothing in the papers," Morávec said. "About the shooting."

"I know," Paul said. "It's not logged in the Incident Books, either."

"This man. Abendschon? Where have they got him?"

"In the SS hospital at Dejvice," Paul said. "No visitors."

"It's damned strange," Morávec said.

"You're damned right," Paul replied. "Have you seen Tonie?"

"Yes."

"How is she?"

"All right," Morávec said. "Considering."

Morávec's group had smuggled Jan Novak's bullet-riddled body across the city to his home. How they had done it, Paul could not begin to imagine. Morávec found a doctor who wrote a death certificate stating that Jan had died of natural causes. Dr Holub in turn found an undertaker named Hanka Tirlov, who furnished a coffin and arranged for a burial plot. The penalty for failing to report a gunshot wound to the Gestapo was death; they did what needed to be done anyway.

"I'll go and see her," Paul said. "What about Maria? Is she all right? Does she need anything?"

"We've taken care of everything," Morávec said. "Tonie is running courier for the paras. Jan's death was just one more reason for her to hate these Nazi bastards."

"As if she didn't have enough," Paul said, thinking of her crying, that night in Stary Smokovec, after they made love. "And Maria?"

"She's strong, Paul. Strong. You should have seen her when we brought Jan's body home. Like a rock, she was. She's helping us. She gave Tonie's room to one of the parachutists. She's organised all her friends to pool their unused ration coupons to get extra food for him. Says it's her way of fighting them. She'll come through fine."

"I ought to go over there," Paul said. "But I don't want to get them involved in what I'm doing any more than I have to. This Abendschon business has unsettled me. I don't know how long he has been on my back. What he knows. What he's found out."

"Do what I do, man!" Morávec said. "Just keep going."

Paul managed a grin. "In the absence of any alternative."

"That's right," Morávec said. "About our parachutists. Can you find out whether the Gestapo knows anything about them?"

"I already know. The answer is yes."

"Christ's nightshirt!" Morávec cursed. "What do they know?"

"They know there are parachutists. They don't know how many. They don't know where they are. As you might imagine, they are trying very hard to come up with something."

"I can imagine," Morávec said grimly. "How did they find out?"

"A farmer near Podebrady found a parachute and some overalls buried in one of his fields. He turned them in to the *gendarmerie*. They passed them on to the Gestapo. They know that if one parachutist landed, there are probably more."

"Christ's nightshirt!" Morávec said, again. "Who's in charge of the investigation?"

"It's nominally *Amt* IVA2," Paul said. "A man named Strubing."

"I know him," Morávec said. "A shit."

Paul smiled. "Aren't they all?"

"What about the biggest one?"

"Leiche? He's still looking for you."

"I'd like him to find me," Morávec said. "In an alley, on a dark night!" He flexed his gloved hands. He never took his gloves off. He noticed Paul's look and wiggled his fingers. One of them didn't wiggle.

"You heard how I lost it?"

"Tonie told me," Paul said. "What are the stitches on your gloves for?"

"Gestapo," Morávec said. "Big stitches for dead ones, little stitches for ones I only wounded."

There were four big stitches and three smaller ones. "Four dead," Paul said. He saw Alben Graumann's eyes open and then close, smelled again the swift reek of cordite and burning cloth. "Does it ever bother you?"

"Killing cockroaches?" Morávec said. "Why should that bother me? It's them or us, Paul. No use thinking about it."

No use thinking about Death? Perhaps not. The better you got to know the Old Man, the less you feared him. Death was only a matter of when, not whether. Death was at the end of every street you had ever walked down, waiting for somebody else. Death was your name on a list, with no date entered yet. Death was the Gestapo breaking down your door at four in the morning.

"Drink up!' Morávec said. They clinked glasses. "*Vitzezstvi!*" Victory. You saw the word everywhere, chalked on factory walls. Sometimes it was just the letter V, or three dots and a dash, the Morse equivalent of the BBC call sign, played on a drum. Bm-bm-bm-boom.

Two men came in. Both of them were Germans, in civilian clothes. They sat at a table opposite the one at which Morávec and Paul were sitting. One fat, one thin. The fat one was about thirty. He had hair like wet black string that did nothing to conceal his bald patch. His friend was thin and dark, and wore horn-rimmed glasses. They ordered *bratwurst* and beer. When the tall, dark, pretty waitress

257

walked away from their table the fat one went *ptschwtschwtsch* with his lips. The girl flushed and pretended not to notice.

The fat one ate noisily. Paul could hear him smacking his lips right across the room. Then he belched noisily, without apology. The thin one appeared not to notice. He kept looking across at Paul and Morávec, as though he was waiting for them to do something. Paul felt a soft, sinister chill.

"Let's get out of here," he said to Morávec.

Morávec looked at him in surprise. When he saw Paul's face, he got up from the table and went across to the cash register to pay their bill. The thin man at the table opposite watched him. The fat one stopped eating long enough to look at Paul. *Come on,* Paul silently urged the Czech. *Let's get out of here.*

Morávec got his coat, and they went out into the street. He looked edgy, poised for action. "Gestapo?" he hissed.

"Set up another meeting," Paul said. "Leave word at one of the drops." They had set up a series of letter boxes: a phone booth near Tyn church, a philatelist's shop, a bookstore in an arcade off the Wenzelplatz.

"Good luck," Morávec said. A biting east wind whistled between the buildings. Paul began to walk up the street in the direction of the Old Town. It was then he saw the black van. It was parked around the corner from the restaurant. At the same moment, the two Gestapo men came out of the restaurant. Morávec was between them and the *Abholwagen*. He saw it in the same moment Paul did. A huge man got out of the van. Morávec saw him and turned on his heel.

"Halt!" Leiche shouted, pulling a pistol from the pocket of his leather coat. Morávec broke into a run, the skirts of his overcoat flapping. Leiche fired at him. The explosion sounded insignificant. Paul saw Morávec falter, then go on. The two Gestapo men who had been in the restaurant pulled out their guns and ran at him. Morávec shot the first one, the thin man with the horn-rimmed glasses. The fat one gave a shout of panic and fell over his own feet trying to get out of Morávec's way. Morávec went past the sprawling man, running.

The Gestapo van roared around the corner. Leiche crouched on the running board. Paul saw Morávec turn, dropping his briefcase. He had a pistol in each hand. He fired them one after the other, left and then right and then left and then right, methodically placing his shots. The windscreen starred in several places, and the van lurched to the left, out of control. Leiche jumped, rolling clear. He lay half-stunned in the gutter as the van smashed into the front of a shop. A man clambered out of it, reeling, trying to level a pistol at Morávec. Morávec shot him. The man slammed back against the hood of the crashed van. Morávec turned and ran towards Volks-strasse.

A man wearing blue overalls tried to grab him. Morávec short-armed him aside. The fat Gestapo agent who had been in the restaurant was blowing his police whistle. Leiche lurched to his feet, shouting at the people in the street to stop Morávec. Before any of them could move, Morávec disappeared down a side street.

Paul turned and walked rapidly away from the scene of the fight. No one tried to stop him. He looked back over his shoulder at the smoking van, the sprawled bodies, the curious crowd edging nearer. Leiche was standing in the middle of the street, his hands on his hips, watching Paul go.

A half hour later, Paul got back to his office in the Glass House. They were waiting for him when he walked in through the door.

Prague, March 20, 1942

"So," Bergmann said. "We begin.""

"By what right have you brought me here?" Paul said. "Am I under arrest?"

He did not know where he was: they had put an eyeless hood over his head. He did not know how many men were in the room, if room it was. But he knew Kurt Bergmann's voice.

"My dear Kramer, of course you are not under arrest," Bergmann said.

"Then what is all this about?"

"We brought you here on a Protective Custody warrant," Bergmann said, smoothly. "Your life is in danger.'"

"From whom?"

"The Czech resistance."

"Why would the Czech resistance want to kill me?"

"They will think you betrayed Morávec yesterday."

"Who is Morávec?"

"Don't play games with me, Kramer!"

"I'm not—"

"State your name and rank. For the record!" It was a different voice this time, higher in pitch. A younger man?

"I wish to place on record my strongest protest at having been brought here in this way," Paul said.

"Your protest is noted," Bergmann said. "State your name and rank."

"Paul Viktor Kramer, *Oberst*."

"You are presently *Abwehr Hauptvertrauensmann* for the Protectorate of Bohemia and Moravia, with responsibility also for the Balkans?"

"I am."

"You will state your NSDAP number and the date on which you joined the Party."

"Is this some sort of hearing?"

"Answer the question!" The first voice again. A Gestapo interrogator, probably, Paul thought.

"Party number 65714," he said. "February 14, 1927."

A little silence followed his words. He was one of the 'first hundred thousand', holder of the Golden Party Badge. All holders were 'known personally' to the Führer. This was dangerous ground to tread.

"You know a man named Vaslav Morávec," another voice said. Two of them, Paul thought. As well as Bergmann.

"Do you mean the Vaslav Morávec who is head of the Czech resistance, or some other Vaslav Moravec?" he said.

"'You know damned well."

"I know nobody named Morávec, except the resistance leader. And I've never seen him face to face."

"You are lying. You were with him yesterday in a café called *Der Kleine Bär*."

"Who says so?"

"I do," said a third voice. Leiche, Paul thought, hope fading.

"The man I was with yesterday is called Léon Karásek."

"The purpose of your meeting?"

"I do not think I have to discuss that here."

"We shall see. Will you take our word for it that Karásek is Morávec?"

"No."

"Why not?" Leiche rumbled. "If as you contend, he is an innocent party, you should have no objection to our interviewing him."

"I would strongly object," Paul said. "He is an informer. I do not want him frightened off by some clumsy oaf in big boots."

"You call us oafs, Kramer?" Bergmann's voice, soft with menace. "You will find that we are not."

"Are you threatening me?"

"We are asking your cooperation."

"I do not have to give it."

"We believed you would want to."

"That's why you brought me here with a hood over my head?"

"We have our reasons."

"I demand to speak to my superiors in Berlin."

"Denied. For your own safety."

It was nonsense, and they knew it. But there was nothing he could do: he had no doubt all the necessary papers had been prepared. *Oberst* Kramer's life was in great danger. It was the duty of the *Sicherheitsdienst* to protect him until that threat had been removed. "Again I protest in the strongest manner."

"Enough of this," he heard one of the other men say. "Let's—"

"No!" Bergmann snapped. "None of that!"

Beneath the hood, Paul smiled. They would have to tread very warily: no violence against the person. He was a senior member of the Party, a high-ranking *Abwehr* officer. The fact that he had been escorted from the Glass House by Gestapo officers would already have been communicated to Berlin. All he had to do was stall as long as possible.

"Tell us about Morávec," a voice shouted, so close to his ear that he jumped.

"I don't know anyone called Morávec."

"Tell us about Karásek, then."

"He is an informer. He has infiltrated one of the Czech resistance cells, and is feeding me information on its members. As soon as I have all the names, I will pass them to the Gestapo for action."

"This Karásek, where does he live?"

"I don't know."

"You expect us to believe that?"

"I don't give a damn what you believe!"

"You'd better——" He felt the tension in the man's voice, the suppressed violence. He'd prefer to talk with a rubber hose, Paul thought. He sat silent and still, waiting.

"How do you contact Karásek?" Bergmann asked.

"Through a drop."

"Where is this drop?"

"A bookstall in Smichov station."

"How often do you meet?"

"As often as necessary."

"You are not being very helpful, *Oberst*."

"Show me where it says I have to."

"You know perfectly well it is your duty to cooperate with the SD and Gestapo at all times."

"Not with a hood over my head, it isn't," Paul said.

"We will remove it," one of the men said. "If you will help us."

"How?"

"Set up a rendezvous with this Karásek, so that we can interrogate him."

"No."

"Then we must assume, *Oberst,* that you have something to conceal in this matter!"

"Assume whatever you please."

He heard a gusty, weary sigh. "Going to do it the hard way, are we?"

"Do it any way you please."

"Very well."

He felt someone place what seemed to be the barrel of a pistol against his head. His blood froze. They could kill him like a dog in some dripping cellar, and no one would ever know. His body would disappear, and, after a protracted but inconclusive search, the Gestapo would offer its regrets to *Zentrale* and that would be the end of that. From up close, the man spoke into Paul's ear.

"We're getting tired of you, Kramer," the voice whispered. "You just ran out of time. I'm going to count to ten, and then . . ."

Paul said nothing. The man started to count. Could it really end like this? Paul wondered. A shabby, despicable death that no one would ever know about? *Tonie, Tonie, I loved you.* It seemed unfair that there had never been any time for their love to flourish and grow.

"Eight," the man said. "Nine."

Goodbye, my darling.

"Ten!" Nothing. The man burst out laughing. The others all joined in. Paul sat silent, shamed by the vast rushing sense of relief that swamped every feeling in his body.

"Nearly pissed yourself then, didn't you, Kramer?"

"Bastards!" he said.

"Let's start again," the man said. "Who is Karásek?"

"I told you."

"Tell us again."

Two hours. Three hours. Four hours.

"Who is Karásek?"

"I told you."

"Tell us again."

"He is an informer. I used him to infiltrate one of the Czech resistance cells."

"Tell us some of the names of the men in this cell."

"If I do that, and you arrest them, you will jeopardise a carefully-planned *Abwehr* operation that has taken more than eight months to set up. I still don't know who is the head of the group."

"Never mind that. Tell us the names."

"I cannot do that without the authorisation of my superiors in Berlin."

"We could beat it out of you."

"I doubt it."

"Would you like us to try?"

Paul said nothing. Without warning one of the men

knocked him off the chair. It was not a hard blow, more of a cuff. He hit the floor hard. Wood, he thought, not stone. At least he was not in a dungeon.

"Once again. Who is Karásek?"

"I told you."

"And you still refuse to set up a rendezvous?"

"I do."

"Then you do have something to conceal!"

"Nothing."

"We prefer to believe otherwise!"

"I cannot prevent that."

Five hours. Six hours. Seven hours. The room smelled of sweat and anger. At one point they had coffee brought in. They did not give any to Paul. He did not ask for any, although his mouth was parched, his throat tight with tension. When he spoke he felt as if someone was scraping the vocal chords with a file.

"All right," the familiar voice said. "Let's start again."

Eight hours. Nine? Twelve? A day? He was beginning to lose count. He did not know any more if it was day or night, how long he had been beneath the sweatsoaked hood. Redness swam upwards through his body. His legs were numb, his feet like blocks of stone. They had tied him to the chair a long time ago because he kept falling off. His clothes stank of sweat and urine.

"Karásek! Karásek! Tell us where to find Karásek!"

He heard them shouting, as if they were far away. I ought to tell them something, he thought. The redness was getting darker, turning to black.

"Alexandrinenstrasse 18," he muttered. "Apartment fourteen."

"Is that where Karásek lives?"

"Yes," Paul mumbled. "Karásek." Morávec would not be there any more. He had stayed out of the hands of the Gestapo all these years by always leaving whatever place he was living in the moment he had any contact whatsoever with the police, even if they only stopped him and checked his papers. But it would keep them busy for a while.

"All right," he heard someone say. "Lock him up."

And then there was only blackness.

* * *

He awoke in a narrow cell. It was not wide enough for him to extend his arms. The walls and floor were wet with condensation. The ceiling, six and a half feet high, dripped constantly. There was no furniture, just a mattress on the floor. It was soaking wet, as was the blanket which Paul found draped across his body. His clothes were soaked and filthy. He rolled up the mattress and sat on it, looking at the steel door. There was a tiny judas window in it. Light came in through a small crack at its base. It was the only light, the only ventilation. In the corner of the cell Paul saw a hole: his toilet.

He got up and banged with his fist on the door. He shouted at the top of his voice, banging again and again on the slimy steel door. They had taken away his watch. He had no idea how long he had been here, nor even where he was. He kept banging on the door. Nobody came.

"Bring him out!"

They put the hood back over his head first, then dragged him along what sounded like a stone corridor, and he heard doors opening and slamming, the sound of keys jangling. A prison? Pankrac? Rough hands jammed him on a wooden chair, others lashed him to it with a rope that burned his upper arms.

"Where am I?" he said, putting anger into his voice. "How long have I been here?"

"You're here to answer questions, Kramer!" someone shouted at him. "Not ask them!"

"Once again, I protest—"

Someone hit him along the side of the head. Quite hard, this time. He went over on his side. His arm was numb from the fall. He felt them grab the chair and set him upright again.

"Tell us about Karásek!" a voice shouted.

"I told you all I know," Paul said.

"You gave us an address. Repeat it!"

"Alexandrinenstrasse 18."

"Apartment?"

"Fourteen."

"Your friend Karásek a comedian, then?"

"I don't understand."

"He wasn't there," the voice said. "But he left something. Two sacks of manure. One marked Goebbels and the other marked Göring."

Paul smiled beneath the hood. Morávec was still at liberty. Perhaps he could use that fact to improve his own situation.

"Well?" he heard the Gestapo interrogator say. "Do you think that's funny?"

"No," Paul said. "Of course not!"

"You said Karásek was your informer."

"I did."

"Yet he commits acts of hostility to the Reich!"

"Perhaps he was being watched," Paul said. "By the resistance."

There was a silence: they hadn't thought of that. One for me, he thought. A small one, perhaps. But one for me.

"Where will he have gone?"

"Karásek? I don't know. I have no idea."

"Then you must set up a *treff* with him."

"I told you, to do so will—"

"There is no longer any choice in the matter, Kramer," Bergmann's voice cut in. So he's here, too, Paul thought. "You are so instructed by the *Reichsprotector* himself, as head of the RSHA and General of the Police."

"I see," said Paul, as if he were thinking it over.

"Untie him," he heard Bergmann say. "Take off the hood."

The lights were dim; he could not see faces well. He recognised Kurt Bergmann, but the others were unfamiliar. Bergmann was sitting on the corner of a table, jackbooted leg swinging.

"Thank you," Paul said.

"Do you want some water?" When Paul nodded, not trusting himself to speak, Bergmann gestured to one of the Gestapo agents. The man filled a glass with water from a carafe on the table and handed it to Paul. Paul drained it in one long swallow: it was flat and brackish, but it tasted like the sweetest he had ever drunk.

266

"Thank you," he said again.

"Now, Kramer, this can't go on," Bergmann said. "You must assist us in our inquiries."

"Yes," Paul said, dully. "I see that."

"Would you like a blanket? Perhaps you'd rather lie down for a while?"

"No."

Bergmann shrugged. "Very well. To business. You are to set up a meeting with the man Karásek immediately."

"Very well," Paul said. There were still ways he could fool them, even now. He and Morávec had all sorts of cutouts and warnings. It would take a long time to use them all. "Where?"

"I think we shall use your apartment," Bergmann said.

"He has never come there."

"All the better," Bergmann said. "He won't suspect it's a trap."

He wrote the coded note and they put it in the drop at the bookstall. Then they drove him to his apartment in Smichov. He could see that it had been carefully and thoroughly searched; that did not worry him. There was nothing at the apartment which could incriminate him. Five Gestapo agents were posted in the apartment, a dozen others all around the building. Six o'clock had been selected as the time of the *treff*.

"He won't come up unless I go down and meet him," Paul told Bergmann. "He'll wait at the trolley stop until he sees me. If I don't come, he'll just go away."

Bergmann looked at him levelly. "Is this some kind of trick, Kramer?"

"No trick."

"Very well, Go down and meet him. But, Kramer . . . try anything and we'll shoot you down like a dog."

"I won't try anything," Paul said. He didn't need to. The moment Morávec saw him on the street alone he would know something was wrong and keep walking. Paul went down the stairs and out into the street. The air was fresh and sweet. He had forgotten that it was spring. There were rainclouds in the sky over Petrin Hill. Late sunlight gilded the tower at its summit. He went up to a man who was waiting for a trolley, and asked him the time. The man looked at his watch, and Paul nodded. Then he walked back to the apartment.

"Well?" Bergmann snapped when he walked in. "Where is he?"

"He sent a courier," Paul said. "You saw me speak to him. He can't come today. He'll try to come tomorrow."

"All right," Bergmann said. "All right, Kramer. One more time. But only one."

They took him back to his cell, hooded so that he would not know where it was. They kept him there all that night and all the next day, bringing him only some bread, cold sausage and weak tea. He wolfed the food down, oblivious to anything except the gnawing hunger. He wished he had a watch, so he would know when to expect them, so he could fortify himself against their coming.

The door clanged open and the guards came in with the hood. They put it over his head and he was taken down the corridor and bundled into a car. At the apartment, Bergmann was waiting, cold and precise. His nostrils twitched with distaste at the smell coming off Paul's unwashed body.

"So," he said. "We try again."

"You want me to go down and meet him?"

"No!" Bergmann snapped. "You will stay here!"

"But he won't come up."

"We'll take that chance," Bergmann said, with a smile. "Sit near the window, Kramer. You wouldn't want to miss anything, would you?"

Paul said nothing. Someone put a chair near the window. He could see down the street. It looked empty, but he knew it was not. There were Gestapo men on the roof opposite, others hidden in doorways and houses all along the street. Three more were hiding in the back of a delivery van parked opposite Paul's apartment. One of them was Gerhard Leiche.

At a few minutes before six, he saw Morávec coming up the street. *Go back,* he pleaded silently with the advancing figure. *Go back!* But Morávec came on, walking with a slight limp. Paul wondered whether he had been wounded during the fight in the street; Morávec had faltered as he ran, he recalled.

Morávec was close to the entrance to the apartment building when he stopped, and bent down to tie his shoelace. *Thank God, he's seen them,* Paul thought. Morávec looked up at the apartment and then crossed the street, walking faster. All at once the street was full of running men. Morávec pulled out his two pistols and started firing. The men who had been hiding in the back of the delivery van piled out. Paul saw that Leiche was carrying a machine-pistol. He raked the street with bullets. Paul saw Morávec stagger and fall, then get up again. He managed to run about forty yards before another bullet knocked him off his feet a second time. The Gestapo men were running towards him, shouting. He rolled over on his back and sat up, the guns banging *bambam-bambabam.* Glass shattered somewhere: a woman screamed. Bergmann cursed and threw open the window, leaning out to watch what was going on below. Morávec had got to his feet again. He ran, staggering, to the end of the street. Gerhard Leiche ran after him, shouting hoarsely. He was too far away for them to hear what he was shouting. Morávec fired at him. Leiche jumped into a doorway. A streetcar ground up the hill, going slowly. When it got level with the end of the street, Morávec ran and jumped on to it. Leiche and his men all ran towards the junction, firing their guns as they went. The tram driver jammed on his brakes. Morávec flinched as though someone had hit him with a stick, and fell into the road. His briefcase fell some yards away from him. He started to crawl towards it. People were jumping off the streetcar in panic, shouting. One of the Gestapo men fired at Morávec. His body arched up in agony and he rolled on to his back, legs kicking high.

As Leiche and his men pounded closer, the little Czech got to his knees. He turned to face the oncoming Leiche, his face contorted with agony.

"Hello, shitface," he said.

Then he put one of his guns into his mouth and pulled the trigger.

London, March 25, 1942

As soon as word came from *'Libuse'* at Pardubice that Kramer was under arrest, three special teams were nominated to go into Czechoslovakia immediately and try to locate and, if possible, liberate him. The men were all volunteers who had trained with Wolf Trap at Camusdarach. The first team, Outdistance, consisted of Adolf Opalka, Karel Curda, and Zdenek Kolarik. The second, Zinc, had Oldrich Pechal, Arnost Miks, and Vilem Gerik as its members. The third, Tin, had only two: Jaroslav Svarc and Ludvik Cupal.

"I want to go in with them," Sam said.

"No, Sam," Mason-Morley said. "Sorry. Not a chance."

"Even if General Donovan okays it?"

"Even then. You know too much. If you were to fall into enemy hands . . ." He let it dangle, like that. Nice of him, Sam thought: always the light touch.

"I speak Czech," Sam said. "German, too. Better than most of your boys do."

"Sam," Mason-Morley said.

"Listen," Sam insisted. "What do you know about me, Noël?" Mason-Morley frowned a trifle guiltily, but did not answer. Well, well, Sam thought, so you've got a dossier on me. I wonder what's in it?

"I'll tell you anyway," he said. "I was born in Germany. When I came out of gymnasium—secondary school—in 1916, my parents sent me to America. So I wouldn't have to go into the German Army."

"Go on," Mason-Morley said, laying down his pen.

"I went to live with my uncle and aunt in a place called Woodmere, on Long Island. They were an elderly couple. They'd never had children, so I became the nearest thing they'd ever had to a son. They put me through college, Columbia Law School. After I passed the State Department examination, I joined the foreign service. I was going to bring my parents to America. That was in 1923. You know what happened in 1923."

"What?"

"A little thing in Munich called a *putsch,* started by a gentleman called Hitler."

270

"Your parents were involved in that?"

"My father was a professor of psychology at the University of Munich," Sam said. "He hated the Nazis. Anyone with any intellect hated them. They were thugs, drunks, jailbirds. He would have voted for Satan sooner than Hitler."

"I don't—"

"On the night of November eighth, Hitler and his henchmen stormed into the Bürgerbräukeller in Munich. There was a political meeting going on. Hitler announced that they were taking control of the Bavarian government. At the same time his *Sturmabteilung* rowdies under Röhm occupied District Army Headquarters in the Schonfeldstrasse. The idea was to take control of Munich, then march on Berlin and bring down the government. They were stopped the next day in the Odeonsplatz."

"Ah," Mason-Morley said. "The famous march."

"The famous march," Sam said. "But that was the next day, around noon. All the preceding night, there were riots, beatings, robberies. Nazi thugs roamed the streets like wolves. They looted shops, they smashed up a newspaper office. They beat people up, smashed up their homes, killed them for no other reason than their names sounded Jewish."

"Your parents. . . ?"

"The family name was Grau," Sam said. "I anglicised it when I joined the service. I suppose it sounded Jewish enough, although we were not. It made no difference. A gang of Nazis broke into the house. They tried to set fire to my father's beard. My mother hit one of them. He hit her with a rifle butt and she fell to the floor, bleeding badly. My father ran at the one who had hit my mother. The man shot him on the spot. Then they splashed kerosene on the furniture and set fire to it."

"Your parents both died," Mason-Morley said. It was not a question.

"Yes," Sam said. "Nobody was ever arrested, or even accused."

"I'm sorry," Mason-Morley said.

"I didn't know about it for a long time," Sam said. "We just got word that my parents had died in a fire. The year Hitler became Chancellor, I was posted to Dresden as com-

271

mercial attaché. I went to Munich, and that was when I found out what had really happened. So you see, Noël, I've got as good reasons as anyone for being at the sharp end. Let me go in with 'Tin'."

"Sam," Mason-Morley said, sympathetically. "I do understand. But, look—you were up at Camusdarach. You know what parachuting is like. It's fine for tough, young kids. I hate to say it, Sam, but you're—"

"Too old, are you going to say?"

"Well, if you put me to it, yes!"

"I'm fifty," Sam said.

Mason-Morley didn't speak. He just looked at Sam. After a few moments he spread his hands, as if to say, what can I tell you?

"I thought you were smart, you British," Sam said. "You're sending in three teams to try to get Kramer out, but you're overlooking something very important."

"Tell me," Mason-Morley said.

"I know what he looks like," Sam said, playing his ace. "Nobody else does."

"Our people in Prague—"

"You have no 'people' in Prague, Noël. They're all under arrest. Nobody in the entire Wolf Trap team knows Kramer. Except me!"

"I hate to say this, Sam," Mason-Morley said, slowly. "But you're right."

"I know."

"We don't even know where he is," Mason-Morley said.

"I know. But maybe we can find out."

"How?"

"I know someone who might tell me," Sam said. "If I put it to him properly." He thought of the loquacious Ludwig Winkel squinting down the barrel of a gun. Yes, if he knew anything, he would talk, Sam thought. The gargoyle face of the Gestapo officer, Leiche, came into his memory. He closed it out, like someone switching off a light. No thank you, memory. He watched Mason-Morley tap his pursed lips with a pencil.

"What about getting out?" Sam said.

"We've got a new fighter bomber," Mason-Morley said. "It has a range of sixteen hundred and fifty miles and it flies

272

like the proverbial manure coming off a shovel. It's called a Mosquito, made by the De Havilland people. All wood. Nothing Jerry has got can touch it for speed. It's just going operational."

Sam spread his hands. "Well, then."

"Sam, it could very well be a one-way trip."

"Noël," Sam said. "Whose life is it, anyway?"

"I can't argue with that," Mason-Morley said. "All right, Sam. If General Donovan okays it, I'll accept you as a volunteer."

"When do they go in?"

"Saturday night," Mason-Morley said. "The twenty-eighth. You haven't got a lot of time."

"It'll be enough," Sam said.

"Do you mind telling me something, Sam?" Mason-Morley asked. "Why is Kramer so important to you?"

"He's a brave man," Sam said. "And I'm in his debt." He didn't think he needed to tell Mason-Morley why. Mason-Morley was the apostle of need-to-know, and this was one time where he was going to take a swig of his own medicine. Sam Gray had his own reasons for wanting to go back to Prague. The man he had been looking for since 1933 was in Prague. Sam had tried a thousand times to locate him. He had never got to first base: his questions met only indifference or hostility. The Nazis looked after their own. So he had waited until he met a man who could ask the questions Sam could not: Paul Kramer. Kramer had access to the kind of documents nobody else ever got to see, Gestapo records, police files, everything. He had come up with the name of the man for whom Sam had been looking all those years, an officer in Heydrich's Reich Main Security Office. His name was Kurt Alfred Bergmann.

"Sam," Mason-Morley said. "Are you sure you're telling me everything?"

"Of course," Sam said. "What's wrong, Noël? Don't you trust me?"

In the circumstances, he thought, that was rather good.

Prague, April 30, 1942

As in everything else, there was a system for interrogation.

General interrogation of suspects was first conducted 'at the lowest level'. This meant that anyone arrested by the Gestapo, or the SD, or any one of the seven security agencies, would be brought under arrest to the Petschek Palace and interrogated by a *Kriminaloberassistant*. The reason for the arrest might be one of many: refusal of a forced labourer to work, idling, remarks construed as being critical of the Reich, being an asocial person. This was routine work, dull, plodding, and often brutal. The lower ranks of the Gestapo were not noted for the subtlety of their methods. They got their information with fists, with boots, and with truncheons.

If, in the course of such interrogation, information was extracted from a prisoner which led to further arrests, for activities more dangerous to the security and safety of the citizens of the Reich, then the prisoner was moved up to the next level of questioning, where he was interrogated 'at a higher level'. There, depending upon his crime—it could perhaps be sabotage, membership of the Communist party, knowledge about important facts, connections or plans hostile to the state or legal system—he would undergo what was known in Gestapo parlance as 'sharpened interrogation'. Sharpened interrogation could consist of any or all of the following: simplest rations (bread and water); hard bed; dark cell; deprivation of sleep; exhaustion exercises; blows with a stick (although in the event of more than twenty blows being administered it was required that a doctor be present).

Interrogation 'at a higher level' was conducted only by officers above the rank of *Kriminalsekretar,* and it was required that the prisoner be at no time alone with only one interrogator. The 'sharpened interrogation' could not be used to make a prisoner confess his own criminal acts, nor upon persons delivered by justice for the purpose of further investigation. Any exceptions to these rules had to be sanctioned by the head of the Gestapo, *Brigadeführer* and *Reichskriminaldirector* Heinrich Müller in Berlin.

Finally, there was interrogation 'at the highest level'. This was a form of interrogation reserved for the most sensitive detainees, such as persons of high rank, or international reputation, persons who were, in the parlance, 'bearers of secrets', and those 'known to the Führer'. Here, and only here, did the security service use kid gloves. Until it could be established beyond doubt that a prisoner was guilty as charged of the offences for which he had been arrested, no coercion and no physical violence could be employed. In other words, if violence was used, it had to be used in a way that left no trace. There were one or two ways this could be done. They had not used any of them on Paul Kramer.

Yet.

He did not know any of his interrogators. There were six or seven of them. They came in no special order, and they did not always continue questioning him from the point at which they had left off. This, as all the other things they did, was to confuse him, to disorient him, to put him off the balance he was so determinedly trying to maintain. It was all he had, and he had to hold on to it. They were going to try and break him down, a bit at a time. He was going to try and prevent them from doing it. He knew the technique as well as they did. Over and over the same ground, probing, poking, testing, checking, double-checking. The same questions, again and again and again, and the same answers. More or less the same answers. He was like Scheherezade, telling her thousand and one stories: the moment there were no more stories, there would be no more Scheherezade. He told them all the small truths, and maintained the one big lie: his innocence. All the small truths had to be checked, verified. That took time. Time was his friend. The longer it took them to break him, the more chance he had to get out of this. It was a dangerous, deadly game, but he had no choice at all any more.

He had pulled every string he knew. Protests at his arrest had poured in; dozens of declarations of his reliability, of his service to the Reich and his impeccable record, had come from the highest echelons in Berlin. Canaris had placed his objections before the Führer himself. Himmler had received letters from Rohleder, Piekenbrock, Dr Ley, a dozen others. It had taken every ounce of Heydrich's not-inconsiderable influence to keep the interrogation open, but he had done it.

He wanted that confession, and he was going to have it. Meanwhile, all Paul could do was to steadfastly protest his innocence, insisting they were making a mistake.

He knew it was no mistake.

So did they.

So it was only a question of how long he could hold them off.

"Again," the interrogator said.

"I've told you everything."

"Tell me again."

Paul looked at the photograph. His eyes swam. He was utterly, bone-achingly weary. They never let him sleep longer than an hour. They never turned off the lights in the cell. He did not know any more whether it was day or night. He had tried to keep track of the time by scratching marks on the wall of the cell, but by the third week of questioning he was too disoriented.

"I have no idea who it is," he said.

"I will tell you," the man said. He was short, thickset, bland. His manner was prim and precise. Schoolmasterish, Paul thought. Come along now, boy. You can do better than this. "His name is Alben Graumann. He is, or rather was, a *Kriminalobersekretar* of *Amt* IVE/1."

"Why don't you call it what it is?" Paul said. "Gestapo."

"All right," the man said, equably. "Gestapo."

"You said 'was'?"

"You know damned well he is dead."

'It's news to me."

"You said that last time."

"That doesn't surprise me," Paul said. "It's the truth."

"You still maintain you do not know this man?"

"Yes."

"Yet during the month of December, 1940, Graumann was assigned to surveillance of your activities."

"May I ask why?"

"You may ask nothing."

"That's what *you* said last time."

"That doesn't surprise me," the man mimicked. "It's the truth. Now, answer my question: have you ever seen this man?"

"Not to my knowledge," Paul said.

"Can you give me an account of your activities on the evening of December 12, 1940?"

This was a new question. They had not asked this one before. "That's over a year ago," Paul said. "I don't think I could remember."

"Let me refresh your memory. You went to a cinema."

"How do you know that?"

"Here is your desk diary," the man said, producing Paul's diary from his briefcase. "On the date in question you have written at the bottom of the page the word 'Ufapalast'."

"I remember now," Paul said. "I went to see a film."

"What film?"

Ohm Kruger.

"The records confirm that the film *Ohm Kruger* was playing at the Ufapalast on the date in question. Did you meet anyone there?"

My God, they even checked the cinema playdates, he thought. "No," he said.

"What did you do after you left the cinema?"

"I can't remember exactly. I think I may have gone for a drink."

"Don't play silly games with us, Kramer!" the man said. "You know where you went!"

Another man came into the interrogation room. He was tall, thin. His eyes had a strange, lacklustre light in them, as if he had learned that his lot in life was to be disappointed in his fellow man.

"Where are we up to?" he asked the interrogator. He pulled an upright chair away from the table and sat down. The first man pointed at the paper on his clipboard. The man nodded.

"All right," he said. "You went for a drink. Where?"

"I told your friend here, I can't remember."

"Do you want us to have the girl brought down here, Kramer?" the thin one snapped. They were changing the pace of the interrogation: the thin one was going to be tougher, less patient. Hard and soft, they called it.

"Girl?" Paul said, thinking fast. "Oh, the tart, you mean?"

"Her name?"

"I never asked."

"That's unusual, isn't it?" Soft asked.

"I wouldn't know," Paul said. "Is it?"

He saw the anger stain Soft's face, and felt a malicious pleasure in scoring a little point. It was imperative that he retain that arrogance, the stance of a man of high status being questioned by inferiors. He had long ago vowed to make them work for every morsel he gave them.

"All right, you picked up the tart. Where was this, by the way?" Hard said, offhandedly.

"The Café Dobren."

"Your memory is improving," Hard said, sarcastically. Paul cursed himself silently for the slip. It was just that he was so damned tired. But he dare not let them know that. Otherwise they would bribe him with sleep. Just tell us what we want to know, and we'll let you sleep as long as you like. Food, warmth, sleep: you had to forget you needed any of them.

"What then?" Soft said, with a reproving glance at Hard.

"I bought some wine."

"How long did you stay there?"

"An hour, maybe two."

"Go on."

"I was going to go to her place," Paul said. "Then when we got outside, I saw she was drunk. And I thought, to the devil with it. I gave her fifty Marks and told her to get a taxi home."

"Fifty Marks, eh? You're free with it, aren't you?" Hard sneered.

Paul smiled, thanking him for the opening. "Some of us can afford to be," he said. He watched Hard's eyes fill with anger: he was a working-class lad, and he had probably hated the wealthy all his life. There were a lot of those in the Party. It was one of the main reasons they joined.

"She was drunk, you say?" Soft said.

"Very. I left her in a doorway. It was all she could do to stand up." Impasse, my friend, he thought. If you did find the tart, all she could tell you was that she went into a doorway with me and when she woke up she was in the car park with Gestapo. If she told you anything else, I can explode it. If she did not, you cannot make a lie out of my 'truth'. Soft looked at Hard. Hard shrugged.

"All right," Hard said. "Let's go over it again."

Kurt Bergmann looked at the photographs which had been found in Morávec's briefcase. They were the faces of young men, ordinary faces you would pass in the street a hundred times a day. Was this the assassination team? He felt a strange undercurrent of excitement and fear. Heydrich knew nothing of these photographs. Bergmann turned them over. On the back was rubber-stamped the words *Sedlácek, Pardubice*. They had been in Pardubice! That would have to be taken care of: the photographer, any contacts. He wished he knew the names of the three men. Somehow that would have made them more real. Morávec had doubtless been bringing the photographs to Kramer, who in turn would have provided forged documents prepared by the *Abwehr*. Bergmann made another mental note to check with Albert Müller of *Abwehr* 1/G. Müller prepared all forged papers for the *Abwehr*. It would be instructive to find out for whom Kramer had requested papers in the past year.

Bergmann put the three photographs back into the envelope and opened his safe. As he locked it, he thought again of Heydrich, who had an identical one. In it, Bergmann knew, where Heydrich's dossiers on all the leaders of the Reich, even the Führer. If one could get one's hands on those, and on the other dossiers which Heydrich called his 'ammunition pack'!

Three men, Bergmann thought. Who were they? What were their names? Were they already in Prague? How would they do it? When would it be?

His telephone rang.

"Yes?"

"Böhm," the voice on the other end said. *Standartenführer* Horst Böhm was head of the Prague *Sicherheitsdienst*.

"What can I do for you, Horst?"

"I thought you'd better know immediately," Böhm said. "The Kladno police just telephoned. A sergeant and a constable caught two men in the forest near Krivoklat. There was shooting. The sergeant is dead, and the policeman wounded."

"And?"

"They killed one of the two men. He's a parachutist, Kurt. A British parachutist."

"I'll come over," Bergmann said. "Don't do anything else till I get there. You understand? Put it in a box!"

"As you wish," Böhm said, coolly, and hung up. I've offended him, Bergmann thought. Fuck him. It wasn't the fawning Böhm he was worried about, it was Heydrich. There would be absolutely no way to keep this from him. His mind raced like a dynamo, weighing the consequences of this new development. Was the man who had been shot in the Krivoklat forest one of the three men whose photographs reposed in the safe behind him? Jesus, Jesus, Jesus, this was dangerous! He felt as if he was walking blindfolded and barefoot through a snakepit. Were there more parachutists? Were they the assassination team? Back-up? Dropped in to do something else? A thousand questions flooded his mind, swamping thought. He buzzed Eckhardt on the internal phone.

"Get the car!" he said.

A fortnight after he returned to active duty, Walter Abendschon was summoned to Bergmann's office in the Hradschin. It was not an interview to which he was particularly looking forward. He felt strangely disinclined to nail down the lid on Paul Kramer's coffin, and he did not know why. He had thought about it a very great deal while he had lain recovering in the hospital. The man was a traitor, no doubt. The question of why nagged at Abendschon like a toothache.

Why would a man betray his country? he wondered. Patriotism was such an abstract thing. He himself did not feel any stirring of pride when the bands played 'Deutschland Über Alles'. Not any more. He had done so, once, but that was in the days when it meant 'Germany before all else', and not 'Germany over everyone', as they preferred it now. He had never felt moved to cheer when the massed black ranks of the SS went goose-stepping past, brass blaring, bells ringing. The mass hysteria of the rallies, the weeping responses to the Führer's speeches, those had never been to his taste. Nor had he wanted war—what sane man did? Yet Hitler had his war, and the war became the will of the people. And he supposed he wanted Germany to win it because a defeated Germany was unthinkable. So like most Germans, Abendschon got on with his job, doing what was expected of him. He had a wife then, and two growing boys to feed; if he fought the system, he would simply lose his job and his pension and his seniority. Someone else would take his place, and the world would keep on turning. What would that prove? So through the years he had watched everything change, and realised that he was deeply unhappy with the way things were, and that he had condoned the changes by not opposing them, while somewhere deep inside himself knowing that they should be opposed.

Was that the difference between a man like himself and a man like Kramer? No, he told himself angrily. It would never have occurred to him to pass state secrets to the British or the Czechs. That was not the way to fight for change. Then what was? If you were a man like Kramer, might you convince yourself it was the only way you could fight? But why, why, why? Why did he hate Germany enough to betray her to her enemies?

The answer, Abendschon felt sure, lay somewhere in the past. As soon as he was able to work, he began to carefully check every aspect of Paul Kramer's life. Something in 1939, perhaps, or 1938, when it had begun? Or something which happened earlier, a hurt buried deep, deep down, burning like slow fire beneath rock for years before erupting as the molten lava of betrayal?

And he found the answer. He knew Bergmann wouldn't be interested. All Bergmann wanted was to break Kramer for Heydrich. Heydrich would use the man for his own purposes. Is that what we do it all for? Abendschon thought, wearily. Two bullets through your body, one so close to the heart the doctors think you'll never pull through, and for what? So Reinhard Heydrich can still further expand his sinister, bloodthirsty empire?

"Well, Walter, you're looking better," Bergmann said. "Come in and sit down!"

"*Standartenführer,*" he said, accepting the chair gratefully. His chest still ached if he stood for a long time. His wounds were healed, yet they made him move warily, constantly reminded of the fragility of his body. None of the doctors had thought he would make it. Well, I fooled them all, he thought. I had a secret weapon: Karin. Something to live for. That was all you needed. They told him he was lucky to be alive. They said one of Novak's bullets had gone within a millimetre of the subclavian artery. They sounded a little piqued, as if it was unfair of him not to die.

"Good to see you back on the job," Bergmann said, with the false bonhomie of a cigar salesman. "How do you feel?"

"I've been chirpier," Abendschon said.

"I thought your report was outstanding," Bergmann said. "Quite outstanding."

"Thank you."

"The thing is," Bergmann said. "They're not getting anywhere with Kramer."

"They?"

"At the Petschek."

"Even with the stuff I gave you?"

"Well," Bergmann said. He's acting, Abendschon thought. Why is he putting this act on? "I didn't give them everything, Walter."

"I see," Abendschon said, although he did not. "Why?"

"I don't want this to go out of our hands," Bergmann said. "The *Reichsprotector* and I agree that it is too sensitive."

"And so?"

"I want you to take over the interrogation of Kramer."

"I see."

"I want him broken, Walter," Bergmann said. "I want him broken wide open!"

I wonder why he hates the man so much? Abendschon wondered. The wife? It seemed unlikely. From what he had found out about Erika Bergmann, her husband didn't give a damn what she did, as long as she didn't do it in the street and frighten the animals.

"Put everything else to one side," Bergmann said. "The *Reichsprotector* is impatient. He wants a confession, Walter. It is our job to get it for him. You understand me?"

Our job, Abendschon thought, wondering why he felt this way. Maybe it was the after-effect of being wounded. He was conscious of mortality, his, everyone else's. Why should a man have to give his life so that someone else could get an extra piece of braid on his shoulders?

"All right," he said, knowing he had no choice. "I'll get started right away."

"Report to me daily," Bergmann said. "I want your report on my desk first thing every day."

"Very good," Abendschon said, thinking, you and your damned reports. He hated reports. Bergmann had given him a very hard time for not having made one on Kramer immediately after his trip to Berlin. You could have died, and then where would we have been? he shouted. And Abendschon thought, you didn't give a damn whether I lived or died, only whether you got your report, only whether you could get Kramer. For the first time in his life, Abendschon was hating what he did, hating the people he did it for. Maybe it all had to do with Karin, he thought. When you had someone to live for you didn't want to deal in death.

"You have until May 20," Bergmann informed him coldly. "No longer."

"Why May 20?" Abendschon asked.

"I suggest you ask the *Reichsprotector,*" Bergmann said. "It was he who chose the date."

"Thank him for me," Abendschon said, and left.

The man who came in was a new one. Paul had never seen him before. He was about fifty, Paul reckoned, with a thin-lipped mouth that turned down at both ends, and heavy eyebrows joined in a frown that seemed habitual. Tall, heavily-built, his hair flecked with grey, the man sat down heavily on the chair opposite Paul and regarded him closely through eyes of a quite extraordinary blueness.

"My name is Walter Abendschon," he said. "From Berlin. *Kripo.*"

Paul nodded. The man looked as if he had been ill. His skin was pasty, and there were pain lines at the corners of the bright blue eyes.

"You don't know me," Abendschon said. "But I know a

283

great deal about you, *Oberst* Kramer. A very great deal."

"Really?" Paul said, unease seeping into his heart. This was all new, all different. Abendschon smiled. It was the smile of someone who has come across Paul's kind of confidence before and knows how to deal with it.

"I want you to tell me something," Abendschon said.

"What's that?"

"Tell me how your father died," Abendschon said, and Paul's spirit dropped like a rock into Hell.

"Again," Abendschon said.

"I've told you everything," Paul said. "There's nothing more."

"Where did you meet Stevens and Best?"

"In the offices of *Het Handelsdient Veer Het Continent*," Paul repeated. "In The Hague."

"And the purpose of your visit there?"

"To convince them that the SD agents with whom they were dealing were, in fact, what they claimed to be."

"You were not there to betray them, at the request of Colonel Alois Frank of Czech Intelligence?"

"Of course not!"

"The Englishman says you were."

"Then how was it that they were not betrayed?"

"It will be the work of but a couple of days to bring them here and confront you, Kramer!" Abendschon snapped. "Do you want me to do that?"

"If you think it would help."

"I think it might," Abendschon said, and Paul's spirits sank still further. There was savage irony in the fact that Best and Stevens were in Oranienburg, and able to testify against him. He had put his own life on the line for them, a long time ago, when he had gone to The Hague to warn them that the SD agents were frauds. They had disregarded his information, and been captured by the SD for their pains. And they had betrayed him as casually as smoking a cigarette.

"Let's go on to something else," Abendschon said.

"All right."

"Tell me about Turnau."

"What?"

"It was Turnau, wasn't it? Where you rendezvoused with Captain Fryc of Czech Intelligence?"

"What are you talking about?"

"February, 1939, *Oberst* Kramer," Abendschon said.

"I was never in Turnau," Paul said. "In 1939 or any other year."

Abendschon sighed. It looked like it was going to take a very long time to break this one.

"Tell me the name of this man," he said, producing a photograph. He laid it face up on the table.

"His name is Samuel Gray. He is, or was, the commercial attaché of the American Embassy in Berlin."

"What is your connection with him?"

"He is an outlet."

"A what?"

"I use him for disinformation purposes."

"Explain."

"How much do you know about counter-espionage?"

"Not much," Abendschon said. "Tell me." He leaned back, inviting Paul to continue. Keep talking, my friend, he thought. The more you talk, the likelier you are to slip. I'll get you. I'll get you.

"One of the main tasks of the counter-espionage operative is negative intelligence," Paul said. This was safe ground. He could talk on this theme for hours. All hours in which he was not being questioned were periods of grace, in which the beleaguered, battered psyche could rest. "His main efforts are directed towards concealing the policies of his country, its diplomatic decisions, its military plans, and any or all of its secret information."

"Yes."

"One of the main ways to achieve those ends is to misinform the agents of other countries."

"You're telling me Gray is an agent?"

"American secret service."

"I didn't know the Americans had a secret service."

"The domestic apparatus which the Americans call their Secret Service is merely a protection squad for the President and other politicians," Paul said. "It was established after the death of Lincoln in 1865. The Federal Bureau of Investigation looks after espionage and counter-espionage on

American soil. Up to last summer, there was no overseas service worthy of the name. Such an agency has been established: the Office of the Coordinator of Information. Gray is one of its senior officers."

"He told you this?"

"Yes. We were exchanging information. That is to say, he was giving me information and I was giving him disinformation."

"How often did you meet?"

"It varied. Perhaps at six- or seven-week intervals."

"When was the last time you saw this man?"

Paul thought very quickly. The long, leisurely chat had led him ineluctably to this question. His foot was directly above the trap. Put it down, or flinch away? He looked at Abendschon's hands. They were slightly tensed.

"Last month," he said. "Here in Prague."

Abendschon could not conceal his disappointment, and Paul allowed himself a small, secret smile at scoring the point. Abendschon had been expecting a lie.

"And what was the nature of your discussion?"

"The reason given for Gray's visit to Prague was 'international trade'. I knew there must be another, covert one. It was a simple matter to contact him."

"How?"

"I followed him when he left his hotel alone."

"And did you discover the reason for his visit?"

"The British had asked him to come to Prague, to see if he could in any way make contact with Vaslav Morávec."

"He told you this?"

"Of course. He was under the impression that I was 'doubled', working inside the Reich for the Allies, as I had led him to believe. He asked me if I could take him to Morávec."

"And did you?"

"I promised I would try."

"Why did you not communicate this matter to the Gestapo or the SD?"

"I planned to, as soon as my own investigations were complete."

"And your code name?"

"I had no code name."

"Surely you don't expect me to believe that?"

Paul shrugged. "I can't make you."

"It wasn't 'Karl', by any chance?"

"No."

"You're good, Kramer," Abendschon said. "Very good."

"Yes," Paul replied. "I am."

Abendschon's eyes sparked with held-back anger, and again Paul let himself relax: they were pinpricks, but they were still points. He watched as Abendschon dipped into his briefcase and brought out yet another photograph. This time it was a picture of Jan Novak.

"You know who this is, of course?"

"Of course. His name is—"

"I know his name. He was shot to death."

"I was told he died of a heart attack."

"Wrong,' Abendschon said, brutally. "He was shot to pieces. I know it for a fact, because I was the one who shot him!"

He saw Kramer's reaction, the immediately-concealed dismay, and a small smile touched his face. Yes, Kramer was good, but he could be hurt. That one had hurt him. A few more like that, and he'd crack.

"I could have him disinterred," he said. "They'd arrest them all. The undertaker, the doctor. The mother. The daughter."

"Bastard!" Paul said.

"You could save them all a lot of grief, Kramer," Abendschon said. "All you have to do is sign a confession."

"Go to hell."

Abendschon smiled. Anger was good. An angry man was easier to trap, an angry man spoke without reflection. Keep him angry, he told himself.

"Tell me about the girl," he said. "She whores, doesn't she?"

The SS squad marched into the cemetery. The gatekeeper watched them, wide-eyed, then hurried away to make a telephone call when he saw where they were digging. An hour later a *Lastwagen* rolled through the cemetery gate, and Jan Novak's disinterred coffin was loaded into it, to be taken to the SS forensic laboratories at the University. Three hours later, Gestapo cars squealed to a stop outside the houses of Dr Vladimir Holub and the mortician Hanka Tirlov. The two men and all the members of the families were hustled into *Abholwagen* and taken to the Petschek, where they were subjected to 'sharpened interrogation' for seventy-two hours. When they had told their interrogators everything they could tell them, they were put into detention cells to await transportation to the KZ-Mauthausen.

The following morning, the Gestapo vehicles drove into the little square in front of the Novak house. Maria Novakova saw them coming from the first-floor bedroom window, where she had been making the beds. At least the parachutists were gone, she thought. Uncle Hajsky moved them around all the time: it was the only way to keep the *Blockleitern* from learning of their existence. She had liked the big American.

Down in the square she saw a huge, ugly man get out of one of the cars and stand with his hands on his hips, looking up. Their eyes met. He ran across the street and banged on the door. Maria smiled, almost dreamily. She sat down on the dressing-table stool and looked at herself in the mirror. Well, old girl, she thought. She had expected to be afraid: she was not. She picked up her husband's photograph and kissed his face. Then she put the cyanide capsule into her mouth and bit down hard on it.

Antonie Novakova was not so lucky. No one could get word to her in the Lufthansa offices. The Gestapo squad arrested her as she came out into the Wenzelplatz at lunchtime. Twenty minutes later, she was sitting in the *kino* at the Petschkarna, shivering. Nobody looked at her. Nobody looked at anybody else. There was no clock on the wall, no way of knowing how long she had been there. From time to time a man in a uniform came to the door and shouted a name. The man or woman named would scramble to their feet and hurry towards the doorway in which the uniformed man stood. The heavy door would close with a bang. The silence would descend again, broken only by the shuffling of a foot, a suppressed cough, the sound of a child whimpering.

* * *

Questions.

And more and more questions.

There was never going to be any end to them. Scheherezade's mind was numb. He could not remember any more exactly what he had told them. They were tripping him on little things. Everyone once in a while, the first, faint tremors of resignation seeped into the back of his mind, and an evil voice whispered, what's the use, tell them, be done with it; what does it matter? And then he would stiffen his resolve and stand straight, and try to act as if he was wearily putting up with a charade whose conclusion was as foregone as its premise was stupid. Where was Rohleder, where was Canaris? Why didn't they get him out of this?

"Tell me again," Abendschon said. "How did your father die?"

"I've told you a dozen times," Paul said. "An accident. A tragic accident."

"He was playing the cello . . ." Abendschon prompted. "And the SS squad burst into the house."

They had Vati by the arms and they were dragging him across the music room. The Sergeant was shouting something but all that Paul could see was the blood on his father's face. He had never before experienced such a surge of blind, animal anguish.

"I told you," he said. "It was all a mistake."

"A mistake," Abendschon said, gently.

"Don't waste your sympathy on me," Paul said. "I don't need it."

"Oh, but you do, Kramer," Abendschon said. "You do."

"Don't," Paul said. "Please don't."

"Come on," Abendschon said. "You've never told anybody, have you?"

"No," Paul said.

"Tell me."

"There's nothing to tell."

"They killed him, didn't they? Took him away and killed him."

"I told you. They made a mistake. They thought he was someone else."

"And then they sent someone to tell you."

"Yes."

"What was his name?"

"I've forgotten. An SS man."

"Think," Abendschon said.

"I don't remember," Paul said, stubbornly.

Abendschon reached into his briefcase and took out some papers. He laid them on the table where Paul could see them.

"This is the report of the officer who came to visit you," he said. "His name is at the bottom. Read it."

Paul stared at the jagged, familiar handwriting, and looked up into Abendschon's eyes. They were the same guileless blue as always. He sighed.

"Reinhard Heydrich," he said.

"It's taking too long," Bergmann said.

"I've got him," Abendschon replied. "I only need a few more days. He'll break. He's ready."

"There's no time," Bergmann said. "The *Reichsprotector* wants his signed confession now."

"You can't hurry these things," Abendschon said.

"Can't I?" Bergmann said. He picked up the telephone and dialled the familiar number of the Petschek. "Leiche? Bergmann here. You picked up the Novakova girl? Good. And the mother? What? God damn it—!" He got control of himself. "I'll discuss that with you when you submit your report," he said, coldly. "No, don't bother. Just tell me, has the Novakova girl been interrogated? She's still on the bench, you say? How long?" He nodded, as though satisfied. Damn your evil soul to Hell, Abendschon thought. He wanted no part of this, but he knew there was no escape.

"Put her in Room 104," Bergmann told Leiche. "Naked."

Room 104 was a former chancellery on the first floor of the Petschek. Just going into it made Abendschon's belly turn over: there were instruments there which looked as if they had come from the dungeon of a medieval castle.

"Yes, right away," Bergmann was saying. "I'll be there in half an hour." He put down the telephone and looked at Abendschon. He knew what Bergmann was going to do. He felt sick, ashamed.

"That bastard has had all the rope I'm going to give

him!" Bergmann said. "It's time we stopped playing games."

"You hate him," Abendschon said.

Bergmann's eyes glowed with evil. "I've always hated him!" he said.

They took him to Room 104. It was only a small room. A window looked out on to the courtyard. Tonie was sitting in a heavy wooden chair, her legs and arms clamped to it with heavy leather straps. She was naked. She looked small and defenceless. Behind her stood a big man with a square face and a broken nose. He had hands like a butcher.

"Oh, sweet Jesus Christ," Paul said, softly. Bergmann smiled.

"I want your confession, Kramer!" he said. "Now."

"Don't!" the girl shouted. "Don't tell them anything!"

Paul shook his head.

"Take him out," Bergmann said.

They sat him on a chair in the corridor. The door closed. There was silence for a long time. Sweat dripped off Paul as if he had been hosed down. He looked at the detective.

"You see what they are," he said.

Abendschon did not answer. His throat was full of bile. He wanted to go somewhere and be sick, but he knew it would not help. He had always known they did this. Every Gestapo headquarters had a room like this one. You blocked it from your consciousness. If you did not think about it, it was not there. But this: this was obscene.

They heard the girl wail softly.

There was another silence, not so long. Then they heard the same soft moan of pain. This time it lasted longer, and rose from a moan to a stifled scream. Abendschon looked at Kramer. Oh, you poor bastard, he thought, you poor miserable fucker. Inside the chancellery the girl screamed. The scream went on and on and on until Abendschon thought his head would explode. Then it stopped. The door opened and Bergmann came out. There was a strange light in his eyes, a madness.

"Bring him in," he said.

The two Gestapo men yanked Paul to his feet. They

marched him into the torture room. The big man with the square face had blood on his hands. There was blood on the inside of Tonie's thighs. Her hair was soaked with sweat. She had bitten through her lip.

"No," she said to Paul. "Don't tell them."

"He'll tell us," Bergmann said.

"No," the girl whispered.

"Becker," Bergmann said, jerking his chin towards the girl. The big man came around the chair and bent down in front of the girl. Her head went back and her eyes opened wide, wide. A howling scream came from her bloody mouth.

"Bastards!" Paul shouted, his mind blank with grief and rage. "You sadistic animal bastards!"

The girl screamed again.

Paul Kramer writhed in the unyielding grip of the two Gestapo guards. He looked at Walter Abendschon, agony in his eyes. Abendschon looked away. His legs were quivering. He could not believe what he had just seen.

"All right," Kramer whispered.

Bergmann was in front of him in one bound.

"What?" he snapped.

"I said, all right. Don't hurt her any more."

"You'll sign the confession?"

"Yes."

"Don't make the mistake of trifling with me, Kramer!"

"No," Paul said. "I'll do whatever you say. Just don't hurt her any more."

Bergmann nodded, smiling. "All right," he said. "Take him back to his cell. I'll be down in a minute."

"Let me say goodbye to her," Paul said.

Bergmann looked at him as if he were a reptile. He made a gesture with his arm and the two Gestapo guards hustled Paul into the corridor. He did not struggle or weep or shout any more. There was nothing left to fight for.

Prague, May 19, 1942

The old man's name was Frantisek Kovarnik. He wore a thin alpaca coat and stained grey trousers. His shoes had run-down heels and scuffed uppers. He had a long, thin face covered with a two-day stubble, a high forehead, and pale, almost shifty eyes.

"It's not far now," he told Sam.

Sam nodded. The streetcar grated and screeched its way up the long broad avenue towards Zizkov. Blocks of apartment houses, devoid of either charm or elegance, grey pavements, cobbled streets, shabbily-dressed people, dingy side streets: Sam felt as if he had lived amidst them all his life. The group he had jumped with had landed in wooded country not far from a village called Lanze Belohrad. With the tall, serious leader of the Outdistance team, Lieutenant Adolf Opalka, Sam had been worked slowly towards Prague. They split up there: it was not safe to stay in one place for very long, no matter how careful the people who were sheltering you. The inquisitive eyes of the Party, the police, the Gestapo, the security police, and even one's neighbours, could not be avoided for very long.

He had lost track of the places he had slept. Sometimes in a warm bed, with a full belly; others on the bare floor of a spare room, or someone's dusty attic. He was no longer astonished at how few people would help the parachutists. Now he was astonished that anyone would. You could die very painfully for doing a lot less than harbouring a saboteur; it was no wonder people were terrified.

As for the parachutists, they were in total disarray. Although Bartos and Potucek, of Silver A, were still in Pardubice, and their transmitter was still in operation, the third member of their team, Valcik, was on the run, blown. Gabcik and Kubis, the two men designated to kill Heydrich, were living in an apartment on Letenska with two girls. To Sam's astonishment, he learned that Gabcik had gotten engaged to one of them. Silver B was lost without trace. Curda and Kolarik of Outdistance were missing. So were Svarc and Cupal of Tin. 'Libuse' asked for reinforcements. Two more teams were dropped on the night of April 28. As they were being found hiding places, Arnost Miks of Zinc found his way into the capital. His team had been dropped hundreds of miles off target. Gerik had surrendered to the Gestapo, he said. Their whole operation was completely compromised.

It was not their incompetence. It was simply that none of them had imagined in his wildest nightmares what the reality of Nazi Occupation was like. Not one person in ten thousand would help them. The smaller the village, the greater was the fear of discovery. Nobody liked the Germans, but nobody was going to risk inviting the execution of his entire family by sheltering parachutists.

A shambles, Sam decided, and cut himself loose from it. He knew where the parachutists were if he needed them. His first priority was to establish what had happened to Paul Kramer. Slowly, painfully, he put the story together. He learned how Morávec had died, Jan Novak, his wife. The daughter? The Gestapo had her. Sweet Antonie, with the madonna face and the red scarf. Sam was utterly saddened: the price of Kramer's treason had been murderously high. He remembered the girl waving to them across the square. She had been such a sweet kid. Notions like that made no difference to the Gestapo.

Finally he made contact with Morávec's one-time 'housing agent', the former schoolmaster Zelenka, known as 'Uncle Hajsky'. He was a small, neat man. He wore horn-rimmed glasses, and he had that didactic manner common to teachers. He had once played as a winger for the Liboc Star football team. He told Sam he had a contact in Police Headquarters on Nationalstrasse who might be able to find out something about Kramer. Sam was to come and see him in Zizkov, when he would give him whatever he had been able to learn.

"We get off here," old Kovarnik said. It was his job to take Sam to Zelenka's apartment. He would remain in the street while the two men talked, keeping watch. If he saw anything suspicious he would ring Zelenka's bell, four times: bz-bz-bz-bzzzz.

The apartment was like the man himself, neat, orderly, comfortable. All along one wall were bookshelves. There were silver trophies on the top of it, some cups, medals in boxes. On another wall hung a framed photograph of a football team. Liboc Star, Sam thought. He could not see a face which looked like Zelenka's.

"That's me," Zelenka said, pointing to a young man kneeling in the front row. "I was the leading scorer that season."

He said it like a man telling someone about a dream he has had: as though it had all happened in another world, another time, a different life.

"Have you been able to learn anything?" he asked.

"It is difficult," Zelenka said. "But we learned something that may help you."

"What is that?"

"Kramer is to be taken to Terezin. Theresienstadt," Zelenka said. "You know what is there?"

"No."

"A concentration camp."

He got a map and showed Sam where the town was, on the Prague-Dresden road, about halfway to the border.

"Can you find out when?" Sam asked.

Zelenka shrugged his shoulders theatrically. "But I would not think until after the big conference is finished," he said. Heydrich had summoned a meeting at the Hradschin. All the big Nazis were there: Müller, head of the Gestapo; Canaris and his staff, the chiefs of the *Abwehr*. Each evening the big official Mercedes brought them down to the centre of town. Loitering inconspicuously near the entrance on the Wenzelplatz, Sam watched them going into the Ambassador Hotel, resplendent in fine uniforms bedecked with gleaming braid and lanyards. From Stechbarths, I'll bet, he thought inconsequentially; the top Berlin brass all bought their uniforms, cut by Herr Cap, there. He knew a few of them by sight, but the one he watched most carefully was a strongly-built man with cold eyes and an unsmiling expression, wearing the uniform of an SS Colonel: Kurt Bergmann.

And he could not get anywhere near him.

He knew where his house was, and where his office was, and how he travelled between each: in a closed Mercedes saloon, with an armed motor-cycle escort. The house itself was secure behind high walls, patrolled by SS guards. There was also a squad of bodyguards in residence at one of the gatehouses. Even on occasions like this it would be hard to get close enough for a killing shot: there were always guards. Once again, Sam felt the angry surge of frustration: why hadn't the British known more about conditions here?

"You've heard what happened to the parachutists?" Zelenka said.

"Oh, Christ, what now?"

"They set up homing devices for the British bombers at Pilsen, to guide them to the Skoda works. They set fire to haystacks to guide them in. It was a complete fiasco. They dropped their bombs everywhere except on the factory."

Sam shook his head. There was nothing you could say. Brave men risking their lives, ordinary people courting Gestapo torture, and for what?

"There's more," Zelenka said. "One of the Bioscope team went back out to Krivoklat with Arnost Miks. They're both dead."

Was there no end to the stupidity? Sam wondered. Every single team that had been dropped had come to grief, losing one or more of its men. They had no sense of purpose, no drive any more. They were scared, Sam thought, that was the trouble. It was easier to lie low, safer. The Gestapo hunters could miss you a thousand times and it would not matter. You only had to slip once and you were dead.

"I have to find out where Kramer is being held," he told Zelenka. "Can you get me any information?" The schoolmaster shook his head, no.

"He could be anywhere," he said. "Pankrac. In the Hradcany. The SS detention barracks. The Petschkarna. They have a lot of prisons, Jenick."

Sam's cover name was Jan Travicnek. His identity card gave his occupation as 'translator and interpreter', his birthplace as Pilsen and his correct date of birth. He had insisted on both: he knew Pilsen well, and spoke Czech with the accent of that city. It was easier to remember your own date of birth than any other: so why change it?

"I must find out," he said.

"There is very little time, Jenick," Zelenka said.

"I know," Sam said.

*   *   *

The village of Jungfern-Breschan lay in a pretty valley about twenty kilometres from Prague. There were two castles—châteaux, really. One stood at the top and the other, in which Heydrich and his family lived, lay at the bottom. It was surrounded by a landscaped park with fine trees, protected by a high wall. In the nearby forest, Heydrich was laying out a race course: he planned to set up a racing stable and breed fine horses.

Whenever he went to Prague, his car was brought to the front door of the lovely white mansion. Klein would wait at attention while Heydrich said his goodbyes: Lina Heydrich, ten years his junior, was pregnant for the fourth time. There was always a special kiss for his baby daughter. Heydrich would then get into the open Mercedes, the huge engine would surge into life and the car glide off down the gravelled drive, out of the gates. The SS guards would snap to attention as the car roared off through the village, up the hill past the second castle, and through a copse of trees about a hundred yards in depth, before reaching the road. There, theoretically, an escort car joined Heydrich's and preceded his into Prague.

The route never varied: from Jungfern-Breschan the road ran straight and level between rows of flowering peach and apple trees. At Klitschan, it joined the main Dresden road leading into town via Sperling, Zdib, and Unter-Habern. There, the road became the cobbled Kirchmayerstrasse, running through the suburb of Kobilis. As Kobilis became Liben, the car made a very sharp turn around a tight right-hand bend into the Klein Holeschowitzerstrasse, proceeding down the hill to the river, across the bridge and on to the Hradschin.

Since the lifting of the State of Emergency in January, Heydrich had more and more frequently dispensed with the escort car and driven into town alone. He was quite confident 'his' Czechs would never hurt him. On the Führer's birthday in April, had he not accepted a fully-equipped hospital train from President Hacha, a 'gift' from the people of the Protectorate? Heydrich felt as safe on the streets of Prague as he would have done in Berlin. Like most Germans, he possessed that characteristic of not noticing that a man dislikes you until he hits you in the face. So it was today. Heydrich sat in the back of his car reading some papers. Klein touched the brakes as he approached the bend, slowing the big car to perhaps fifteen kilometres an hour.

Gabcik and Kubis watched it go by.

They were narrowing down the options. A plan to wreck the special train in which Heydrich travelled to Berlin had been abandoned because there was no guarantee Heydrich would be killed. A plan to stretch a steel cable across the road into Prague had been discarded for the same reason. They had explored every kilometre of the *Reichsprotector*'s route into town, checking and double-checking the speed of the car as it went by, the amount of time they would have to make the attack. They walked around the corner. Ornamental railings set between brick pillars contained a much-overgrown garden which concealed a paint factory. Mature trees shaded the sidewalk on the Klein Holeschowitzerstrasse. Trams stopped directly on the corner: their tracks curved to within a couple of yards of the sidewalk.

Gabcik smiled his quick smile. He was very sunburned. Kubis nodded.

"Here?" Gabcik said.

"Here," Kubis told him.

Prague, May 26, 1942

"Everything ready?" Heydrich said.

"Everything, *Reichsprotector*," Bergmann said.

"Good," Heydrich said. "I'd stay longer, but I've got to go to that damned concert tonight." A concert of chamber music, which was to be performed by the Bohnhardt Quartet at the Valdstejn Palace, had been organised by the German Music Society. It was all part of the annual Prague Music Festival which had just begun. The quartet was to play a work by Heydrich's father, Bruno. Despite the fact

298

that what he really wanted to do was to finish his presentation for the Führer and Himmler, Heydrich could not evade the evening. As a result, he had been even more impatient than usual, and as a result the atmosphere at the Hradschin was so tense it almost twanged. No one there was more tense than Kurt Bergmann. In fact, he was worried sick. Heydrich was winning all the way down the line, and Himmler seemed powerless to stop him. Had Bergmann backed the wrong horse?

"What about those damned parachutists?" Heydrich said, looking up from the task of carefully putting red GRS folders into his briefcase.

"You read my report?" Bergmann asked.

"You've done well, Bergmann," Heydrich said. "But I want all of them. Damned saboteurs! I don't want all my hard work here ruined by a couple of kids with home-made bombs!"

The British were dropping their parachutists with the most incredible inaccuracy. Three of them had come down near Kbely, in Slovakia. They had been the ones who had the fight with the policemen. One of them had killed himself, one escaped. The third, one Vilem Gerik, was enthusiastically helping the Gestapo. To Bergmann's enormous relief, none of the British teams had any idea what the others' missions were. So if there was an assassination team, no one would know unless those men were captured. Bergmann looked at Heydrich. He doesn't know, he thought. He can't know. He believes he has won, everything.

Has he?

Does he know?

Could he be playing that damned cat and mouse game with me, too?

On the face of it, Heydrich had it all. He had summoned Admiral Canaris, Piekenbrock and the *Abwehr* Chief of Staff, Oster, to Prague. There, in a conference attended by Gestapo Müller and senior representatives of the *Kripo* and SD, he had presented them with the evidence of Kramer's treason. There was no argument, he told them. It was a signed confession. It had not been obtained under duress: they were at liberty to interview the prisoner.

"What do you want, Heydrich?" Canaris said.

"It has always been my belief that the security services of the Reich should be under the control of one office," Heydrich said. "One central authority. I propose to ask the Führer for this responsibility. You will do me the honour of supporting it."

"And if we do not?"

"You have no choice," Heydrich said, coldly, and they knew he was right. For almost a week—they arrived in Prague on Thursday, May 16 until their departure the following Tuesday—Canaris and his staff fought a rearguard action, seeking concessions, trying to bargain. Heydrich was relentless. The *Abwehr* would hand control of the Secret *Feldgendarmerie* to the RSHA, as an adjunct of the Gestapo. Counter-espionage would be the sole province of his department. Nor would *Abwehr* any longer have the power to interfere in Gestapo investigations.

"You ask too much, Heydrich!" Canaris protested. "You ask us to abrogate most of our power to you."

"May I remind the Admiral," Heydrich said, smoothly. "that I am not *asking* anything?"

They were silent. Canaris shook his head slightly, as though to say, how can this be? Nobody in the room doubted that Heydrich would get his way. With the Kramer confession in his hands—and God alone knew what else from that armour-plated safe of his—he could probably convince Hitler of anything he wanted.

Would Himmler let that happen? Bergmann wondered. Damn the man, what was he doing?

He reported daily to the *Reichsführer* by secret scrambler telephone. Himmler was, as always, infuriatingly vague. He seemed not to be aware of the danger he was asking Bergmann to face. The Warsaw Gestapo had picked up a Russian agent who claimed he was on his way to Prague to assassinate Heydrich. He hanged himself in his cell before they could find out more. The report was forwarded to Bergmann, and he concealed it from Heydrich.

That was the right thing to do, Himmler told him.

Himmler had told him Heydrich's plan was to become Minister of the Interior. Heydrich said he was going to ask for the position of *Reichsprotector* of Western Europe and commander of intelligence. One of them was lying. Which one?

Heydrich could be telling the truth. Why would he lie?

He was going to Berlin tomorrow.

Jesus Maria, what to do? Hitler would welcome him with open arms. He had spectacularly exposed the traitorous activities of the *Abwehr*. He had tamed the Czechs and turned the Protectorate into a smoothly-running industrial machine. He had drafted a new Occupation Statute for Belgium, France and the Low Countries. It seemed nothing could stop the man.

I should never have put my money on Himmler, Bergmann thought. I should have known Heydrich would win.

Heydrich always won.

"Give Klein a buzz, will you?" Heydrich said, picking up his briefcase. He closed the drawers of his desk, locking each one in turn. Then he swung the heavy door of the safe shut, and locked it with another key from the same bunch.

"Wish me luck, Bergmann," he said. "Glory or a coffin, yes?"

"Do you think the Führer will remove Canaris?"

"The Führer is hard to predict," Heydrich said. "Perhaps when he reads the Kramer dossier . . ." He let the sentence trail off in that typical way he had. "You've done fine work, Bergmann. I'm going to see if I can't get you an extra oak leaf for your collar while I'm at *Wolfschanze*."

"The *Reichsprotector* honours me," Bergmann murmured.

"No, no, my dear fellow, you've earned it!" Heydrich said, smiling. At that moment Heydrich's chauffeur knocked on the door and was bidden to enter. He came in and saluted. Well over six and a half feet tall, with the battered face of a fairground boxer, the sergeant was the very antithesis of his name: *klein* meant small.

"What time do you leave tomorrow?" Bergmann asked.

"Oh, about midday," Heydrich said. "I'll call here first. You'll have left by the time I get here, I imagine?"

"At ten," Bergmann said. "I can leave later, of course. . . ?"

"No, no!" Heydrich said, waving a hand. "You're going with him all the way to Theresienstadt?"

"All the way," Bergmann said. "I'm taking the Novakova girl, too." Heydrich smiled. He understood that kind of hate. "Good," he said. "See to it they are . . . well looked-after, Bergmann. Until we have it all in our hand." He extended his hand, palm up. "And then . . ." He closed it into a fist. The lynx eyes were cold and distant.

After Heydrich left, Bergmann went back to his own office and stood looking out of the window. The red roofs of Prague shone beneath the sinking sun. Lilac was in blossom; the horse-chestnuts were bright with flowers. Far below, the Moldau looked like silk ribbon. Somewhere in those teeming streets the British parachutists were hiding.

Where are you? Bergmann silently screamed.

Where the hell are you?

"I want a go-anywhere pass," Abendschon said.

"Walter . . ." Eckhardt said. "I'll have to check with the Chief."

"By all means," Abendschon said, sweetly. "And you know what he'll say, don't you? 'Why the devil are you . . .'"

"'. . . bothering me with trifles,' all right, all right!" Eckhardt said, irritably. "When do you want it?"

"Yesterday," Abendschon said.

Eckhardt rolled his eyes up towards the heavens, and went across the room to one of the secretaries. Then he came back to where Abendschon was standing. "It'll be ready in a moment," he said. "Where are you going?"

"Hunting parachutists," Abendschon said, and it was the truth.

He had decided to turn traitor.

He was still astonished at the decision. He hoped he would be able to go through with it: every step he took added to the burden of fear that was building inside him. Yet something forced him on. It had been surprisingly easy so far. There was no reason for anyone to suspect him, after all. He was still covered in glory from the Kramer affair. Bergmann and Heydrich might have taken all the credit in Berlin, but here in Prague everyone knew who had done it. The praise lacerated Abendschon worse than whips. He hated himself.

"You know where they're sending you?" he asked Kramer, the last time he saw him.

"They told me," Kramer said.

He was much thinner, and there was a great deal of pain in his eyes. He was still being intensively questioned: there were a great many people involved. The case would keep a hundred Gestapo investigators busy for years. That was why Kramer was being sent to Theresienstadt, why the girl had been kept alive. They were to remain available until all the inquiries were completed. Then—Abendschon decided not to think about 'then'. At that last meeting, he asked Kramer why he had turned traitor.

"Was it because of your father?" he said. "What happened to him in Munich?"

"Mostly that," Kramer admitted. "Not altogether. I'd joined the Party on fire to change the world, to fight Communism, to restore German greatness. I believed all that shit, Abendschon, the way you people still do."

"Go on," Abendschon said, refusing to be angered.

"When that SS squad came and dragged my father away, I realised what people like me had done. We had created a monster, and the monster was out of control. No one could fight it from the bottom up. So I decided to get to the top, and fight it from there."

"But you must have known you would be caught," Abendschon said. "Sooner or later."

"Yes, I knew."

"Yet still you did it."

"Someone has to fight you bastards, Abendschon," Kramer said. "Someone has to."

You mean *them,* Abendschon protested silently.

He could not get what Kramer had said out of his mind. All these years he had thought of himself as not being part of the dirty business of the SS, the business with the Jews, and the concentration camps, and the rest of it. That was being done by *them.* There is no *them,* he thought. *I* am them. The Bergmanns of this world cannot exist without me.

He kept seeing Kramer in his cell, the lines of pain around the man's eyes, the stiff way he held his body. They had tortured him: there was no embargo any more. He was a self-confessed traitor, a spy, a murderer. Abendschon remembered his own anger over the death of Alben Graumann. That anyone should commit murder on the streets of Berlin, *his* Berlin. He had seen a tree and missed the forest: what were Himmler's black-uniformed minions doing, what were Heydrich and Bergmann doing but committing murder on the streets of every city in Europe? If Kramer was a murderer, what were they?

After many sleepless nights he telephoned Karin Graumann and told her that the man who had killed her husband had been arrested and would be sent to a KZ.

"You'll be coming back to Berlin, then?" she said. Her voice was breathy, excited. He pictured the pert face, the green eyes shining with excitement.

"Not right away," he said.

"But soon."

"As soon as I can." I ought to tell her, he thought. I ought to tell her that I love her.

"Oh, Walter, that will be wonderful!" she said. "*Auf Wiedersehen.*"

"*Wiederschau'n,*" he said, and hung up without saying it.

He went through the files at the Petschek and extracted a few names. Most of them were already under intensive surveillance, suspected of illegal activities or sympathy with the resistance. The Novakova girl had named a number, as well as confessing that she had been in contact with the parachutists hidden somewhere near Pardubice. On Bergmann's strict instructions, they had not yet been rounded up.

"I want a clean sweep," he had said. "According to the girl there are fifteen or more of them. Take three and the others will all go to ground. Watch them. Report to me. But take no action."

Abendschon got into his car and drove towards Zizkov. Twenty minutes later, he pulled up outside the apartment building on the Bischofsstrasse where the schoolteacher Zelenka lived.

He stood for a long, long moment staring at the bell pushes. The next step was the irrevocable one, the one which would make him as much a traitor to his country as Paul Kramer had ever been. He sighed and pushed the bell: bz-bz-bz-bzzzz.

Prague, May 27, 1942

The big Mercedes W150 saloon slid to a stop in front of the pillared portico of the Petschek Palace. The sergeant driver got out and ran around the front, opening the doors at front and back, leaving the 7·7-litre engine running. The car had three sets of seats, front, centre, and rear. Two Gestapo sergeants brought Kramer and the girl out. Both of them walked like old, old people. Kramer looked up at the sky and took a deep breath, blinking in the bright sunshine. The Gestapo officers tipped forward the centre seats and got into the back, machine pistols ready. Kramer and the girl got into the centre seats. They did not speak: talking was *verboten*. The driver closed the rear door. He saluted as *Standartenführer* Kurt Bergmann came down the steps. His uniform was smartly pressed; his varnished boots gleamed. He slid into the front seat without even deigning to look at the prisoners. He pointed forward. The driver put the car into gear and the huge black car glided into motion.

Bergmann's driver was an *SS-Unterscharführer* named Conrad Memling. He was very proud of his driving. He enjoyed controlling the huge machine—privately, he thought of it as The Beast—taking corners at just the right speed, reading the road well ahead, braking carefully, never accelerating abruptly. If people were thrown about, if their heads jerked, Memling chided himself silently. He wanted to be the best driver in the SS. Perhaps one day he would drive the Führer. The Beast was a beauty: 394 horses under the hood. She drank ten gallons of petrol and a quart of oil every hundred and five kilometres. She had bulletproof glass, armoured doors, two-way radio telephone, security locks. The news this morning was good. Rommel on the attack, the Red Army halted in the Donetz basin. Memling read the Prague paper *Der Neue Tag* from cover to cover every day, as well as the *Volkischer Beobachter*. There was always a lot of waiting around in his job. He didn't mind at all: it was a lot better than being at Bir Hacheim or in the Donetz basin. He pulled to a gentle stop as a traffic light turned red. Nobody looked at the car. It was as if it was the head of the Gorgon, and they would be turned to stone if they attracted its baleful glare.

The car moved forward, across the Smermuv bridge. Off to the left, the Hradschin shone on its high hill, the purple spires of St Vitus's sharp against the beaming sky. There were hundreds of ducks on the Moldau. A lovely day, Memling thought. Shame to waste it going to a damned KZ.

Behind him, Paul Kramer touched Tonie's hand with his own. They were not manacled. There was no need for that: where would they escape to? He lifted his chin and she followed his gaze. They were forbidden to speak, of course, but she knew what he meant. They gazed for the last time at the river, the hills dressed in bright spring green, the soaring spires of the cathedral where the faithful still chanted to St Wenceslas, their patron saint, 'Czech prince, pray for us.' Then the view was shut out as the car entered the tunnel running beneath the Letensky gardens.

They emerged from the tunnel and turned right at Letensky-platz, taking the left fork towards Holeschowitz. They passed beneath a railway bridge. The ten thousand-pound car rumbled smoothly over the cobblestoned streets. Off to the left Memling could see the sun striking flashes of light off the glass frontage of the Kongresspalast. They were approaching Holeschowitz station: beneath the railway bridge beyond it, the road would swing right at an angle of almost ninety degrees.

Kurt Bergmann looked at his watch: 10.20. It was about sixty kilometres to Theresienstadt. They ought to be there comfortably by noon. He switched on the radio-telephone and picked up the microphone. It was answered immediately by Exchange.

"Bergmann," he said. "*Danke.* Contact my office. Have them call the Commandant at Theresienstadt. I would like lunch ready for my arrival. Say, twelve-thirty. Good. *Schluss.*"

He put the microphone back on its hook. Memling changed down and touched the brakes as the Holeschowitz railway bridge loomed ahead.

Gabcik and Kubis took a streetcar to the garage in Zizkov where they kept their borrowed bicycles. They fixed their briefcases to the handlebars and headed for the corner in

Liben. Valcik was waiting for them at the turning. He told them Opalka was already in place. Girls in nurse's uniforms got off a streetcar, and walked up the grassy bank around the clinic to the Bulovka hospital. The sky was bright blue, with not a cloud in sight. Gabcik leaned against the low garden wall. Kubis stood at the edge of the pavement. He could see Valcik, further up the Kirchmayerstrasse. The moment Valcik saw Heydrich's car, he would signal with a mirror. Gabcik carefully took the Sten gun out of the briefcase and draped his borrowed raincoat over it.

All they had to do now was wait.

Sam Gray gave the signal.

The two Czechs across the street released their hold on the handcart. They had been holding it against the slope of the street leading to the station. It was piled high with old, heavy furniture, and it ran out into the middle of the road in the exact second that the big Mercedes came around the corner. The driver hit the brakes and swerved, but he was too late. The car ploughed into the cart, smashing it to pieces. The furniture which had been piled on top of it collapsed into a smashed heap, blocking the street. Steam rose from the radiator of the big car. Memling got out, shouting at people on the street to help him clear the debris away. He looked at the car and swore. One of the tyres was flat.

"Get out and help him!" Bergmann snapped to the two Gestapo men. They jumped. Memling opened the door on the sidewalk side, gesturing at Kramer and the girl to get out. The two Gestapo men tipped the seats forward and scrambled out. As soon as they were out of the car, Sam shot them. They went down like targets in a fairground, legs thrashing.

"Jesus Maria!" Memling shouted, scrabbling with panicked fingers at the fastening of his holster. He pulled out the Luger, eyes wide with fear. Kramer pulled Tonie away from the car and into a doorway. Bergmann yelled "Stop them!" but Memling was too frightened. He saw a big, sandy-haired man coming towards him. He lifted the gun. He had never fired it. His whole body was shaking with fear. I'm a *chauffeur*, he wanted to scream. It's not fair! The sandy-haired man shot him in the head as Bergmann, alone inside the big Mercedes, hit the locks on the doors. At the same time he set off the alarm. A shrill whooping sound was emitted by the car: at the same time a homing device began sending. He grabbed the radio telephone. Once again the Exchange replied immediately.

"*Hilfe!*" he shouted. "This is Bergmann. My car is under attack in Holeschowitz! Have you got that? Beneath the railway bridge at Holeschowitz station! Send assistance instantly!"

"All units are engaged, sir!" Exchange said.

"What?" Bergmann screamed. "I am under attack here! Send help immediately, do you hear me?"

"Sir, there has been an attempt on the life of *Obergruppenführer* Heydrich. All units—"

"Help me!" Bergmann screeched. "For God's sake, help me!"

Through the windshield he saw the sandy-haired man run towards the car. He was waving people back, shouting something. A beat policeman was running along the sidewalk. The sandy-haired man fired the gun into the air. The policeman skidded to a stop, ducking into a doorway. Bergmann saw the sandy-haired man run around the rear of the Mercedes. He heard a metallic sound beneath the car. He could not believe all this. People were standing, as if transfixed, watching.

The sandy-haired man appeared in front of the car. He got up on the running board. Bergmann watched, hypnotised, as the man clamped a limpet mine to the windshield. Bergmann's bowels turned to water: now he understood what the metallic sound had been. There was another fixed to the petrol tank. He was dead if he got out, dead if he stayed where he was.

Sam Gray tripped the fuse. He jumped off the running board of the car and ran for cover, shouting as he ran.

"Clear the street!" he yelled in Czech. "It's a bomb!"

People ran, screaming. Sam flattened himself behind one of the buttresses of the stone bridge. Kramer and the girl were huddled in a shop doorway, her body shielded by his. The mines went off with a sharp flashing thud. The back of the car lifted slightly off the ground, and the petrol tank exploded with a rushing *whommmppppfff!* Sam felt the searing scorch of the burned air. He stepped clear of cover. Smoke climbed in a black, stinking column Into the silence bored a thin, awful scream. One of the doors of the car fell open, its hinges making a protesting crack. What was left of Kurt Bergmann fell into the street. He had no face. His uniform was smouldering. He got to his knees, the weird mewling sound emerging from the bloody pudding at the front of his head.

Sam put the gun against what was left of Bergmann's temple and pulled the trigger. Bergmann went down as if he had been hit with a bat. Sam walked across to where Kramer and the girl were standing.

"Come on," he said urgently. "We've got to get out of here."

"No," Kramer said. "There's nowhere to run to, Sam. Nowhere in the whole wide world."

"We've got help," Sam said. "Look!" He pointed across the street. A car stood parked at the corner, engine running. Beside it stood the burly figure of Walter Abendschon.

Paul shook his head, smiling. "Well, I'll be damned!" he said. "So that's how you knew!"

"Come on!" Sam said.

"Get out of here, Sam!" Paul said. "Those cars are all connected to the Petschek. There'll be a Gestapo squad here any minute!"

"They'll be having a busy morning," Sam said. "Heydrich has been assassinated."

"My God!" Paul said. Tonie had come over to stand by his side. "Did you hear that?" he said to her.

"I heard," she said. "A lot of innocent people will pay for all this."

"I'm going to stay. Fight it out," Sam said.

"No!" Paul said. He put his hand on Sam's shoulder. "Try to get back, Sam. Do what you can about the Final Solution. Make them understand."

"Why do you care so much?"

"Someone's got to," Paul said.

"Come with us," Sam said, agonisedly. In the distance he

heard the par-pee-par-pee-par of Gestapo cars drawing nearer. Tonie stood on tiptoe and kissed him. "Sam," she said. "I always liked that name."

Sam shrugged and stuck out his hand. Paul grasped it. Then he took the gun and limped over to the barricade past the burning car. Shielding her face from the heat with one arm, Tonie picked up the machine pistols the Gestapo guards had dropped and followed him. He was humming a song, very quietly, as if to himself. *'Morgenrot, Morgenrot, leuchtest uns zu frühen Tod . . .'* A shiver touched her skin. She looked over her shoulder. A crowd was forming, edging closer. Tonie fired one of the guns into the sky. The crowd melted back. The sound of the Gestapo sirens was very close now. Sam ran across the street to where Abendschon was standing, his face twisted with anxiety.

"Let's go, let's go!" he shouted. "What are they doing?"

"They're not coming," Sam said.

"What?" Abendschon said. "You mean we did all this for nothing?"

"No," Sam said, getting into the car. "I wouldn't say that." Abendschon slammed his door and swung the car around the corner under the bridge. Sam caught a last fleeting glimpse of Paul Kramer's face through the rolling smoke, Tonie Novakova beside him. As Abendschon gunned the car down Kongressstrasse, three Gestapo vans, loaded with men, roared past them in the opposite direction, sirens blaring. They were in for a surprise when they turned the corner, Sam thought.

"Tell me," Abendschon said to the American. "Did . . . he recognise me?" It was important; he needed to know.

"He recognised you," Sam said.

"What did he say?"

"He said, 'Well, I'll be damned!'."

Abendschon grinned. The car roared past Dejvice station. Up on the hill to their left the Hradschin loomed. Sam tried to imagine the turmoil and confusion there: phones ringing incessantly, teleprinters chattering the news to Berlin, alerts ringing in barracks. The Hradschin fell behind. They roared through Smichov and picked up the main highway to Pilsen.

"Where are we heading?" Sam said.

"Munich," Abendschon said. "Then the Swiss border."

"You think we can make it?"

"I don't know," Walter Abendschon said. He felt good. He felt very good indeed, better than for years. "I don't know, Mr. Gray. But by God, we're going to try!"

Author's Note

At approximately ten thirty in the morning on May 27, 1942 *Obergruppenführer* Reinhard Heydrich was severely wounded by shrapnel from a grenade thrown at his car by the Czech parachutist, Jan Kubis. Heydrich was rushed to the nearby Bulovka hospital, where he died of his injuries, compounded by septicemia, on Thursday, June 4.

When Heinrich Himmler visited the dying man for the last time on May 31, Heydrich lectured his leader on Fate, and quoted these lines from his father's opera, *Amen*:

> *Yes, the world is merely a barrel-organ*
> *Played by God himself*
> *We must all dance to the tune*
> *Which just happens to be on the roll.*

Reichsführer Himmler's reaction is not recorded.